ACKNOWLEDGMENTS

Special thanks to the following, for permission to reprint:

Bantam Books, Inc.—"Immortality" by Fredric Brown, from *Nightmares and Geezenstacks,* © Copyright 1961 by Fredric Brown.

Ballantine Books, Inc.—"The Rocket of 1955" by C. M. Kornbluth, from *The Explorers,* © 1954 by C. M. Kornbluth.

Berkley Publishing Corporation—"Chronopolis" by J. G. Ballard, © 1961 by Nova Publications Ltd., London. Reprinted by arrangement.

John C. M. Brust—"Red White and Blue Rum Collins" by John C. M. Brust. First appeared in the *Harvard Lampoon.*

Doubleday & Company, Inc.—"There Will Come Soft Rains" by Ray Bradbury, from *The Martian Chronicles* by Ray Bradbury. Copyright 1950 by The Crowell-Collier Publishing Company.

Martin Gardner—"No-Sided Professor" by Martin Gardner, Copyright 1946 by Martin Gardner. First appeared in *Esquire.*

Damon Knight—"Analogues" by Damon Knight, Copyright 1952 by Damon Knight. First appeared in *Astounding Science Fiction.*

Alfred A. Knopf, Inc.—"The Great Automatic Grammatisator" by Roald Dahl, from *Someone Like You,* Copyright 1953 by Roald Dahl.

Little, Brown & Company—"I Kill Myself" by Julian Kawalec, from *The Modern Polish Mind,* edited by Maria Kuncewicz, Copyright © 1962 by Little, Brown & Co. (Inc.).

Mercury Press, Inc., and the authors—"The Men Who Murdered Mohammed" by Alfred Bester, Copyright 1958 by Mercury Press, Inc.; "An Egg a Month from All Over" by Idris Seabright, Copyright 1952 by Mercury Press, Inc. Both stories first appeared in the *Magazine of Fantasy and Science Fiction.*

Harold Matson Company, Inc.—"Something for Nothing" by Robert Sheckley, Copyright 1954 by Galaxy Publishing Corporation; "A Canticle for Leibowitz" by Walter M. Miller, Jr., © 1955 by Walter M. Miller, Jr. A novel of the same title was based, in part, on the latter story.

Scott Meredith Literary Agency, Inc.—"Patent Pending," Copyright 1954 by Arthur C. Clarke; "Or All the Seas with Oysters," © 1957 by Avram Davidson; and "Random Quest," © 1961 by John Wyndham.

Sheed & Ward, Inc.—"The Death of the Sea" by José María Gironella, from *Phantoms and Fugitives* by José María Gironella, © 1964 by Sheed & Ward.

Simon & Schuster, Inc.—"Shadow Show" by Clifford D. Simak, from *Strangers in the Universe,* © 1950, 1951, 1952, 1953, 1954, and 1956 by Clifford D. Simak.

Theodore Sturgeon—"And Now the News," © 1956 by Theodore Sturgeon. First appeared in the *Magazine of Fantasy and Science Fiction.*

William Styron—"Pie in the Sky," first published in this volume.

❋ *Introduction*

The day of the old-fashioned "space opera" is dying. The launching of Sputnik in 1957 was a near-mortal blow—no one wants to read about Interstellar Officer Candidate Larkin's trip to Betelgeuse when he can pick up a newspaper and read an equally exciting account of man's actual experiments in space.

But the advance of space-age science has not, as might have been expected, brought an abrupt end to the genre of science fantasy. On the contrary, it has helped to turn science-fiction writers away from technology as an end in itself, and, consequently, has led them to subordinate their scientific imagination to an increased concern with human attitudes and emotions, on the one hand, and with the field of sociology on the other. This new trend, which can be traced back to the end of World War II, has succeeded in raising noticeably the literary standards of the science-fiction story.

This should not be surprising, for, theoretically at least, science fantasy presents virtually all the possibilities open to the writer of "mainstream" fiction, with one added dimension: the setting or situation is left, without limits, to the author's imagination. This freedom can be used to advantage in any number of ways. J. G. Ballard, for example, examines a psychological consequence of overpopulation by creating a complex society, "Chronopolis," in which overpopulation is an obsessive problem. Roald Dahl conceives an electronic gadget, "The Great Automatic Grammatisator," so that he may comment satirically on the art of modern fiction. José Maria Gironella finds that he can probe deeply into human emotions by expressing them in the form of a fantastic natural phenomenon. And Alfred

Bester invents a time machine for the sheer purpose of letting his imagination run absolutely wild.

This is not to claim that science fiction today has reached the status of great literature—certainly, the majority of good science fantasy stories are written primarily to entertain. The point of this anthology is to illustrate that at least some of the body of work broadly classified as fantasy is literate, provocative, and absorbing. To that end, a wide variety of stories, from four different countries, have been assembled here. Some may be familiar to science-fiction readers; others have never been anthologized previously. (Included in this latter category is a story by William Styron which is being published here for the first time.) Hopefully, this collection will serve to show that critics are being unfortunately short-sighted when, as Kingsley Amis writes,

> "S.f.'s no good," they bellow till we're deaf.
> "But this is good!" "Well then it's not s.f."

CHRISTOPHER CERF

✿ *Contents*

INTRODUCTION *vii*

ROALD DAHL: *The Great Automatic
Grammatisator* 3

IDRIS SEABRIGHT: *An Egg a Month from
All Over* 22

RAY BRADBURY: *There Will Come Soft Rains* 30

THEODORE STURGEON: *And Now the News* 37

MARTIN GARDNER: *No-Sided Professor* 59

JOHN WYNDHAM: *Random Quest* 71

C. M. KORNBLUTH: *The Rocket of 1955* 111

ROBERT SHECKLEY: *Something for Nothing* 113

JOSÉ MARIA GIRONELLA: *The Death of the Sea* 126

JOHN C. M. BRUST: *The Red White and Blue
Rum Collins* 140

WILLIAM STYRON: *Pie in the Sky* 142

DAMON KNIGHT: *The Analogues* 160

FREDRIC BROWN: *Immortality* 172

CLIFFORD D. SIMAK: *Shadow Show* 174

J. G. BALLARD: *Chronopolis* 213

AVRAM DAVIDSON: *Or All the Seas with Oysters* 239

ARTHUR C. CLARKE: *Patent Pending* 249

x] **Contents**

JULIAN KAWALEC: *I Kill Myself*   260

ALFRED BESTER: *The Men Who Murdered
                    Mohammed*   268

WALTER M. MILLER, JR.: *A Canticle for
                    Leibowitz*   282

BIOGRAPHICAL NOTES   305

The Vintage Anthology of

❁

SCIENCE FANTASY

❂ *Roald Dahl*

THE GREAT AUTOMATIC GRAMMATISATOR

"Well, Knipe, my boy. Now that it's all finished, I just called you in to tell you I think you've done a fine job."

Adolph Knipe stood still in front of Mr. Bohlen's desk. There seemed to be no enthusiasm in him at all.

"Aren't you pleased?"

"Oh, yes, Mr. Bohlen."

"Did you see what the papers said this morning?"

"No, sir, I didn't."

The man behind the desk pulled a folded newspaper toward him, and began to read: "The building of the great automatic computing engine, ordered by the government some time ago, is now complete. It is probably the fastest electronic calculating machine in the world today. Its function is to satisfy the ever-increasing need of science, industry, and administration for rapid mathematical calculation which, in the past, by traditional methods, would have been physically impossible, or would have required more time than the problems justified. The speed with which the new engine works, said Mr. John Bohlen, head of the firm of electrical engineers mainly responsible for its construction, may be grasped by the fact that it can provide the correct answer in five seconds to a problem that would occupy a mathematician for a month. In three minutes, it can produce a calculation that by hand (if it were possible) would fill half a million sheets of foolscap paper. The automatic computing engine uses pulses of electricity, generated at the rate of a million a second, to solve all calculations that resolve themselves into addition, subtraction, multiplication, and division. For practical purposes there is no limit to what it can do . . ."

Mr. Bohlen glanced up at the long, melancholy face of the younger man. "Aren't you proud, Knipe? Aren't you pleased?"

"Of course, Mr. Bohlen."

"I don't think I have to remind you that your own contribution, especially to the original plans, was an important one. In fact, I might go so far as to say that without you and some of your ideas, this project might still be on the drawing boards today."

Adolph Knipe moved his feet on the carpet, and he watched the two small white hands of his chief, the nervous fingers playing with a paper clip, unbending it, straightening out the hairpin curves. He didn't like the man's hands. He didn't like his face either, with the tiny mouth and the narrow purple-colored lips. It was unpleasant the way only the lower lip moved when he talked.

"Is anything bothering you, Knipe? Anything on your mind?"

"Oh no, Mr. Bohlen. No."

"How would you like to take a week's holiday? Do you good. You've earned it."

"Oh, I don't know, sir."

The older man waited, watched this tall, thin person who stood so sloppily before him. He was a difficult boy. Why couldn't he stand up straight? Always drooping and untidy, with spots on his jacket, and hair falling all over his face.

"I'd like you to take a holiday, Knipe. You need it."

"All right, sir. If you wish."

"Take a week. Two weeks if you like. Go somewhere warm. Get some sunshine. Swim. Relax. Sleep. Then come back, and we'll have another talk about the future."

Adolph Knipe went home by bus to his two-room apartment. He threw his coat on the sofa, poured himself a drink of whiskey, and sat down in front of the typewriter that was on the table. Mr. Bohlen was right. Of course he was right. Except that he didn't know the half of it. He probably thought it was a woman. Whenever a young man gets depressed, everybody thinks it's a woman.

He leaned forward and began to read through the half-finished sheet of typing still in the machine. It was headed "A Narrow Escape," and it began *"The night was dark and stormy, the wind whistled in the trees, the rain poured down like cats and dogs . . ."*

Adolph Knipe took a sip of whiskey, tasting the malty-bitter flavor, feeling the trickle of cold liquid as it traveled down his throat and settled in the top of his stomach, cool at first, then spreading and becoming warm, making a little area of warmness in the gut. To hell with Mr. John Bohlen anyway. And to hell with the great electrical computing machine. To hell with . . .

At exactly that moment, his eyes and mouth began slowly to open, in a sort of wonder, and slowly he raised his head and became still, absolutely motionless, gazing at the wall opposite with this look that was more perhaps of astonishment than of wonder, but quite fixed now, unmoving, and remaining thus for forty, fifty, sixty seconds. Then gradually (the head still motionless), a subtle change spreading over the face, astonishment becoming pleasure, very slight at first, only around the corners of the mouth, increasing gradually, spreading out until at last the whole face was open wide and shining with extreme delight. It was the first time Adolph Knipe had smiled in many, many months.

"Of course," he said, speaking aloud, "it's completely ridiculous." Again he smiled, raising his upper lip and baring his teeth in a queerly sensual manner.

"It's a delicious idea, but so impracticable it doesn't really bear thinking about at all."

From then on, Adolph Knipe began to think about nothing else. The idea fascinated him enormously, at first because it gave him a promise—however remote—of revenging himself in a most devilish manner upon his greatest enemies. From this angle alone, he toyed idly with it for perhaps ten or fifteen minutes; then all at once he found himself examining it quite seriously as a practical possibility. He took paper and made some preliminary notes. But he didn't get far. He found himself, almost immediately, up against the old truth that a machine, however ingenious, is incapable of original thought. It can handle no problems except those that resolve themselves into mathematical terms—problems that contain one, and only one, correct answer.

This was a stumper. There didn't seem any way around it. A machine cannot have a brain. On the other hand, it *can* have a memory, can it not? Their own electronic calculator had a marvelous memory. Simply by converting electric pulses, through a column of mercury, into supersonic waves, it could store away at least a thousand numbers at a time, extracting any one of them at the precise moment it was needed. Would it not be possible, therefore, on this principle, to build a memory section of almost unlimited size?

Now what about that?

Then suddenly he was struck by a powerful but simple little truth, and it was this: *That English grammar is governed by rules that are almost mathematical in their strictness!* Given the words, and given the sense of what is to be said, then there is only one correct order in which those words can be arranged.

No, he thought, that isn't quite accurate. In many sentences there are several alternative positions for words and phrases, all of which may be grammatically correct. But what the hell. The theory itself is basically true. Therefore, it stands to reason that an engine built along the lines of the electric computer could be adjusted to arrange words (instead of numbers) in their right order according to the rules of grammar. Give it the verbs, the nouns, the adjectives, the pronouns, store them in the memory section as a vocabulary, and arrange for them to be extracted as required. Then feed it with plots and leave it to write the sentences.

There was no stopping Knipe now. He went to work immediately, and there followed during the next few days a period of intense labor. The living room became littered with sheets of paper: formulae and calculations; lists of words, thousands and thousands of words; the plots of stories, curiously broken up and subdivided; huge extracts from *Roget's Thesaurus*; pages filled with the first names of men and women; hundreds of surnames taken from the telephone directory; intricate drawings of wires and circuits and switches and thermionic valves; drawings of machines that could punch holes of different shapes in little cards,

and of a strange electrical typewriter that could type ten
thousand words a minute. Also, a kind of control panel
with a series of small push buttons, each one labeled with
the name of a famous American magazine.

He was working in a mood of exultation, prowling
around the room amidst this littering of paper, rubbing his
hands together, talking out loud to himself; and sometimes,
with a sly curl of the nose, he would mutter a series of
murderous imprecations in which the word "editor" seemed
always to be present. On the fifteenth day of continuous
work, he collected the papers into two large folders which
he carried—almost at a run—to the offices of John Bohlen,
Inc., electrical engineers.

Mr. Bohlen was pleased to see him back.

"Well, Knipe, good gracious me, you look a hundred per
cent better. You have a good holiday? Where'd you go?"

He's just as ugly and untidy as ever, Mr. Bohlen thought.
Why doesn't he stand up straight? He looks like a bent
stick. "You look a hundred per cent better, my boy." I
wonder what he's grinning about. Every time I see him,
his ears seem to have got larger.

Adolph Knipe placed the folders on the desk. "Look, Mr.
Bohlen!" he cried. "Look at these!"

Then he poured out his story. He opened the folders
and pushed the plans in front of the astonished little man.
He talked for over an hour, explaining everything, and
when he had finished, he stepped back, breathless, flushed,
waiting for the verdict.

"You know what I think, Knipe? I think you're nuts."
Careful now, Mr. Bohlen told himself. Treat him carefully.
He's valuable, this one is. If only he didn't look so awful,
with that long horse face and the big teeth. The fellow
had ears as big as rhubarb leaves.

"But, Mr. Bohlen! It'll work! I've proved to you it'll
work! You can't deny that!"

"Take it easy now, Knipe. Take it easy, and listen to me."
Adolph Knipe watched his man, disliking him more every
second.

"This idea," Mr. Bohlen's lower lip was saying, "is very
ingenious—I might almost say brilliant—and it only goes to
confirm my high opinion of your abilities, Knipe. But don't
take it too seriously. After all, my boy, what possible use

can it be to us? Who on earth wants a machine for writing stories? And where's the money in it, anyway? Just tell me that."

"May I sit down, sir?"

"Sure, take a seat."

Adolph Knipe seated himself on the edge of a chair. The older man watched him with alert brown eyes, wondering what was coming now.

"I would like to explain something, Mr. Bohlen, if I may, about how I came to do all this."

"Go right ahead, Knipe." He would have to be humored a little now, Mr. Bohlen told himself. The boy was really valuable—a sort of genius, almost—worth his weight in gold to the firm. Just look at these papers here. Darndest thing you ever saw. Astonishing piece of work. Quite useless, of course. No commercial value. But it proved again the boy's ability.

"It's a sort of confession, I suppose, Mr. Bohlen. I think it explains why I've always been so . . . so kind of worried."

"You tell me anything you want, Knipe. I'm here to help you—you know that."

The young man clasped his hands together tight on his lap, hugging himself with his elbows. It seemed as though suddenly he was feeling very cold.

"You see, Mr. Bohlen, to tell the honest truth, I don't really care much for my work here. I know I'm good at it and all that sort of thing, but my heart's not in it. It's not what I want to do most."

Up went Mr. Bohlen's eyebrows, quick like a spring. His whole body became very still.

"You see, sir, all my life I've wanted to be a writer."

"A writer!"

"Yes, Mr. Bohlen. You may not believe it, but every bit of spare time I've had, I've spent writing stories. In the last ten years I've written hundreds, literally hundreds of short stories. Five hundred and sixty-six, to be precise. Approximately one a week."

"Good heavens, man! What on earth did you do that for?"

"All I know, sir, is I have the urge."

"What sort of urge?"

"The creative urge, Mr. Bohlen." Every time he looked

up he saw Mr. Bohlen's lips. They were growing thinner and thinner, more and more purple.

"And may I ask you what you do with these stories, Knipe?"

"Well, sir, that's the trouble. No one will buy them. Each time I finish one, I send it out on the rounds. It goes to one magazine after another. That's all that happens, Mr. Bohlen, and they simply send them back. It's very depressing."

Mr. Bohlen relaxed. "I can see quite well how you feel, my boy." His voice was dripping with sympathy. "We all go through it one time or another in our lives. But now—now that you've had proof—positive proof—from the experts themselves, from the editors, that your stories are—what shall I say—rather unsuccessful, it's time to leave off. Forget it, my boy. Just forget all about it."

"No, Mr. Bohlen! No! That's not true! I *know* my stories are good. My heavens, when you compare them with the stuff some of those magazines print—oh my word, Mr. Bohlen—the sloppy, boring stuff you see in the magazines week after week—why, it drives me mad!"

"Now wait a minute, my boy . . ."

"Do you ever read the magazines, Mr. Bohlen?"

"You'll pardon me, Knipe, but what's all this got to do with your machine?"

"Everything, Mr. Bohlen, absolutely everything! What I want to tell you is, I've made a study of the magazines, and it seems that each one tends to have its own particular type of story. The writers—the successful ones—know this, and they write accordingly."

"Just a minute, my boy. Calm yourself down, will you? I don't think all this is getting us anywhere."

"*Please,* Mr. Bohlen, hear me through. It's all terribly important." He paused to catch his breath. He was properly worked up now, throwing his hands around as he talked. The long, toothy face, with the big ears on either side, simply shone with enthusiasm, and there was an excess of saliva in his mouth which caused him to speak his words wet. "So you see, on my machine, by having an adjustable coordinator between the 'plot-memory' section and the 'word-memory' section, I am able to produce any type of story I desire simply by pressing the required button."

"Yes, I know, Knipe, I know. This is all very interesting, but what's the point of it?"

"Just this, Mr. Bohlen. The market is limited. We've got to be able to produce the right stuff, at the right time, whenever we want it. It's a matter of business, that's all. I'm looking at it from *your* point of view now—as a commercial proposition."

"My dear boy, it can't possibly be a commercial proposition—ever. You know as well as I do what it costs to build one of these machines."

"Yes, sir, I do. But with due respect, I don't believe you know what the magazines pay writers for stories."

"What do they pay?"

"Anything up to twenty-five hundred dollars. It probably averages around a thousand."

Mr. Bohlen jumped.

"*Yes, sir,* it's true."

"Absolutely impossible, Knipe! Ridiculous!"

"No, sir, it's true."

"You mean to sit there and tell me that these magazines pay out money like that to a man for . . . just for scribbling off a story! Good heavens, Knipe! Whatever next! Writers must all be millionaires!"

"That's exactly it, Mr. Bohlen! That's where the machine comes in. Listen a minute, sir, while I tell you some more. I've got it all worked out. The big magazines are carrying approximately three fiction stories in each issue. Now, take the fifteen most important magazines—the ones paying the most money. A few of them are monthlies, but most of them come out every week. All right. That makes, let us say, around forty big-money stories being bought each week. That's forty thousand dollars. So with our machine—when we get it working properly—we can collar nearly the whole of this market!"

"My dear boy, you're mad!"

"No, sir, honestly, it's true what I say. Don't you see that with volume alone we'll completely overwhelm them? This machine can produce a five-thousand-word story, all typed and ready for dispatch, in thirty seconds. How can the writers compete with that? I ask you, Mr. Bohlen, *how?*"

At that point, Adolph Knipe noticed a slight change in

the man's expression, an extra brightness in the eyes, the nostrils distending, the whole face becoming still, almost rigid. Quickly, he continued. "Nowadays, Mr. Bohlen, the hand-made article hasn't a hope. It can't possibly compete with mass production, especially in this country—you know that. Carpets . . . chairs . . . shoes . . . bricks . . . crockery . . . anything you like to mention—they're all made by machinery now. The quality may be inferior, but that doesn't matter. It's the cost of production that counts. And stories—well—they're just another product, like carpets or chairs, and no one cares how you produce them so long as you deliver the goods. We'll sell them wholesale, Mr. Bohlen! We'll undercut every writer in the country! We'll corner the market!"

Mr. Bohlen edged up straighter in his chair. He was leaning forward now, both elbows on the desk, the face alert, the small brown eyes resting on the speaker.

"I still think it's impracticable, Knipe."

"Forty thousand a week!" cried Adolph Knipe. "And if we halve the price, making it twenty thousand a week, that's still a million a year!" And softly he added, "You didn't get any million a year for building the old electronic calculator, did you, Mr. Bohlen?"

"But seriously now, Knipe. D'you really think they'd buy them?"

"Listen, Mr. Bohlen. Who on earth is going to want custom-made stories when they can get the other kind at half the price? It stands to reason, doesn't it?"

"And how will you sell them? Who will you say has written them?"

"We'll set up our own literary agency, and we'll distribute them through that. And we'll invent all the names we want for the writers."

"I don't like it, Knipe. To me, that smacks of trickery, does it not?"

"And another thing, Mr. Bohlen. There's all manner of valuable by-products once you've got started. Take advertising, for example. Beer manufacturers and people like that are willing to pay good money these days if famous writers will lend their names to their products. Why, my heavens, Mr. Bohlen! This isn't any children's plaything we're talking about. It's big business."

"Don't get too ambitious, my boy."

"And another thing. There isn't any reason why we shouldn't put *your* name, Mr. Bohlen, on some of the better stories, if you wished it."

"My goodness, Knipe. What should I want that for?"

"I don't know, sir, except that some writers get to be very much respected—like Mr. Erle Gardner or Kathleen Norris, for example. We've got to have names, and I was certainly thinking of using my own on one or two stories, just to help out."

"A writer, eh?" Mr. Bohlen said, musing. "Well, it would surely surprise them over at the club when they saw my name in the magazines—the good magazines."

"That's right, Mr. Bohlen."

For a moment, a dreamy, faraway look came into Mr. Bohlen's eyes, and he smiled. Then he stirred himself and began leafing through the plans that lay before him.

"One thing I don't quite understand, Knipe. Where do the plots come from? The machine can't possibly invent plots."

"We feed those in, sir. That's no problem at all. Everyone has plots. There's three or four hundred of them written down in that folder there on your left. Feed them straight into the 'plot-memory' section of the machine."

"Go on."

"There are many other little refinements too, Mr. Bohlen. You'll see them all when you study the plans carefully. For example, there's a trick that nearly every writer uses, of inserting at least one long, obscure word into each story. This makes the reader think the man is very wise and clever. So I have the machine do the same thing. There'll be a whole stack of long words stored away just for this purpose."

"Where?"

"In the 'word-memory' section," he said, epexegetically.

Through most of that day the two men discussed the possibilities of the new engine. In the end, Mr. Bohlen said he would have to think about it some more. The next morning, he was quietly enthusiastic. Within a week, he was completely sold on the idea.

"What we'll have to do, Knipe, is to say that we're merely building another mathematical calculator, but of a new type. That'll keep the secret."

"Exactly, Mr. Bohlen."

And in six months the machine was completed. It was housed in a separate brick building at the back of the premises, and now that it was ready for action, no one was allowed near it excepting Mr. Bohlen and Adolph Knipe.

It was an exciting moment when the two men—the one, short plump, breviped—the other tall, thin and toothy—stood in the corridor before the control panel and got ready to run off the first story. All around them were walls dividing up into many small corridors, and the walls were covered with wiring and plugs and switches and huge glass valves. They were both nervous, Mr. Bohlen hopping from one foot to the other, quite unable to keep still.

"Which button?" Adolph Knipe asked, eyeing a row of small white discs that resembled the keys of a typewriter. "You choose, Mr. Bohlen. Lots of magazines to pick from—*Saturday Evening Post, Collier's, Ladies' Home Journal*—any one you like."

"Goodness me, boy! How do I know?" He was jumping up and down like a man with hives.

"Mr. Bohlen," Adolph Knipe said gravely, "do you realize that at this moment, with your little finger alone, you have it in your power to become the most versatile writer on this continent?"

"Listen, Knipe, just get on with it, will you please—and cut out the preliminaries."

"Okay, Mr. Bohlen. Then we'll make it . . . let me see—this one. How's that?" He extended one finger and pressed down a button with the name TODAY'S WOMAN printed across it in diminutive black type. There was a sharp click, and when he took his finger away, the button remained down, below the level of the others.

"So much for the selection," he said. "Now—here we go!" He reached up and pulled a switch on the panel. Immediately, the room was filled with a loud humming noise, and a crackling of electric sparks, and the jingle of many, tiny, quickly moving levers; and almost in the same instant, sheets of quarto paper began sliding out from a slot to the right of the control panel and dropping into a basket below. They came out quick, one sheet a second, and in less than half a minute it was all over. The sheets stopped coming.

"That's it!" Adolph Knipe cried. "There's your story!"

They grabbed the sheets and began to read. The first one they picked up started as follows: "Aifkjmbsaoegwcz-gwcztpplnvoqudskigt&,fuhpekanvbertyuiolkjhgfdsazxcvbnm, peruitrehdjkgmvnb,wmsuy . . ." They looked at the others. The style was roughly similar in all of them. Mr. Bohlen began to shout. The younger man tried to calm him down.

"It's all right, sir. Really it is. It only needs a little adjustment. We've got a connection wrong somewhere, that's all. You must remember, Mr. Bohlen, there's over a million feet of wiring in this room. You can't expect everything to be right first time."

"It'll never work," Mr. Bohlen said.

"Be patient, sir. Be patient."

Adolph Knipe set out to discover the fault, and in four days' time he announced that all was ready for the next try.

"It'll never work," Mr. Bohlen said. "I know it'll never work."

Knipe smiled and pressed the selector button marked *Reader's Digest*. Then he pulled the switch, and again the strange, exciting, humming sound filled the room. One page of typescript flew out of the slot into the basket.

"Where's the rest?" Mr. Bohlen cried. "It's stopped! It's gone wrong!"

"No, sir, it hasn't. It's exactly right. It's for the *Digest*, don't you see?"

This time, it began: "Fewpeopleyetknowthatarevolution-arynewcurehasbeendiscoveredwhichmaywellbringpermanent relieftosufferersofthemostdreadeddiseaseofourtime . . ." And so on.

"It's gibberish!" Mr. Bohlen shouted.

"No, sir, it's fine. Can't you see? It's simply that she's not breaking up the words. That's an easy adjustment. But the story's there. Look, Mr. Bohlen, look! It's all there except the words are joined together."

And indeed it was.

On the next try a few days later, everything was perfect, even the punctuation. The first story they ran off, for a famous women's magazine, was a solid, plotty story of a boy who wanted to better himself with his rich employer. This boy arranged, so the story went, for a friend to hold up the rich man's daughter on a dark night when she was driving home. Then the boy himself, happening by, knocked the gun out of his friend's hand and rescued the girl. The girl was grateful. But the father was suspicious. He questioned the boy sharply. The boy broke down and confessed. Then the father, instead of kicking him out of the house, said that he admired the boy's resourcefulness. The girl admired his honesty—and his looks. The father promised him to be head of the Accounts Department. The girl married him.

"It's tremendous, Mr. Bohlen! It's exactly right!"

"Seems a bit sloppy to me, my boy."

"No, sir, it's a seller, a real seller!"

In his excitement, Adolph Knipe promptly ran off six more stories in as many minutes. All of them—except one, which for some reason came out a trifle lewd—seemed entirely satisfactory.

Mr. Bohlen was now mollified. He agreed to set up a literary agency in an office downtown, and to put Knipe in charge. In a couple of weeks, this was accomplished. Then Knipe mailed out the first dozen stories. He put his own name to four of them, Mr. Bohlen's to one, and for the others he simply invented names.

Five of these stories were promptly accepted. The one with Mr. Bohlen's name on it was turned down with a letter from the fiction editor saying, "This is a skilful job, but in our opinion it doesn't quite come off. We would like to see more of this writer's work . . ." Adolph Knipe took a cab out to the factory and ran off another story for the same magazine. He again put Mr. Bohlen's name to it, and mailed it out immediately. That one they bought.

The money started pouring in. Knipe slowly and carefully stepped up the output, and in six months' time he was delivering thirty stories a week, and selling about half.

He began to make a name for himself in literary circles as a prolific and successful writer. So did Mr. Bohlen; but not quite such a good name, although he didn't know it. At the same time, Knipe was building up a dozen or more fictitious persons as promising young authors. Everything was going fine.

At this point it was decided to adapt the machine for writing novels as well as stories. Mr. Bohlen, thirsting now for greater honors in the literary world, insisted that Knipe go to work at once on this prodigious task.

"I want to do a novel," he kept saying. "I want to do a novel."

"And so you will, sir. And so you will. But please be patient. This is a very complicated adjustment I have to make."

"Everyone tells me I ought to do a novel," Mr. Bohlen cried. "All sorts of publishers are chasing after me day and night begging me to stop fooling around with stories and do something really important instead. A novel's the only thing that counts—that's what they say."

"We're all going to do novels," Knipe told him. "Just as many as we want. But please be patient."

"Now listen to me, Knipe. What I'm going to do is a *serious* novel, something that'll make 'em sit up and take notice. I've been getting rather tired of the sort of stories you've been putting my name to lately. As a matter of fact, I'm none too sure you haven't been trying to make a monkey out of me."

"A monkey, Mr. Bohlen?"

"Keeping all the best ones for yourself, that's what you've been doing."

"Oh no, Mr. Bohlen! No!"

"So this time I'm going to make damn sure I write a high-class intelligent book. You understand that."

"Look, Mr. Bohlen. With the sort of switchboard I'm rigging up, you'll be able to write any sort of book you want."

And this was true, for within another couple of months, the genius of Adolph Knipe had not only adapted the machine for novel writing, but had constructed a marvelous new control system which enabled the author to pre-select literally any type of plot and any style of writing he desired. There were so many dials and levers on the thing, it looked like the instrument panel of some enormous airplane.

First, by depressing one of a series of master buttons, the writer made his primary decision: historical, satirical, philosophical, political, romantic, erotic, humorous, or straight. Then, from the second row (the basic buttons), he chose his theme: army life, pioneer days, civil war, world war, racial problem, wild west, country life, childhood memories, seafaring, the sea bottom, and many, many more. The third row of buttons gave a choice of literary style: classical, whimsical, racy, Hemingway, Faulkner, Joyce, feminine, etc. The fourth row was for characters, the fifth for wordage—and so on and so on—ten long rows of pre-selector buttons.

But that wasn't all. Control had also to be exercised during the actual writing process (which took about fifteen minutes per novel), and to do this the author had to sit, as it were, in the driver's seat, and pull (or push) a battery of labeled stops, as on an organ. By so doing, he was able continually to modulate or merge fifty different and variable qualities such as tension, surprise, humor, pathos, and mystery. Numerous dials and gauges on the dashboard itself told him throughout exactly how far along he was with his work.

Finally, there was the question of "passion." From a careful study of the books at the top of the best-seller lists for the past year, Adolph Knipe had decided that this was the most important ingredient of all—a magical catalyst that somehow or other could transform the dullest novel into a howling success—at any rate financially. But Knipe also knew that passion was powerful, heady stuff, and must be prudently dispensed—the right proportions at the right moments; and to ensure this, he had devised an independent control consisting of two sensitive sliding adjustors operated by footpedals, similar to the throttle and brake in a car. One pedal governed the percentage of passion to be injected, the other regulated its intensity. There was no doubt, of course—and this was the only drawback —that the writing of a novel by the Knipe method was going to be rather like flying a plane and driving a car and playing an organ all at the same time, but this did not trouble the inventor. When all was ready, he proudly escorted Mr. Bohlen into the machine house and began to explain the operating procedure for the new wonder.

"Good God, Knipe! I'll never be able to do all that! Dammit, man, it'd be easier to write the thing by hand!"

"You'll soon get used to it, Mr. Bohlen, I promise you. In a week or two, you'll be doing it without hardly thinking. It's just like learning to drive."

Well, it wasn't quite as easy as that, but after many

hours of practice, Mr. Bohlen began to get the hang of it, and finally, late one evening, he told Knipe to make ready for running off the first novel. It was a tense moment, with the fat little man crouching nervously in the driver's seat, and the tall toothy Knipe fussing excitedly around him.

"I intend to write an important novel, Knipe."

"I'm sure you will, sir. I'm sure you will."

With one finger, Mr. Bohlen carefully pressed the neces-sary pre-selector buttons:

Master button—*satirical*

Subject—*racial problem*

Style—*classical*

Characters—*six men, four women, one infant*

Length—*fifteen chapters.*

At the same time he had his eye particularly upon three organ stops marked *power, mystery, profundity.*

"Are you ready, sir?"

"Yes, yes, I'm ready."

Knipe pulled the switch. The great engine hummed. There was a deep whirring sound from the oiled movement of fifty thousand cogs and rods and levers; then came the drumming of the rapid electrical typewriter, setting up a shrill, almost intolerable clatter. Out into the basket flew the typewritten pages—one every two seconds. But what with the noise and the excitement, and having to play upon the stops, and watch the chapter-counter and the pace-indicator and the passion-gauge, Mr. Bohlen began to panic. He reacted in precisely the way a learner driver does in a car—by pressing both feet down hard on the pedals and keeping them there until the thing stopped.

"Congratulations on your first novel," Knipe said, picking up the great bundle of typed pages from the basket.

Little pearls of sweat were oozing out all over Mr. Bohlen's face. "It sure was hard work, my boy."

"But you got it done, sir. You got it done."

"Let me see it, Knipe. How does it read?"

He started to go through the first chapter, passing each finished page to the younger man.

"Good heavens, Knipe! What's this?" Mr. Bohlen's thin purple fish-lip was moving slightly as it mouthed the words, his cheeks were beginning slowly to inflate.

"But look here, Knipe! This is outrageous!"

"I must say it's a bit fruity, sir."

"*Fruity!* It's perfectly revolting! I can't possibly put my name to this!"

"Quite right, sir. Quite right."

"Knipe! Is this some nasty trick you've been playing on me?"

"O no, sir! No!"

"It certainly looks like it."

"You don't think, Mr. Bohlen, that you mightn't have been pressing a little hard on the passion-control pedals, do you?"

"My dear boy, how should *I* know?"

"Why don't you try another?"

So Mr. Bohlen ran off a second novel, and this time it went according to plan.

Within a week, the manuscript had been read and accepted by an enthusiastic publisher. Knipe followed with one in his own name, then made a dozen more for good measure. In no time at all, Adolph Knipe's Literary Agency had become famous for its large stable of promising young novelists. And once again the money started rolling in.

It was at this stage that young Knipe began to display a real talent for big business.

"See here, Mr. Bohlen," he said. "We still got too much competition. Why don't we just absorb all the other writers in the country?"

Mr. Bohlen, who now sported a bottle-green velvet jacket and allowed his hair to cover two-thirds of his ears, was quite content with things the way they were. "Don't know what you mean, my boy. You can't just absorb writers."

"Of course you can, sir. Exactly like Rockefeller did with his oil companies. Simply buy 'em out, and if they won't sell, squeeze 'em out. It's easy!"

"Careful now, Knipe. Be careful."

"I've got a list here, sir, of fifty of the most successful writers in the country, and what I intend to do is offer each one of them a lifetime contract with pay. All *they* have to do is undertake never to write another word; and, of course, to let us use their names on our own stuff. How about that?"

"They'll never agree."

"You don't know writers, Mr. Bohlen. You watch and see."

"What about that creative urge, Knipe?"

"It's bunk! All they're really interested in is the money —just like everybody else."

In the end, Mr. Bohlen reluctantly agreed to give it a try, and Knipe, with his list of writers in his pocket, went off in a large chauffeur-driven Cadillac to make his calls.

He journeyed first to the man at the top of the list, a very great and wonderful writer, and he had no trouble getting into the house. He told his story and produced a suitcase full of sample novels, and a contract for the man to sign which guaranteed him so much a year for life. The man listened politely, decided he was dealing with a lunatic, gave him a drink, then firmly showed him to the door.

The second writer on the list, when he saw Knipe was serious, actually attacked him with a large metal paperweight, and the inventor had to flee down the garden followed by such a torrent of abuse and obscenity as he had never heard before.

But it took more than this to discourage Adolph Knipe. He was disappointed but not dismayed, and off he went in his big car to seek his next client. This one was a female, famous and popular, whose fat romantic books sold by the million across the country. She received Knipe graciously, gave him tea, and listened attentively to his story.

"It all sounds very fascinating," she said. "But of course I find it a little hard to believe."

"Madam," Knipe answered. "Come with me and see it with your own eyes. My car awaits you."

So off they went, and in due course, the astonished lady was ushered into the machine house where the wonder was kept. Eagerly, Knipe explained its workings, and after a while he even permitted her to sit in the driver's seat and practice with the buttons.

"All right," he said suddenly. "You want to do a book now?"

"Oh yes!" she cried. "Please!"

She was very competent and seemed to know exactly what she wanted. She made her own pre-selections, then ran off a long, romantic, passion-filled novel. She read through the first chapter and became so enthusiastic that she signed up on the spot.

"That's one of them out of the way," Knipe said to Mr. Bohlen afterwards. "A pretty big one too."

"Nice work, my boy."

"And you know *why* she signed?"

"Why?"

"It wasn't the money. She's got plenty of that."

"Then why?"

Knipe grinned, lifting his lip and baring a long pale upper gum. "Simply because she saw the machine-made stuff was better than her own."

Thereafter, Knipe wisely decided to concentrate only upon mediocrity. Anything better than that—and there were so few it didn't matter much—was apparently not quite so easy to seduce.

In the end, after several months of work, he had persuaded something like seventy per cent of the writers on his list to sign the contract. He found that the older ones, those who were running out of ideas and had taken to drink, were the easiest to handle. The younger people were more troublesome. They were apt to become abusive, sometimes violent when he approached them; and more than once Knipe was slightly injured on his rounds.

But on the whole, it was a satisfactory beginning. This last year—the first full year of the machine's operation—it was estimated that at least one half of all the novels and stories published in the English language were produced by Adolph Knipe upon the Great Automatic Grammatisator.

Does this surprise you?

I doubt it.

And worse is yet to come. Today, as the secret spreads, many more are hurrying to tie up with Mr. Knipe. And all the time the screw turns tighter for those who hesitate to sign their names.

This very moment, as I sit here listening to the howling of my nine starving children in the other room, I can feel my own hand creeping closer and closer to that golden contract that lies over on the other side of the desk.

Give us strength, O Lord, to let our children starve.

⚙ *Idris Seabright*

AN EGG A MONTH FROM ALL OVER

When the collector from Consolidated Eggs found the mnxx bird egg on the edge of the cliff, he picked it up unsuspiciously. A molded mnxx bird egg looks almost exactly like the chu lizard eggs the collector was hunting, and this egg bore no visible signs of the treatment it had received at the hands of Jreel just before Krink's hatchet men caught up with him. The collector was paid by the egg; everything that came along was grist to his mill. He put the molded mnxx bird egg in his bag.

George Lidders lived alone in a cabin in the desert outside Phoenix. The cabin had only one room, but at least a third of the available space was taken up by an enormous incubator. George was a charter member of the Egg-of-the-Month Club, and he never refused one of their selections. He loved hatching eggs.

George had come to Phoenix originally with his mother for her health. He had taken care of her faithfully until her death, and now that she was gone, he missed her terribly. He had never spoken three consecutive words to any woman except her in his life. His fantasies, when he was base enough to have any, were pretty unpleasant. He was forty-six.

On Thursday morning he walked into Phoenix for his mail. As he scuffled over the sand toward the post office substation, he was hoping there would be a package for him from the Egg-of-the-Month Club. He was feeling tired, tired and depressed. He had been sleeping badly, with lots of nightmares. A nice egg package would cheer him up.

The South American mail rocket, cleaving the sky overhead, distracted him momentarily. If he had enough money, would he travel? Mars, Venus, star-side? No, he didn't think so. Travel wasn't really interesting. Eggs . . . Eggs (but the thought was a little frightening), eggs were the only thing he had to go on living for.

The postmistress greeted him unsmilingly. "Package for you, Mr. Lidders. From the egg club. You got to brush for it." She handed him a slip.

George brushed, his hand shaking with excitement. This must be his lucky morning. It might even be a double selection; the package seemed unusually big. His lips began to lift at the corners. With a nod in place of thanks, he took the parcel from the postmistress, and went out, clutching it.

The woman looked after him disapprovingly. "I want you to stay away from that gesell, Fanny," she said to her eleven-year-old daughter, who was reading a postcard in the back of the cubicle. "There's something funny about him and his eggs."

"Oksey-snoksey, mums, if you say so. But lots of people hatch eggs."

The postmistress sniffed. "Not the way he hatches eggs," she said prophetically.

On the way home George tore the wrapper from the box. He couldn't wait any longer. He pulled back the flaps eagerly.

Inside the careful packing there was a large, an unusually large, pale blue-green egg. Its surface stood up in tiny bosses, instead of being smooth as eggs usually were, and the shell gave the impression of being more than ordinarily thick. According to the instructions with the parcel, it was a chu lizard egg from the planet Morx, a little-known satellite of Amorgos. It was to be incubated at a temperature of 76.3 C. with high humidity. It would hatch in about eight days.

George felt the surface of the egg lovingly. If only Mother were here to see it! She had always been interested in his egg hatching; it was the only thing he had ever wanted to do that she had really approved of. And this was an unusually interesting egg.

When he got home he went straight to the incubator. Tenderly he laid the *soi-disant* chu lizard egg in one of the compartments; carefully he adjusted the temperature control. Then he sat down on the black and red afghan on his cot (his mother had crocheted the coverlet for him just before she passed away), and once more read the brochure that had come with the egg.

When he had finished it, he sighed. It was too bad there weren't any other eggs in the incubator now, eggs that were on the verge of hatching. Eight days was a long time to wait. But this egg looked wonderfully promising; he didn't know when the club had sent out an egg that attracted him so. And from one point of view it was a good thing he hadn't any hatchings on hand. Hatching, for all its excitement, was a sort of ordeal. It always left him feeling nervously exhausted and weak.

He had lunch, and after lunch, lying under the red and black afghan, he had a little nap. When he woke it was late afternoon. He went over to the incubator and looked in. The egg hadn't changed. He hadn't expected it would.

His nap hadn't cheered or refreshed him. He was almost more tired than he had been when he lay down to sleep. Sighing, he went around to the other side of the incubator and stared at the cage where he kept the things he had hatched out. After a moment he took his eyes away. They weren't interesting, really—lizards and birds and an attractive small snake or two. He wasn't interested in the things that were in eggs after they had hatched out.

In the evening he read a couple of chapters in the *Popular Guide to Egg Hatchery.*

He woke early the next morning, his heart hammering. He'd had another of those nightmares. But—his mind wincingly explored the texture of the dream—but it hadn't been all nightmare. There'd been a definitely pleasurable element in it, and the pleasure had been somehow connected with the egg that had come yesterday. Funny. (Jreel, who had molded the mnxx bird egg from its original cuboid into the present normal ovoid shape, wouldn't have found it funny at all.) It was funny about dreams.

He got grapes from the cupboard and made *café à la*

crême on the hotplate. He breakfasted. After breakfast he looked at his new egg.

The temperature and humidity were well up. It was about time for him to give the egg a quarter of a turn, as the hatching booklet suggested. He reached in the compartment, and was surprised to find it full of a dry, brisk, agreeable warmth. It seemed to be coming from the egg.

How odd! He stood rubbing the sprouting whiskers on his upper lip. After a moment he tapped the two gauges. No, the needles weren't stuck; they wobbled normally. He went around to the side of the incubator and checked the connections. Everything was sound and tight, nothing unusual. He must have imagined the dry warmth. Rather apprehensively, he put his hand back in the compartment—he still hadn't turned the egg—and was relieved to find the air in it properly humid. Yes, he must have imagined it.

After lunch he cleaned the cabin and did little chores. Abruptly, when he was half through drying the lunch dishes, the black depression that had threatened him ever since Mother died swallowed him up. It was like a physical blackness; he put down the dish undried and groped his way over to a chair. For a while he sat unmoving, his hands laced over his little stomach, while he sank deeper and deeper into despair. Mother was gone; he was forty-six; he had nothing to live for, not a thing . . . He escaped from the depression at last, with a final enormous guilty effort, into one of his more unpleasant fantasies. The imago within the molded mnxx bird egg, still plastic within its limey shell, felt the strain and responded to it with an inaudible grunt.

On the third day of the hatching, the egg began to enlarge. George hung over the incubator, fascinated. He had seen eggs change during incubation before, of course. Sometimes the shells got dry and chalky; sometimes they were hygroscopic and picked up moisture from the air. But he had never seen an egg act like this one. It seemed to be swelling up like an inflating balloon.

He reached in the compartment and touched the egg lightly. The shell, that had been so limey and thick when he first got it, was now warm and yielding and gelatinous. There was something uncanny about it. Involuntarily, George rubbed his fingers on his trouser leg.

He went back to the incubator at half-hour intervals. Every time it seemed to him that the egg was a little bigger than it had been. It was wonderfully interesting; he had never seen such a fascinating egg.

He got out the hatching instructions booklet and studied it. No, there was nothing said about changes in shell surface during incubation, and nothing about the egg's incredible increase in size. And the booklets were usually careful about mentioning such things. The directors of the Egg-of-the-Month Club didn't want their subscribers to overlook anything interesting that would happen during the incubation days. They wanted you to get your money's worth.

There must be some mistake. George, booklet in hand, stared at the incubator doubtfully. Perhaps the egg had been sent him by mistake; perhaps he hadn't been meant to have it. (He was right in both these suppositions: Jreel had meant the egg for Krink, as a little gift.) Perhaps he ought to get rid of the egg. An unauthorized egg might be dangerous.

Hesitantly he raised the incubator lid. It would be a shame, but—yes, he'd throw the egg out. Anything, anything at all might be inside an egg. There was no sense in taking chances. He approached his hand. The imago, dimly aware that it was at a crucial point in its affairs, exerted itself.

George's hand halted a few inches from the egg. He had broken into a copious sweat, and his forearm was one large cramp. Why, he must have been crazy. He didn't want—he couldn't possibly want to—get rid of the egg. What had been the matter with him? He perceived very clearly now what he thought he must have sensed dimly all along; that there was a wonderful promise in the egg.

A promise of what? Of—he couldn't be sure—but of warmth, of sleep, of rest. A promise of something he'd been wanting all his life. He couldn't be any more specific than that. But if what he thought might be in the egg was actually there, it wouldn't matter any more that Mother was dead and that he was forty-six and lonely. He'd—he gulped and sighed deeply—he'd be happy. Satisfied.

The egg kept on enlarging, though more slowly, until late that evening. Then it stopped.

George was in a froth of nervous excitement. In the

course of watching the egg's slow growth, he had chewed his fingernails until three of them were down to the quick and ready to bleed. Still keeping his eyes fixed on the egg, he went to the dresser, got a nail file, and began to file his nails. The operation soothed him. By midnight, when it became clear that nothing more was going to happen immediately, he was calm enough to go to bed. He had no dreams.

The fourth and fifth days passed without incident. On the sixth day George perceived that though the egg was of the same size, its shell had hardened and become once more opaque. And on the eighth day—to this extent the molded mnxx bird egg was true to the schedule laid down in the booklet for the chu lizard—the egg began to crack.

George felt a rapturous excitement. He hovered over the incubator breathlessly, his hands clutching the air-and-water conduits for support. As the tiny fissure enlarged, he kept gasping and licking his lips. He was too agitated to be capable of coherent thought, but it occurred to him that what he really expected to come out of the egg was a bird of some sort, some wonderful, wonderful bird.

The faint pecking from within the egg grew louder. The dark fissure on the pale blue-green background widened and spread. The halves of the shell fell back suddenly, like the halves of a door. The egg was open. There was nothing inside.

Nothing. Nothing. For a moment George felt that he had gone mad. He rubbed his eyes and trembled. Disappointment and incredulity were sickening him. He picked up the empty shell.

It was light and chalky and faintly warm to the touch. He felt inside it unbelievingly. There was nothing there.

His frustration was stifling. For a moment he thought of crumpling up newspapers and setting the cabin on fire. Then he put the halves of the shell down on the dresser and went wobblingly toward the door. He'd—go for a walk.

The mnxx bird imago, left alone within the cabin, flitted about busily.

The moon had risen when George got back. In the course of his miserable wanderings, he had stopped on a slight rise and shed a few salty tears. Now he was feeling, if not better, somewhat more resigned. His earlier hopes, his later disappointment, had been succeeded by a settled hope-lessness.

The mnxx bird was waiting behind the door of the cabin for him.

In its flittings in the cabin during his absence, it had managed to assemble for itself a passable body. It had used newspapers, grapes, and black wool from the afghan as materials. What it had made was short and squat and ex-cessively female, not at all alluring, but it thought George would like it. It held the nail file from the dresser in its one completed hand.

George shut the cabin door behind him. His arm moved toward the light switch. He halted, transfixed by the great-est of the surprises of the day. He saw before him, glim-mering wanly in the moonlight from the window, the woman of his—let's be charitable—dreams.

She was great-breasted, thighed like an idol. Her face was only a blur; there the mnxx bird had not felt it neces-sary to be specific. But she moved toward George with a heavy sensual swaying; she was what George had always wanted and been ashamed of wanting. She was here. He had no questions. She was his. Desire was making him drunk. He put out his hands.

The newspaper surface, so different from what he had been expecting, startled him. He uttered a surprised cry. The mnxx bird saw no reason for waiting any longer. George was caressing one grape-tipped breast uncertainly. The mnxx raised its right arm, the one that was complete, and drove the nail file into his throat.

The mnxx bird was amazed at the amount of blood in its victim. Jreel, when he had been molding the imago with his death wishes for Krink, had said nothing about this. The inhabitants of the planet Morx do not have much blood.

After a momentary disconcertment, the mnxx went on with its business. It had, after all, done what it had been molded to do. Now there awaited it a more personal task.

It let the woman's body it had shaped collapse behind it carelessly. The newspapers made a whuffing sound. In a kind of rapture it threw itself on George. His eyes would be admirable for mnxx bird eyes, it could use his skin, his hair, his teeth. Admirable material! Trembling invisibly with the joy of creation, the mnxx bird set to work.

When it had finished, George lay on the sodden carpet flaccidly. His eyes were gone, and a lot of his vital organs. Things were over for him. He had had, if not all he wanted, all he was ever going to get. He was quiet. He was dead. He was satisfied.

The mnxx bird, on the fine strong wings it had plaited for itself out of George's head hair, floated out into the night.

✸ *Ray Bradbury*

THERE WILL COME SOFT RAINS

In the living room the voice-clock sang, *Tick-tock, seven o'clock, time to get up, time to get up, seven o'clock!* as if it were afraid that nobody would. The morning house lay empty. The clock ticked on, repeating and repeating its sounds into the emptiness. *Seven-nine, breakfast time, seven-nine!*

In the kitchen the breakfast stove gave a hissing sigh and ejected from its warm interior eight pieces of perfectly browned toast, eight eggs sunnyside up, sixteen slices of bacon, two coffees, and two cool glasses of milk.

"Today is August 4, 2026," said a second voice from the kitchen ceiling, "in the city of Allendale, California." It repeated the date three times for memory's sake. "Today is Mr. Featherstone's birthday. Today is the anniversary of Tilita's marriage. Insurance is payable, as are the water, gas, and light bills."

Somewhere in the walls, relays clicked, memory tapes glided under electric eyes.

Eight-one, tick-tock, eight-one o'clock, off to school, off to work, run, run, eight-one! But no doors slammed, no carpets took the soft tread of rubber heels. It was raining outside. The weather box on the front door sang quietly: "Rain, rain, go away; rubbers, raincoats for today . . ." And the rain tapped on the empty house, echoing.

Outside, the garage chimed and lifted its door to reveal the waiting car. After a long wait the door swung down again.

At eight-thirty the eggs were shriveled and the toast

was like stone. An aluminum wedge scraped them into the sink, where hot water whirled them down a metal throat which digested and flushed them away to the distant sea. The dirty dishes were dropped into a hot washer and emerged twinkling dry.

Nine-fifteen, sang the clock, *time to clean*.

Out of warrens in the wall, tiny robot mice darted. The rooms were acrawl with the small cleaning animals, all rubber and metal. They thudded against chairs, whirling their mustached runners, kneading the rug nap, sucking gently at hidden dust. Then, like mysterious invaders, they popped into their burrows. Their pink electric eyes faded. The house was clean.

Ten o'clock. The sun came out from behind the rain. The house stood alone in a city of rubble and ashes. This was the one house left standing. At night the ruined city gave off a radioactive glow which could be seen for miles.

Ten-fifteen. The garden sprinklers whirled up in golden founts, filling the soft morning air with scatterings of brightness. The water pelted windowpanes, running down the charred west side where the house had been burned evenly free of its white paint. The entire west face of the house was black, save for five places. Here the silhouette in paint of a man mowing a lawn. Here, as in a photograph, a woman bent to pick flowers. Still farther over, his image burned on wood in one titanic instant, a small boy, hands flung into the air; higher up, the image of a thrown ball, and opposite him a girl, hands raised to catch a ball which never came down.

The five spots of paint—the man, the woman, the children, the ball—remained. The rest was a thin charcoaled layer.

The gentle sprinkler rain filled the garden with falling light.

Until this day, how well the house had kept its peace. How carefully it had inquired, "Who goes there? What's the password?" and, getting no answer from lonely foxes and whining cats, it had shut up its windows and drawn shades in an old-maidenly preoccupation with self-protection which bordered on a mechanical paranoia.

It quivered at each sound, the house did. If a sparrow brushed a window, the shade snapped up. The bird, startled, flew off! No, not even a bird must touch the house!

The house was an altar with ten thousand attendants, big, small, servicing, attending, in choirs. But the gods had gone away, and the ritual of the religion continued senselessly, uselessly.

Twelve noon.

A dog whined, shivering, on the front porch.

The front door recognized the dog voice and opened. The dog, once huge and fleshy, but now gone to bone and covered with sores, moved in and through the house, tracking mud. Behind it whirred angry mice, angry at having to pick up mud, angry at inconvenience.

For not a leaf fragment blew under the door but what the wall panels flipped open and the copper scrap rats flashed swiftly out. The offending dust, hair, or paper, seized in miniature steel jaws, was raced back to the burrows. There, down tubes which fed into the cellar, it was dropped into the sighing vent of an incinerator which sat like evil Baal in a dark corner.

The dog ran upstairs, hysterically yelping at each door, at last realizing, as the house realized, that only silence was here.

It sniffed the air and scratched the kitchen door. Behind the door, the stove was making pancakes which filled the house with a rich baked odor and the scent of maple syrup.

The dog frothed at the mouth, lying at the door, sniffing, its eyes turned to fire. It ran wildly in circles, biting at its tail, spun in a frenzy, and died. It lay in the parlor for an hour.

Two o'clock, sang a voice.

Delicately sensing decay at last, the regiments of mice hummed out as softly as blown gray leaves in an electrical wind.

Two-fifteen.

The dog was gone.

In the cellar, the incinerator glowed suddenly and a whirl of sparks leaped up the chimney.

Two thirty-five.

Bridge tables sprouted from patio walls. Playing cards fluttered onto pads in a shower of pips. Martinis manifested on an oaken bench with egg-salad sandwiches. Music played.

But the tables were silent and the cards untouched.

At four o'clock the tables folded like great butterflies back through the paneled walls.

Four-thirty.

The nursery walls glowed.

Animals took shape: yellow giraffes, blue lions, pink antelopes, lilac panthers cavorting in crystal substance. The walls were glass. They looked out upon color and fantasy. Hidden films clocked through well-oiled sprockets, and the walls lived. The nursery floor was woven to resemble a crisp, cereal meadow. Over this ran aluminum roaches and iron crickets, and in the hot still air butterflies of delicate red tissue wavered among the sharp aroma of animal spoors! There was the sound like a great matted yellow hive of bees within a dark bellows, the lazy bumble of a purring lion. And there was the patter of okapi feet and the murmur of a fresh jungle rain, like other hoofs, falling upon the summer-starched grass. Now the walls dissolved into distances of parched weed, mile on mile, and warm endless sky. The animals drew away into thorn brakes and water holes.

It was the children's hour.

Five o'clock. The bath filled with clear hot water.

Six, seven, eight o'clock. The dinner dishes manipulated like magic tricks, and in the study a *click*. In the metal stand, opposite the hearth where a fire now blazed up warmly, a cigar popped out, half an inch of soft gray ash on it, smoking, waiting.

Nine o'clock. The beds warmed their hidden circuits, for nights were cool here.

Nine-five. A voice spoke from the study ceiling.

"Mrs. McClellan, which poem would you like this evening?"

The house was silent.

The voice said at last, "Since you express no preference, I shall select a poem at random." Quiet music rose to back the voice. "Sara Teasdale. As I recall, your favorite . . .

"There will come soft rains and the smell of the ground,
And swallows circling with their shimmering sound;
And frogs in the pools singing at night,
And wild plum trees in tremulous white;
Robins will wear their feathery fire,
Whistling their whims on a low fence-wire;
And not one will know of the war, not one
Will care at last when it is done.
Not one would mind, neither bird nor tree,
If mankind perished utterly;
And Spring herself, when she woke at dawn,
Would scarcely know that we were gone."

The fire burned on the stone hearth and the cigar fell away into a mound of quiet ash on its tray. The empty chairs faced each other between the silent walls, and the music played.

At ten o'clock the house began to die.

The wind blew. A falling tree bough crashed through the kitchen window. Cleaning solvent, bottled, shattered over the stove. The room was ablaze in an instant!

"Fire!" screamed a voice. The house lights flashed, water pumps shot water from the ceilings. But the solvent spread on the linoleum, licking, eating, under the kitchen door, while the voices took it up in chorus: "Fire, fire, fire!"

The house tried to save itself. Doors sprang tightly shut, but the windows were broken by the heat and the wind blew and sucked upon the fire.

The house gave ground as the fire in ten billion angry sparks moved with flaming ease from room to room and then up the stairs. While scurrying water rats squeaked from the walls, pistoled their water, and ran for more. And the wall sprays let down showers of mechanical rain.

But too late. Somewhere, sighing, a pump shrugged to a stop. The quenching rain ceased. The reserve water supply which had filled baths and washed dishes for many quiet days was gone.

The fire crackled up the stairs. It fed upon Picassos and Matisses in the upper halls, like delicacies, baking off the oily flesh, tenderly crisping the canvases into black shavings.

Now the fire lay in beds, stood in windows, changed the colors of drapes!

And then, reinforcements.

From attic trapdoors, blind robot faces peered down with faucet mouths gushing green chemical.

The fire backed off, as even an elephant must at the sight of a dead snake. Now there were twenty snakes whipping over the floor, killing the fire with a clear cold venom of green froth.

But the fire was clever. It had sent flame outside the house, up through the attic to the pumps there. An explosion! The attic brain which directed the pumps was shattered into bronze shrapnel on the beams.

The fire rushed back into every closet and felt of the clothes hung there.

The house shuddered, oak bone on bone, its bared skeleton cringing from the heat, its wires, its nerves revealed as if a surgeon had torn the skin off to let the red veins and capillaries quiver in the scalded air. Help, help! Fire! Run, run! Heat snapped mirrors like the first brittle winter ice. And the voices wailed Fire, fire, run, run, like a tragic nursery rhyme, a dozen voices, high, low, like children dying in a forest, alone, alone. And the voices faded as the wires popped their sheathings like hot chestnuts. One, two, three, four, five voices died.

In the nursery the jungle burned. Blue lions roared, purple giraffes bounded off. The panthers ran in circles, changing color, and ten million animals, running before the fire, vanished off toward a distant steaming river . . .

Ten more voices died. In the last instant under the fire avalanche, other choruses, oblivious, could be heard announcing the time, playing music, cutting the lawn by remote-control mower, or setting an umbrella frantically out and in the slamming and opening front door, a thousand things happening, like a clock shop when each clock strikes the hour insanely before or after the other, a scene of maniac confusion, yet unity; singing, screaming, a few last cleaning mice darting bravely out to carry the horrid ashes away! And one voice, with sublime disregard for the situation, read poetry aloud in the fiery study, until all the film spools burned, until all the wires withered and the circuits cracked.

The fire burst the house and let it slam flat down, puffing out skirts of spark and smoke.

In the kitchen, an instant before the rain of fire and timber, the stove could be seen making breakfasts at a psychopathic rate, ten dozen eggs, six loaves of toast, twenty dozen bacon strips, which, eaten by fire, started the stove working again, hysterically hissing!

The crash. The attic smashing into kitchen and parlor. The parlor into cellar, cellar into sub-cellar. Deep freeze, armchair, film tapes, circuits, beds, and all like skeletons thrown in a cluttered mound deep under.

Smoke and silence. A great quantity of smoke.

Dawn showed faintly in the east. Among the ruins, one wall stood alone. Within the wall, a last voice said, over and over again and again, even as the sun rose to shine upon the heaped rubble and steam:

"Today is August 5, 2026, today is August 5, 2026, today is . . ."

✸ *Theodore Sturgeon*

AND NOW THE NEWS . . .

The man's name was MacLyle, which by looking at you can tell wasn't his real name, but let's say this is fiction, shall we? MacLyle had a good job in—well—a soap concern. He worked hard and made good money and got married to a girl called Esther. He bought a house in the suburbs and after it was paid for he rented it to some people and bought a home a little farther out and a second car and a freezer and a power mower and a book on landscaping, and settled down to the worthy task of giving his kids all the things he never had.

He had habits and he had hobbies, like everybody else and (like everybody else) his were a little different from anybody's. The one that annoyed his wife the most, until she got used to it, was the news habit, or maybe hobby. MacLyle read a morning paper on the 8:14 and an evening paper on the 6:10, and the local paper his suburb used for its lost dogs and auction sales took up forty after-dinner minutes. And when he read a paper he read it, he didn't mess with it. He read Page 1 first and Page 2 next, and so on all the way through. He didn't care too much for books but he respected them in a mystical sort of way, and he used to say a newspaper was a kind of book, and so would raise particular hell if a section was missing or in upside down, or if the pages were out of line. He also heard the news on the radio. There were three stations in town with hourly broadcasts, one on the hour, one on the half-hour, and one five minutes before the hour, and he was usually able to catch them all. During these five-minute

periods he would look you right in the eye while you talked
to him and you'd swear he was listening to you, but he
wasn't. This was a particular trial to his wife, but only for
five years or so. Then she stopped trying to be heard while
the radio talked about floods and murders and scandal and
suicide. Five more years, and she went back to talking
right through the broadcasts, but by the time people are
married ten years, things like that don't matter; they talk
in code anyway, and nine-tenths of their speech can be
picked up anytime like ticker tape. He also caught the
7:30 news on Channel 2 and the 7:45 news on Channel 4
on television.

Now it might be imagined from all this that MacLyle
was a crotchety character with fixed habits and a neurotic
neatness, but this was far from the case. MacLyle was
basically a reasonable guy who loved his wife and children
and liked his work and pretty much enjoyed being alive.
He laughed easily and talked well and paid his bills. He
justified his preoccupation with the news in a number of
ways. He would quote Donne: "... *any man's death
diminishes me, because I am involved in mankind. ...*"
which is pretty solid stuff and hard to argue down. He
would point out that he made his trains and his trains
made him punctual, but that because of them he saw the
same faces at the same time day after endless day, before,
during, and after he rode those trains, so that his immediate
world was pretty circumscribed, and only a constant awareness of what was happening all over the earth kept him
conscious of the fact that he lived in a bigger place than a
thin straight universe with his house at one end, his office
at the other, and a railway track in between.

It's hard to say just when MacLyle started to go to
pieces, or even why, though it obviously had something to
do with all that news he exposed himself to. He began to
react, very slightly at first; that is, you could tell he was
listening. He'd *shh!* you, and if you tried to finish what you
were saying he'd run and stick his head in the speaker
grille. His wife and kids learned to shut up when the news
came on, five minutes before the hour until five minutes
after (with MacLyle's switching stations) and every hour
on the half-hour, and from 7:30 to 8 for the TV, and
during the forty minutes it took him to read the local paper.

He was not so obvious about it when he read his paper, because all he did was freeze over the pages like a cata- tonic, gripping the top corners until the sheets shivered, knotting his jaw and breathing from his nostrils with a strangled whistle.

Naturally all this was a weight on his wife Esther, who tried her best to reason with him. At first he answered her, saying mildly that a man has to keep in touch, you know; but very quickly he stopped responding altogether, giving her the treatment a practiced suburbanite gets so expert in, as when someone mentions a lawn mower just too damn early on Sunday morning. You don't say yes and you don't say no, you don't even grunt, and you don't move your head or even your eyebrows. After a while your inter- locutor goes away. Pretty soon you don't hear these ill- timed annoyances any more than you appear to.

It needs to be said again here that MacLyle was, outside his peculiarity, a friendly and easygoing character. He liked people and invited them and visited them, and he was one of those adults who can really listen to a first- grade child's interminable adventures and really care. He never forgot things like the slow leak in the spare tire or antifreeze or anniversaries, and he always got the storm windows up in time, but he didn't rub anyone's nose in his reliability. The first thing in his whole life he didn't take as a matter of course was this news thing that started so small and grew so quickly.

So after a few weeks of it his wife took the bull by the horns and spent the afternoon hamstringing every receiver in the house. There were three radios and two TV sets, and she didn't understand the first thing about them, but she had a good head and she went to work with a will and the can-opening limb of a pocket knife. From each receiver she removed one tube, and one at a time, so as not to get them mixed up, she carried them into the kitchen and meticulously banged their bases against the edge of the sink, being careful to crack no glass and bend no pins, until she could see the guts of the tube rolling around loose inside. Then she replaced them and got the back panels on the sets again.

MacLyle came home and put the car away and kissed her and turned on the living-room radio and then went to hang up his hat. When he returned the radio should have warmed up but it didn't. He twisted the knobs a while and bumped it and rocked it back and forth a little, grunting, and then noticed the time. He began to feel a little frantic, and raced back to the kitchen and turned on the little ivory radio on the shelf. It warmed up quickly and cheerfully and gave him a clear sixty-cycle hum, but that was all. He behaved badly from then on, roaring out the information that the sets didn't work, either of them, as if that wasn't pretty evident by that time, and flew upstairs to the boys' room, waking them explosively. He turned on their radio and got another sixty-cycle note, this time with a shattering microphonic when he rapped the case, which he did four times, whereupon the set went dead altogether.

Esther had planned the thing up to this point, but no further, which was the way her mind worked. She figured she could handle it, but she figured wrong. MacLyle came downstairs like a pallbearer, and he was silent and shaken until 7:30, time for the news on TV. The living-room set wouldn't peep, so up he went to the boys' room again, waking them just as they were nodding off again, and this time the little guy started to cry. MacLyle didn't care. When he found out there was no picture on the set, he almost started to cry too, but then he heard the sound come in. A TV set has an awful lot of tubes in it and Esther didn't know audio from video. MacLyle sat down in front of the dark screen and listened to the news. *"Everything seemed to be under control in the riot-ridden border country in India,"* said the TV set. Crowd noises and a background of Beethoven's "Turkish March." *"And then——"* Cut music. Crowd noise up: gabble-wurra and a scream. Announcer over: *"Six hours later, this was the scene."* Dead silence, going on so long that MacLyle reached out and thumped the TV set with the heel of his hand. Then, slow swell, Ketelbey's "In a Monastery Garden." *"On a more cheerful note, here are the six finalists in the Miss Continuum contest."* Background music, "Blue Room," interminably, interrupted only once, when the announcer said through a childish chuckle *". . . and she meant it!"* MacLyle pounded himself on the temples. The little guy continued to sob. Esther stood at the foot of the stairs wringing her hands. It went on for thirty minutes like this. All

MacLyle said when he came downstairs was that he wanted the paper—that would be the local one. So Esther faced the great unknown and told him frankly she hadn't ordered it and wouldn't again, which of course led to a full and righteous confession of her activities of the afternoon.

Only a woman married better than fourteen years can know a man well enough to handle him so badly. She was aware that she was wrong but that was quite overridden by the fact that she was logical. It would not be logical to continue her patience, so patience was at an end. That which offendeth thee, cast it out, yea, even thine eye and thy right hand. She realized too late that the news was so inextricably part of her husband that in casting it out she cast him out too. And out he went, while whitely she listened to the rumble of the garage door, the car door speaking its sharp syllables, clear as *Exit* in a playscript; the keen of a starter, the mourn of a motor. She said she was glad and went in the kitchen and tipped the useless ivory radio off the shelf and retired, weeping.

And yet, because true life offers few clean cuts, she saw him once more. At seven minutes to three in the morning she became aware of faint music from somewhere; unaccountably it frightened her, and she tiptoed about the house looking for it. It wasn't in the house, so she pulled on MacLyle's trench coat and crept down the steps into the garage. And there, just outside in the driveway, where steel beams couldn't interfere with radio reception, the car stood where it had been all along, and MacLyle was in the driver's seat dozing over the wheel. The music came from the car radio. She drew the coat tighter around her and went to the car and opened the door and spoke his name. At just that moment the radio said ". . . *and now the news*" and MacLyle bolted upright and *shh'*d furiously. She fell back and stood a moment in a strange transition from unconditional surrender to total defeat. Then he shut the car door and bent forward, his hand on the volume control, and she went back into the house.

After the news report was over and he had recovered himself from the stab wounds of a juvenile delinquent, the grinding agonies of a derailed train, the terrors of the near-crash of a C-119, and the fascination of a cabinet officer, charter member of the We Don't Trust Nobody Club, saying in exactly these words that there's a little bit of good in the worst of us and a little bit of bad in the best of us, all of which he felt keenly, he started the car (by rolling it down the drive because the battery was almost dead) and drove as slowly as possible into town.

At an all-night garage he had the car washed and greased while he waited, after which the automat was open and he sat in it for three hours drinking coffee, holding his jaw set until his back teeth ached, and making occasional, almost inaudible noises in the back of his throat. At nine he pulled himself together. He spent the entire day with his astonished attorney, going through all his assets, selling, converting, establishing, until when he was finished he had a modest packet of cash and his wife would have an adequate income until the children went to college, at which time the house would be sold, the tenants in the older house evicted, and Esther would be free to move to the smaller home with the price of the larger one added to the base capital. The lawyer might have entertained fears for MacLyle except for the fact that he was jovial and loquacious throughout, behaving like a happy man—a rare form of insanity, but acceptable. It was hard work but they did it in a day, after which MacLyle wrung the lawyer's hand and thanked him profusely and checked into a hotel.

When he awoke the following morning he sprang out of bed, feeling years younger, opened the door, scooped up the morning paper and glanced at the headlines.

He couldn't read them.

He grunted in surprise, closed the door gently, and sat on the bed with paper in his lap. His hands moved restlessly on it, smoothing and smoothing until the palms were shadowed and the type hazed. The shouting symbols marched across the page like a parade of strangers in some unrecognized lodge uniform, origins unknown, destination unknown, and the occasion for marching only to be guessed at. He traced the letters with his little finger, he measured the length of a word between his index finger and thumb and lifted them up to hold them before his wondering eyes. Suddenly he got up and crossed to the desk, where signs and placards and printed notes were trapped like a butterfly collection under glass—the breakfast menu, something about valet service, something about checking out. He remembered them all and had an idea of their significance—but he couldn't read them. In the drawer was stationery, with a picture of the building and no other buildings around it, which just wasn't so, and an inscription which might have been in Cyrillic for all he knew. Telegram blanks, a bus schedule, a blotter, all bearing hieroglyphs and runes, as far as he was concerned. A phone book full of strangers' names in strange symbols.

He requested of himself that he recite the alphabet. "A," he said clearly, and "Eh?" because it didn't sound right and he couldn't imagine what would. He made a small foolish grin and shook his head slightly and rapidly, but grin or no, he felt frightened. He felt glad, or relieved—mostly happy anyway, but still a little frightened.

He called the desk and told them to get his bill ready, and dressed and went downstairs. He gave the doorman his parking check and waited while they brought the car round. He got in and turned the radio on and started to drive west.

He drove for some days, in a state of perpetual, cold, and (for all that) happy fright—roller-coaster fright, horror-movie fright—remembering the significance of a stop sign without being able to read the word STOP across it, taking caution from the shape of a railroad-crossing notice. Restaurants look like restaurants, gas stations like gas stations; if Washington's picture denotes a dollar and Lincoln's five, one doesn't need to read them. MacLyle made out just fine. He drove until he was well into one of those square states with all the mountains and cruised until he recognized the section where, years before he was married, he had spent a hunting vacation. Avoiding the lodge he had used, he took back roads until, sure enough, he came to that deserted cabin in which he had sheltered one night, standing yet, rotting a bit but only around the edges. He wandered in and out of it for a long time, memorizing details because he could not make a list, and then got back into his car and drove to the nearest town, not very near and not very much of a town. At the general store he bought shingles and flour and nails and paint—all sorts of paint, in little cans, as well as big containers of house paint—and canned goods and tools. He ordered a knock-down windmill and a generator, eighty pounds of modeling clay, two loaf pans and a mixing bowl, and a war-surplus jungle hammock. He paid cash and promised to be back in two weeks for the things the store didn't stock, and wired (because it could be done over the phone) his lawyer to arrange for the predetermined eighty dollars a month which was all he cared to take for himself from his assets. Before he left he stood in wonder before a monstrous piece of musical plumbing called an ophicleide which stood, dusty and majestic, in a corner. (While it might be easier on the reader to make this a French horn or a sousaphone—which would answer narrative purposes quite as well—we're done telling lies here. MacLyle's real name is concealed, his home town cloaked, and his occupation disguised, and dammit it really was a twelve-keyed, 1824, fifty-inch, obsolete brass ophicleide.) The storekeeper explained how his great-grandfather had brought it over from the old country and nobody had played it for two generations except an itinerant tuba player who had turned pale green on the first three notes and put it down as if it were full of percussion caps. MacLyle asked how it sounded and the man told him, terrible. Two weeks later MacLyle was back to pick up the rest of his stuff, nodding and smiling and not saying a word. He still couldn't read, and now he couldn't speak. Even more, he had lost the power to understand speech. He had paid for the purchases with a hundred-dollar bill and a wistful expression, and then another hundred-dollar bill, and the storekeeper, thinking he had turned deaf and dumb, cheated him roundly but at the same time felt so sorry for him that he gave him the ophicleide. MacLyle loaded up his car happily and left. And that's the first part of the story about Mac-Lyle's being in a bad way.

MacLyle's wife Esther found herself in a peculiar position. Friends and neighbors offhandedly asked her questions to which she did not know the answers, and the only person who had any information at all—MacLyle's attorney —was under bond not to tell her anything. She had not, in the full and legal sense, been deserted, since she and the children were provided for. She missed MacLyle, but in a specialized way; she missed the old reliable MacLyle, and he had, in effect, left her long before that perplexing night when he had driven away. She wanted the old MacLyle back again, not this untrolleyed stranger with the grim and spastic preoccupation with the news. Of the many unpleasant facets of this stranger's personality, one glowed brightest, and that was that he was the sort of man who would walk out the way he did and stay away as long as he had. Ergo, he was that undesirable person just as long as he stayed away, and tracking him down would, if it returned him against his will, return to her only a person who was not the person she missed.

Yet she was dissatisfied with herself, for all that she was the injured party and had wounds less painful that the pangs of conscience. She had always prided herself on being a good wife, and had done many things in the past which were counter to her reason and her desires purely because they were consistent with being a good wife. So as time went on she gravitated from the "what shall I do?" area into the "what ought a good wife to do?" spectrum, and after a great deal of careful thought, went to see a psychiatrist.

He was a fairly intelligent psychiatrist which is to say he caught on to the obvious a little faster than most people. For example he became aware in only four minutes of conversation that MacLyle's wife Esther had not come to him on her own behalf, and further, decided to hear her out completely before resolving to treat her. When she had quite finished and he had dug out enough corroborative detail to get the picture, he went into a long silence and cogitated. He matched the broad pattern of MacLyle's case with his reading and his experience, recognized the challenge, the clinical worth of the case, the probable value of the heirloom diamond pendant worn by his visitor. He placed his finger tips together, lowered his fine young head, gazed through his eyebrows at MacLyle's wife Esther, and took up the gauntlet. At the prospects of getting her husband back safe and sane, she thanked him quietly and left the office with mixed emotions. The fairly intelligent psychiatrist drew a deep breath and began making arrangements with another headshrinker to take over his other patients, both of them, while he was away, because he figured to be away quite a while.

It was appallingly easy for him to trace MacLyle. He did not go near the lawyer. The solid foundation of all skip tracers and Bureaus of Missing Persons, in their *modus operandi,* is the piece of applied psychology which dictates that a man might change his name and his address, but he will seldom—can seldom—change the things he does, particularly the things he does to amuse himself. The ski addict doesn't skip to Florida, though he might make Banff instead of an habitual Mount Tremblant. A philatelist is not likely to mount butterflies. Hence when the psychiatrist found, among MacLyle's papers, some snapshots and brochures, dating from college days, of the towering Rockies, of bears feeding by the roadside, and especially of season after season's souvenirs of a particular resort to which he had never brought his wife and which he had not visited since he married her, it was worth a feeler, which went out in the form of a request to that state's police for information on a man of such-and-such description driving so-and-so with out-of-state plates, plus a request that the man not be detained nor warned, but only that he, the fairly intelligent psychiatrist, be notified. He threw out other lines, too, but this is the one that hooked the fish. It was a matter of weeks before a state patrol car happened by MacLyle's favorite general store: after that it was a matter of minutes before the information was in the hands of the psychiatrist. He said nothing to MacLyle's wife Esther except good-by for a while, and this bill is payable now, and then took off, bearing with him a bag of tricks.

He rented a car at the airport nearest MacLyle's hideout and drove a long, thirsty, climbing way until he came to the general store. There he interviewed the proprietor, learning some eighteen hundred items about how bad business could get, how hot it was, how much rain hadn't fallen and how much was needed, the tragedy of being blamed for high markups when anyone with the brains God gave a goose ought to know it cost plenty to ship things out here, especially in the small quantities necessitated by business being so bad and all; and betwixt and between, he learned eight or ten items about MacLyle—the exact location of his cabin, the fact that he seemed to have turned into a deaf-mute who was also unable to read, and that he must be crazy because who but a crazy man would want eighty-four different half-pint cans of house paint or, for that matter, live out here when he didn't have to?

The psychiatrist got loose after a while and drove off, and the country got higher and dustier and more lost every mile, until he began to pray that nothing would go wrong with the car, and sure enough, ten minutes later something had. Any car that made a noise like the one he began to hear was strictly a shot-rod, and he pulled over to the side to worry about it. He turned off the motor and the noise went right on, and he began to realize that the sound was not in the car or even near it, but came from somewhere uphill. There was a mile and a half more of the hill to go, and he drove it in increasing amazement, because that sound got louder and more impossible all the time. It was sort of like music, but like no music currently heard on this or any other planet. It was a solo voice, brass, with muscles. The upper notes, of which there seemed to be about two octaves, were wild and unmusical, the middle was rough, but the low tones were like the speech of these mountains themselves, big up to the sky, hot, and more natural than anything ought to be, basic as a bear's fang. Yet all the notes were perfect—their intervals were perfect—this awful noise was tuned like an electronic organ. The psychiatrist had a good ear, though for a while he wondered how long he'd have any ears at all, and he realized all these things about the sound, as well as the fact that it was rendering one of the more primitive fingering studies from Czerny, Book One, the droning little horror that goes: *do mi fa sol la sol fa mi, re fa sol la si la sol fa, mi sol la* . . . etcetera, inchworning up the scale and then descending hand over hand.

He saw blue sky almost under his front tires and wrenched the wheel hard over, and found himself in the grassy yard of a made-over prospector's cabin, but that he didn't notice right away because sitting in front of it was what he described to himself, startled as he was out of his professional detachment, as the craziest-looking man he had ever seen.

He was sitting under a parched, wind-warped Engle-mann spruce. He was barefoot up to the armpits. He wore the top half of a skivvy shirt and a hat the shape of one of those conical Boy Scout tents when one of the Boy

Scouts has left the pole home. And he was playing, or anyway practicing, the ophicleide, and on his shoulders was a little moss of spruce needles, a small shower of which descended from the tree every time he hit on or under the low B♭. Only a mouse trapped inside a tuba during band practice can know precisely what it's like to stand that close to an operating ophicleide.

It was MacLyle all right, looming well fed and filled out. When he saw the psychiatrist's car he went right on playing, but, catching the psychiatrist's eye, he winked, smiled with the small corner of lip which showed from behind the large cup of the mouthpiece, and twiddled three fingers of his right hand, all he could manage of a wave without stopping. And he didn't stop either until he had scaled the particular octave he was working on and let himself down the other side. Then he put the ophicleide down carefully and let it lean against the spruce tree, and got up. The psychiatrist had become aware, as the last stupendous notes rolled away down the mountain, of his extreme isolation with this offbeat patient, of the unconcealed health and vigor of the man, and of the presence of the precipice over which he had almost driven his car a moment before, and had rolled up his window and buttoned the door lock and was feeling grateful for them. But the warm good humor and genuine welcome on MacLyle's sunburned face drove away fright and even caution, and almost before he knew what he was doing the psychiatrist had the door open and was stooping up out of the car, thinking, merry is a disused word but that's what he is, by God, a merry man. He called him by name but either MacLyle did not hear him or didn't care; he just put out a big warm hand and the psychiatrist took it. He could feel hard flat calluses in MacLyle's hand, and the controlled strength an elephant uses to lift a bespangled child in its trunk; he smiled at the image, because after all MacLyle was not a particularly large man, there was just that feeling about him. And once the smile found itself there it wouldn't go away.

He told MacLyle that he was a writer trying to soak up some of this magnificent country and had just been driving wherever the turn of the road led him, and here he was; but before he was half through he became conscious of MacLyle's eyes, which were in some indescribable way very much on him but not at all on anything he said; it was precisely as if he had stood there and hummed a tune. MacLyle seemed to be willing to listen to the sound until it was finished, and even to enjoy it, but that enjoyment was going to be all he got out of it. The psychiatrist finished anyway and MacLyle waited a moment as if to see if there would be any more, and when there wasn't he gave out more of that luminous smile and cocked his head toward the cabin. MacLyle led the way, with his visitor bringing up the rear with some platitudes about nice place you got here. As they entered, he suddenly barked at that unresponsive back, "Can't you hear me?" and MacLyle, without turning, only waved him on.

They walked into such a clutter and clabber of colors that the psychiatrist stopped dead, blinking. One wall had been removed and replaced with glass panes; it overlooked the precipice and put the little building afloat on haze. All the walls were hung with plain white chenille bedspreads, and the floor was white, and there seemed to be much more light indoors here than outside. Opposite the large window was an oversized easel made of peeled poles, notched and lashed together with baling wire, and on it was a huge canvas, most non-objective, in the purest and most uncompromising colors. Part of it was unquestionably this room, or at least its air of colored confusion here and all infinity beyond. The ophicleide was in the picture, painstakingly reproduced, looking like the hopper of some giant infernal machine, and in the foreground, some flowers; but the central figure repulsed him—more, it repulsed everything which surrounded it. It did not look exactly like anything familiar and, in a disturbed way, he was happy about that.

Stacked on the floor on each side of the easel were other paintings, some daubs, some full of ruled lines and overlapping planes, but all in this achingly pure color. He realized what was being done with the dozens of colors of house paint in little cans which had so intrigued the storekeeper.

In odd places around the room were clay sculptures, most mounted on pedestals made of sections of tree trunks large enough to stand firmly on their sawed ends. Some of the pedestals were peeled, some painted, and in some the bark texture or the bulges or clefts in the wood had been carried right up into the model, and in others clay had been knived or pressed into the bark all the way down to the floor. Some of the clay was painted, some not, some ought to have been. There were free forms and gollywogs, a marsupial woman and a guitar with legs, and some, but not an overweening number, of the symbolisms which pre-occupy even fairly intelligent psychiatrists. Nowhere was there any furniture per se. There were shelves at all levels and of varying lengths, bearing nail kegs, bolts of cloth, canned goods, tools and cooking utensils. There was a sort of table but it was mostly a workbench, with a vise at one end and at the other, half finished, a crude but exceedingly ingenious foot-powered potter's wheel.

He wondered where MacLyle slept, so he asked him, and again MacLyle reacted as if the words were not words, but a series of pleasant sounds, cocking his head and waiting to see if there would be any more. So the psychiatrist re-sorted to sign language, making a pillow of his two hands, laying his head on it, closing his eyes. He opened them to see MacLyle nodding eagerly, then going to the white-draped wall. From behind the chenille he brought a ham-mock, one end of which was fastened to the wall. The other end he carried to the big window and hung to a hook screwed to a heavy stud between the panes. To lie in that hammock would be to swing between heaven and earth like Mahomet's tomb, with all that sky and scenery virtu-ally surrounding the sleeper. His admiration for this idea ceased as MacLyle began making urgent indications for him to get into the hammock. He backed off warily, expos-tulating, trying to convey to MacLyle that he only won-dered, he just wanted to know: no, *no*, he wasn't tired, dammit; but MacLyle became so insistent that he picked the psychiatrist up like a child sulking at bedtime and carried him to the hammock. Any impulse to kick or quarrel was quenched by the nature of this and all other hammocks to be intolerant of shifting burdens, and by the proximity of the large window, which he now saw was built leaning outward, enabling one to look out of the hammock straight down a minimum of four hundred and eighty feet. So all right, he concluded, if you say so. I'm sleepy.

So for the next two hours he lay in the hammock watching MacLyle putter about the place, thinking more or less professional thoughts.

He doesn't or can't speak (he diagnosed): aphasia, motor. He doesn't or can't understand speech: aphasia, sensory. He won't or can't read and write: alexia. And what else?

He looked at all that art—if it *was* art, and any that was, was art by accident—and the gadgetry: the chuntering windmill outside, the sash-weight door closer. He let his eyes follow a length of clothesline dangling unobtrusively down the leaning center post to which his hammock was fastened, and the pulley and fittings from which it hung, and its extension clear across the ceiling to the back wall, and understood finally that it would, when pulled, open two long, narrow horizontal hatches for through ventilation. A small door behind the chenille led to what he correctly surmised was a primitive powder room, built to overhang the precipice, the most perfect no-plumbing solution for that convenience he had ever seen.

He watched MacLyle putter. That was the only word for it, and his actions were the best example of puttering he had ever seen. MacLyle lifted, shifted, and put things down, backed off to judge, returned to lay an approving hand on the thing he had moved. Net effect, nothing tangible—yet one could not say there was no effect, because of the intense satisfaction the man radiated. For minutes he would stand, head cocked, smiling slightly, regarding the half-finished potter's wheel, then explode into activity, sawing, planing, drilling. He would add the finished piece to the cranks and connecting rods already completed, pat it as if it were an obedient child, and walk away, leaving the rest of the job for some other time. With a wood-rasp he carefully removed the nose from one of his dried clay figures, and meticulously put on a new one. Always there was this absorption in his own products and processes, and the air of total reward in everything. And there was time, there seemed to be time enough for everything, and always would be.

Here is a man, thought the fairly intelligent psychiatrist, in retreat, but in retreat the like of which my science has not yet described. For observe: he has reacted toward the primitive in terms of supplying himself with his needs with his own hands and by his own ingenuity, and yet there is nothing primitive in those needs themselves. He works constantly to achieve the comforts which his history has conditioned him to in the past—electric lights, cross-ventilation, trouble-free waste disposal. He exhibits a profound humility in the low rates he pays himself for his labor: he is building a potter's wheel apparently in order to make his own cooking vessels, and since wood is cheap and clay free, his vessel can only cost him less than engine-turned aluminum by a very low evaluation of his own efforts.

His skills are less than his energy (mused the psychiatrist). His carpentry, like his painting and sculpture, shows considerable intelligence, but only moderate training; he can construct but not beautify, draw but not draft, and reach the artistically pleasing only by not erasing the random shake, the accidental cut; so that real creation in his work is, like any random effect, rare and unpredictable. Therefore his reward is in the area of satisfaction—about as wide a generalization as one can make.

What satisfaction? Not in possessions themselves, for this man could have bought better for less. Not in excellence in itself, for he obviously could be satisfied with less than perfection. Freedom, perhaps, from routine, from dominations of work? Hardly, because for all that complexity of this cluttered cottage, it had its order and its systems; the presence of an alarm clock conveyed a good deal in this area. He wasn't dominated by regularity—he used it. And his satisfaction? Why, it must lie in this closed circle, himself to himself, and in the very fact of non-communication!

Retreat . . . retreat. Retreat to savagery and you don't engineer your cross-ventilation or adjust a five-hundred-foot gravity flush for your john. Retreat into infancy and you don't design and build a potter's wheel. Retreat from people and you don't greet a stranger like . . .

Wait.

Maybe a stranger who had something to communicate, or some way of communication, wouldn't be so welcome. An unsettling thought, that. Running the risk of doing something MacLyle didn't like would be, possibly, a little more unselfish than the challenge warranted.

MacLyle began to cook.

Watching him, the psychiatrist reflected suddenly that this withdrawn and wordless individual was a happy one, in his own matrix; further, he had fulfilled all his obligations and responsibilities and was bothering no one.

It was intolerable.

It was intolerable because it was a violation of the prime directive of psychiatry—at least, of that school of psychiatry which he professed, and he was not going to confuse himself by considerations of other, less-tried theories—*It is the function of psychiatry to adjust the aberrate to society, and to restore or increase his usefulness to it.* To yield, to rationalize this man's behavior as balance, would be to fly in the face of science itself; for this particular psychiatry finds its most successful approaches in the scientific method, and it is unprofitable to debate whether or not it is or is not a science. To its practitioner it is, and that's that; it has to be. Operationally speaking, what has been found true, even statistically, must be Truth, and all other things, even Possible, kept the hell out of the toolbox. No known Truth allowed a social entity to secede this way, and, for one, this fairly intelligent psychiatrist was not going to give this—this *suicide* his blessing.

He must, then, find a way to communicate with Mac-Lyle, and when he had found it, he must communicate to him the error of his ways. Without getting thrown over the cliff.

He became aware that MacLyle was looking at him, twinkling. He smiled back before he knew what he was doing, and obeyed MacLyle's beckoning gesture. He eased himself out of the hammock and went to the workbench, where a steaming stew was set out in earthenware bowls. The bowls stood on large plates and were surrounded by a band of carefully sliced tomatoes. He tasted them. They were obviously vine-ripened and had been speckled with a dark green paste which, after studious attention to its aftertaste, he identified as fresh basil mashed with fresh garlic and salt. The effect was symphonic.

He followed suit when MacLyle picked up his own bowl and they went outside and squatted under the old Engelmann spruce to eat. It was a quiet and pleasant occasion, and during it the psychiatrist had plenty of opportunity to size up his man and plan his campaign. He was quite sure now how to proceed, and all he needed was opportunity, which presented itself when MacLyle rose, stretched, smiled, and went indoors. The psychiatrist followed him to the door and saw him crawl into the hammock and fall almost instantly asleep.

The psychiatrist went to his car and got out his bag of tricks. And so it was late in the afternoon, when MacLyle emerged stretching and yawning from his nap, he found his visitor under the spruce tree, hefting the ophicleide and twiddling its keys in a perplexed and investigatory fashion. MacLyle strode over to him and lifted the ophicleide away with a pleasant I'll-show-you smile, got the monstrous contraption into position, and ran his tongue around the inside of the mouthpiece, large as a demitasse. He had barely time to pucker up his lips at the strange taste before his irises rolled up completely out of sight and he collapsed like a grounded parachute. The psychiatrist was able only to snatch away the ophicleide in time to keep the mouthpiece from knocking out MacLyle's front teeth.

He set the ophicleide carefully against the tree and straightened MacLyle's limbs. He concentrated for a moment on the pulse, and turned the head to one side so saliva would not drain down the flaccid throat, and then went back to his bag of tricks. He came back and knelt, and MacLyle did not even twitch at the bite of the hypodermics: a careful blend of the non-soporific tranquilizers Frenquel, chlorpromazine and Reserpine, and a judicious dose of scopolamine, a hypnotic.

The psychiatrist got water and carefully sponged out the man's mouth, not caring to wait out another collapse the next time he swallowed. Then there was nothing to do but wait, and plan.

Exactly on schedule, according to the psychiatrist's wrist watch, MacLyle groaned and coughed weakly. The psychiatrist immediately and in a firm quiet voice told him not to move. Also not to think. He stayed out of the immediate range of MacLyle's unfocused eyes and explained that MacLyle must trust him, because he was there to help, and not to worry about feeling mixed-up or disoriented. "You don't know where you are or how you got here," he informed MacLyle. He also told MacLyle, who was past forty, that he was thirty-seven years old, but he knew what he was doing.

MacLyle just lay there obediently and thought these things over and waited for more information. He didn't know where he was or how he got here. He did know that he must trust this voice, the owner of which was here to help him; that he was thirty-seven years old; and his name. In these things he lay and marinated. The drugs kept him conscious, docile, submissive and without guile. The psychiatrist observed and exulted: oh you azacyclonol, he chanted silently to himself, you pretty piperidyl, handsome hydrochloride, subtle Serpasil . . . Confidently he left MacLyle and went into the cabin where, after due search, he found some decent clothes and some socks and shoes and brought them out and wrapped the supine patient in them. He helped MacLyle across the clearing and into his car, humming as he did so, for there is none so happy as an expert faced with excellence in his specialty. MacLyle sank back into the cushions and gave one wondering glance at the cabin and at the glare of late light from the bell of the ophicleide; but the psychiatrist told him firmly that these things had nothing to do with him, nothing at all, and MacLyle smiled relievedly and fell to watching the scenery go by, passive as a Pekingese. As they passed the general store MacLyle stirred, but said nothing about it. Instead he asked the psychiatrist if the Ardsmere station was open yet, whereupon the psychiatrist could barely answer him for the impulse to purr like a cat: the Ardsmere station, two stops before MacLyle's suburban town, had burned down and been rebuilt almost six years ago; so now he knew for sure that MacLyle was living in a time preceding his difficulties—a time during which, of course, MacLyle had been able to talk. He crooned his appreciation for chlorpromazine (which had helped MacLyle be tranquil) and he made up a silent song, o doll o' mine, scopolamine, which had made him so very suggestible. But all of this the psychiatrist kept to himself, and answered gravely that yes, they had the Ardsmere station operating again. And did he have anything else on his mind?

MacLyle considered this carefully, but since all the immediate questions were answered—unswervingly, he *knew* he was safe in the hands of this man, whoever he was; he knew (he thought) his correct age and that he was expected to feel disoriented; he was also under a command not to think—he placidly shook his head and went back to watching the road unroll under their wheels. "Fallen Rock Zone," he murmured as they passed a sign. The psychiatrist drove happily down the mountain and across the flats, back to the city where he had hired the car. He left it at the railroad station ("Rail Crossing Road," murmured MacLyle) and made reservations for a compartment on the train, aircraft being too open and public for his purposes and far too fast for the hourly rate he suddenly decided to apply.

They had time for a silent and companionable dinner before train time, and then at last they were aboard, solid ground beneath, a destination ahead, and the track joints applauding.

The psychiatrist turned off all but one reading lamp and leaned forward. MacLyle's eyes dilated readily to the dimmer light, and the psychiatrist leaned back comfortably and asked him how he felt. He felt fine and said so. The psychiatrist asked him how old he was and MacLyle told him, thirty-seven, but he sounded doubtful.

Knowing that the scopolamine was wearing off but the other drugs, the tranquilizers, would hang on for a bit, the psychiatrist drew a deep breath and removed the suggestion; he told MacLyle the truth about his age, and brought him up to the here and now. MacLyle just looked puzzled for a few minutes and then his features settled into an expression that can only be described as not unhappy. "Porter," was all he said, gazing at the push button on the partition with its little metal sign, and announced that he could read now.

The psychiatrist nodded sagely and offered no comment, being quite willing to let a patient stew in his own juice as long as he produced essence.

MacLyle abruptly demanded to know why he had lost the powers of speech and reading. The psychiatrist raised his eyebrows a little and his shoulders a good deal and smiled one of those "You-tell-me" smiles, and then got up and suggested they sleep on it. He got the porter in to fix the beds and as an afterthought told the man to come back with the evening papers. Nothing can orient a cultural expatriate better than the evening papers. The man did. MacLyle paid no attention to this, one way or the other. He just climbed into the psychiatrist's spare pajamas thoughtfully and they went to bed.

The psychiatrist didn't know if MacLyle had awakened him on purpose or whether the train's slowing down for a watering stop had done it, or both; anyway he awoke about three in the morning to find MacLyle standing beside his bunk looking at him fixedly. He closed his eyes and screwed them tight and opened them again, and MacLyle was still there, and now he noticed that MacLyle's reading lamp was lit and the papers were scattered all over the floor. MacLyle said, "You're some kind of a doctor," in a flat voice.

The psychiatrist admitted it.

MacLyle said, "Well, this ought to make some sense to you. I was skiing out here years ago when I was a college kid. Accident, fellow I was with broke his leg. Compound. Made him comfortable as I could and went for help. Came back, he'd slid down the mountain, thrashing around, I guess. Crevasse, down in the bottom; took two days to find him, three days to get him out. Frostbite. Gangrene."

The psychiatrist tried to look as if he was following this.

MacLyle said, "The only thing I always remember, him pulling back the bandages all the time to look at his leg. Knew it was gone, couldn't keep himself from watching the stuff spread around and upward. Didn't like to; *had* to. Tried to stop him, finally had to help him or he'd hurt himself. Every ten, fifteen minutes all the way down to the lodge, fifteen hours, looking under the bandages."

The psychiatrist tried to think of something to say and couldn't, so he looked wise and waited.

MacLyle said, "That Donne, that John Donne I used to spout, I always believed that."

The psychiatrist began to misquote the thing about send not to ask for whom the bell . . .

"Yeah, that, but especially *'any man's death diminishes me, because I am involved in mankind.'* I believed that," MacLyle repeated. "I believed more than that. Not only death. Damn foolishness diminishes me because I am involved. People all the time pushing people around diminishes me. Everybody hungry for a fast buck diminishes me." He picked up a sheet of newspaper and let it slip away; it flapped off to the corner of the compartment like a huge grave-moth. "I was getting diminished to death and I had to watch it happening to me like that kid with the gangrene, so that's why." The train, crawling now, lurched suddenly and yielded. MacLyle's eyes flicked to the window, where neon beer signs and a traffic light were reluctantly being framed. MacLyle leaned close to the psychiatrist. "I just had to get uninvolved with mankind before I got diminished altogether, everything mankind did was my fault. So I did and now here I am involved again." MacLyle abruptly went to the door. "And for that, thanks."

From a dusty throat the psychiatrist asked him what he was going to do.

"Do?" asked MacLyle cheerfully. "Why, I'm going out there and diminish mankind right back." He was out in the corridor with the door closed before the psychiatrist so much as sat up. He banged it open again and leaned in. He said in the sanest of all possible voices, "Now mind you, doctor, this is only one man's opinion," and was gone. He killed four people before they got him.

⚙ *Martin Gardner*

NO-SIDED PROFESSOR

Dolores—a tall, black-haired striptease at Chicago's Purple Hat Club—stood in the center of the dance floor and began the slow gyrations of her Cleopatra number, accompanied by soft Egyptian music from the Purple Hatters. The room was dark except for a shaft of emerald light that played over her filmy Egyptian costume and smooth, voluptuous limbs.

A veil draped about her head and shoulders was the first to be removed. Dolores was in the act of letting it drift gracefully to the floor when suddenly a sound like the firing of a shotgun came from somewhere above and the nude body of a large man dropped head first from the ceiling. He caught the veil in mid-air with his chin and pinned it to the floor with a dull thump.

Pandemonium reigned.

Jake Bowers, the master of ceremonies, yelled for lights and tried to keep back the crowd. The club's manager, who had been standing by the orchestra watching the floor show, threw a tablecloth over the crumpled figure and rolled it over on its back.

The man was breathing heavily, apparently knocked unconscious by the blow on his chin, but otherwise unharmed. He was well over fifty, with a short, neatly trimmed red beard and mustache, and a completely bald head. He was built like a professional wrestler.

With considerable difficulty three waiters succeeded in transporting him to the manager's private office in the back, leaving a roomful of bewildered, near-hysterical men and women gaping at the ceiling and each other, and arguing heatedly about the angle and manner of the man's fall. The only hypothesis with even a slight suggestion of sanity was that he had been tossed high into the air from somewhere on the side of the dance floor. But no one saw the tossing. The police were called.

Meanwhile, in the back office the bearded man recovered consciousness. He insisted that he was Dr. Stanislaw Slapenarski, professor of mathematics at the University of Warsaw, and at present a visiting lecturer at the University of Chicago.

Before continuing this curious narrative, I must pause to confess that I was not an eyewitness of the episode just described, having based my account on interviews with the master of ceremonies and several waiters. However, I did participate in a chain of remarkable events which culminated in the professor's unprecedented appearance.

These events began several hours earlier when members of the Moebius Society gathered for their annual banquet in one of the private dining rooms on the second floor of the Purple Hat Club. The Moebius Society is a small, obscure Chicago organization of mathematicians working in the field of topology, one of the youngest and most mysterious of the newer branches of transformation mathematics. To make clear what happened during the evening, it will be necessary at this point to give a brief description of the subject matter of topology.

Topology is difficult to define in nontechnical terms. One way to put it is to say that topology studies the mathematical properties of an object which remain constant regardless of how the object is distorted.

Picture in your mind a doughnut made of soft pliable rubber that can be twisted and stretched as far as you like in any direction. No matter how much this rubber doughnut is distorted (or "transformed" as mathematicians prefer to say), certain properties of the doughnut will remain unchanged. For example, it will always retain a hole. In topology the doughnut shape is called a "torus." A soda straw is merely an elongated torus, so—from a topological point of view—a doughnut and a soda straw are identical figures.

Topology is completely disinterested in quantitative

measurements. It is concerned only with basic properties of shape which are unchanged throughout the most radical distortions possible without breaking off pieces of the object and sticking them on again at other spots. If this breaking off were permitted, an object of a given structure could be transformed into an object of any other type of structure, and all original properties would be lost. If the reader will reflect a moment he will soon realize that topology studies the most primitive and fundamental mathematical properties that an object can possess.[1]

A sample problem in topology may be helpful. Imagine a torus (doughnut) surface made of thin rubber like an inner tube. Now imagine a small hole in the side of this torus. Is it possible to turn the torus inside out through this hole, as you might turn a balloon inside out? This is not an easy problem to solve in the imagination.

Although many mathematicians of the eighteenth century wrestled with isolated topological problems, one of the first systematic works in the field was done by August Ferdinand Moebius, a German astronomer who taught at the University of Leipzig during the first half of the last century. Until the time of Moeibus it was believed that any surface, such as a piece of paper, had two sides. It was the German astronomer who made the disconcerting discovery that if you take a strip of paper, give it a single half-twist, then paste the ends together, the result is a "unilateral" surface—a surface with only one side!

If you will trouble to make such a strip (known to topologists as the "Moebius surface") and examine it carefully, you will soon discover that the strip actually does consist of one continuous side and of one continuous edge.

It is hard to believe at first that such a strip can exist, but there it is—a visible, tangible thing that can be constructed in a moment. And it has the indisputable property

[1] The reader who is interested in obtaining a clearer picture of this new mathematics will find excellent articles on topology in the *Encyclopaedia Britannica* (Fourteenth Edition) under *Analysis Situs;* and under *Analysis Situs* in the *Encyclopedia Americana.* There also are readable chapters on elementary topology in two recent books—*Mathematics and the Imagination* by Kasner and Newman, and *What Is Mathematics?* by Courant and Robbins. Slapenarski's published work has not yet been translated from the Polish.

of one-sidedness, a property it cannot lose no matter how much it is stretched or how it is distorted.[2]

But back to the story. As an instructor in mathematics at the University of Chicago with a doctor's thesis in topology to my credit, I had little difficulty in securing admittance into the Moebius Society. Our membership was small—only twenty-six men, most of them Chicago topologists but a few from universities in neighboring towns.

We held regular monthly meetings, rather academic in character, and once a year on November 17 (the anniversary of Moebius' birth) we arranged a banquet at which an outstanding topologist was brought to the city to act as a guest speaker.

The banquet always had its less serious aspects, usually in the form of special entertainment. But this year our funds were low and we decided to hold the celebration at the Purple Hat where the cost of the dinner would not be too great and where we could enjoy the floor show after the lecture. We were fortunate in having been able to obtain as our guest the distinguished Professor Slapenarski, universally acknowledged as the world's leading topologist and one of the greatest mathematical minds of the century.

Dr. Slapenarski had been in the city several weeks giving a series of lectures at the University of Chicago on the topological aspects of Einstein's theory of space. As a result of my contacts with him at the university, we became good friends and I had been asked to introduce him at the dinner.

We rode to the Purple Hat together in a taxi, and on the way I begged him to give me some inkling of the content of his address. But he only smiled inscrutably and told me, in his thick Polish accent, to wait and see. He had announced his topic as "The No-Sided Surface"—a topic which had aroused such speculation among our members

[2] The Moebius strip has many terrifying properties. For example, if you cut the strip in half lengthwise, cutting down the center all the way around, the result is not two strips, as might be expected, but one single large strip. But if you begin cutting a third of the way from the side, cutting *twice* around the strip, the result is one large and one small strip, interlocked. The smaller strip can then be cut in half to yield a single large strip, still interlocked with the other large strip. These weird properties are the basis of an old magic trick with cloth, known to the conjuring profession as the "Afghan bands."

that Dr. Robert Simpson of the University of Wisconsin wrote he was coming to the dinner, the first meeting that he had attended in over a year.[3]

Dr. Simpson is the outstanding authority on topology in the Middle West and the author of several important papers on topology and nuclear physics in which he vigorously attacks several of Slapenarski's major axioms.

The Polish professor and I arrived a little late. After introducing him to Simpson, then to our other members, we took our seats at the table and I called Slapenarski's attention to our tradition of brightening the banquet with little topological touches. For instance, our napkin rings were silver-plated Moebius strips. Doughnuts were provided with the coffee, and the coffee itself was contained in specially designed cups made in the shape of "Klein's bottle."[4]

After the meal we were served Ballantine ale, because of the curious trademark,[5] and pretzels in the shapes of the two basic "trefoil" knots.[6] Slapenarski was much amused by these details and even made several suggestions for additional topological curiosities, but the suggestions are too complex to explain here.

After my brief introduction, the Polish doctor stood up,

[3] Dr. Simpson later confided to me that he had attended the dinner not to hear Slapenarski but to see Dolores.

[4] Named after Felix Klein, a brilliant German mathematician, Klein's bottle is a completely closed surface, like the surface of a globe, but without inside or outside. It is unilateral like a Moebius strip, but unlike the strip it has no edges. It can be bisected in such a way that each half becomes a Moebius surface. It will hold a liquid. Nothing frightful happens to the liquid.

[5] This trademark is a topological manifold of great interest. Although the three rings are interlocked, no *two* rings are interlocked. In other words, if any one of the rings is removed, the other two rings are completely free of each other. Yet the three together cannot be separated.

[6] The trefoil knot is the simplest form of knot that can be tied in a closed curve. It exists in two forms, one a mirror image of the other. Although the two forms are topologically identical, it is impossible to transform one into the other by distortion, an upsetting fact that has caused topologists considerable embarrassment. The study of the properties of knots forms an important branch of topology, though very little is understood as yet about even the simplest knots.

acknowledged the applause with a smile, and cleared his throat. The room instantly became silent. The reader is already familiar with the professor's appearance—his portly frame, reddish beard, and polished pate—but it should be added that there was something in the expression of his face that suggested he had matters of considerable import to disclose to us.

It would be impossible to give with any fullness the substance of Slapenarski's brilliant, highly technical address. But the gist of it was this. Ten years ago, he said, he had been impressed by a statement of Moebius, in one of his lesser known treatises, that there was no theoretical reason why a surface could not lose *both* its sides—to become, in other words, a "nonlateral" surface.

Of course, the professor explained, such a surface was impossible to imagine, but so is the square root of minus one or the hypercube of fourth-dimensional geometry. That a concept is inconceivable has long ago been recognized as no basis for denying either its validity or usefulness in mathematics and modern physics.

We must remember, he added, that even the one-sided surface is inconceivable to anyone who has not seen and handled a Moebius strip. And many persons, with well-developed mathematical imaginations, are unable to understand how such a strip can exist even when they have one in hand.

I glanced at Dr. Simpson and thought I detected a skeptical smile curving the corners of his mouth.

Slapenarski continued. For many years, he said, he had been engaged in a tireless quest for a no-sided surface. On the basis of analogy with known types of surfaces he had been able to analyze many of the properties of the no-sided surface. Finally one day—and he paused here for dramatic emphasis, sweeping his bright little eyes across the motionless faces of his listeners—he had actually succeeded in constructing a no-sided surface.

His words were like an electric impulse that transmitted itself around the table. Everyone gave a sudden start and shifted his position and looked at his neighbor with raised eyebrows. I noticed that Simpson was shaking his head vigorously. When the speaker walked to the end of the room where a blackboard had been placed, Simpson bent his head and whispered to the man on his left, "It's sheer nonsense. Either Slappy has gone completely mad or he's playing a deliberate prank on all of us."

I think it had occurred to the others also that the lecture was a hoax because I noticed several were smiling to themselves while the professor chalked some elaborate diagrams on the blackboard.

After a somewhat involved discussion of the diagrams (which I was wholly unable to follow) the professor announced that he would conclude his lecture by constructing one of the simpler forms of the no-sided surface. By now we were all grinning at each other. Dr. Simpson's face had more of a smirk than a grin.

Slapenarski produced from his coat pocket a sheet of pale-blue paper, a small pair of scissors, and a tube of paste. He cut the paper into a figure that had a striking resemblance, I thought, to a paper doll. There were five projecting strips or appendages that resembled a head and four limbs. Then he folded and pasted the sheet carefully. It was an intricate procedure. Strips went over and under each other in an odd fashion until finally only two ends projected. Dr. Slapenarski then applied a dab of paste to one of these ends.

"Gentlemen," he said, holding up the twisted blue construction and turning it about for all to see, "you are about to witness the first public demonstration of the Slapenarski surface."

So saying, he pressed one of the projecting ends against the other.

There was a loud pop, like the bursting of a light bulb, and the paper figure vanished in his hands!

For a moment we were too stunned to move, then with one accord we broke into laughter and applause.

We were convinced, of course, that we were the victims of an elaborate joke. But it had been beautifully executed. I assumed, as did the others, that we had witnessed an ingenious chemical trick with paper—paper treated so it could be ignited by friction or some similar method and caused to explode without leaving an ash.

But I noticed that the professor seemed disconcerted by

the laughter, and his face was beginning to turn the color of his beard. He smiled in an embarrassed way and sat down. The applause subsided slowly.

Falling in with the preposterous mood of the evening we all clustered around him and congratulated him warmly on his remarkable discovery. Then the man in charge of arrangements reminded us that a table had been reserved below so those interested in remaining could enjoy some drinks and see the floor show.

The room gradually cleared of everyone except Slapenarski, Simpson, and myself. The two famous topologists were standing in front of the blackboard. Simpson was smiling broadly and gesturing toward one of the diagrams.

"The fallacy of your proof was beautifully concealed, Doctor," he said. "I wonder if any of the others caught it."

The Polish mathematician was not amused.

"There is no fallacy in my proof," he said impatiently.

"Oh, come now, Doctor," Simpson said. "Of course there's a fallacy." Still smiling, he touched a corner of the diagram with his thumb. "These lines can't possibly intersect within the manifold. The intersection is somewhere out here." He waved his hand off to the right.

Slapenarski's face was growing red again.

"I tell you there is no fallacy," he repeated, his voice rising. Then slowly, speaking his words carefully and explosively, he went over the proof once more, rapping the blackboard at intervals with his knuckles.

Simpson listened gravely, and at one point interrupted with an objection. The objection was answered. A moment later he raised a second objection. The second objection was answered. I stood aside without saying anything. The discussion was too far above my head.

Then they began to raise their voices. I have already spoken of Simpson's long-standing controversy with Slapenarski over several basic topological axioms. Some of these axioms were now being brought into the argument.

"But I tell you the transformation is *not* bicontinuous and therefore the two sets cannot be homeomorphic," Simpson shouted.

The veins on the Polish mathematician's temples were standing out in sharp relief. "Then suppose you explain to me why my manifold vanished," he yelled back.

"It was nothing but a cheap conjuring trick," snorted Simpson. "I don't know how it worked and I don't care, but it certainly wasn't because the manifold became nonlateral."

"Oh it wasn't, wasn't it?" Slapenarski said between his teeth. Before I had a chance to intervene he had sent his huge fist crashing into the jaw of Dr. Simpson. The Wisconsin professor groaned and dropped to the floor. Slapenarski turned and glared at me wildly.

"Get back, young man," he said. As he outweighed me by at least one hundred pounds, I got back.

Then I watched in horror what was taking place. With insane fury still flaming on his face, Slapenarski had knelt beside the limp body and was twisting the arms and legs into fantastic knots. He was, in fact, folding the Wisconsin topologist as he had folded his piece of paper! Suddenly there was a small explosion, like the backfire of a car, and under the Polish mathematician's hands lay the collapsed clothing of Dr. Simpson.

Simpson had become a nonlateral surface.

Slapenarski stood up, breathing with difficulty and holding in his hands a tweed coat with vest, shirt, and underwear top inside. He opened his hands and let the garments fall on top of the clothing on the floor. Great drops of perspiration rolled down his face. He muttered in Polish, then beat his fists against his forehead.

I recovered enough presence of mind to move to the entrance of the room, and lock the door. When I spoke my voice sounded weak. "Can he . . . be brought back?"

"I do not know, I do not know," Slapenarski wailed. "I have only begun the study of these surfaces—only just begun. I have no way of knowing where he is. Undoubtedly it is one of the higher dimensions, probably one of the odd-numbered ones. God knows which one."

Then he grabbed me suddenly by my coat lapels and shook me so violently that a bridge on my upper teeth came loose. "I must go to him," he said. "It is the least I can do—the very least."

He sat down on the floor and began interweaving arms and legs.

"Do not stand there like an idiot!" he yelled. "Here—some assistance."

I adjusted my bridge, then helped him twist his right

arm under his left leg and back around his head until he was able to grip his right ear. Then his left arm had to be twisted in a somewhat similar fashion. "Over, not under," he shouted. It was with difficulty that I was able to force his left hand close enough to his face so he could grasp his nose.

There was another explosive noise, much louder than the sound made by Simpson, and a sudden blast of cold wind across my face. When I opened my eyes I saw the second heap of crumpled clothing on the floor.

While I was staring stupidly at the two piles of clothing there was a muffled sort of "pfft" sound behind me. I turned and saw Simpson standing near the wall, naked and shivering. His face was white. Then his knees buckled and he sank to the floor. There were vivid red marks at various places where his limbs had been pressed tightly against each other.

I stumbled to the door, unlocked it, and started down the stairway after a strong drink—for myself. I became conscious of a violent hubbub on the dance floor. Slapenarski had, a few moments earlier, completed his sensational dive.

In a back room below I found the other members of the Moebius Society and various officials of the Purple Hat Club in a noisy, incoherent debate. Slapenarski was sitting in a chair with a tablecloth wrapped around him and holding a handkerchief filled with ice cubes against the side of his jaw.

"Simpson is back," I said. "He fainted but I think he's okay."

"Thank heavens," Slapenarski mumbled.

The officials and patrons of the Purple Hat never understood, of course, what happened that wild night, and our attempts to explain made matters worse. The police arrived, adding to the confusion.

We finally got the two professors dressed and on their feet, and made an escape by promising to return the following day with our lawyers. The manager seemed to think the club had been the victim of an outlandish plot, and threatened to sue for damages against what he called the club's "refined reputation." As it turned out, the incident proved to be magnificent word-of-mouth advertising and eventually the club dropped the case. The papers heard the story, of course, but promptly dismissed it as an uncouth publicity stunt cooked up by Phanstiehl, the Purple Hat's press agent.

Simpson was unhurt, but Slapenarski's jaw had been broken. I took him to Billings Hospital, near the university, and in his hospital room late that night he told me what he thought had happened. Apparently Simpson had entered a higher dimension (very likely the fifth) on level ground.

When he recovered consciousness he unhooked himself and immediately reappeared as a normal three-dimensional torus with outside and inside surfaces. But Slapenarski had worse luck. He had landed on some sort of slope. There was nothing to see—only a gray, undifferentiated fog on all sides—but he had the distinct sensation of rolling down a hill.

He tried to keep a grip on his nose but was unable to maintain it. His right hand slipped free before he reached the bottom of the incline. As a result, he unfolded himself and tumbled back into three-dimensional space and the middle of Dolores' Egyptian routine.

At any rate, that was the way Slapenarski had it figured out.

He was several weeks in the hospital, refusing to see anyone until the day of his release, when I accompanied him to the Union Station. He caught a train to New York and I never saw him again. He died a few months later of a heart attack in Warsaw. At present Dr. Simpson is in correspondence with his widow in an attempt to obtain his notes on nonlateral surfaces.

Whether these notes will or will not be intelligible to American topologists (assuming we can obtain them) remains to be seen. We have made numerous experiments with folded paper, but so far have produced only commonplace bilateral and unilateral surfaces. Although it was I who helped Slapenarski fold himself, the excitement of the moment apparently erased the details from my mind.

But I shall never forget one remark the great topologist made to me the night of his accident, just before I left him at the hospital.

"It was fortunate," he said, "that both Simpson and I released our right hand before the left."

"Why?" I asked.

Slapenarski shuddered.

"We would have been inside out," he said.

☼ *John Wyndham*

RANDOM QUEST

The sound of a car coming to a stop on the gravel caused
Dr. Harshom to look at his watch. He closed the book in
which he had been writing, put it away in one of his desk
drawers, and waited. Presently Stephens opened the door
to announce: "Mr. Trafford, sir."

The doctor got up from his chair, and regarded the
young man who entered, with some care. Mr. Colin Trafford turned out to be presentable, just in his thirties, with
brown hair curling slightly, clean-shaven, a suit of good
tweed well cut, and shoes to accord. He looked pleasant
enough though not distinguished. It would not be difficult
to meet thirty or forty very similar young men in a day. But
when one looked more closely, as the doctor now did, there
were signs of fatigue to be seen, indications of anxiety in
the expression and around the mouth, a strained dogged-
ness in the set of the mouth.

They shook hands.

"You'll have had a long drive," said the doctor. "I expect
you'd like a drink. Dinner won't be for half an hour yet."

The younger man accepted, and sat down. Presently, he
said:

"It was kind of you to invite me here, Dr. Harshom."

"Not really altruistic," the doctor told him. "It is more
satisfactory to talk than to correspond by letter. Moreover,
I am an inquisitive man recently retired from a very hum-
drum country practice, Mr. Trafford, and on the rare occasions that I do catch the scent of a mystery my curiosity
urges me to follow it up." He, too, sat down.

"Mystery?" repeated the young man.

"Mystery," said the doctor.

The young man took a sip of his whisky.

"My inquiry was such as one might receive from—well, from any solicitor," he said.

"But you are not a solicitor, Mr. Trafford."

"No," Colin Trafford admitted, "I am not."

"But you do have a very pressing reason for your inquiry. So there is the mystery. What pressing, or indeed leisurely, reason could you have for inquiries about a person of whose existence you yourself appear to be uncertain —and of whom Somerset House has no record?"

The young man regarded him more carefully, as he went on:

"How do I know that? Because an inquiry there would be your natural first step. Had you found a birth certificate, you would not have pursued the course you have. In fact, only a curiously determined person would have persisted in a quest for someone who had no official existence. So, I said to myself: 'When this persistence in the face of reason addresses itself to me I will try to resolve the mystery."

The young man frowned.

"You imply that you said that *before* you had my letter?"

"My dear fellow, Harshom is not a common name—an unusual corruption of Harvesthome, if you are interested in such things—and, indeed, I never yet heard of a Harshom who was not traceably connected with the rest of us. And we do, to some extent, keep in touch. So, quite naturally, I think, the incursion of a young man entirely unknown to any of us, but persistently tackling us one after another with his inquiries regarding an unidentifiable Harshom, aroused our interest. Since it seemed that I myself came low on your priority list I decided to make a few inquiries of my own. I—"

"But why should you judge yourself low on a list," Colin Trafford interrupted.

"Because you are clearly a man of method. In this case, geographical method. You began your inquiries with Harshoms in the central London area, and worked outwards, until you are now in Herefordshire. There are only two further-flung Harshoms now on your list: Peter, down in

the toe of Cornwall, and Harold, a few miles from Durham
—am I right?"

Colin Trafford nodded, with a trace of reluctance.

"You are," he admitted.

Dr. Harshom smiled, a trifle smugly.

"I thought so. There is—" he began, but the young man
interrupted him again.

"When you answered my letter, you invited me here,
but you evaded my question," he remarked.

"That is true. But I have answered it now by insisting
that the person you seek not only does not exist, but never
did exist."

"But if you're quite satisfied on that, why ask me here
at all?"

"Because—" The doctor broke off at the sound of a gong.
"Dear me, Phillips allows one just ten minutes to wash.
Let me show you your room, and we can continue over
dinner."

A little later when the soup was before them, he resumed:

"You were asking me why I invited you here. I think
the answer is that since you feel entitled to be curious
about a hypothetical relative of mine, I feel no less entitled
to be curious about the motives that impel your curiosity.
Fair enough?—as they say."

"Dubious," replied Mr. Trafford after consideration. "To
inquire into my motives would, I admit, be not unreasonable if you knew this person to exist—but, since you assure
me she does not exist, the question of my motives surely
becomes academic."

"My interest *is* academic, my dear fellow, but none the
less real. Perhaps we might progress a little if I might put
the problem as it appears from my point of view?"

Trafford nodded. The doctor went on:

"Well, now, this is the situation: Some seven or eight
months ago a young man, unknown to any of us, begins a
series of approaches to my relatives. His concern, he says,
is to learn the whereabouts, or to gain any clues which
may help him to trace the whereabouts, of a lady called
Ottilie Harshom. She was born, he believes, in 1928,
though it could be a few years to either side of that—and

she may, of course, have adopted another surname through marriage.

"In his earlier letters there is an air of confidence suggesting his feeling that the matter will easily be dealt with, but as one Harshom after another fails to identify the subject of his inquiries his tone becomes less confident though not less determined. In one or two directions he does learn of young Harshom ladies—none of them called Ottilie, by the way, but he nevertheless investigates them with care. Can it be, perhaps, that he is as uncertain about the first name as about everything else concerning her? But apparently none of these ladies fulfills his requirements, for he presses on. In the face of unqualified unsuccess, his persistence in leaving no Harshom stone unturned begins to verge upon the unreasonable. Is he an eccentric, with a curious obsession?

"Yet by all the evidence he was—until the spring of 1953, at any rate—a perfectly normal young man. His full name is Colin Wayland Trafford. He was born in 1921, in Solihull, the son of a solicitor. He went to Chartowe School 1934. Enlisted in the army 1939. Left it, with the rank of Captain 1945. Went up to Cambridge. Took a good degree in Physics 1949. Joined Electro-Physical Industries on the managerial side that same year. Married Della Stevens 1950. Became a widower 1951. Received injuries in a laboratory demonstration accident early in 1953. Spent the following five weeks in St. Merryn's Hospital. Began his first approaches to members of the Harshom family for information regarding Ottilie Harshom about a month after his discharge from hospital."

Colin Trafford said coldly:

"You are very fully informed, Dr. Harshom."

The doctor shrugged slightly.

"Your own information about the Harshoms must by now be almost exhaustive. Why should you resent some of us knowing something of you?"

Colin did not reply to that. He dropped his gaze, and appeared to study the tablecloth. The doctor resumed:

"I said just now—has he an obsession? The answer has appeared to be yes—since sometime last March. Prior to that, there seems to have been no inquiry whatever regarding Miss Ottilie Harshom.

"Now when I had reached this point I began to feel that I was on the edge of a more curious mystery than I had expected." He paused. "I'd like to ask you, Mr. Trafford, had you ever been aware of the name Ottilie Harshom before January last?"

The young man hesitated. Then he said, uneasily:

"How can one possibly answer that? One encounters myriad names on all sides. Some are remembered, some seem to get filed in the subconscious, some apparently fail to register at all. It's unanswerable."

"Perhaps so. But we have the curious situation that before January Ottilie Harshom was apparently not on your mental map, yet since March she has, without any objective existence, dominated it. So I ask myself, what happened between January and March . . . ?

"Well, I practice medicine. I have certain connections, I am able to learn the external facts. One day late in January you were invited, along with several other people, to witness a demonstration in one of your company's laboratories. I was not told the details, I doubt if I would understand them if I were: the atmosphere around the higher flights of modern physics is so rarefied—but I gather that during this demonstration something went amiss. There was an explosion, or an implosion, or perhaps a matter of a few atoms driven berserk by provocation. In any case, the place was wrecked. One man was killed outright, another died later, several were injured. You yourself were not badly hurt. You did get a few cuts, and bruises—nothing serious, but you were knocked out—right out . . .

"You were, indeed, so thoroughly knocked out that you lay unconscious for twenty-four days . . .

"And when at last you did come round you displayed symptoms of considerable confusion—more strongly, perhaps, than would be expected in a patient of your age and type, and you were given sedatives. The following night you slept restlessly, and showed signs of mental distress. In particular you called again and again for someone named Ottilie.

"The hospital made what inquiries they could, but none of your friends or relatives knew of anyone called Ottilie associated with you.

"You began to recover, but it was clear you had something heavily on your mind. You refused to reveal what it was, but you did ask one of the doctors whether he could have his secretary try to find the name Ottilie Harshom in any directory. When it could not be found, you became depressed. However, you did not raise the matter again—at least, I am told you did not—until after your discharge when you set out on this quest for Ottilie Harshom, in which, in spite of completely negative results, you continue.

"Now, what must one deduce from that?" He paused to look across the table at his guest, left eyebrow raised.

"That you are even better informed than I thought," Colin said, without encouragement. "If I were your patient your inquiries might be justified, but as I am not, and have not the least intention of consulting you professionally, I regard them as intrusive, and possibly unethical."

If he had expected his host to be put out he was disappointed. The doctor continued to regard him with interested detachment.

"I'm not yet entirely convinced that you ought not to be someone's patient," he remarked. "However, let me tell you why it was I, rather than another Harshom, who was led to make these inquiries. Perhaps you may then think them less impertiment. But I am going to preface that with a warning against false hopes. You must understand that the Ottilie Harshom you are seeking *does not exist and has not existed.* That is quite definite.

"Nevertheless, there *is* one aspect of this matter which puzzled me greatly, and that I cannot bring myself to dismiss as coincidence. You see, the name Ottilie Harshom was not entirely unknown to me. No—" He raised his hand. "—I repeat, no false hopes. There *is no* Ottilie Harshom, but there has been—or, rather, there have in the past been, two Ottilie Harshoms."

Colin Trafford's resentful manner had entirely dropped away. He sat, leaning a little forward, watching his host intently.

"But," the doctor emphasized, "it was all long ago. The first was my grandmother. She was born in 1832, married Grandfather Harshom in 1861, and died in 1866. The other was my sister: she, poor little thing, was born in 1884 and died in 1890 . . ."

He paused again. Colin made no comment. He went on:

"I am the only survivor of this branch so it is not altogether surprising that the others have forgotten there was
ever such a name in the family, but when I heard of your
inquiries I said to myself: There is something out of order
here. Ottilie is not the rarest of names, but on any scale
of popularity it would come a very long way down indeed;
and Harshom *is* a rare name. The odds against these two
being coupled by mere chance must be some quite astronomical figure. Something so large that I can not believe
it *is* chance. Somewhere there must be a link, some cause
. . .

"So, I set out to discover if I could find out why this
young man Trafford should have hit upon this improbable
conjunction of names—and, seemingly, become obsessed
by it.—You would not care to help me at this point?"

Colin continued to look at him, but said nothing.

"No? Very well. When I had all the available data assembled the conclusion I had to draw was this: that as a
result of your accident you underwent some kind of trau-
matic experience, an experience of considerable intensity
as well as unusual quality. Its intensity one deduces from
your subsequent fixation of purpose; the unusual quality
partly from the pronounced state of confusion in which
you regained consciousness, and partly from the consist-
ency with which you deny recollecting anything from the
moment of the accident until you awoke.

"Now, if that were indeed a blank, why did you awake
in such a confused condition? There must have been some
recollection to cause it. And if there was something akin to
ordinary dream images, why this refusal to speak of them?
There must have been, therefore, some experience of great
personal significance wherein the name Ottilie Harshom
was a very potent element indeed.

"Well, Mr. Trafford. Is the reasoning good, the conclusion valid? Let me suggest, as a physician, that such things
are a burden that should be shared."

Colin considered for some little time, but when he still
did not speak the doctor added:

"You are almost at the end of the road, you know. Only
two more Harshoms on the list, and I assure you they
won't be able to help—so what then?"

Colin said, in a flat voice:

"I expect you are right. You should know. All the same, I must see them. There might be something, some clue . . . I can't neglect the least possibility . . . I had just a little hope when you invited me here. I knew that you had a family . . ."

"I *had*," the doctor said, quietly. "My son Malcolm was killed racing at Brooklands in 1927. He was unmarried. My daughter married, but she had no children. She was killed in a raid on London in 1941 . . . So there it ends . . ." He shook his head slowly.

"I am sorry," said Colin. Then: "Have you a picture of your daughter that I may see?"

"She wasn't of the generation you are looking for."

"I realize that, but nevertheless . . ."

"Very well—when we return to the study. Meanwhile, you've not yet said what you think of my reasoning."

"Oh, it was good."

"But you are still disinclined to talk about it? Well, I am not. And I can still go a little further. Now, this experience of yours cannot have been a kind to cause a feeling of shame or disgust, or you would be trying to sublimate it in some way, which manifestly you are not. Therefore it is highly probable that the cause of your silence is fear. Something makes you afraid to discuss the experience. You are not, I am satisfied, afraid of facing it; therefore your fear must be of the consequences of communicating it. Consequences possibly to someone else, but much more probably to yourself . . ."

Colin went on regarding him expressionlessly for a moment. Then he relaxed a little and leaned back in his chair. For the first time he smiled faintly.

"You do get there in the end, don't you, Doctor? But do you mind if I say that you make quite Germanically heavy-going of it? And the whole thing is so simple, really. It boils down to this. If a man, any man, claims to have had an experience which is outside all normal experience, it will be inferred, will it not, that he is in some way not quite a normal man? In that case, he cannot be entirely relied upon to react to a particular situation as a normal man should—and if his reactions may be nonnormal, how can he be really dependable? He may be, of course—

but would it not be sounder policy to put authority into the hands of a man about whom there is *no* doubt? Better to be on the safe side. So he is passed over. His failure to make the expected step is not unnoticed. A small cloud, a mere wrack, of doubt and risk begins to gather above him. It is tenuous, too insubstantial for him to disperse, yet it casts a faint, persistent shadow.

"There is, I imagine, no such thing as a normal human being, but there is a widespread feeling that there ought to be. Any organization has a conception of 'the type of man we want here,' which is regarded as the normal for its purposes. So every man there attempts more or less to accord to it—organizational man, in fact—and anyone who diverges more than slightly from the type in either his public, or in his private, life does so to the peril of his career. There is, as you said, fear of the results to myself: it is, as I said, so simple."

"True enough," the doctor agreed. "But you have not taken any care to disguise the consequence of the experience—the hunt for Ottilie Harshom."

"I don't need to. Could anything be more reassuringly normal than 'man seeks girl'? I have invented a background which has quite satisfied any interested friends—and even several Harshoms."

"I dare say. None of them being aware of the 'coincidence' in the conjunction of 'Ottilie' with 'Harshom.' But I am."

He waited for Colin Trafford to make some comment on that. When none came, he went on:

"Look, my boy. You have this business very heavily on your mind. There are only the two of us here. I have no links whatever with your firm. My profession should be enough safeguard for your confidence, but I will undertake a special guarantee if you like. It will do you good to unburden—and I should like to get to the bottom of this . . ."

But Colin shook his head.

"You won't, you know. Even if I were to tell you, you'd only be the more mystified—as I am."

"Two heads are better than one. We could try," said the doctor, and waited.

Colin considered again, for some moments. Then he lifted his gaze, and met the doctor's steadily.

"Very well then. I've tried. You shall try. But first I would like to see a picture of your daughter. Have you one taken when she was about twenty-five?"

They left the table and went back to the study. The doctor waved Colin to a chair, and crossed to a corner cupboard. He took out a small pile of cardboard mounts and looked through them. He selected three, gazed at them thoughtfully for a few seconds, and then handed them over. While Colin studied them he busied himself with pouring brandy from a decanter.

Presently Colin looked up.

"No," he said. "And yet there is something . . ." He tried covering parts of the full-face portrait with his hand. "Something about the setting and shape of the eyes—but not quite. The brow, perhaps, but it's difficult to tell with the hair done like that . . ." He pondered the photographs a little longer, and then handed them back. "Thank you for letting me see them."

The doctor picked up one of the others and passed it over.

"This was Malcolm, my son."

It showed a laughing young man standing by the fore-part of a car which bristled with exhaust manifold and had its bonnet held down by straps.

"He loved that car," said the doctor, "but it was too fast for the old track there. It went over the banking, and hit a tree."

He took the picture back, and handed Colin a glass of brandy.

Colin swirled it. Neither of them spoke for some little time. Then he tasted the brandy, and, presently, lit a cigarette.

"Very well," he said again. "I'll try to tell you. But first I'll tell you what *happened*—whether it was subjective, or not, it happened for me. The implications and so on we can look at later—if you want to."

"Good," agreed the doctor. "But tell me first, do we start from the moment of the accident—or was there anything at all relevant before that?"

"No," Colin Trafford said, "that's where it *does* start."

It was just another day. Everything and everybody perfectly ordinary—except that this demonstration was something a bit special. What it concerned is not my secret, and not, as far as I know, relevant. We all gathered round the apparatus. Deakin, who was in charge, pulled down a switch. Something began to hum, and then to whine, like a motor running faster and faster. The whine became a shriek as it went up the scale. There was a quite piercingly painful moment or two near the threshold of audibility, then a sense of relief because it was over and gone, with everything seeming quiet again. I was looking across at Deakin watching his dials, with his fingers held ready over the switches, and then, just as I was in the act of turning my head towards the demonstration again, there was a flash . . . I didn't hear anything, or feel anything: there was just this dazzling white flash . . . Then nothing but black . . . I heard people crying out, and a woman's voice screaming . . . screaming . . . screaming . . .

I felt crushed by a great weight. I opened my eyes. A sharp pain jabbed through them into my head, but I struggled against the weight, and found it was due to two or three people being on top of me; so I managed to shove a couple of them off, and sit up. There were several other people lying about on the ground, and a few more picking themselves up. A couple of feet to my left was a large wheel. I looked further up and found that it was attached to a bus—a bus that from my position seemed to tower like a scarlet skyscraper, and appeared, moreover, to be tilted and about to fall on me. It caused me to get up very quickly, and as I did I grabbed a young woman who had been lying across my legs, and dragged her to a safer place. Her face was dead white, and she was unconscious.

I looked around. It wasn't difficult to see what had happened. The bus, which must have been traveling at a fair speed, had, for some reason got out of control, run across the crowded pavement, and through the plate-glass window of a shop. The forepart of the top deck had been telescoped against the front of the building, and it was up there that the screaming was going on. Several people were still lying on the ground, a woman moving feebly, a man groaning, two or three more quite still. Three streams of blood were meandering slowly across the pavement among the crystals of broken glass. All the traffic had stopped, and I could see a couple of policemen's helmets bobbing through the crowd towards us.

I moved my arms and legs experimentally. They worked perfectly well, and painlessly. But I felt dazed, and my head throbbed. I put my hand up to it and discovered a quite tender spot where I must have taken a blow on the left occiput.

The policemen got through. One of them started pushing back the gaping bystanders, the other took a look at the casualties on the ground. A third appeared and went up to the top deck of the bus to investigate the screaming there.

I tried to conquer my daze, and looked round further. The place was Regent Street, a little up from Piccadilly Circus; the wrecked window was one of Austin Reed's. I looked up again at the bus. It was certainly tilted, but not in danger of toppling, for it was firmly wedged into the window opening to within a yard of the word "General," gleaming in gold letters on its scarlet side.

At this point it occurred to me that I was supernumerary, and that if I were to hang around much longer I should find myself roped in as a witness—not, mind you, that I would grudge being a witness in the ordinary way, if it would do anyone any good, but I was suddenly and acutely aware that this was not at all in the ordinary way. For one thing I had no knowledge of anything whatever but the aftermath—and, for another, what was I doing here anyway . . . ? One moment I had been watching a demonstration out at Watford; the next, there was this. How the devil did I come to be in Regent Street at all . . . ?

I quietly edged my way into the crowd, then out of it again, zigzagged across the road amid the held-up traffic, and headed for the Café Royal, a bit further down.

They seemed to have done things to the old place since I was there last, a couple of years before, but the important thing was to find the bar, and that I did, without difficulty.

"A double brandy, and some soda," I told the barman.

He gave it me, and slid along the siphon. I pulled some money out of my pocket, coppers and a little small silver. So I made to reach for my notecase.

"Half a crown, sir," the barman told me, as if fending off a note.

I blinked at him. Still, he said it. I slid over three shillings. He seemed gratified.

I added soda to the brandy, and took a welcome drink. It was as I was putting the glass down that I caught sight of myself in the mirror behind the bar . . .

I used to have a mustache. I came out of the army with it, but decided to jettison it when I went up to Cambridge. But there it was—a little less luxuriant, perhaps, but resurrected. I put up my hand and felt it. There was no illusion, and it was genuine, too. At almost the same moment I noticed my suit. Now, I used to have a suit pretty much like that, years ago. Not at all a bad suit either, but still, not quite the thing we organization men wear in E.P.I. . . .

I had a swimming sensation, took another drink of the brandy, and felt, a little unsteadily, for a cigarette. The packet I pulled out of my pocket was unfamiliar—have you ever heard of Player's "Mariner" cigarettes—No? Neither had I, but I got one out, and lit it with a very unsteady match. The dazed feeling was not subsiding; it was growing, rapidly . . .

I felt for my inside pocket. No wallet. It should have been there—perhaps some opportunist in the crowd round the bus had got it . . . I sought through the other pockets—a fountain pen, a bunch of keys, a couple of cash receipts from Harrods, a check book—containing checks addressed to the Knightsbridge branch of the Westminster Bank. Well, the bank was all right, but why Knightsbridge?—I live in Hampstead . . .

To try to get some kind of grip on things I began to recapitulate from the moment I had opened my eyes and found the bus towering over me. It was quite vivid. I had a sharp recollection of staring up at that scarlet menace, with the gilded word "General" shining brightly . . . yes, in gleaming gold—only, as you know, the word "General" hasn't been seen on London buses since it was replaced by "London Transport" in 1933 . . .

I was getting a little rattled by now, and looked round the bar for something to steady my wits. On one table I noticed a newspaper that someone had discarded. I went across to fetch it, and got carefully back onto my stool before I looked at it. Then I took a deep breath and regarded the front page. My first response was dismay for the whole thing was given up to a single display advertisement. Yet there was some reassurance, of a kind, at the top, for it read: "*Daily Mail*, London, Wednesday 27 January 1954." So it was at least the right day—the one we had fixed for the demonstration at the labs.

I turned to the middle page, and read: "Disorders in Delhi. One of the greatest exhibitions of civil disobedience so far staged in India took place here today demanding the immediate release of Nehru from prison. For nearly all the hours of daylight the city has been at a standstill—" Then an item in an adjoining column caught my eye: "In answer to a question from the Opposition front bench Mr. Butler, the Prime Minister, assured the House that the Government was giving serious consideration——" In a dizzy way I glanced at the top of the page: the date there agreed with that on the front, 27 January 1954, but just below it there was a picture with the caption: "A scene from last night's production of *The Lady Loves,* at the Laughton Theatre, in which Miss Amanda Coward plays the lead in the last of her father's many musical plays. *The Lady Loves* was completed only a few days before Noel Coward's death last August, and a moving tribute to his memory was paid at the end of the performance by Mr. Ivor Novello who directed the production."

I read that again, with care. Then I looked up and about, for reassurance, at my fellow drinkers, at the furniture, at the barman, at the bottles: it was all convincingly real.

I dropped the paper, and finished the rest of my brandy. I could have done with another, but it would have been awkward if, with my wallet gone, the barman should change his mind about his modest price. I glanced at my watch—and there was a thing, too! It was a very nice watch, gold, with a crocodile strap, and hands that stood at twelve-thirty, but I had never seen it before. I took it off and looked at the back. There was a pretty bit of engraving there; it said: "C. forever O. 10.x.50." And it jolted me quite a little, for 1950 was the year I was married—though not in October, and not to anyone called O. My wife's name was Della. Mechanically I restrapped the watch on my wrist, and left.

The interlude and the brandy had done me some good. When I stepped out of Regent Street again I was feeling less dazed (though, if it is not too fine a distinction, more bewildered) and my head had almost ceased to ache, so that I was able to pay more attention to the world about me.

At first sight Piccadilly Circus gave an impression of being much as usual, and yet a suggestion that there was something a bit wrong with it. After a few moments I perceived that it was the people and the cars. Surprising numbers of the men and women, too, wore clothing that looked shabby, and the flower girls below Eros seemed like bundles of rags. The look of the women who were not shabby took me completely aback. Almost without exception their hats were twelve-inch platter-like things balanced on the top of their heads. The skirts were long, almost to their ankles, and, worn under fur coats, gave an impression that they were dressed for the evening, at midday. Their shoes were pointed, overornamented, pinheeled, and quite hideous. I suppose all high-fashion would look ludicrous if one were to come upon it unprepared, but then one never does—at least one never had until now . . . I might have felt like Rip van Winkle newly awakened, but for the dateline on that newspaper . . . The cars were odd, too. They seemed curiously high-built, small, and lacking in the flashy effects one had grown accustomed to, and when I paid more attention I did not see one make I could readily identify—except a couple of unmistakable Rollses.

While I stood staring curiously a plate-hatted lady in a well-worn fur coat posted herself beside me and addressed me as "dearie" in a somewhat grim way. I decided to move on, and headed for Piccadilly. On the way, I looked across at St. James's Church. The last time I had seen it it was clothed in scaffolding, with a hoarding in the garden to help to raise funds for the rebuilding—that would have been about a fortnight before—but now all that was gone, and it looked as if it had never been bombed at all. I crossed the road to inspect it more closely, and was still more impressed with the wonderful job they had made of the restoration.

Presently I found myself in front of Hatchard's windows, and paused to examine their contents. Some of the books had authors whose names I knew; I saw works by Priestley, C. S. Lewis, Bertrand Russell, T. S. Eliot, and others, but scarcely a title that I recognized. And then, down in the front, my eye was caught by a book in a predominantly pink jacket: *Life's Young Day*, a novel by Colin Trafford.

I went on goggling at it, probably with my mouth open. I once had ambitions in that direction, you know. If it had not been for the war I'd probably have taken an Arts degree, and tried my hand at it, but as things happened I made a friend in the regiment who turned me to science, *and* could put me in the way of a job with E.P.I. later. Therefore it took me a minute or two to recover from the coincidence of seeing my name on the cover, and, when I did, my curiosity was still strong enough to take me into the shop.

There I discovered a pile of half a dozen copies lying on a table. I picked up the top one, and opened it. The name was plain enough on the titlepage—and opposite was a list of seven other titles under "author of." I did not recognize the publisher's name, but overleaf there was the announcement: "First published January 1954."

I turned it over in my hand, and then all but dropped it. On the back was a picture of the author; undoubtedly me—and with the mustache . . . The floor seemed to tilt slightly beneath my feet.

Then, somewhere over my shoulder, there was a voice; one that I seemed to recognize. It said:

"Well met, Narcissus! Doing a bit of sales promotion, eh? How's it going?"

"Martin!" I exclaimed. I had never been so glad to see anyone in all my life. "Martin. Why we've not met since —when was it?"

"Oh, for at least three days, old boy," he said, looking a little surprised.

Three days! I'd seen a lot of Martin Falls at Cambridge, but only run across him twice since we came down, and the last of those was two years ago. But he went on:

"What about a spot of lunch, if you're not booked?" he suggested.

And that wasn't quite right either. I'd not heard anyone speak of a *spot* of lunch for years. However, I did my best to feel as if things were becoming more normal.

"Fine," I said, "but you'll have to pay. I've had my wallet pinched."

He clicked his tongue.

"Hope there wasn't much in it. Anyway, what about the club? They'll cash you a check there."

I put the book I was still holding back on the pile, and we left.

"Funny thing," Martin said. "Just ran into Tommy— Tommy Westhouse. Sort of blowing sulphur—hopping mad with his American agent. You remember that godawful thing of Tommy's—*The Thornèd Rose*—kind of Ben Hur meets Cleopatra, with the Marquis de Sade intervening? Well, it seems this agent—" He rambled on with a shoppy, anecdotal recital full of names that meant nothing to me, but lasted through several streets and brought us almost to Pall Mall. At the end of it he said: "You didn't tell me how *Life's Young Day's* doing. Somebody said it was over-subscribed. Saw the Lit Sup wagged a bit of a finger at you. Not had time to read it myself yet. Too much on hand."

I chose the easier—the noncommittal way. It seemed easier than trying to understand, so I told him it was doing just about as expected.

The club, when in due course we reached it, turned out to be the Savage. I am not a member, but the porter greeted me by name, as though I were in the habit of dropping in every day.

"Just a quick one," Martin suggested. "Then we'll look in and see George about your check."

I had misgivings over that, but it went off all right, and during lunch I did my best to keep my end up. I had the same troubles that I have now—true it was from the other end, but the principle still holds: if things are *too* queer people will find it easier to think you are potty than to help you; so you keep up a front.

I am afraid I did not do very well. Several times I caught Martin glancing at me with a perplexed expression.

Once he asked: "Quite sure you're feeling all right, old man?"

But the climax did not come until, with cheese on his plate, he reached out his left hand for a stick of celery. And as he did so I noticed the gold signet ring on his little finger, and that jolted me right out of my caution—for, you see, Martin doesn't have a little finger on his left hand, or a third finger, either. He left both of them somewhere near the Rhine in 1945 . . .

"Good God!" I exclaimed. For some reason that pierced me more sharply than anything yet. He turned his face towards me.

"What on earth's the matter, man? You're as white as a sheet."

"Your hand—" I said.

He glanced at it curiously, and then back at me, even more curiously.

"Looks all right to me," he said, eyes a little narrowed.

"But—but you lost the two last fingers—in the war," I exclaimed. His eyebrows rose, and then came down in an anxious frown. He said, with kind intention:

"Got it a bit mixed, haven't you, old man? Why, the war was over before I was born."

Well, it goes a bit hazy just after that, and when it got coherent again I was lying back in a big chair, with Martin sitting close beside, saying:

"So take my advice, old man. Just you trot along to the quack this afternoon. Must've taken a bit more of a knock than you thought, you know. Funny thing, the brain—can't be too careful. Well, I'll have to go now I'm afraid. Appointment. But don't you put it off. Risky. Let me know how it goes." And then he was gone.

I lay back in the chair. Curiously enough I was feeling far more myself than I had since I came to on the pavement in Regent Street. It was as if the biggest jolt yet had shaken me out of the daze, and got the gears of my wits into mesh again . . . I was glad to be rid of Martin, and able to think . . .

I looked round the lounge. As I said, I am not a member, and did not know the place well enough to be sure of details, but I rather thought the arrangement was a little

different, and the carpet, and some of the light fittings, from
when I saw it last . . .

There were few people around. Two talking in a corner,
three napping, two more reading papers; none taking any
notice of me. I went over to the periodicals table, and
brought back *The New Statesman*, dated January 22, 1954.
The front-page leader was advocating the nationalization of
transport as a first step towards putting the means of production into the hands of the people and so ending unem-
ployment. There was a wave of nostalgia about that. I
turned on, glancing at articles which baffled me for lack
of context. I was glad to find Critic present, and I noticed
that among the things that were currently causing him
concern was some experimental work going on in Germany.
His misgivings were, it seemed, shared by several eminent
scientists, for, while there was little doubt now that nuclear
fission was a theoretical possibility, the proposed methods
of control were inadequate. There could well be a chain
reaction resulting in a disaster of cosmic proportions. A con-
sortium which included names famous in the arts as well
as many illustrious in the sciences was being formed to
call upon the League of Nations to protest to the German
government in the name of humanity against reckless r·
search . . .

Well, well . . . !

With returning confidence in myself I sat and pondered.

Gradually, and faintly at first, something began to glimmer . . . Not anything about the how, or the why—I still
have no useful theories about those—but about *what* could
conceivably have happened.

It was vague—set off, perhaps, by the thought of that
random neutron which I knew in one set of circumstances
to have been captured by a uranium atom, but which, in
another set of circumstances, apparently had not . . .

And there, of course, one was brought up against Einstein and relativity which, as you know, denies the possibility of determining motion absolutely and consequently
leads into the idea of the four-dimensional space-time continuum. Well, then, since you cannot determine the motions
of the factors in the continuum, any pattern of motion
must be illusory, and there cannot be any determinable

consequences. Nevertheless, where the factors are closely similar—are composed of similar atoms in roughly the same relation to the continuum, so as to speak—you *may* quite well get similar consequences. They can never be identical, of course, or determination of motion would be possible. But they could be very similar, and capable of consideration in terms of Einstein's Special Theory, and they *could* be determined further by a set of closely similar factors. In other words although the infinite point which we may call a moment in 1954 *must* occur throughout the continuum, it *exists* only in relation to each observer, and *appears* to have similar existence in relation to certain close groups of observers. However, since no two observers can be identical—that is, the same observer—each must perceive a different past, present, and future from that perceived by any other; consequently, what he perceives arises only from the factors of his relationship to the continuum, and exists only for him.

Therefore I began to understand that *what* had happened must be this: in some way—which I cannot begin to grasp—I had somehow been translated to the position of a different observer—one whose angle of view was in some respects very close to my own, and yet different enough to have relationships, and therefore realities, unperceived by me. In other words, he must have lived in a world real only to him, just as I had lived in a world real only to me—until this very peculiar transposition had occurred to put me in the position of observing *his* world, with, of course, its relevant past and future, instead of the one I was accustomed to.

Mind you, simple as it is when you consider it, I certainly did not grasp the form of it all at once, but I did argue my way close enough to the observer-existence relationship to decide that whatever might have gone amiss, my own mind was more or less all right. The trouble really seemed to be that it was in the wrong place, and getting messages not intended for me; a receiver somehow hooked into the wrong circuit.

Well, that's not good, in fact, it's bad; but it's still a lot better than a faulty receiver. And it braced me a bit to realize that.

I sat there quite a time trying to get it clear, and wondering what I should do, until I came to the end of my packet of "Mariner" cigarettes. Then I went to the telephone.

First I dialed Electro-Physical Industries. Nothing happened. I looked them up in the book. It was quite a different number, on a different exchange. So I dialed that.

"Extension one three three," I told the girl on the desk, and then, on second thoughts, named my own department.

"Oh. You want extension five nine," she told me.

Somebody answered. I said:

"I'd like to speak to Mr. Colin Trafford."

"I'm sorry," said the girl. "I can't find that name in this department," the voice told me.

Back to the desk. Then a longish pause.

"I'm sorry," said the girl. "I can't find that name in our staff list."

I hung up. So, evidently, I was not employed by E.P.I. I thought a moment, and then dialed my Hampstead number. It answered promptly. "Transcendental Belts and Corsets," it announced brightly. I put down the receiver.

It occurred to me to look myself up in the book. I was there, all right: "Trafford, Colin W., 54 Hogarth Court, Duchess Gardens, S.W.7. SLOane 67021." So I tried that. The phone at the other end rang . . . and went on ringing . . .

I came out of the box wondering what to do next. It was an extremely odd feeling to be bereft of orientation, rather as if one had been dropped abruptly into a foreign city without even a hotel room for a base—and somehow made worse by the city being foreign only in minor and personal details.

After further reflection I decided that the best protective coloration would come from doing what *this* Colin Trafford might reasonably be expected to do. If he had no work to do at E.P.I., he did at least have a home to go to . . .

A nice block of flats, Hogarth Court, springy carpet and illuminated floral arrangement in the hall, that sort of thing, but, at the moment no porter in view, so I went straight to the lift. The place did not look big enough to contain fifty-four flats, so I took a chance on the five meaning the fifth floor, and sure enough I stepped out to find "54" on the door facing me. I took out my bunch of keys, tried the most likely one, and it fitted.

Inside was a small hall. Nothing distinctive—white paint, lightly patterned paper, close maroon carpet, occasional table with telephone and a few flowers in a vase, with a nice gilt-framed mirror above, the hard occasional chair, a passage off, lots of doors. I paused.

"Hullo," I said, experimentally. Then a little louder: "Hullo! Anyone at home?"

Neither voice nor sound responded. I closed the door behind me. What now? Well—well, hang it, I was—am— Colin Trafford! I took off my overcoat. Nowhere to put it. Second try revealed the coat closet . . . Several other coats already in there. Male and female, a woman's overshoes, too . . . I added mine.

I decided to get the geography of the place, and see what home was really like . . .

Well, you won't want an inventory, but it was a nice flat. Larger than I had thought at first. Well furnished and arranged; not with extravagance, but not with stint, either. It showed taste too; though not my taste—but what is taste? Either feeling for period, or refined selection from a fashion. I could feel that this was the latter, but the fashion was strange to me, and therefore lacked attraction.

The kitchen was interesting. A fridge, no washer, single-sink, no plate racks, no laminated tops, old-fashioned-looking electric cooker, packet of soap powder, no synthetic detergents, curious light panel about three feet square in the ceiling, no mixer . . .

The sitting room was airy, chairs comfortable. Nothing spindly. A large radiogram, rather ornate, no F.M. on its scale. Lighting again by ceiling panels, and square things like glass cakeboxes on stands. No television.

I prowled round the whole place. Bedroom feminine, but not fussy. Twin beds. Bathroom tiled, white. Spare bedroom, small double bed. And so on. But it was a room at the end of the passage that interested me most. A sort of study. One wall all bookshelves, some of the books familiar—the older ones—others not. An easy chair, a lighter chair. In front of the window a broad, leather-topped desk, with a view across the bare-branched trees in the Gardens, roofs beyond, plenty of sky. On the desk a covered typewriter, adjustable lamp, several folders with sheets of paper untidily projecting, cigarette box, metal ashtray, clean and empty, and a photograph in a leather frame.

I looked at the photograph carefully. A charming study. She'd be perhaps twenty-four—twenty-five? Intelligent, happy-looking, somebody one would like to know—but not anyone I did know . . .

There was a cupboard on the left of the desk, and, on it, a glass-fronted case with eight books on it; the rest was empty. The books were all in bright paper jackets, looking as new. The one on the right-hand end was the book that I had seen in Hatchard's that morning—*Life's Young Day*; all the rest, too, bore the name Colin Trafford. I sat down in the swivel chair at the desk and pondered them for some moments. Then, with a curious, schizoid feeling I pulled out *Life's Young Day*, and opened it.

It was, perhaps, half an hour, or more, later that I caught the sound of a key in the outer door. I decided that, on the whole, it would be better to disclose myself than wait to be discovered. So I opened the door. Along at the end of the passage a figure in three-quarter length gray suede coat which showed a tweed skirt beneath was dumping parcels onto the hall table. At the sound of my door she turned her head. It was the original of the photograph, all right; but not in the mood of the photograph. As I approached, she looked at me with an expression of surprise, mixed with other feelings that I could not identify; but certainly it was not an adoring-wife-greets-husband look.

"Oh," she said. "You're in, what happened?"

"Happened?" I repeated, feeling for a lead.

"Well, I understand you had one of those so-important meetings with Dickie at the BBC fixed for this afternoon," she said, a little curtly I thought.

"Oh. Oh, that, yes. Yes, he had to put it off," I replied, clumsily.

She stopped still, and inspected me carefully. A little oddly, too, I thought. I stood looking at her, wondering what to do, and wishing I had had the sense to think up some kind of plan for this inevitable meeting instead of wasting my time over *Life's Young Day*. I hadn't even had the sense to find out her name. It was clear that I'd got away wrong somehow the moment I opened my mouth. Besides, there was a quality about her that upset my balance altogether . . . It hit me in a way I'd not known for years, and more shrewdly than it had then . . . Somehow, when you are thirty-three you don't expect these things to happen—well, not to happen quite like that, any more . . . Not with a great surge in your heart, and everything coming suddenly bright and alive as if she had just switched it all into existence . . .

So we stood looking at one another; she with a half-frown, I trying to cope with a turmoil of elation and confusion, unable to say a word.

She glanced down, and began to unbutton her coat. She, too, seemed uncertain.

"If——" she began. But at that moment the telephone rang.

With an air of welcoming the interruption, she picked up the receiver. In the quiet of the hall I could hear a woman's voice ask for Colin.

"Yes," she said, "he's here." And she held the receiver out to me, with a very curious look.

"Hullo," I said. "Colin here."

"Oh, indeed," replied the voice, "and why, may I ask?"

"Er—I don't quite——" I began, but she cut me short.

"Now, look here, Colin, I've already wasted an hour waiting for you, thinking that if you couldn't come you might at least have had the decency to ring me up and tell me. Now I find you're just sitting at home. Not quite good enough, Colin."

"I—um—who is it? Who's speaking?" was the only temporizing move I could think of. I was acutely conscious that the young woman beside me was frozen stock-still in the act of taking off her coat.

"Oh, for God's sake," said the voice, exasperated. "What silly game is this? Who do you *think* it is?"

"That's what I'm asking," I said.

"Oh, don't be such a clown, Colin. If it's because Ottilie's still there—and I bet she is—you're just being stupid. She answered the phone herself, so she *knows* it's me."

"Then perhaps I'd better ask her who you are," I suggested.

"Oh—you must be tight as an owl. Go and sleep it off," she snapped, and the phone went dead.

I put the receiver back in the rest. The young woman was looking at me with an expression of genuine bewilderment. In the quietness of the hall she must have been able to hear the other voice almost as clearly as I had. She turned away, and busied herself with taking her coat off and putting it on a hanger in the closet. When she'd carefully done that she turned back.

"I don't understand," she said. "You aren't tight, are you? What's it all about? What has dear Dickie done?"

"Dickie?" I inquired. The slight furrow between her brows deepened.

"Oh, really, Colin. If you think I don't know Dickie's voice on the telephone by this time . . ."

"Oh," I said. A bloomer of a peculiarly cardinal kind, that. In fact, it is hard to think of a more unlikely mistake than that a man should confuse the gender of his friends. Unless I wanted to be thought quite potty, I must take steps to clarify the situation.

"Look, can't we go into the sitting room? There's something I want to tell you," I suggested.

I took the chair opposite, and wondered how to begin. Even if I had been clear in my own mind about what had happened, it would have been difficult enough. But how to convey that though the physical form was Colin Trafford's, and I myself was Colin Trafford, yet I was not *that* Colin Trafford; not the one who wrote books and was married to her, but a kind of alternative Colin Trafford astray from an alternative world? What seemed to be wanted was some kind of approach which would not immediately suggest a call for an alienist and it wasn't easy to perceive.

"Well?" she repeated.

"It's difficult to explain," I temporized, but truthfully enough.

"I'm sure it is," she replied, without encouragement, and added: "Would it perhaps be easier if you didn't look at me like that? I'd prefer it, too."

"Something very odd has happened to me," I told her.

"Oh, dear, again?" she said. "Do you want my sympathy, or something?"

I was taken aback, and a little confused.

"Do you mean it's happened to him before?" I asked.

She looked at me hard.

"Him? Who's him? I thought you were talking about you? And what I mean is last time it happened it was Dickie, and the time before that it was Frances, and before that it was Lucy . . . And now you've given Dickie a most peculiar kind of brushoff . . . Am I supposed to be surprised . . . ?"

I was learning about my *alter ego* quite fast, but we were off the track. I tried:

"No, you don't understand. This is something quite different."

"Of course not. Wives never do, do they? And it's always different. Well, if that's all that's so important . . ." She began to get up.

"No, please . . ." I said anxiously.

She checked herself, looking very carefully at me again. The half-frown came back.

"No," she said. "No, I don't think I do understand. At least, I—I hope not . . ." And she went on examining me, with something like growing uncertainty, I thought.

When you plead for understanding you can scarcely keep it on an impersonal basis, but when you don't know whether the best address would be "my dear," or "darling," or some more intimate variant, nor whether it should be prefaced by first name, nickname, or pet name, the way ahead becomes thorny indeed. Besides, there was this persistent misunderstanding on the wrong level.

"Ottilie, darling," I tried—and that was clearly no usual form, for, momentarily, her eyes almost goggled, but I plowed on: "It isn't at all what you're thinking—nothing a bit like that. It's—well, it's that in a way I'm not the same person . . ."

She was back in charge of herself.

"Oddly enough, I've been aware of that for some time," she said. "*And* I could remind you that you've said something like that before, more than once. All right then, let me go on for you; so you're not the same person I married, so you'd like a divorce—or is it that you're afraid Dickie's husband is going to cite you this time? Oh, God! How sick I am of all this . . ."

"No, no," I protested desperately. "It's not that sort of thing at all. Do please be patient. It's a thing that's terribly difficult to explain . . ." I paused, looking at her. That did not make it any easier. Indeed, it was far from helping the rational processes. She sat looking back at me, still with that half-frown, but now it was a little more uneasy than displeased.

"Something *has* happened to you . . ." she said.

"That's what I'm trying to tell you about," I told her, but I doubt whether she heard it. Her eyes grew wider as she looked. Suddenly they avoided mine.

"No!" she said. "Oh, *no!*" She looked as if she were about to cry, and wound her fingers tightly together in her lap. She half-whispered: "Oh, no! . . . Oh, please God, no! . . . Not again . . . Haven't I been hurt enough? . . . I won't . . I won't . . . !"

Then she jumped up, and, before I was halfway out of my chair, she was out of the room.

Colin Trafford paused to light a fresh cigarette, and took his time before going on. At length he pulled his thoughts back.

"Well," he went on, "obviously you will have realized by now that *that* Mrs. Trafford was born Ottilie Harshom. It happened in 1928, and she married *that* Colin Trafford in 1949. Her father was killed in a plane crash in 1938—I don't remember her ever mentioning his first name. That's unfortunate—there are a lot of things that are unfortunate: had I any idea that I might be jerked back here I'd have taken notice of a lot of things. But I hadn't . . . Something exceedingly odd had happened, but that was no reason to suppose that an equally odd thing would happen, in reverse . . .

"I did do my best, out of my own curiosity, to discover when the schism had taken place. There must, as I saw it, have been some point where, perhaps by chance, some pivotal thing had happened, or failed to happen, and finding it could bring one closer to knowing the moment, the atom of time, that had been split by some random neutron to give two atoms of time diverging into different futures. Once that had taken place, consequences gradually accumulating would make the conditions on one plane progressively different from those on the other.

"Perhaps that is always happening. Perhaps chance is

continually causing two different outcomes so that in a dimension we cannot perceive there are infinite numbers of planes, some so close to our own and so recently split off that they vary only in minor details, others vastly different. Planes on which some misadventure caused Alexander to be beaten by the Persians, Scipio to fall before Hannibal, Caesar to stay beyond the Rubicon; infinite, infinite planes of the random split and resplit by the random. Who can tell? But, now that we know the Universe for a random place, why not?

"But I couldn't come near fixing the moment. It was, I *think*, somewhere in late 1926, or early 1927. Further than that one seemed unable to go without the impossible data of quantities of records from both planes for comparison. Something happening, or not happening, about then had brought results which prevented, among other things, the rise of Hitler, and thus the Second World War—and consequently postponed the achievement of nuclear fission on this plane of our dichotomy—if that is a good word for it.

"Anyway, it was for me, and as I said, simply a matter of incidental curiosity. My active concerns were more immediate. And the really important one was Ottilie . . .

"I have, as you know, been married—and I was fond of my wife. It was, as people say, a successful marriage, and it never occurred to me to doubt that—until this thing happened to me. I don't want to be disloyal to Della now, and I don't think she was unhappy—but I am immensely thankful for one thing: that this did not happen while she was alive; she never knew, because I didn't know then, that I had married the wrong woman—and I hope she never thought it . . .

"And Ottilie had married the wrong man . . . We found that out. Or perhaps one should put it that she had not married the man she thought she had. She had fallen in love with him; and, no doubt, he had loved her, to begin with—but in less than a year she became torn between the part she loved, and the side she detested . . .

"Her Colin Trafford looked like me—right down to the left thumb which had got mixed up in an electric fan and never quite matched the other side—indeed, up to a point, that point somewhere in 1926-27 he *was* me. We had, I gathered, some mannerisms in common, and voices that

were similar—though we differed in our emphases, and in
our vocabularies, as I learnt from a tape, and in details:
the mustache, the way we wore our hair, the scar on the
left side of the forehead which was exclusively his; yet, in
a sense, I was him and he was me. We had the same parents, the same genes, the same beginning, and—if I was
right about the time of the dichotomy—we must have had
the same memory of our life, for the first five years or so.

But later on, things on our different planes must have
run differently for us. Environment, or experiences, had
developed qualities in him which, I have to think, lie latent
in me—and, I suppose, vice versa.

"I think that's a reasonable assumption, don't you? After
all, one begins life with a kind of armature which has individual differences and tendencies, though a common general plan, but whatever is modeled on that armature later
consists almost entirely of stuff from contacts and influ-
ences. What these had been for the other Colin Trafford I
don't know, but I found the results somewhere painful—
rather like continually glimpsing oneself in unexpected distorting mirrors.

"There were certain cautions, restaints, and expectations
in Ottilie that taught me a number of things about him,
too. Moreover, in the next day or two I read his novels
attentively. The earliest was not displeasing, but as the
dates grew later and the touch surer, I cared less and less
for the flavor; no doubt the widening streaks of brutality
showed the calculated development of a selling point, but
there was something a little more than that—besides, one
has a choice of selling points . . . With each book, I re-
sented seeing my name on the title page a little more.

"I discovered the current 'work in progress,' too. With
the help of his notes I could, I believe, have produced a
passable forgery, but I knew I would not. If I had to continue his literary career, it would be with my kind of books,
not his. But, in any case, I had no need to worry over
making a living: what with the war and one thing and
another, physics on my own plane was a generation ahead
of theirs. Even if they had got as far as radar it was
still someone's military secret. I had enough knowledge to
pass for a genius, and make my fortune if I cared to use
it . . ."

He smiled, and shook his head. He went on:

"You see, once the first shock was over and I had begun to perceive what must have happened, there was no cause for alarm, and, once I had met Ottilie, none for regret. The only problem was adjustment. It helped in general, I found, to try to get back to as much as I could remember of the prewar world. But details were not difficult: unrecognized friends, lapsed friends, all with unknown histories, some of them with wives, or husbands, I knew (though not necessarily the same ones); some with quite unexpected partners. There were queer moments, too—an encounter with a burly cheerful man in the bar of the Hyde Park Hotel. He didn't know me, but I knew him; the last time I had seen him he was lying by a road with a sniper's bullet through his head. I saw Della, my wife, leaving a restaurant looking happy, with her arm through that of a tall legal-looking type; it was uncanny to have her glance at me as at a complete stranger—I felt as if both of us were ghosts—but I was glad she had got past 1951 all right on that plane. The most awkward part was frequently running into people that it appeared I should know; the other Colin's acquaintanceship was evidently vast and curious. I began to favor the idea of proclaiming a breakdown from overwork, to tide me over for a bit.

"One thing that did not cross my mind was the possibility of what I took to be a unique shift of plane occurring again, this time in reverse . . .

"I am thankful it did not. It would have blighted the three most wonderful weeks in my life. I thought it was, as the engraving on the back of the watch said: 'C. forever O.'

"I made a tentative attempt to explain to her what I thought had happened, but it wasn't meaning anything to her, so I gave it up. I think she had it worked out for herself that somewhere about a year after we were married I had begun to suffer from overstrain, and that now I had got better and become again the kind of man she had thought I was . . . something like that . . . but theories about it did not interest her much—it was the consequence that mattered . . .

"And how right she was—for me too. After all, what else did matter? As far as I was concerned, nothing. I was in love. What did it matter *how* I had found the one unknown woman I had sought all my life. I was happy, as I had never expected to be . . . Oh, all the phrases are trite, but 'on top of the world' was suddenly half ridiculously vivid. I was full of a confidence rather like that of the slightly drunk. I could take anything on. With her beside me I could keep on top of that, or any, world . . . I think she felt like that, too. I'm sure she did. She'd wiped out the bad years. Her faith was regrowing, stronger every day . . . If I'd only known—but how could I know? What could I do . . . ?"

Again he stopped talking, and stared into the fire, this time for so long that at last the doctor fidgeted in his chair to recall him, and then added:

"What happened?"

Colin Trafford still had a faraway look.

"Happened?" he repeated. "If I knew that I could perhaps—but I *don't* know . . . There's nothing *to* know . . . *It's* random, too . . . One night I went to sleep with Ottilie beside me—in the morning I woke up in a hospital bed—back here again . . . That's all there was to it. All there is . . . Just random . . ."

In the long interval that followed, Dr. Harshom unhurriedly refilled his pipe, lit it with careful attention, assured himself it was burning evenly and drawing well, settled himself back comfortably, and then said, with intentional matter-of-factness:

"It's a pity you don't believe that. If you did, you'd never have begun this search; if you'd come to believe it, you'd have dropped the search before now. No, you believe that there is a pattern, or rather, that there were two patterns, closely similar to begin with, but gradually, perhaps logically, becoming more variant—and that you, your psyche, or whatever you like to call it, was the aberrant, the random factor.

"However, let's not go into the philosophical, or metaphysical consideration of what you call the dichotomy now—all that stuff will keep. Let us say that I accept the validity of your experience, for you, but reserve judgment on its nature. I accept it on account of several features—not the least being as I have said, the astronomical odds against the conjunction of names, Ottilie and Harshom,

occurring fortuitously. Of course, you *could* have seen the
name somewhere and lodged it in your subconscious, but
that, too, I find so immensely improbable that I put it aside.

"Very well, then, let us go on from there. Now, you appear to me to have made a number of quite unwarrantable
assumptions. You have assumed, for instance, that because
an Ottilie Harshom exists on what you call *that* plane,
she must have come into existence on this plane also. I
cannot see that that is justified by anything you have told
me. That she *might* have existed here, I admit, for the
name Ottilie is in my branch of the family; but the chances
of her having no existence at all are considerably greater—
did not you yourself mention that you recognized friends
who in different circumstances were married to different
wives—is it not, therefore, highly probable that the circumstances which produced an Ottilie Harshom there failed
to occur here, with the result that she could not come into
existence at all? And, indeed, that must be so.

"Believe me, I am not unsympathetic. I do understand
what your feelings must be, but are you not, in effect, in
the state we all have known—searching for an ideal young
woman who has never been born? We must face the
facts: if she exists, or did exist, I should have heard of her,
Somerset House would have a record of her, your own
extensive researches would have revealed *something* positive. I do urge you for your own good to accept it, my
boy. With all this against you, you simply have no case."

"Only my own positive conviction," Colin put in. "It's
against reason, I know—but I still have it."

"You must try to rid yourself of it. Don't you see there
are layers of assumptions? If she did exist she might be
already married."

"But to the wrong man," Colin said promptly.

"Even that does not follow. Your counterpart varied
from you, you say. Well, her counterpart if she existed
would have had an entirely different upbringing in different circumstances from the other; the probability is that
there would only be the most superficial resemblance. You
must see that the whole thing goes into holes wherever
you touch it with reason." He regarded Colin for a moment, and shook his head. "Somewhere at the back of
your mind you are giving houseroom to the proposition

that unlike causes can produce like results. Throw it out."

Colin smiled.

"How Newtonian, Doctor. No, a random factor is random. Chance therefore exists."

"Young man, you're incorrigible," the doctor told him. "If there weren't little point in wishing success with the impossible I'd say your tenacity deserves it. As things are, I advise you to apply it to the almost attainable."

His pipe had gone out, and he lit it again.

"That," he went on, "was a professional recommendation. But now, if it isn't too late for you, I'd like to hear more. I don't pretend to guess at the true nature of your experience, but the speculations your plane of might-have-been arouses are fascinating. Not unnaturally one feels a curiosity to know how one's own counterpart made out there—and failing that, how other people's did. Our present Prime Minister, for instance—did both of him get the job? And Sir Winston—or is he not *Sir* Winston over there?— how on earth did he get along with no Second World War to make his talents burgeon? And what about the poor old Labour Party . . . ? The thing provokes endless questions . . ."

After a late breakfast the next morning Dr. Harshom helped Colin into his coat in the hall, but held him there for a final word.

"I spent what was left of the night thinking about this," he said, earnestly. "Whatever the explanation may be, you must write it down, every detail you can remember. Do it anonymously if you like, but do it. It may not be unique, someday it may give valuable confirmation of someone else's experience, or become evidence in support of some theory. So put it on record—but then leave it at that . . . Do your best to forget the assumptions you jumped at— they're unwarranted in a dozen ways. *She does not exist.* The only Ottilie Harshoms there have been in this world died long ago. Let the image fade. But thank you for your confidence. Though I am inquisitive, I am discreet. If there should be any way I can help you . . ."

Presently he was watching the car down the drive. Colin waved a hand just before it disappeared round the corner. Dr. Harshom shook his head. He knew he might as well have saved his breath, but he felt in duty bound to make one last appeal. Then he turned back into the house, frowning. Whether the obsession was a fantasy, or something more than a fantasy, was almost irrelevant to that fact that sooner or later the young man was going to drive himself into a breakdown . . .

During the next few weeks Dr. Harshom learnt no more, except that Colin Trafford had not taken his advice, for word filtered through that both Peter Harshom in Cornwall and Harold in Durham had received requests for information regarding a Miss Ottilie Harshom who, as far as they knew, was nonexistent.

After that there was nothing more for some months. Then a picture postcard from Canada. On one side was a picture of the Parliament Buildings, Ottawa. The message on the other was brief. It said simply:

"Found her. Congratulate me. C.T."

Dr. Harshom studied it for a moment, and then smiled slightly. He was pleased. He had thought Colin Trafford a likable young man; too good to run himself to pieces over such a futile quest. One did not believe it for a moment, of course, but if some sensible young woman had managed to convince him that she was the reincarnation, so to speak, of his beloved, good luck to her—and good luck for him . . . The obsession could now fade quietly away. He would have liked to respond with the requested congratulations, but the card bore no address.

Several weeks later there was another card, with a picture of St. Mark's Square, Venice. The message was again laconic, but headed this time by a hotel address. It read:

"Honeymoon. May I bring her to see you after?"

Dr. Harshom hesitated. His professional inclination was against it; a feeling that anything likely to recall the young man to the mood in which he had last seen him was best avoided. On the other hand, a refusal would seem odd as well as rude. In the end he replied, on the back of a picture of Hereford Cathedral:

"Do. When?"

Half August had already gone before Colin Trafford did make his reappearance. He drove up looking sunburnt and

in better shape all round than he had on his previous visit.
Dr. Harshom was glad to see it, but surprised to find that
he was alone in the car.

"But I understand the whole intention was that I should
meet the bride," he protested.

"It was—it is," Colin assured him. "She's at the hotel.
I—well, I'd like to have a few words with you first."

The doctor's gaze became a little keener, his manner
more thoughtful.

"Very well. Let's go indoors. If there's anything I'm not
to mention, you could have warned me by letter, you know."

"Oh, it's not that. She knows about that. Quite what she
makes of it, I'm not sure, but she knows, and she's anxious
to meet you. No, it's—well, it won't take—more than ten
minutes."

The doctor led the way to his study. He waved Colin to
an easy chair, and himself took the swivel chair at the desk.

"Unburden yourself," he invited.

Colin sat forward, forearms on knees, hands dangling between them.

"The most important thing, Doctor, is for me to thank
you. I can never be grateful enough to you—never. If you
had not invited me here as you did, I think it is unlikely
I ever would have found her."

Dr. Harshom frowned. He was not convinced that the
thanks were justified. Clearly, whoever Colin had found
was possessed of a strong therapeutic quality, nevertheless:

"As I recollect, all I did was listen, and offer you un-
welcome advice for your own good—which you did not
take," he remarked.

"So it seemed to me at the time," Colin agreed. "It
looked as if you had closed all the doors. But then, when
I thought it over, I saw one, just one, that hadn't quite
latched."

"I don't recall giving you *any* encouragement," Dr. Harshom asserted.

"I am sure you don't, but you did. You indicated to me
the last, faintly possible line—and I followed it up—No,
you'll see what it was later, if you'll just bear with me a
little.

"When I did see the possibility, I realized it meant a
lot of groundwork that I couldn't cover on my own, so

I had to call in the professionals. They were pretty good, I thought, and they certainly removed any doubt about the line being the right one, but what they could tell me ended on board a ship bound for Canada. So then I had to call in some inquiry agents over there. It's a large country. A lot of people go to it. There was a great deal of routine searching to do, and I began to get discouraged, but then they got a lead, and in another week they came across with the information that she was a secretary working in a lawyer's office in Ottawa.

"Then I put it to E.P.I. that I'd be more valuable after a bit of unpaid recuperative leave——"

"Just a minute," put in the doctor. "If you'd asked me I could have told you there are *no* Harshoms in Canada. I happen to know that because——"

"Oh, I'd given up expecting that. Her name wasn't Harshom—it was Gale," Colin interrupted, with the air of one explaining.

"Indeed. And I suppose it wasn't Ottilie, either?" Dr. Harshom said heavily.

"No. It was Belinda," Colin told him.

The doctor blinked slightly, opened his mouth, and then thought better of it. Colin went on:

"So then I flew over, to make sure. It was the most agonizing journey I'd ever made. But it was all right. Just one distant sight of her was enough. I couldn't have *mistaken* her for Ottilie, but she was so very, very nearly Ottilie that I would have known her among ten thousand. Perhaps if her hair and her dress had been——" He paused speculatively, unaware of the expression on the doctor's face. "Anyway," he went on. "I *knew*. And it was damned difficult to stop myself rushing up to her there and then, but I did just have enough sense to hold back.

"Then it was a matter of managing an introduction. After that it was as if there were—well, an inevitability, a sort of predestination about it."

Curiosity impelled the doctor to say:

"Comprehensible, but sketchy. What, for instance, about her husband?"

"Husband?" Colin looked momentarily startled.

"Well, you did say her name was Gale," the doctor pointed out.

"So it was, Miss Belinda Gale—I thought I said that. She was engaged once, but she didn't marry. I tell you there was a kind of—well, fate, in the Greek sense, about it."

"But if—" Dr. Harshom began, and then checked himself again. He endeavored, too, to suppress any sign of skepticism.

"But it would have been just the same if she had had a husband," Colin asserted, with ruthless conviction. "He'd have been the wrong man."

The doctor offered no comment, and he went on:

"There were no complications, or involvements—well, nothing serious. She was living in a flat with her mother, and getting quite a good salary. Her mother looked after the place, and had a widow's pension—her husband was in the R.C.A.F.; shot down over Berlin—so between them they managed to be reasonably comfortable.

"Well, you can imagine how it was. Considered as a phenomenon I wasn't any too welcome to her mother, but she's a fair-minded woman, and we found that, as persons, we liked one another quite well. So that part of it, too, went off more easily than it might have done."

He paused here. Dr. Harshom put in:

"I'm glad to hear it, of course. But I must confess I don't quite see what it has to do with your not bringing your wife along with you."

Colin frowned.

"Well, I thought—I mean she thought—well, I haven't quite got to the point yet. It's rather delicate."

"Take your time. After all, I've retired," said the doctor, amiably.

Colin hesitated.

"All right. I think it'll be fairer to Mrs. Gale if I tell it the way it fell out.

"You see, I didn't intend to say anything about what's at the back of all this—about Ottilie, I mean, and why I came to be over in Ottawa—not until later, anyway. You were the only one I had told, and it seemed better that way . . . I didn't want them wondering if I was a bit off my rocker, naturally. But I went and slipped up.

"It was on the day before our wedding. Belinda was out getting some last-minute things, and I was at the flat doing my best to be reassuring to my future mother-in-law. As nearly as I can recall it, what I said was:

" 'My job with E.P.I. is quite a good one, and the prospects are good, but they do have a Canadian end, too, and I dare say that if Ottilie finds she really doesn't like living in England——'

"And then I stopped because Mrs. Gale had suddenly sat upright with a jerk, and was staring at me open-mouthed. Then in a shaky sort of voice she asked:

" '*What* did you say?'

"I'd noticed the slip myself, just too late to catch it. So I corrected: 'I was just saying that if Belinda finds she doesn't like——'

"She cut in on that.

" 'You didn't say Belinda. You said Ottilie.'

" 'Er—perhaps I did,' I admitted, 'but, as I say, if she doesn't——'

" 'Why?' she demanded. '*Why* did you call her Ottilie?'

"She was intense about that. There was no way out of it.

" 'It's well, it's the way I think of her,' I said.

" 'But why? *Why* should you think of Belinda as Ottilie?' she insisted.

"I looked at her more carefully. She had gone quite pale, and the hand that was visible was trembling. She was afraid, as well as distressed. I was sorry about that, and I gave up bluffing.

" 'I didn't mean this to happen,' I told her.

"She looked at me steadily, a little calmer.

" 'But now it has, you *must* tell me. What do you know about us?' she asked.

" 'Simply that if things had been different she wouldn't be Belinda Gale. She would be Ottilie Harshom,' I told her.

"She kept on watching my face, long and steadily, her own face still pale.

" 'I don't understand,' she said more than half to herself. 'You *couldn't* know. Harshom—yes, you might have found that out somehow, or guessed it—or did she tell you?' I shook my head. 'Never mind, you could find out,' she went on. 'But Ottilie . . . You *couldn't* know that—just that one name out of all the thousands of names in the world . . . *Nobody* knew that—nobody but me . . .' She shook her head.

" 'I didn't even tell Reggie . . . When he asked me if we could call her Belinda, I said yes; he'd been so very good to me . . . He had no idea that I had meant to call her Ottilie—nobody had. I've never told anyone, before or since . . . So how *can* you know.'

"I took her hand between mine, and pressed it, trying to comfort her and calm her.

" 'There's nothing to be alarmed about,' I told her. 'It was a—a dream, a kind of vision—I just knew . . .'

"She shook her head. After a minute she said quietly:

" 'Nobody knew but me . . . It was in the summer, in 1927. We were on the river, in a punt, pulled under a willow. A white launch swished by us, we watched it go, and saw the name on its stern. Malcolm said' "—if Colin noticed Dr. Harshom's sudden start, his only acknowledgment of it was a repetition of the last two words—" 'Malcolm said: "Ottilie—pretty name, isn't it? It's in our family. My father had a sister Ottilie who died when she was a little girl. If ever I have a daughter I'd like to call her Ottilie." ' "

Colin Trafford broke off, and regarded the doctor for a moment. Then he went on:

"After that she said nothing for a long time, until she added:

" 'He never knew, you know. Poor Malcolm, he was killed before even I knew she was coming . . . I did so want to call her Ottilie for him . . . He'd have liked that . . . I wish I had . . .' And then she began quietly crying . . ."

Dr. Harshom had one elbow on his desk, one hand over his eyes. He did not move for some little time. At last he pulled out a handkerchief, and blew his nose decisively.

"I did hear there was a girl," he said. "I even made inquiries, but they told me she had married soon afterwards. I thought she—— But why didn't she come to me? I would have looked after her."

"She couldn't know that. She was fond of Reggie Gale. He was in love with her, and willing to give the baby his name," Colin said.

After a glance towards the desk, he got up and walked over to the window. He stood there for several minutes with his back to the room until he heard a movement behind him. Dr. Harshom had got up and was crossing to the cupboard.

"I could do with a drink," he said. "The toast will be the restoration of order, and the rout of the random element."

"I'll support that," Colin told him, "but I'd like to couple it with the confirmation of your contention, Doctor—after all, you are right at last, you know; Ottilie Harshom *does not exist*—not any more. And then, I think, it will be high time you were introduced to your granddaughter, Mrs. Colin Trafford."

❂ *C. M. Kornbluth*

THE ROCKET OF 1955

The scheme was all Fein's, but the trimmings that made it more than a pipe dream, and its actual operation, depended on me. How long the plan had been in incubation I do not know, but Fein, one spring day, broke it to me in crude form. I pointed out some errors, corrected and amplified on the thing in general, and told him that I'd have no part of it—and changed my mind when he threatened to reveal certain indiscretions committed by me some years ago.

It was necessary that I spend some months in Europe, conducting research work incidental to the scheme. I returned with recorded statements, old newspapers, and photostatic copies of certain documents. There was a brief, quiet interview with that old, bushy-haired Viennese worshiped incontinently by the mob; he was convinced by the evidence I had compiled that it would be wise to assist us.

You all know what happened next—it was the professor's historic radio broadcast. Fein had drafted the thing, I had rewritten it, and told the astronomer to assume a German accent while reading. Some of the phrases were beautiful: "American dominion over the very planets! . . . veil at last ripped aside . . . man defies gravity . . . travel through limitless space . . . plant the red-white-and-blue banner in the soil of Mars!"

The requested contributions poured in. Newspapers and magazines ostentatiously donated yard-long checks of a few thousand dollars; the government gave a welcome half-million; heavy sugar came from the "Rocket Contribution

Week" held in the nation's public schools; but independent contributions were the largest. We cleared seven million dollars, and then started to build the spaceship.

The virginium that took up most of the money was tinplate; the monoatomic fluorine that gave us our terrific speed was hydrogen. The take-off was a party for the newsreels: the big, gleaming bullet extravagant with vanes and projections; speeches by the professor; Farley, who was to fly it to Mars, grinning into the cameras. He climbed an outside ladder to the nose of the thing, then dropped into the steering compartment. I screwed down the sound-proof door, smiling as he hammered to be let out. To his surprise, there was no duplicate of the elaborate dummy controls he had been practicing on for the past few weeks.

I cautioned the pressmen to stand back under the shelter, and gave the professor the knife switch that would send the rocket on its way. He hesitated too long—Fein hissed into his ear: "Anna Pareloff of Cracow, Herr Professor . . ."

The triple blade clicked into the sockets. The vaned projectile roared a hundred yards into the air with a wabbling curve—then exploded.

A photographer, eager for an angle-shot, was killed; so were some kids. The steel roof protected the rest of us. Fein and I shook hands, while the pressmen screamed into the telephones which we had provided.

But the professor got drunk, and, disgusted with the part he had played in the affair, told all and poisoned himself. Fein and I left the cash behind and hopped a freight. We were picked off it by a vigilance committee (headed by a man who had lost fifty cents in our rocket). Fein was too frightened to talk or write so they hanged him first, and gave me a paper and pencil to tell the story as best I could. Here they come, with an insulting thick rope.

⚙ *Robert Sheckley*

SOMETHING FOR NOTHING

But had he heard a voice? He couldn't be sure. Reconstructing it a moment later, Joe Collins knew he had been lying on his bed, too tired even to take his waterlogged shoes off the blanket. He had been staring at the network of cracks in the muddy yellow ceiling, watching water drip slowly and mournfully through.

It must have happened then. Collins caught a glimpse of metal beside his bed. He sat up. There was a machine on the floor, where no machine had been.

In that first moment of surprise, Collins thought he heard a very distant voice say, "There! *That* does it!"

He couldn't be sure of the voice. But the machine was undeniably there.

Collins knelt to examine it. The machine was about three feet square and it was humming softly. The crackle-gray surface was featureless, except for a red button in one corner and a brass plate in the center. The plate said, CLASS-A UTILIZER, SERIES AA-1256432. And underneath, WARNING! THIS MACHINE SHOULD BE USED ONLY BY CLASS-A RATINGS!

That was all.

There were no knobs, dials, switches or any of the other attachments Collins associated with machines. Just the brass plate, the red button and the hum.

"Where did you come from?" Collins asked. The Class-A Utilizer continued to hum. He hadn't really expected an answer. Sitting on the edge of his bed, he stared thoughtfully at the Utilizer. The question now was—what to do with it?

He touched the red button warily, aware of his lack of experience with machines that fell from nowhere. When he turned it on, would the floor open up? Would little green men drop from the ceiling?

But he had slightly less than nothing to lose. He pressed the button lightly.

Nothing happened.

"All right—*do* something," Collins said, feeling definitely let down. The Utilizer continued to hum softly.

Well, he could always pawn it. Honest Charlie would give him at least a dollar for the metal. He tried to lift the Utilizer. It wouldn't lift. He tried again, exerting all his strength, and succeeded in raising one corner an inch from the floor. He released it and sat down on the bed, breathing heavily.

"You should have sent a couple of men to help me," Collins told the Utilizer. Immediately, the hum grew louder and the machine started to vibrate.

Collins watched, but still nothing happened. On a hunch, he reached out and stabbed the red button.

Immediately, two bulky men appeared, dressed in rough work-clothes. They looked at the Utilizer appraisingly. One of them said, "Thank God, it's the small model. The big ones is brutes to get a grip on."

The other man said, "It beats the marble quarry, don't it?"

They looked at Collins, who stared back. Finally the first man said, "Okay, Mac, we ain't got all day. Where you want it?"

"Who are you?" Collins managed to croak.

"The moving men. Do we look like the Vanizaggi Sisters?"

"But where do you come from?" Collins asked. "And *why*?"

"We come from the Powha Minnile Movers, Incorporated," the man said. "And we come because you wanted movers, that's why. Now, where you want it?"

"Go away," Collins said. "I'll call for you later."

The moving men shrugged their shoulders and vanished.

For several minutes, Collins stared at the spot where they had been. Then he stared at the Class-A Utilizer, which was humming softly again.

Utilizer? He could give it a better name.

A Wishing Machine.

Collins was not particularly shocked. When the miraculous occurs, only dull, workaway mentalities are unable to accept it. Collins was certainly not one of those. He had an excellent background for acceptance.

Most of his life had been spent wishing, hoping, praying that something marvelous would happen to him. In high school, he had dreamed of waking up some morning with an ability to know his homework without the tedious necessity of studying it. In the army, he had wished for some witch or jinn to change his orders, putting him in charge of the day room, instead of forcing him to do close-order drill like everyone else.

Out of the army, Collins had avoided work, for which he was psychologically unsuited. He had drifted around, hoping that some fabulously wealthy person would be induced to change his will, leaving him Everything.

He had never really expected anything to happen. But he was prepared when it did.

"I'd like a thousand dollars in small unmarked bills," Collins said cautiously. When the hum grew louder, he pressed the button. In front of him appeared a large mound of soiled singles, five- and ten- dollar bills. They were not crisp, but they certainly were money.

Collins threw a handful in the air and watched it settle beautifully to the floor. He lay on his bed and began making plans.

First, he would get the machine out of New York—upstate, perhaps—some place where he wouldn't be bothered by nosy neighbors. The income tax would be tricky on this sort of thing. Perhaps, after he got organized, he should go to Central America, or . . .

There was a suspicious noise in the room.

Collins leaped to his feet. A hole was opening in the wall, and someone was forcing his way through.

"*Hey,* I didn't ask you anything!" Collins told the **machine.**

The hole grew larger, and a large, red-faced man was halfway through, pushing angrily at the hole.

At that moment, Collins remembered that machines usually have owners. Anyone who owned a wishing machine wouldn't take kindly to having it gone. He would go to any lengths to recover it. Probably, he would stop short of—

"Protect me!" Collins shouted at the Utilizer, and stabbed the red button.

A small, bald man in loud pajamas appeared, yawning sleepily. "Sanisa Leek, Temporal Wall Protection Service," he said, rubbing his eyes. "I'm Leek. What can I do for you?"

"Get him out of here!" Collins screamed. The red-faced man, waving his arms wildly, was almost through the hole.

Leek found a bit of bright metal in his pajamas pocket. The red-faced man shouted, "Wait! You don't understand! That man—"

Leek pointed his piece of metal. The red-faced man screamed and vanished. In another moment the hole had vanished too.

"Did you kill him?" Collins asked.

"Of course not," Leek said, putting away the bit of metal. "I just veered him back through his glommatch. He won't try *that* way again."

"You mean he'll try some other way?" Collins asked.

"It's possible," Leek said. "He could attempt a microtransfer, or even an animation." He looked sharply at Collins. "This is your Utilizer, isn't it?"

"Of course," Collins said, starting to perspire.

"And you're an A-rating?"

"Naturally," Collins told him. "If I wasn't, what would I be doing with a Utilizer?"

"No offense," Leek said drowsily; "just being friendly." He shook his head slowly. "How you A's get around! I suppose you've come back here to do a history book?"

Collins just smiled enigmatically.

"I'll be on my way," Leek said, yawning copiously. "On the go, night and day. I'd be better off in a quarry."

And he vanished in the middle of a yawn.

Rain was still beating against the ceiling. Across the air-shaft, the snoring continued, undisturbed. Collins was alone again, with the machine.

And with a thousand dollars in small bills scattered around the floor.

He patted the Utilizer affectionately. Those A-ratings had it pretty good. Want something? Just ask for it and press a button. Undoubtedly, the real owner missed it.

Leek had said that the man might try to get in some other way. What way?

What did it matter? Collins gathered up the bills, whistling softly. As long as he had the wishing machine, he could take care of himself.

The next few days marked a great change in Collins' fortunes. With the aid of the Powha Minnile Movers he took the Utilizer to Upstate New York. There, he bought a medium-sized mountain in a neglected corner of the Adirondacks. Once the papers were in his hands, he walked to the center of his property, several miles from the highway. The two movers, sweating profusely, lugged the Utilizer behind him, cursing monotonously as they broke through the dense underbrush.

"Set it down here and scram," Collins said. The last few days had done a lot for his confidence.

The moving men sighed wearily and vanished. Collins looked around. On all sides, as far as he could see, was closely spaced forest of birch and pine. The air was sweet and damp. Birds were chirping merrily in the treetops, and an occasional squirrel darted by.

Nature! He had always loved nature. This would be the perfect spot to build a large, impressive house with swimming pool, tennis courts and, possibly, a small airport.

"I want a house," Collins stated firmly, and pushed the red button.

A man in a neat gray business suit and pince-nez appeared. "Yes, sir," he said, squinting at the trees, "but you really must be more specific. Do you want something classic, like a bungalow, ranch, split-level, mansion, castle or palace? Or primitive, like an igloo or hut? Since you are an A, you could have something up-to-the-minute, like a semiface, an extended new or a sunken miniature."

"Huh?" Collins said. "I don't know. What would you suggest?"

"Small mansion," the man said promptly. "They usually start with that."

"They do?"

"Oh, yes. Later, they move to a warm climate and build a palace."

Collins wanted to ask more questions, but he decided against it. Everything was going smoothly. These people thought he was an A, and the true owner of the Utilizer. There was no sense in disenchanting them.

"You take care of it all," he told the man.

"Yes, sir," the man said. "I usually do."

The rest of the day, Collins reclined on a couch and drank iced beverages while the Maxima Olph Construction Company materialized equipment and put up his house.

It was a long-slung affair of some twenty rooms, which Collins considered quite modest under the circumstances. It was built only of the best materials, from a design of Mig of Degma, interior by Towige, a Mula swimming pool and formal gardens by Vierien.

By evening, it was completed, and the small army of workmen packed up their equipment and vanished.

Collins allowed his chef to prepare a light supper for him. Afterward, he sat in his large, cool living room to think the whole thing over. In front of him, humming gently, sat the Utilizer.

Collins lighted a cheroot and sniffed the aroma. First of all, he rejected any supernatural explanations. There were no demons or devils involved in this. His house had been built by ordinary human beings, who swore and laughed and cursed like human beings. The Utilizer was simply a scientific gadget, which worked on principles he didn't understand or care to understand.

Could it have come from another planet? Not likely. They wouldn't have learned English just for him.

The Utilizer must have come from the Earth's future. But how?

Collins leaned back and puffed his cheroot. Accidents will happen, he reminded himself. Why couldn't the Utilizer have just *slipped* into the past? After all, it could create something from nothing, and that was much more complicated.

What a wonderful future it must be, he thought. Wishing machines! How marvelously civilized! All a person had to do was think of something. Presto! There it was. In time, perhaps, they'd eliminate the red button. Then there'd be no manual labor involved.

Of course, he'd have to watch his step. There was still the owner—and the rest of the A's. They would try to take the machine from him. Probably, they were a hereditary clique . . .

A movement caught the edge of his eye and he looked up. The Utilizer was quivering like a leaf in a gale.

Collins walked up to it, frowning blackly. A faint mist of steam surrounded the trembling Utilizer. It seemed to be overheating.

Could he have overworked it? Perhaps a bucket of water . . .

Then he noticed that the Utilizer was perceptibly smaller. It was no more than two feet square and shrinking before his eyes.

The owner! Or perhaps the A's! This must be the microtransfer that Leek had talked about. If he didn't do something quickly, Collins knew, his wishing machine would dwindle to nothingness and disappear.

"Leek Protection Service," Collins snapped. He punched the button and withdrew his hand quickly. The machine was very hot.

Leek appeared in a corner of the room, wearing slacks and a sports shirt, and carrying a golf club. "Must I be disturbed every time I—"

"*Do something!*" Collins shouted, pointing to the Utilizer, which was now only a foot square and glowing a dull red.

"Nothing I can do," Leek said. "Temporal wall is all I'm licensed for. You want the microcontrol people." He hefted his golf club and was gone.

"Microcontrol," Collins said, and reached for the button. He withdrew his hand hastily. The Utilizer was only about four inches on a side now and glowing a hot cherry red. He could barely see the button, which was the size of a pin.

Collins whirled around, grabbed a cushion and punched down.

A girl with horn-rimmed glasses appeared, notebook in hand, pencil poised. "With whom did you wish to make an appointment?" she asked sedately.

"Get me help fast!" Collins roared, watching his precious Utilizer grow smaller and smaller.

"Mr. Vergon is out to lunch," the girl said, biting her pencil thoughtfully. "He's de-zoned himself. I can't reach him."

"Who *can* you reach?"

She consulted her notebook. "Mr. Vis is in the Dieg Continuum and Mr. Elgis is doing field work in Paleolithic Europe. If you're really in a rush, maybe you'd better call Transferpoint Control. They're a smaller outfit, but—"

"Transferpoint Control. Okay—scram." He turned his full attention to the Utilizer and stabbed down on it with the scorched pillow. Nothing happened. The Utilizer was barely half an inch square, and Collins realized that the cushion hadn't been able to depress the almost invisible button.

For a moment Collins considered letting the Utilizer go. Maybe this was the time. He could sell the house, the furnishings, and still be pretty well off . . .

No! He hadn't wished for anything important yet! No one was going to take it from him without a struggle.

He forced himself to keep his eyes open as he stabbed the white-hot button with a rigid forefinger.

A thin, shabbily dressed old man appeared, holding something that looked like a gaily colored Easter egg. He threw it down. The egg burst and an orange smoke billowed out and was sucked directly into the infinitesimal Utilizer. A great billow of smoke went up, almost choking Collins. Then the Utilizer's shape started to form again. The old man nodded curtly.

"We're not fancy," he said, "but we're reliable." He nodded again and disappeared.

Collins thought he could hear a distant shout of anger.

Shakily, he sat down on the floor in front of the machine. His hand was throbbing painfully.

"Fix me up," he muttered through dry lips, and punched the button with his good hand.

The Utilizer hummed louder for a moment, then was silent. The pain left his scorched finger and, looking down,

Collins saw that there was no sign of a burn—not even scar tissue to mark where it had been.

Collins poured himself a long shot of brandy and went directly to bed. That night, he dreamed he was being chased by a gigantic letter A, but he didn't remember it in the morning.

Within a week, Collins found that building his mansion in the woods had been precisely the wrong thing to do. He had to hire a platoon of guards to keep away sightseers, and hunters insisted on camping in his formal gardens.

Also, the Bureau of Internal Revenue began to take a lively interest in his affairs.

But, above all, Collins discovered he wasn't so fond of nature after all. Birds and squirrels were all very well, but they hardly ranked as conversationalists. Trees, though quite ornamental, made poor drinking companions.

Collins decided he was a city boy at heart.

Therefore, with the aid of the Powha Minnile Movers, the Maxima Olph Construction Corporation, the Jagton Instantaneous Travel Bureau and a great deal of money placed in the proper hands, Collins moved to a small Central American republic. There, since the climate was warmer and income tax nonexistent, he built a large, airy, ostentatious palace.

It came equipped with the usual accessories—horses, dogs, peacocks, servants, maintenance men, guards, musicians, bevies of dancing girls and everything else a palace should have. Collins spent two weeks just exploring the place.

Everything went along nicely for a while.

One morning Collins approached the Utilizer, with the vague intention of asking for a sports car, or possibly a small herd of pedigreed cattle. He bent over the gray machine, reached for the red button . . .

And the Utilizer backed away from him.

For a moment, Collins thought he was seeing things, and he almost decided to stop drinking champagne before breakfast. He took a step forward and reached for the red button.

The Utilizer sidestepped him neatly and trotted out of the room.

Collins sprinted after it, cursing the owner and the A's. This was probably the animation that Leek had spoken about—somehow, the owner had managed to imbue the machine with mobility. It didn't matter. All he had to do was catch up, punch the button and ask for the Animation Control people.

The Utilizer raced down a hall, Collins close behind. An under-butler, polishing a solid gold doorknob, stared open-mouthed.

"Stop it!" Collins shouted.

The under-butler moved clumsily into the Utilizer's path. The machine dodged him gracefully and sprinted toward the main door.

Collins pushed a switch and the door slammed shut.

The Utilizer gathered momentum and went right through it. Once in the open, it tripped over a garden hose, regained its balance and headed toward the open countryside.

Collins raced after it. If he could get just a little closer . . .

The Utilizer suddenly leaped into the air. It hung there for a long moment, then fell to the ground. Collins sprang at the button.

The Utilizer rolled out of the way, took a short run and leaped again. For a moment, it hung twenty feet above his head—drifted a few feet straight up, stopped, twisted wildly and fell.

Collins was afraid that, on a third jump, it would keep going up. When it drifted unwillingly back to the ground, he was ready. He feinted, then stabbed at the button. The Utilizer couldn't duck fast enough.

"Animation Control!" Collins roared triumphantly.

There was a small explosion, and the Utilizer settled down docilely. There was no hint of animation left in it.

Collins wiped his forehead and sat on the machine. Closer and closer. He'd better do some big wishing now, while he still had the chance.

In rapid succession, he asked for five million dollars, three functioning oil wells, a motion-picture studio, perfect health, twenty-five more dancing girls, immortality, a sports car and a herd of pedigreed cattle.

He thought he heard someone snicker. He looked around. No one was there.

When he turned back, the Utilizer had vanished.

He just stared. And, in another moment, *he* vanished.

When he opened his eyes, Collins found himself standing in front of a desk. On the other side was the large, red-faced man who had originally tried to break into his room. The man didn't appear angry. Rather, he appeared resigned, even melancholy.

Collins stood for a moment in silence, sorry that the whole thing was over. The owner and the A's had finally caught him. But it had been glorious while it lasted.

"Well," Collins said directly, "you've got your machine back. Now, what else do you want?"

"*My* machine?" the red-faced man said, looking up incredulously. "It's not my machine, sir. Not at all."

Collins stared at him. "Don't try to kid me, mister. You A-ratings want to protect your monopoly, don't you?"

The red-faced man put down his paper. "Mr. Collins," he said stiffly, "my name is Flign. I am an agent for the Citizens Protective Union, a nonprofit organization, whose aim is to protect individuals such as yourself from errors of judgment."

"You mean you're not one of the A's?"

"You are laboring under a misapprehension, sir," Flign said with quiet dignity. "The A-rating does not represent a social group, as you seem to believe. It is merely a credit rating."

"A what?" Collins asked slowly.

"A credit rating." Flign glanced at his watch. "We haven't much time, so I'll make this as brief as possible. Ours is a decentralized age, Mr. Collins. Our businesses, industries and services are scattered through an appreciable portion of space and time. The utilization corporation is an essential link. It provides for the transfer of goods and services from point to point. Do you understand?"

Collins nodded.

"Credit is, of course, an automatic privilege. But, eventually, everything must be paid for."

Collins didn't like the sound of that. *Pay?* This place

wasn't as civilized as he had thought. No one had mentioned paying. Why did they bring it up now?

"Why didn't someone stop me?" he asked desperately. "They must have known I didn't have a proper rating."

Flign shook his head. "The credit ratings are suggestions, not laws. In a civilized world, an individual has the right to his own decisions. I'm very sorry, sir." He glanced at his watch again and handed Collins the paper he had been reading. "Would you just glance at this bill and tell me whether it's in order?"

Collins took the paper and read:

One Palace, with Accessories ....Cr.	450,000,000
Services of Maxima Olph Movers	111,000
122 Dancing Girls	122,000,000
Perfect Health	888,234,031

He scanned the rest of the list quickly. The total came to slightly better than eighteen billion Credits.

"Wait a minute!" Collins shouted. "I can't be held to this! The Utilizer just dropped into my room by accident!"

"That's the very fact I'm going to bring to their attention," Flign said. "Who knows? Perhaps they will be reasonable. It does no harm to try."

Collins felt the room sway. Flign's face began to melt before him.

"Time's up," Flign said. "Good luck."

Collins closed his eyes.

When he opened them again, he was standing on a bleak plain, facing a range of stubby mountains. A cold wind lashed his face and the sky was the color of steel.

A raggedly dressed man was standing beside him. "Here," the man said and handed Collins a pick.

"What this?"

"This is a pick," the man said patiently. "And over there is a quarry, where you and I and a number of others will cut marble."

"Marble?"

"Sure. There's always some idiot who wants a palace," the man said with a wry grin. "You can call me Jang. We'll be together for some time."

Collins blinked stupidly. "How long?"

"You work it out," Jang said. "The rate is fifty credits a month until your debt is paid off."

The pick dropped from Collins' hand. They couldn't do this to him! The Utilization Corporation must realize its mistake by now! *They* had been at fault, letting the machine slip into the past. Didn't they realize that?

"It's all a mistake!" Collins said.

"No mistake," Jang said. "They're very short of labor. Have to go recruiting all over for it. After the first thousand years you won't mind it."

Collins started to follow Jang toward the quarry. He stopped.

"The first *thousand* years? I won't live that long!"

"Sure you will," Jang assured him. "You got immortality, didn't you?"

Yes, he had. He had wished for it, just before they took back the machine. Or had they taken back the machine *after* he wished for it?

Collins remembered something. Strange, but he didn't remember seeing immortality on the bill Flign had showed him.

"How much did they charge me for immortality?" he asked.

Jang looked at him and laughed. "Don't be naïve, pal. You should have it figured out by now."

He led Collins toward the quarry. "Naturally, they give *that* away for nothing."

☼ José Maria Gironella

THE DEATH OF THE SEA

TRANSLATED FROM THE SPANISH BY *Terry Broch Fontseré*

Basilio Hernandez—Basilio to all the neighbors of the town —possessed nothing in the world but his son, Felix, thirteen years old, and the sea. At his wife's death, he requested the post of lighthouse-keeper and obtained it. Basilio and the boy had been living alone in the tower for ten years now, taking care of the beacon. From up there they dominated the small port, the bay, the white town and the foot of the mountains. "We're like aviators," Basilio would say. They were a pair apart, two islands, at whom the beacon winked its eye and whom the waves, down there, caressed or furiously assailed, according to their mood. The sea—its visible surface, and even down to a certain depth—had no secrets for them. They knew the rhythm of the tides by memory, the significance of the water's coloring, the location of the reefs. They could interpret the sudden silences, predict the arrival of a school of fish or a ship, measure the potency and direction of the winds. They used to say that they could read the form and wrinkles of the water, but the truth is that in their knowledge of the sea there was habit, the five senses, and perhaps one more. Naturally, scent was essential. They had only to climb to the platform that encircled the beacon, and their nostrils widened; the salt air and the humidity were a Morse code that tapped at their brains. "There'll be a storm." "Three days of complete calm." "The water is suffering." "A drunken purpoise is roving nearby who's lost his school." Lately, Basilio, the father, noticed his eyes were tired and he often introduced his little finger into his left ear and probed with a certain exasperation; Felix, the son, on the contrary, was surging ahead. One would have said he gathered from the floor the faculties that were dropping from his father. It was a transferring of powers, the law of continuity.

Basilio loved his son. More than the telescope, more than the compass, more than the sea. He would have spent hours and lifetimes sitting on the cot caressing his hair. When he went down to the town he never forgot to buy him some trifle: a beret, decal decorations, a licorice stick. Felix was grateful for these gifts and he reciprocated by telling him stories. While he lit the alcohol stove to warm his coffee—coffee was the atavistic habit of the tower-keeper—Felix invented stories of what had occurred in his father's absence. A powerful fleet had crossed the horizon. He had had to kill a green rat that looked in at the stair door. The radio had announced that the moon had split in two. The compass had suddenly made a speech. It spoke to him of the North, of the South, of how much it liked to tremble and of how it wanted to die in the pocket of a boy. Basilio, tall and with thick shaggy eyebrows, listened smiling to Felix. He recognized in the boy what he had once been himself. Basilio had always lived in an unreal world, suspecting that behind each thing and inside each bulk there beat an ignored existence. Felix was given to poetizing: so much the better! "If it were otherwise, the lighthouse would be insupportable!" When the boy tired and Basilio had finished his coffee, they would light a cigarette and smoke it by turns—three puffs per man—playing cards, checkers, thinking of the dead mother or silhouetting not only rabbits and donkeys on the wall, but also Felix's profile, and fish. Felix often studied arithmetic and geography, what he liked most, or he would sit next to the radio, on the alert, trying to catch distant messages.

The neighbors from the town loved the pair. On Sunday, many couples climbed to the beacon, and Basilio and Felix entertained them as best they could. They offered them the binoculars. "Take a look, there's your window!" "Look, that's my balcony!"—and they showed them the maps and the old logbooks in which were noted shipwrecks along the coast, storms and the story of a Chinese ship that was found intact and, of course, without a crew. "Marry and spend your honeymoon here." The girls would look down at the cliffs of the tower and exclaim, "Heavens!" They felt the giddiness of Sunday, of love and of a controllable danger. The fellows seemed foolish and considered Basilio a sort of magician who protected the town and the lives of the town. "Thanks to you, we've peace of mind." "If something happened, you would give the alarm." Of course he would! If something happened, the tower-keeper would awaken the whole province. That's because they were father and son, and serious and serviceable.

There were no two ways about the appreciation the townspeople felt for Basilio and Felix. The dockworkers loved them very much and so did the men of the small shipyard, and the women who mended nets on the beach, and the fishermen. Felix was the mascot of these last and there was even a black and white boat named "Felix." The priest, who had unsuccessfully tried to make an altar boy out of Felix, also loved them very much. "Let him be," Basilio said to him. "This business of the candles doesn't suit the kid." The teacher, who taught Felix to add and, especially, to multiply, also loved them. And the pharmacist loved them—Felix had a habit of weighing himself on the scales in the pharmacy—and the storekeepers loved them and a manufacturer of fireworks who, every year, at the end of the Fiesta Mayor, asked them how the final burst had looked, seen from the beacon. And the vagabond dogs loved them and, of course, the old men who awaited death taking the sun on the benches of the walk. The beacon tower was for everyone a point of reference, security. Without its inevitable and robust presence the town would have felt abandoned.

Basilio and Felix were happy, in their fashion. Especially the former. When other tower-keepers called him on the telephone and he asked them, "Well, how are things over there?" he couldn't understand when they answered in a bored tone, "As always. A lot of water." True that the water was generally always the same, and from the height that he and Felix were, all men seemed the same and their preoccupations and strivings were somewhat ridiculous.

But, what was a seagull? What was a telescope? Why were there green rats and why did Felix go on growing day after day in an almost palpable manner? Indubitably, everything was not obvious and those tower-keepers would do well to look at themselves attentively in the mirror. The example of Felix was worthy of imitation: he contemplated one thing and drew from it, in a chain reaction, exciting conclusions. Of course, temperament influenced all this. There were tower-keepers who were found one day hanging from the beacon, there were those who became brutish, looking more and more like simians, and there were those who were almost happy, like Basilio.

As for Felix, he was all heart. He had never been out of the town and this, in fact, allowed him to create the already created in his own way, and to become ecstatic not only before the stars, but before the decalcomanias that his father brought for him. In reality, he had never seen a train, nor a race horse, nor a field of wheat, nor a bad woman. More than half his forehead was virginal. "It doesn't seem to me that I'm an aviator," he said to his father, "but a circus performer, a trapeze artist." It required a certain effort for him to look horizontally. He did not know what being happy meant, unless it meant gazing at the seagulls and taking four puffs on the cigarette in his turn, instead of three. The sea was for Felix the restless plain, the trampoline, and it sheltered in its coffer laughter and doubt and an incalculable number of desires. He was sure that the earth killed, but not the sea. He was sure the drowned continued living, that there existed submarine cities equipped with everything necessary for breathing and well-being. "In the sea there are no cemeteries." "Salt conserves everything." In the sea lookouts would be unnecessary and it would not occur to anyone to light candles to ask for this or that favor.

The first day of the year—Felix was fourteen—the unexpected occurred. He and his father had spent a good part of the night, "Nochevieja," night of San Silvestre, laughing, and loving their solitude. Basilio had gone down to the town and refused all invitations, thinking only of Felix. He took back to the tower a calendar showing a beautiful woman, wine, cognac, sweets and two paper hats: one pointed, for him; the other round, for Felix. The two tower-keepers chatted quietly for a long while, passing the time until midnight. Suddenly, the first gong sounded on the church clock. It was heard so clearly from the beacon that it almost intimidated them. They put on the hats, toasted with the wine, embraced and kissed, and as the twelve gongs sounded they had the impression that they were being united more and more. They even danced around the rotunda, careful not to knock down the table and chairs, and winking at the woman on the calendar, freezing in her bathing suit. It was, in there, a warm and beautiful year's ending; outside, the firmament shivered and the stranded boats on the beach rocked with humility.

At one o'clock sharp, father and son sat down to play cards, chewing grains of coffee. The stove crackled as though splintered sins burned in it. Basilio won all the hands, since Felix, on holidays, simulated a lack of luck. At two they went to sleep, each in his cot. The usual inspection of the beacon, on the outside platform, was done by Felix and he did not observe anything abnormal. A regular rhythm, frozen whiplashes, the fan of the light glistening on the water. "Brrr . . . !" He came in again and got into bed. Shortly afterwards father and son were snoring, while the stove died down and, in the town below, the taverns overflowed with promises of friendship and promises of a new life, honorable and worthy.

At six Felix awoke with a start. He had dreamt that the water of the sea was sweet. What nonsense! It would be subversive. He fell asleep again and dreamt that the water of the sea was red. How absurd! Blood was red, fire was red. He found himself sitting up in bed and chattering from the cold, while his father slept soundly . . . Felix listened. The sea beat deep at the base of the tower. The sea attacked. Felix knew its ire. A yellowish light filtered through the window pane. Why yellowish? He covered himself with his scarf. It seemed strange that the wind didn't whistle. Why was the light yellow while the sky appeared livid, purple, as it did so many times before sun-up? Felix looked at the clock: it was seven. He went back to bed again and tried to fall asleep, but a strange uneasiness prevented him. And, suddenly, a great flock of seagulls were hammering at the large window. Felix turned towards them, watched them. They seemed wild, as though searching for something vital, very much theirs, and which they had lost. And how they screamed! What was happening?

Brusquely determined, Felix pushed the blankets aside and got up. Grains of coffee crunched under his feet. He pulled his cap down and went to the window panes, which were frosted. The seagulls, seeing him, fled. The beacon continued living; Felix, with his hand, drew an oval on the frosted pane and faced the sea.

A strange spectacle met his eyes. Had he been bird and not man, he also would have screamed. The sky was in fact livid, an immense crypt of Good Friday, the color of coagulated blood. And the sea was violent . . . but not out to its limits. On the contrary, the horizon appeared motionless, rigid. With a pious stillness, that gave horror, that seemed pressed, mineral, and from which a front of waves rose galloping in the direction of the coast, as though fleeing from that distant petrified plain. Giant waves, that approached Felix's eyes with the same wild tremor as the seagulls, Waves with craters, vomiting foam insanely. Aquatic spines wounded by a harpoon. Himalayas excavated from below with extraordinary violence.

Felix felt a superstitious dread. With a reflex movement he wrapped the scarf around him further and opened a small window on the right. And instantly, a stench which reminded him of a morgue penetrated his nostrils. He shut it immediately. He looked at the compass: it spun without direction. He brushed something metallic, it gave him a jolt. He didn't dare disconnect the beacon light. Invisible presences besieged him. He remained rooted in his place, a child, incapable of seeing a law in all this. Lightning bolts did not frighten Felix, but sparks from the radio did. (He had never even seen a train.) The sky was empurpling more and more, staining the water and cliffs with a deep melancholy. It seemed to him that everything was stilled. There was a silence without depth, as though neither the rocks, nor time, nor the sea existed. He found himself alone in the rotunda, holding his breath.

Felix looked at his father. It hurt him to awaken him, but he did, shaking him. Basilio opened his eyes, startled. "What's the matter?" Felix pointed to the wide window.

"The sea . . ." Basilio jumped from his bed. "What's happened?" His eyes interrogated Felix and in doing so he seemed to grow old. Felix whimpered and the tower-keeper, slowly, went to the window and looked through the oval. And immediately, his hands grasped the sill convulsively and he muttered something which could have been a curse or a prayer.

Basilio had the immediate suspicion that the phenomenon was transcendental and unique. It had nothing to do with the imminence of a cyclone or the caprices of undercurrents. He saw clearly that the petrification of the distant sea was not an optic effect, but a fact. Nevertheless, he went to the telescope and looked through it, fixedly. It was evident that the galloping waves were attempting to escape. It was evident that many of them suddenly collapsed, defeated from behind, extending the rigid plain. This crushing was produced with an almost geometrical rigor, from west to east, as though an occult power directed the operation step by step. Basilio, thanks to the telescope, also located two ships, which converted his suspicions into certainty; in fact, within a very brief interval, one, and then the other, were overtaken by the mineralization and were immobilized and fell sideways, like toys, as they would have done on terra firma.

Basilio abandoned the telescope and looked at Felix, who continued trembling, with his cap on. The sea suffered! How to understand that? It stiffened and became like parchment. And that distant placidness! Wasn't it reminiscent of the placidness of the dead? Could the sea die like men, like years or like seagulls? Felix remembered his dead mother. The stiffness! The silence!

"Father, the sea is dying . . ."

Basilio threatened the youngster with his shaggy brows. But, unexpectedly, he drew back. Good Lord! Why not? Dark Biblical memories assailed him.

"Open the little window and smell."

Basilio, shaken, looked at his son again and obeyed. And a cold and pestilent stench lashed his face.

"It's true!" muttered the tower-keeper. "The sea is dying!"

Felix, hearing this confirmation, burst out in a hysterical sob. "Why, why?" Basilio looked at the ceiling, then at the compass and finally, painfully slammed the little window shut.

Then he remembered that he was the lookout and reacted.

"Go to the town and warn them. I'll call the other tower-keepers on the telephone."

Felix could not move. Was it not the end of the world? Finally he started running and went down the curling staircase like a thunderbolt.

Once down he covered the cement ramp which separated the tower from the docks in a few strides. But there was no one on the docks. It was the first day of the year. Boxes piled up, barrels and canvas covers, a crane. Felix kept running until he reached the small shipyard and the beach. There he found a few men smoking, close to the boats. He didn't know what to say. "The sea is dying!" he stammered. "The sea is dying!" And with a stupid expression and holding his cap in his hand he pointed to the lighthouse, where his father was, and he pointed to an imprecise distance and the celestial crypt the color of Good Friday.

The men looked at each other and smiled. What was the matter with little Felix? Had he gotten drunk with the wine and the sweets? Or with the woman on the calendar? It was too early yet to go to the pharmacy to weigh himself . . .

"What's wrong with you, young man?"

"I'm not lying, I'm not lying! My father has seen it! The sea . . . !"

A fisherman came near him affectionately and tried putting his hand on his shoulder. But Felix jumped back and lifted his arms like a small prophet.

"Climb up to the beacon, and you'll see!" Felix sniffed intensely. "Don't you smell death?"

At that moment, Basilio appeared up there, on the platform of the lighthouse. He had already called two tower-keepers and he was hurrying to transmit the news by Morse code, in an official capacity.

The men who smoked beside the boats watched him, puzzled. There was a moment of suspense. Basilio's silhouette (the perfect tower-keeper) was solemn.

"Attention, attention! Wide strips of the sea are petrifying. The petrification advances, always from west to east, and is approaching the coast. Should it follow the same pattern, it will reach the port by mid-morning."

The men were dumbfounded. They looked at each other and then at the sea. In all that their vision encompassed, there was nothing to be seen. However, Felix continued with the same expression and with his hands raised, holding his cap.

"Let's go up to the lighthouse!" said one of them. And the others imitated him and began walking.

Another declared, "I'm going to the Fishermen's Co-operative to give them the alarm."

"No, wait."

"Why? I'm going to warn them."

Felix gave another sob and, hardly realizing what he was doing, started running toward the town. His intention was to alert the whole community, but when he reached the first streets and saw the doors and windows shut, the words wouldn't come out of him. He remembered the church and went to it. The door was open. He found the priest. "The sea is dying! We must ring the bells!" The priest tried unsuccessfully to restrain the boy. Felix went directly to the base of the belfry and, grabbing the rope, pulled with all his strength. The bells pealed in an unknown rhythm. It was not fire, it was not a baptism, it was not resurrection! It was a lugubrious peal, but strange. The priest was trying to restrain Felix, but at each pull the boy rose, hoisted to an incredible height. "I'm not lying! Not lying! Go and see!"

The bells wrought the miracle. Besides, the news had also been received in the small telephone office. Sleepy faces, disheveled hair, appeared in the windows. "What's happened? What's the matter?" The men buttoned their trousers drowsily and descended the stairs quickly or went out to the doorway. Dogs and cats, guided by pure instinct, were going toward the beach. "Basilio has communicated I don't know what. The sea is turning to stone!"

"What foolishness!"

"He must be drunk!"

The arrival of the neighbors at the beach coincided with the return of the fishermen who had climbed to the beacon. They confirmed the event. They had seen it with their own eyes, by now without the need of a telescope. Death advanced so fast! It was a cataclysm with nothing to palliate it, "transcendental and unique."

"The waves rise, and fall dead."

"They're like yawns."

"The water turns yellow."

"What will become of us?"

Basilio, firm at his post, continued sending the communiqué to the authorities. At eight the whole town had congregated at the breakwater. Some women wore black kerchiefs on their heads. Only the grave-digger had refused to abandon the cemetery. "Foolishness! They must be drunk!"

The phenomenon was already so clearly visible from the breakwater, that soon all the neighbors, grouped in families, with each hand searching for another hand, withdrew helter-skelter to the beach. Many climbed up the little hill of the shipyard and some solitary ones scattered over the cliffs that closed the bay on the right. A few sobs were heard, but the silence that had so moved Felix was heard even louder. What was there to do? The bell had stopped pealing and Felix now ran in the direction of the lighthouse, to join his father.

At nine sharp Basilio communicated, "Death reaches the mouth of the port." And it was true. And it was the first time that Basilio officially employed that word. The water at the foot of the beacon trembled and became immobile. The sun climbed in the sky above, but it was also the color of Golgotha! The air smelled of decayed vegetables, of decomposition. Fish jumped as though searching for a refuge. Where? How?

The water at the docks stopped lapping. It receded, seemed to rise and the boats anchored in a corner—the black and white one named "Felix"—leaned over and fell sideways, like toys. The whole bay began to turn yellow. The water did not change to stone but to marble. Polished, shining. The mussel beds were imprisoned and seemed to wither. In their turn, the buoys were immobilized.

In fact, death advanced slowly, but it seemed a dizzying pace to the community. At ten everyone waited for the death rattle, the final one. It came at ten-thirty and was witnessed by all. From one end of the bay to the other, an agonizing wave rose which was like a cry—until it collapsed and was laid out on the sand, where it remained rigid, like a hypnotized lizard. The lip of foam became a fringe of lime, solid and cutting.

The community feared that other phenomena on earth and in the heavens would succeed this one, and the people near the priest crossed themselves. The mass escape of the seagulls toward the mountains seemed to justify this fear; however, they soon realized that their own thoughts would be the most painful. In fact, each brain was an ache and each ache different. Without the sea the town lost its life, but in this awareness each man and each woman felt the amputation in his own way. The fishermen thought of thousands of nights on the open sea, which would not be repeated, and of the pathetic and absurd end of their trade and sustenance. The women who mended the nets felt annihilated. The man in charge of Lifeguards bewailed the irony of his uselessness. The old men were arriving, having been left behind, and were asking everyone what was happening. The doctor understood his limitations, once and for all. The lovers, for whom the sea had been a gazing point and a matrix for dreams and beautiful words, were suffering untold solitude and doubt. Death was spattering heads, baptizing them in one way or another. The man of the fireworks, a great early-riser, held a half-made firecracker in his hand, as though it were a candle. The rod fishermen bit their nails as though they were fish-hooks. The children approached the dead water as though they wanted to touch it! Perhaps, perhaps, the only living beings who seemed happy were the grave-digger and the worms. The grave-digger was a cross-word puzzle enthusiast, and he was asking himself how it would be possible to bury the sea. "I'd like to see you try it!" he challenged himself. As for the worms, at the bottom of the boats, they moved with unmistakable impatience and exhilaration.

Confusion gave way to pity. The neighbors understood that the death of the sea implied myriad deaths, and felt pity. Pity for the fish, big and small. Fossilized, on the spot! Pity for the banks of coral, of nacre, pity for sea snails. Pity for the boats, large and small, for the ocean liners, for the submarines! Ah, the messages of captains surprised in mid-ocean! The islands must have ceased to be islands, the underwater cities—equipped with breathing and well-being —of which Felix had dreamt, must have died. And the telephone cables and the sounding mines and the depth mines. All must have died. Each drop, a cadaver; each whirlpool, a good-bye; the sea, the largest cemetery ever known. A strange symbolism took hold the populace, opening a path in their minds. The nets appeared to them as shrouds; the boats, biers; the lighthouse-tower, a torch worthy of the magnitude of the sea. And the rivers—what would they do when they emptied into the solid sea? And what must have happened in the frozen seas? The men were looking at the bay; the sea was, in effect, dead. It even seemed to shrink. It seemed it would exhale gas through some crevice, at any moment. A photographer had mounted his tripod and was taking photographs. The cats were moving away, instead, and suddenly an old woman came running, carrying a wreath of wild flowers with a purple ribbon whose letters no one was quick enough to read as she flung it to the sea.

Now then, at a given moment, all the pain and all the compassion of the community was concentrated on the figures of Basilio and Felix, who finally decided to abandon the beacon and join the townspeople on the beach. Yes, someone mused, "There they are!" And many eyes turned and saw the two tower-keepers slowly crossing the cement ramp that separated, that joined, the tower and the docks, saw them reach these and continue toward them. From a distance, they both seemed older than they were in reality, and their scarfs danced in the wind. A lacerating expectation arose, because no one could ignore that that father and that son, happy in their fashion, with their alcohol stove and silhouetting Chinese shadows on the wall, would be the principal orphans, the most concrete victims of the death of the sea. Basilio, without a beacon, without the telescope, without the logbook of shipwrecks! He would never adapt to the new circumstance! And Felix . . . ! without the sea, he had no reason for existing. When he tolled the bells, he tolled them for himself. The boy had tattooed two oars on his chest, and whenever he visited his mother's grave, he said to her, "I love you as I do the sea."

The priest came out to meet the two tower-keepers, but Basilio paid no attention. On the one hand, it seemed that nothing mattered to him; on the other, he gave the impression of having arrived at a decision. The priest stepped aside. Actually, everyone made way for them, while far away the solitary figures posted on the rocks asked themselves, "And how do you take a death mask of the dead sea?"

Basilio and Felix came to the middle of the beach and stood on the shore; they neared the edge. Like the children, it seemed as though they wanted to touch with their hands that which had been water. But it was not so. In fact, they were meditating and they were hardly aware of the crowd's presence. They were meditating on an idea that had occurred to Felix in his eagerness to save the unsaveable: on the possibility that not all the seas had died on earth, that in some distant place a piece of sea had escaped petrification. "Perhaps on the Northern coasts, where they say everything is hard and strong." "Perhaps a warm sea." The tower-keepers of the region, nearby, had confirmed by telephone. "It has died here also." But, what about the Arctic? Wouldn't it still be alive, under the ice, in between the icebergs? And the Southern seas? And the Dead Sea?

Felix carried the compass with him and, like it, trembled. They saw the teacher, the mayor, the photographer, who was photographing them, the old woman who threw the wreath of wild flowers onto the sea. They saw all their friends of the town, and of the spirit; and the trees on the promenade and the nets and the masts of the boats. Their look had a double aspect. It reaffirmed that they loved their fellow men and the earth; but also that their fellow men and the earth were not enough to live for . . .

Thus, then, unexpectedly, they consulted the compass, and then looked into each other's eyes. And without needing to utter a single syllable they made, in accord, the supreme decision. Facing their neighbors, they said, "Luck . . ." in a voice not heard by all, but which other mouths transmitted up to the last in line: the man with the unfinished firecracker, who, for the first time in his life, broke down and wept.

Seconds later, Basilio and Felix, the first with his right arm around his son's neck, were entering on the solid surface that had been the sea. The fringe of lime—the lip of the foam—obliged them to lift their feet slightly; then, all was smooth and easy as in a royal salon.

A voice was heard, "Get back! Get back! You're crazy!" Other voices were heard, "Get back Get back!"

There was nothing to be done. Father and son were advancing, with firmer step each time, and no one, not even the dogs, dared go out after them and make them turn back.

The silence in the bay became total. Basilio and Felix were going off in the distance, drunk on their search and their own condition. The compass had righted itself. Soon they would be at the level of the lighthouse-tower, a moment at which perhaps they too would break down and cry. However, it was certain that hope was gaining on them. Oh, yes, they dominated all, except fantasy! Surely a piece of sea had been saved, in some place there still existed a piece of live sea, salt water, sweet to the heart, and with fish also alive, like human tremors. To it, then! To the piece of live sea!

Their hearts had hit the mark. The whole community, posted in a semicircle on the cliffs and on the beach, learned of it thanks to the observers with binoculars. The piece of live sea existed and meant the instantaneous death of Basilio and Felix. It existed a little further beyond the breakers, on the open sea, next to a reef named the Serpiente. It had a circular form, with a hole large enough to swallow two bodies. Basilio and Felix had not foreseen the suction. It didn't give them time to stop. Their feet sang in the water and father and son disappeared. Their diminutive figures ceased to be. While the people whimpered on the beach and the sun, streaking purple, was suddenly rising very high, bloody and eternal.

✿ *John C. M. Brust*

THE RED WHITE AND BLUE RUM COLLINS

As Martin Slee awoke from uneasy dreams, he discovered he had been transformed into a large rum collins. He was resting, as it were, on a leather-covered table in what appeared to be the office in a consulate. He was filled with ice, which was cold. "Brrrrr," thought Martin Slee.

Then he began to wonder what had happened.

Suddenly the door opened, and he stopped wondering. "I can't waste time wondering," thought Martin Slee. "I must act . . . for America. Hooray!"

No sooner was this thought out than he remembered where he was. "I remember now," thought Martin Slee. "I'm a spy, and I'm in disguise. This man is a R——n consul. I must spy on him. Three cheers for America!"

Then he began to spy.

For fifteen minutes he watched every move the R——n made, and gloated all the time. "I knew this disguise would work," thought Martin Slee. "I am able to watch every move this R——n makes. Oh, hooray for American ingenuity!"

Suddenly his prey took a sip out of Martin Slee. But Martin Slee wasn't embarrassed.

"Ho, ho," thought Martin Slee. "I suppose, Mr. Enemy-of-Freedom-Loving-Peoples, you think I didn't foresee this possibility. Little do you know that I filled myself with poison. Ho, ho!"

"I see you behind your disguise," the Enemy-of-Freedom-Loving-Peoples was muttering, totally unaware of his impending doom.

"Three cheers for America!" thought Martin Slee. "Alan Dulles would be proud of me!" Then he repeated the Declaration of Independence, until the last drop of him gurgled down the R——n's hateful throat.

The Stars and Stripes had triumphed again.

❂ *William Styron*

PIE IN THE SKY

The whole thing began in a midsummer of the 1950's, following a heat wave which from the Mississippi Valley to
the Atlantic had left the population of the country smoldering and desperate. Automobile tires had melted in Providence. Down in Atlanta a girl in a bathing suit fried eggs
on the corner of Peachtree Street. Entire tar roads liquified
for the benefit of sweltering photographers. Throughout
the countryside rows of cornstalks stood sere and blasted in
fields hovering perilously close to flame, and these, too,
had their pictures taken. It was, the newspapers proclaimed, the hottest spell in half a century, and there were
few among the population—almost too listless even to take
to the beaches—who did not believe it. Then a curious
break (some, though thankful for the mild relief it brought,
thought it not just curious but downright ludicrous) came
in the weather. A vast low-pressure area centered itself
over the Appalachians, engulfing the Coastal Plain and
the upper Ohio Valley in a muggy, unseasonable overcast
and torrents of lukewarm rain. It was indeed peculiar,
everyone said, yet it was welcome: the heat was only to a
slight degree lowered by the deluge, but at least the crops
would survive. Many people pondering the events which
ensued in the Middle West immediately after the remarkable climate set in (Walter Winchell called it the "Doom
Monsoon"), saw some connection between them. Others,
less imaginative or perhaps only more circumspect, bustled
around among the weather records and brought forth incontrovertible data; it had been rare weather, true, but
hardly unique: look at 1912. Whatever these facts may be,

one thing is certain: the full moon came up dazzling bright in the Middle West that night in July and, no matter what a Missourian or Iowan saw, there was no Easterner, drowned in his clammy fog, who could logically dispute him.

The story about the moon rang the bell on the teletypes in the nation's newsrooms on July 7 at a few minutes past 5 A.M. Eastern Daylight Saving Time, too late, of course, for the morning papers but in good time for the first radio and television broadcasters, who began paying fascinated, if in one or two cases rather facetious, attention to the item as early as six o'clock. The dispatch itself, which originated in the Manhattan headquarters of one of the nation's leading wire services, came at an awkward time in history. That during those first hours the story was treated by a few people with some levity—with an actual ho-hum sort of contempt by one prominent New York morning-show star, whose flustered apologies later became famous in television circles—can perhaps be laid to the current to-do over flying saucers (at that moment somewhat in disrepute) and to the implications of the dispatch itself, which might have strained the credulity of some people even in an age numb to new wonders:

ST. LOUIS, July 7—Reports of a celestial phenomenon so unprecedented as to be termed by experts "bordering on the miraculous" are flooding police stations and newspaper offices all over the Iowa-Illinois-Missouri area early today. Reliable eyewitnesses from lower Minnesota as far west as Kansas and Nebraska are reported as having observed a huge ragged fissure which opened on the face of the moon at a little past 3:15 A.M. (E.S.T.) Remaining in this situation for approximately thirty seconds, the fissure reportedly closed as suddenly and mysteriously as it opened. Authorities state that dependable sources, some of whose accounts are still largely incoherent due to the awesome nature of the spectacle, described the sight as being like a great jagged gash rent into the side of hell. Another source, from the little hamlet of Blakesburg near Ottumwa in southeastern Iowa, told of looking up and "seeing a rugged crevasse yawning for about half a minute on the side of the moon, as if a big chunk had been blown off by a thousand H-bombs." Authorities seeking to coordinate details of the phenomenon have been working with hastily summoned scientists from institutions in the area, who have so far pointed out that a search for any scientific corroboration of the unusual pageant would likely prove fruitless, since the moon for some years has been devoid of serious astronomic observation. Officials of the area, anxious to sift and authenticate accounts of the spectacular display, are urging eyewitnesses to communicate with their local newspapers and law enforcement agencies. Meanwhile, late reports from trustworthy observers at Columbia, Missouri, home of Stephens College, reveal that a holocaust . . .

This, then, was the first communiqué as received by several thousand newspaper, radio, and television subscribers to the wire service. Astonishing enough in itself, it was nothing compared to the apparition which floated in, minutes later, on the machines of those bureaus whose services included wirephoto coverage. This celebrated picture was shown widely that morning on television. Accompanied by the single explanatory line, "Photo taken of ravaged moon by unknown Missouri amateur with Baby Brownie," it was fuzzed and indistinct, unquestionably the work of an amateur, but it was nonetheless phenomenal: a silvery full moon flawlessly lunar in appearance, except for the presence of a large jagged area of darkness cut away from its circumference. In terms of the face of a clock, this area would include most of the surface between ten and twelve, describing a sort of splintered crescent which at its furthest extent from the rim reached to a point about halfway from the center. There was one important point about the picture, it might be mentioned here, that later tended to remove a lot of scientific skepticism, much of which had revolved around the contention that thousands of eyewitnesses had been deluded by some bleak meteorological shadow or cloud originating on earth. For, smack in the middle of the black area, tiny and remote in space and almost overwhelmed by the moon's brilliance, a star peeked through.

By eight o'clock that morning in St. Louis, where the report was datelined, the furor in the newsroom was outlandish. *Post-Dispatch* men reporting for work found the night staff red-eyed and frantic from the strain of answering telephone calls. Lawton Manship—an assistant city editor whose nonfiction account was for many months a best seller—vividly set down those early moments of bewilderment and confusion:

"I had not seen it on television myself. When I arrived at work the city room was pandemonium. There were phones ringing all over the place. I remember thinking to myself, 'What on earth goes on here? An atomic attack?' Then somebody—I believe it was Bert Flynn, who later went on to the old Chicago *Tribune*—hurried up in great agitation and showed me the wirephoto and the flash from the teletype. I recall asking Flynn where the story had originated, and who had dug it up. To this query he could only reply with a wry 'Maybe you'd better ask some of the *Globe-Democrat* boys.'

"In those days we did not go to press very early in the day so I had some time to dig up information. I hoped a few reliable eyewitnesses were phoning in. Most of the calls, however, which by then were turning the place into a veritable bedlam, were from people panicked into believing that the world was coming to an end. They had received the news via their radio or television sets. I tried to reassure them, but like most Americans that morning I was apprehensive myself, and I'm afraid my attempts to put forth a pacifying word were rather futile. I shifted to another tack, and called Father O'Byrne (the Rev. Thomas E. O'Byrne, S.J., now Monsignor), who then taught astronomy at St. Louis University.

"'Hiya, my boy,' he exclaimed, 'I was wondering when I'd become one of those "hastily summoned scientists."' Jovial as usual, the good padre said that he, too, had received the news via television, but would have none of it. Such a phenomenon, he said, besides being impossible without wreaking a tidal catastrophe upon the earth, could simply not occur, then vanish without leaving a trace behind. Then I asked him that question which many perplexed Americans, similarly uninformed scientifically, were asking themselves that morning, namely, whether the moon's rotation could not carry the gash, or whatever it was, out of sight after it had once been seen. But the friendly cleric-astronomer pointed out the now well-known fact that the moon always presents the same face to the earth, adding genially, 'It's mass hallucination, my boy, mass hallucination. I heard the report and I saw the picture. It's still mass hallucination.'

"Father O'Byrne's words allayed my anxiety for a while, but I'm afraid not for long. It was then shortly before nine o'clock. In order to find out how conditions were on the East Coast I tried to get in touch with our New York bureau man, Roland Pleasants, only to find everything so jammed up, telephone- and telegraph-wise, that communication with any point that far out of the city was virtually impossible. Besides, only a few minutes passed before I was informed of the first two of those eyewitness accounts which were to overwhelm us in the next few hours. Taking over a phone from Flynn, I spoke to Mrs. Vernice Dudley, forty-one, wife of a jobber of dinette furniture who lived in suburban Richmond Heights. Her account, one of the first on record and therefore one of the most famous, has long since passed into the archives of our time. I quote it here verbatim, hoping that by doing so the anxieties of that day may in some measure be reflected. It is impossible, of course, to suggest the tension and frenzy with which her voice was laden:

"'No, not Bernice. V as in vitamins. Vernice. They said there on TV to phone in, so I'm phoning in. Yes, I saw it, and you can bet your boots, mister, it was something out of this world. What was I doing up at that hour? Just what anybody would be doing up at that hour who'd had insomnia for ten years. I was down in the kitchen getting a glass of warm milk. I hadn't turned the lights on yet and I just happened to gaze out of the window. My God, it was just ghastly! No, it wasn't any shadow. I may have migraine but my eyes are bright. I just looked out of the window and there it was: this awful moon shining down on the city with this hunk torn out of its side. Sort of like a part of it had been blown away by some atom bomb or something. I tell you, it was just horrible! It looked like the end of the world. I started reeling around like crazy and screamed out for Mac, my husband, and then I fainted dead away. It was terrible, I tell you! When I woke up Mac was standing there in his pajamas pouring water on me and I was laying up against the side of the Bendix, and when I looked up at the moon it was round and bright again.'

"That terminated Mrs. Dudley's account. Frankly, I was baffled. Coming so quickly on the heels of Father O'Byrne's reassuring words, Mrs. Dudley's statement left me utterly disconcerted. I was inclined with the padre to believe that perhaps she was one of many who had partaken of some mass hallucination; however, only a minute later another report caused me to slightly shift my position. This second account I received from a man who described himself as Guy Junior Larkin, sixty-three, an installer of storm windows from nearby Clayton, Missouri. More composed than Mrs. Dudley's voice, Larkin's unlettered drawl nonetheless betrayed the emotions of a man who had peered, if ever so briefly, into the abyss: 'Well, I'll tell you, sir, I ain't a man to go around telling tall stories. I've lived a sober, godly life, raised me up a fine brood of boys I hope and pray get a chance in life I never had. I ain't one to blow my own whistle, but I'll tell you this: I been an elder in the Calvary Baptist Church of Clayton for running on eight years. Folks around this part of Clayton'll tell you one or two things about Larkin: he might be a little slow, but he's steady and sober, and he ain't a man to go around believing something he ain't smelt or heard with his own five senses. I don't pretend to be one of those eggheads and I ain't had much time for reading or learning . . . What'd you say? The moon? Yes, sir, I seen it all right. I woke up a little after three-fifteen to get me a glass of water. It was shining right outside the bathroom window with this great big round hunk broke out of it, just like that picture they showed on TV. It was like that for—oh, I'd say about half a minute—then it shut up again —pop!—just like that. Well, sir, I guess it wasn't no proper place to do what I done, but I got down on my knees right there up aside the water closet, and I prayed.'

"That these two accounts of the Moongash, freighted as they were with the ring of truth, were nonetheless phantasms of an hysterical woman and a primitive religious zealot, was a suspicion that for a few minutes nagged at my mind. My doubts were soon dispelled, however, by the number of eyewitness versions (forty-six) that flooded in within the next half-hour alone, and finally by the call I received, at about nine-thirty, from Jack Jessup, editor of the weekly *Gasconade County Enterprise* in Owensville, some seventy miles west of St. Louis. Jessup, an old newspaper friend of years standing, told me in taut, nervous tones that the situation in Owensville and the surrounding countryside had approached 'stampede proportions,' and that from hurried calls he had made to authorities in nearby communities he was able to judge that conditions there were the same. Eyewitnesses were simply everywhere.

"This information I put out as soon as possible on the wires, along with a digest of the forty-six accounts we had received, Mrs. Dudley's and Larkin's among them. Would anyone in my position, I have often wondered since, have acted differently?"

By midmorning of July 7, Manship was not alone in his battered predicament. Throughout the Midwest, from Chicago as far west as Omaha and from St. Paul to the southern Missouri border, newspaper offices had their most strenuous day within memory. In whatever place in the Middle West over which the bright moon had shone that night an imposing number of people had come forth to attest that they had seen, way up in the tranquil heavens, something sinister and strange. Alone, the town of Alton, Illinois, a community of 32,000 souls, claimed eighty-eight witnesses, or 0.003 per cent of the town's population—a diminutive fraction which loomed staggeringly and convincingly large when placed in the light of the late hour of the phenomenon, its short duration, and the laws of probability determininng the number of onlookers upon any moon at a given instant. By noon in Hillsboro, Illinois, a town of 4,000 in the heart of the Lincoln country, officials had compiled a list of twenty-three separate accounts by eyewitnesses comprising roughly 0.056 per cent of the citizenry; this was the highest incidence of reports, in terms of per capita ratio, to issue from any single locality (it was trailed closely by Moberly, Missouri, and the Blakesburg mentioned in the teletype dispatch by 0.053 and 0.049 respectively), a fact which for a few weeks thereafter caused astronomers to theorize that Hillsboro for unknown reasons had presented optimum conditions for observation, and, in hope of some "repeat performance," to set up tons of equipment in the community.

Despite Manship's quoting of Jessup as to the "stampede" in and around Owensville, students of the period have often noted the relative lack of hysteria, the equanimity, with which the news was received. Although the Moongash (Manship had coined the word, which was not very inspired, but it somehow stuck) was one of the most outstanding events ever to engage the attention of a highly strung human race, the shock of its happening, even among the tiny minority which had actually witnessed it, seemed very soon to be replaced only by a kind of rueful universal wonder. In the metropolises of the nation, which had always been considered rich breeding grounds for panic, the general composure was everywhere apparent and exemplary. And by noon of that first day in overcast, sweltering Manhattan, the crowds which gathered marveling around the newsstands, where the afternoon *Post* displayed the wirephoto beneath the shocking banner, PORTENT OF DOOM? —these crowds, according to one rather florid observer, "saw the dreadful photograph and were not dismayed, saw the lists and the accounts and the descriptions, saw the terrible testimonials of their fellow men, and remained undaunted."

Nevertheless, there was at least on that first day, as a jauntier correspondent put it, "a hell of a lot of people wondering whether they'd still be around for supper." For one thing, much of whatever initial skepticism there was (and there was skepticism, mostly among scientists and urban sophisticates of various stripes, even after all the columns and columns of circumstantiating data had been printed) became dispelled by the accounts from two sources of awesome reliability. The accounts were prominently featured that day in the late afternoon editions; the status of the people involved gave the whole event a kind of final and unalterable stamp of truth.

The first of these witnesses was Captain Frank Bello, of La Jolla, California, the pilot of a DC-6 flying from Los Angeles to Chicago. At the time of the event, Captain Bello calculated, his plane was cruising at 330 miles per hour in clear, bright air over western Iowa. A man of forty-four with a solid muscular jaw and eyes peering intently, though not without humor, from beneath gray busy eyebrows, Captain Bello, veteran of nineteen years with commercial airlines, was "certainly not a person to be lured into any weird fantasies," as the description of him which accompanied his account stated.

"Like I say," he said, in his recorded interview with reporters, "it was a routine flight in every other respect. Unlimited visibility and ceiling. Tailwinds of twenty to forty miles per hour. Bonnie Lee (Bonnie Lee Hedrick, twenty-three, the stewardess, of Glendale, California) had just been up yakking with me. We'd shot the breeze around a bit about various things, then she'd gone back to the passengers. Audrey Hepburn was aboard, one of my favorite stars. I can remember thinking how I'd hate to have anything go haywire with a plane, while I was flying it, with someone like Audrey Hepburn aboard. A pilot starts to think about such things every now and then. You've got a damn big responsibility. Once on the New York-L.A. run I had on board Terry Moore and Edmund Purdom and Louella Parsons, when my number one engine conked out. I guess you can imagine how I felt for a while, but it turned out to be nothing serious, thank God. Anyway, as I say, I had just turned around in my seat after the stewardess left, when I saw it. I just happened to look up and there it was. The biggest full moon I ever saw in my life with this huge hunk blasted out of its side. God, it was terrifying! No, there wasn't any noise or anything. It couldn't have been a cloud shadow, because we were a good three thousand feet over where the clouds would have been, even if there had been any that night. Yes, the gash was right where everyone said it was—between ten and twelve o'clock. It couldn't have been a shadow, I tell you. There was that star shining through, just as there was in the picture. I turned to Stroup (Calvin C. Stroup, thirty, the co-pilot, of Whittier, California) and started to say something, but he had gone back to the can. When I turned again, this tremendous gash had filled up again, and the moon was normal. The passengers were all asleep and none of the crew had seen anything. I thought I was nuts for a while. Boy, was I glad to hear that report on the radio when we got over Chicago."

The federal organization set up by nightfall of the seventh, an advisory group composed of five prominent educators, was called the President's Emergency Commission on the Present Danger. Although its investigative subgroup, the Committee on Authentications, finally listed among its 18,060 authenticated witnesses five mayors, three city managers, three members of state legislatures, and police chiefs too numerous to count, the most highly placed political figure on record as having observed the phenomenon was the extraordinary E. Barton Raynolds. At the time Lieutenant-Governor of Iowa, Raynolds was flying alone in his Beechcraft from his home in Des Moines to a conference of Corn Belt lieutenant-governors in Springfield. It was Raynolds whose picture was joined with that of Captain Bello side by side on the front pages, and whose testimony lent a last decisive note of confirmation to the whole upheaval. He described his experience that afternoon, in an address to his fellow lieutenant-governors broadcast nationally by television and radio from the Illinois capital. Flying high through a night "bright with the brightness of the Creation," Raynolds said he was over the Mississippi, "that noble waterway shared alike by the great commonwealth of Illinois and by our own great state of Iowa," a few minutes before the thing happened. Raynolds, notably self-possessed during his speech, went on to describe the landscape of the night, the prairies below, the moon-drenched little hamlets, "the lights sparkling, far off to the north of me, of the great Quad Cities, their fruits of commerce and industry participated in alike by our two great commonwealths." This, of course, was a reference to the closely grouped cities of Davenport, Rock Island, Moline, and East Moline. To the south, he said, he could pick out the lights of Burlington and of Fort Madison—"home of Shaeffer fountain pens"—"progressive Keokuk," and, twenty-five miles across the prairies to the east, the faint street lamps of Galesburg, "birthplace of the great and beloved Carl Sandburg—a son of Illinois, it is true, but honored by Iowans everywhere.

" 'Pile up the bodies at Austerlitz and Waterloo. Shovel

them under and let me work—' There is no Iowan breathing who does not cherish those lines."

Yet Raynolds was not thinking of poetry at the moment when the moon gaped open, he told his fellow assistant chief executives. He was pondering, rather, the "terrible onus" they all bore, removed as they were but a heartbeat from the concerns of high office—"concerns which now, as of three-seventeen this morning, reach out beyond our great midland area of America to touch the mysteries of the universe."

As for the moon, he said, when he finally got around to describing it, "it opened up upon its stricken side a crevasse equal to a million Grand Canyons, a sight reminding me of the face of Hell . . . Surely, I thought, this is a visible manifestation of the hand of the Creator Himself . . ."

Raynolds and Bello, of course, as well as the scores of other people whose descriptions of the phenomen were especially colorful, or whose situations at the time were unique (a railroad detective, for instance, who, stalking a robber in the yards at Fairmont, Minnesota, was so dazzled by the spectacle that his prey got away), became celebrities overnight. A farm woman not far from Davenport witnessed the Moongash during the agonies of a solitary childbirth; another woman, speeding toward her gravely ill husband in a Kansas City hospital, was so terrified by the sight that she cracked up her car against a bridge abutment. Such stories occupied the pages of most of American newspapers for a solid week; the supplemental publicity—television interviews, magazine articles, a half-dozen hastily fabricated books, and the like—for several months almost exclusively commanded the nation's attention. Meanwhile, as the telescopes of the world became trained each night upon the moon and as people everywhere, with curiosity, with fear, or with tremulous wisecracks, awaited in vain a reappearance of the sight, the President's Emergency Commission brought forth its vast report.

Early the Commission deplored the fact that natural conditions had prevented all but a relatively small area of the nation from being exposed to the phenomenon: "Notwithstanding the fact that the entire Eastern third of the country was shrouded in the overcast of an unusual meteorological disturbance, and that inclement weather covered much of the Far West as well, the Commission was led initially to several conjectures. Chief among these was that some temperamental quirk, and one peculiarly Midwestern, had provided fertile soil, as it were, for a riotous mass hallucination." So reads a part of the report, written mainly by Easterners. However, the Commission eventually admitted that such a conjecture was a "statistical monstrosity, bearing no relation to reality." And finally the Commission concluded that it was "highly persuasive a fact" that of the some 26,000 investigated accounts (the 18,060 figure related only to those sworn to, notarized, or otherwise solemnly deposed) an overwhelming 99.3 per cent *was* from that Midwestern area where the spectacle could have been seen. It indicated that no "countrywide craze" was at work, while at the same time the other 0.7 per cent was shown to comprise crackpot accounts from such impossible sources as Nyack and Maine and Idaho, and even from one old Kansan who was discovered to be blind. What mostly troubled the Commission was the lack of any consistent data concerning the manner in which the gash disappeared.

"Testimony as to the physical appearance of the fissure has been notable for its unanimity, 99.81 per cent of the descriptions having coincided precisely with the Brandenburg photograph." (This refers to the picture taken by the unknown Missouri amateur, nineteen-year-old Leo Brandenburg, who showed up with his Baby Brownie in the offices of a Kansas City newspaper during the first hours of confusion, and who claimed to have been "messing around in the backyard" when he took the photograph. He later received the Pulitzer Prize—the youngest recipient in history and the first prize awarded to an amateur in over ten years.) "As to the manner in which the fissure closed, however, there is less agreement. This Commission has not been fully satisfied with such vague descriptions as 'Well, it just filled up there like some melted cheese' (*Anders,* Gentry Co., Mo., p. 965), or 'It just kind of gradually come together, like a kind of a fan,' (*Smallwood,* Van Buren Co., Ia., p. 1020), especially when these accounts are at such variance with 'Wham! First there was that gash there, then it closed up—wham!' (*Bogardus,* Moberly Co., Mo., p. 1051)." Nor was the Commission at all happy with what it termed

the "emotional response differential," by which it meant
the extraordinary range of feelings which the Moongash
inspired in its onlookers. "How is it possible," a section of
the report begins, in a tone almost of despair, "to achieve
even the inkling of any scientific verification, when re-
sponses to the phenomenon range from 'The most spine-
chilling sight I've never seen,' to 'thrillingly lovely,' to 'I
guess you might just say I didn't feel nothing at all.'
(*Watts, Harper, Belk*, all Peoria Heights, Ill., pp. 1081-4)?"

Nonetheless, the Commission was finally, if reluctantly,
convinced. "The Commission is therefore moved, at least
tentatively, to accept the phenomenon as reality," the report
states, at the conclusion of its 4,000-odd pages. "That all
scientific efforts to corroborate the appearance of the fissure
have so far been in vain, that the phenomenon is unparal-
lelled in recorded history, that the fissure has not presented
itself again for observation—these facts nonetheless cannot
and do not nullify, in the opinion of this Commission, the
sworn testimony of 18,060 persons. The Commission desires
to reassert its fervent conviction that modern scientific
resources will, in due time, offer an explanation of the
phenomenon; until that time, however, it is the Commission's hope that the people of America will be urged, by
Presidential appeal, to place their faith in God as they
always have. *Animis Opibusque Parati.*"

And what were the consequences of all this? Well, the
Moongash for a while without doubt altered things considerably, although in certain ways not nearly so much as
might be imagined. As mentioned before, there was little
panic or terror; on the other hand, it soon became apparent
that the crisis had put few people in the mood for any
sudden and excessive merriment. It is surprising to note
in the literature of the period how few of the jokes—even
the bawdy ones—are involved in word-plays on the phenomenon. Also, there were hardly any fads and very little
commercialization. No Moongash toys, no Moongash con-
fectionery, no cute hats. One song about the Moongash,
to be sure, gained some brief popularity, but it climbed
only through the lower ranks of the Hit Parade. No Gallup
polls were needed to discover that people everywhere had
become sobered by the event—not made solemn, not paralyzed, merely sobered—and while little was seen in the way

of a rush to the libraries, or in anything like a cultural or intellectual revival, there was, in the words of one friendly British observer, "a kind of mysterious calm in the American air, a new, almost palpable mood of decorum, as if the phenomenon, whatever else it might represent, had been in the nature of a visible 'Shhh' from the universe, a cosmic call for quiet and reflection." Although the short period of the Moongash saw no respite from wars and no religious renaissance whatever (outside of the merger, sought for ever since the Civil War, of the Northern and Southern Presbyterians, who discovered in the spectacle a divine signal for union), it did see a strangely tranquillized American people. "During its all too brief duration," this same Englishman concluded, "the period brought abundant rewards to the foreign observer. Greatest among these was the sight of the average American, a man who, in quiet absorption with this baffling riddle from the outer regions, had wrapped himself in the unaccustomed cloak of contemplation, and in the process acquired new dignity and a startling grace."

The credit for uncovering the whole gigantic hoax must go to the indefatigable Spafford Wheelis, an editor of one of America's largest magazines. A rather self-effacing man in his middle forties, Wheelis in his writings was in the habit of describing himself as "asparagus grower and perennial skeptic." Contemporary accounts portray him as "rumpled in appearance"; in the absence of further particulars, this will have to do. The details of Wheelis' exposure of the fraud came to the attention of a dumfounded public almost a year to the day after the Moongash's appearance, at a time when most people had just about become used to living with the ghost of their heavenly omen.

Wheelis described his early forebodings in *his* sensational best seller when he said, "It is of course not to the discredit of the American people that they were taken in by the tragic hoax. I might possibly have been myself deluded, except that from the very beginning there was something about the whole thing that smelled of Sheldon Frame. Many years before, when Sheldon and I were friends and fellow reporters at the wire service, I had noticed this idiosyncrasy of his: an uncontrollable passion for fooling around with the teletype machines. At the time I regarded the habit as somewhat irritating, but childish enough and certainly harmless. Would that I had been able to fathom then the darker psychopathology! Even in that summer of 1939, when Sheldon got drunk one night and sent out on the wires, three weeks early, the news of Hitler's march on Poland, I thought little enough of this obsession of his. Fortunately I had the presence of mind to kill the story in time, and Sheldon was very contrite the next day, but I'm afraid that true contrition was never among Sheldon's many virtues.

"Many of my critics, rudely jarred out of the pseudo-occult reverie induced by the Moongash, have asked why, if I had been aware all along that the Moongash was only a false teletype flash and a trumped-up wirephoto, I did not step forward earlier with some accusation. As if friend-ship were a meretricious bauble to be cast in the corner with the rest of the broken toys! The reports are true, indeed, that in 1944 Sheldon and I fell out over a ten-dollar bet, but whatever enmity there was between us was certainly Sheldon's, not mine. And although we never en-countered each other for over a decade, my feeling toward Sheldon Frame was always one of tremendous warmth. Yet I could not stand to see a mankind bowed under the weight of a perpetually unexplained enigma. Perhaps now calmer reflection on the part of those who have reviled me will enable them to understand the agony of my conflict, and my long indecision."

Frame was picked up by police at his Brooklyn apart-ment on a day unsurpassed in America for public con-sternation. REFUTES MOONGASH, HOAX!—this was one of the headlines, and what was going on in the minds of at least 18,060 citizens may be imagined. Whisked by federal agents to Washington, Frame was lodged under guard in St. Elizabeth's hospital, where he underwent mental ob-servation for a week. He was judged sane (although a qualifying affidavit termed him "rather peculiar") and was released to authorities for trial, when someone in the Attorney General's office suggested that perhaps a simple investigation would be more appropriate, because Frame, in spite of everything, had committed nothing which even remotely resembled a crime. Accordingly, the soon-to-be-defunct President's Emergency Commission made plans for a single public hearing, at which Frame was to present his testimony. Details of Frame's stunt leaked out to the public before the hearing. At first, some few Americans were incensed, and there were buzzings about immediate punishment, even execution, but after their readjustment to normality most people were inclined to laugh it all off. Even the Midwestern witnesses, following a few days of shame-faced disavowals and half-hearted explanations, admitted that they had been colossally and rather comically bamboozled, and, after some good-natured joshing from their neighbors, settled down as ordinary citizens again. In fact, only one really tragic consequence of the whole episode is on record, and that is the death, by his own hand, of young Leo Brandenburg, who drowned himself "out of mortification" when the Pulitzer Committee asked for its $500 back.

In the meantime, as Frame under custody awaited his investigation, an affectionate and even gallant legend grew up around him. Millions of people felt that they had rather enjoyed the mystery and the ruminative stimulation of the Moongash period; surely there was something bold and glamorous, even Promethean, about a person who in one stroke could sway the imagination of so many men. Unfortunately for his admiring contemporaries and for history, Frame managed to drop completely out of sight after his hearing—a feat which must have called for great cunning in an age when the extent of intrusions upon privacy numb the imagination. There were rumors that he went to Manitoba and for a number of years prospected for uranium, but this has never been verified. At any rate, descriptions of him are sketchy, mainly because reporters were kept at bay during his detention, and because TV and photographers were banned from his hearing. It is known, though, that he was a bachelor, and that "he'd certainly never drive a girl nuts," which was the comment after the hearing of one female spectator, who added with more charity, "Just kind of sweet and dumpy and sad. Lonesome, I guess." Concluding is an excerpt from the testimony, the interrogator being the counsel to the Commission, Edward Holt, Jr.:

HOLT: What did you expect to gain by all this, Sheldon?

FRAME: I don't know. I can't tell you. I think I was just bored.

H: Think? Don't you know?

F: I was just bored, then. Fed up.

H: Then you did it on the spur of the moment?

F: That's right, sir.

H: You had access, you say, to the teletype machines and a camera and the wirephoto apparatus, and you say that at the time you used these machines there was no one around to see you?

F: Yes, sir, that's correct.

H: Do you take intoxicants?

F: Yes, sir, I guess I'm actually sort of a drunk if you want to know the truth.

H: Then were you drunk when you sent out the teletype dispatch and the wirephoto?

F: Well, in a manner of speaking.

H: What do you mean by 'a manner of speaking'? You're a reporter, aren't you? Can't you try to articulate a little better for the Commission?

F: Yes, I am.

H: Yes, I am what?

F: Yes, I'm a reporter. Though I don't guess I'm a very successful—

H: Look, Sheldon, don't get flip with the Commission. What I want to know is whether or not you were drunk at the time you sent out the dispatch. Try to describe your state of mind.

F: Well, I guess I *was* drunk. It wasn't all booze, though. I had all these crazy things floating around in my head. This thing I'd played on my phonograph at home. Did you ever hear that thing by Bach? It has all these crazy, tremendous trumpets soaring up in it. I don't know. I was thinking of green things suddenly, something off far away, this kind of serene, fantastic lawn—

H: All right. So you had some sort of half-insane hallucination before you did it. Now approximately what time was this?

F: Oh, I guess about five o'clock in the morning.

H: Sheldon, tell me this. Do you love your country?

F: Yes, sir, I do.

H: Then why did you do it? Didn't you realize the calamity, the havoc—

F: I guess I simply didn't think that anybody would take it seriously, that it would go on and on like it did. It was just a thing I'd thought up. I'd seen the weather reports. I knew people in the East couldn't tell, on account of the rain. It just somehow worked out too well, I guess. I didn't think people would eat it up like they did.

H: You mean that in an age of such scientific advancemest, when already a crash program is contemplated to erect a strategic space station—

F: That's what I'm getting at. I was bored, I tell you, fed up! Crash programs, I mean. Missiles. Things in the air. Dependable sources. Eyewitnesses! Orbits! Batmen!—

H: Control yourself!

F: I'm sorry, sir.

H: That's better. Now how about that 'holocaust'?

F: What holocaust?

H: At the end of your otherwise perfectly counterfeited dispatch. That gibberish. You just stopped.

F: I got terribly sleepy all of a sudden. I must have slumped down there on the keys.

H: I see. Now there's one thing else the Commission wants to know. This concerns the photograph. How were you able in your wirephoto to so perfectly simulate the moon?

F: Oh, it wasn't too hard, really. It's sad about that fellow Brandenburg, that he had to go and drown himself over it.

H: Stick to the point. Will you please describe how you faked the original photograph?

F: Well, you know, working the hours I do I get pretty hungry. As long as I've been on the night staff there I've always dropped into this Hanscom's before work and picked up some pastry for a snack. Sometimes one of those little bitty pies—

H: You mean—

F: Well, I'd already taken a bite out of it.

H: You mean that you— But how about the star?

F: I've thought and thought about that star everybody was talking about. I think it must have been a little crumb that got in there.

❋ *Damon Knight*

THE ANALOGUES

The creature was like an eye, a globular eye that could see in all directions, encysted in the gray, cloudy mind that called itself Alfie Strunk. In that dimness thoughts squirmed, like dark fish darting; and the eye followed them without pity.

It knew Alfie, knew the evil in Alfie; the tangled skein of impotence and hatred and desire; the equation: Love equals death. The roots of that evil were beyond its reach; it was only an eye. But now it was changing. Deep in its own center, little electric tingles came and went. Energy found a new gradient, and flowed.

A thought shone in the gray cloud that was Alfie—only half-formed, but unmistakable. And a channel opened. Instantly, the eye thrust a filament of itself into the passage.

Now it was free. Now it could act.

The man on the couch stirred and moaned. The doctor, who had been whispering into his ear, drew back and watched his face. At the other end of the couch, the technician glanced alertly at the patient, then turned again to his meters.

The patient's head was covered to the ears by an ovoid shell of metal. A broad strap of webbing, buckled under his jaw, held it securely. The heads of screw clamps protruded in three circles around the shell's circumference, and a thick bundle of insulated wires issued from its center, leading ultimately to the control board at the foot of the couch.

The man's gross body was restrained by a rubber sheet.

the back of his head resting in the trough of a rubber block fixed to the couch.

"No!" he shouted suddenly. He mumbled, his loose features contorting. Then, "I wasn't gonna—No! Don't—" He muttered again, trying to move his body, the tendons in his neck sharply outlined. *"Please,"* he said, and tears glistened in his eyes.

The doctor leaned forward and whispered in his ear. "You're going away from there. You're going away. It's five minutes later."

The patient relaxed and seemed to be asleep. A teardrop spilled over and ran slowly down his cheek.

The doctor stood up and nodded to the technician, who slowly moved his rheostat to zero before he cut the switches. "A good run," the doctor mouthed silently. The technician nodded and grinned. He scribbled on a pad. "Test him this aft.?" The doctor wrote, "Yes. Can't tell till then, but think we got him solid."

Alfie Strunk sat in the hard chair and chewed rhymically, staring at nothing. His brother had told him to wait here while he went down the hall to see the doctor. It seemed to Alfie that he had been gone a long time.

Silence flowed around him. The room he sat in was almost bare—the chair he sat in, the naked walls and floor, a couple of little tables with books on them. There were two doors; one, open, led into the long bare hall outside. There were other doors in the hall, but they were all closed and their windows were dark. At the end of the hall was a door, and that was closed, too. Alfie had heard his brother close it behind him, with a solid click, when he left. He felt very safe and alone.

He heard something, a faint echo of movement, and turned his head swiftly, automatically. The noise came from beyond the second door in the room, the one that was just slightly ajar. He heard it again.

He stood up cautiously, not making a sound. He tiptoed to the door, looked through the crack. At first he saw nothing; then the footsteps came again and he saw a flash of color: a blue print skirt, a white sweater, a glimpse of coppery hair.

Alfie widened the crack, very carefully. His heart was

pounding and his breath was coming faster. Now he could
see the far end of the room. A couch, and the girl sitting
on it, opening a book. She was about eleven, slender and
dainty. A reading lamp by the couch gave the only light.
She was alone.

Alfie's blunt fingers went into his trousers pocket and
clutched futilely. They had taken his knife away. Then he
glanced at the little table beside the door, and his breath
caught. There it was, his own switchblade knife, lying beside the books. His brother must have left it there and forgotten to tell him. He reached for it—

And an angry female voice said, *"ALFIE!"*

He whirled, cringing. His mother stood there, towering
twice his height, with wrath in her staring gray eyes, every
line of her so sharp and real that he could not doubt her—
though he knew she had been dead these fifteen years.

She had a willow switch in her hand.

"No!" gasped Alfie, retreating to the wall. "Don't—I
wasn't gonna do nothing."

She raised the switch. "You're no good, no good, no
good," she spat. "You've got the devil in you, and it's just
got to be whipped out."

"Don't, *please*—" said Alfie. Tears leaked out of his eyes.

"Get away from that girl," she said, advancing. "Get
clean away and don't ever go back. Go on—"

Alfie turned and ran, sobbing in his throat.

In the next room, the girl went on reading until a voice
said, "O.K., Rita. That's all."

She looked up. "Is that *all*? Well, I didn't do much."

"You did enough," said the voice. "We'll explain to you
what it's all about some day. Come on, let's go."

She smiled, stood up—and vanished as she moved out of
range of the mirrors in the room below. The two rooms
where Alfie had been tested were empty. Alfie's mother was
already gone—gone with Alfie, inside his mind where he
could never escape her again, as long as he lived.

Martyn's long, cool fingers pressed the highball glass.
The glass accepted the pressure, a very little; the liquid
rose almost imperceptibly inside it. This glass would not
break, he knew; it had no hard edges and if thrown it
would not hurt anybody much. It was a symbol, perhaps;

but only in the sense that nearly everything around him was a symbol.

The music of the five-piece combo down at the end of the long room was like a glass—muted, gentle, accommodating. And the alcohol content of the whiskey in his drink was twenty-four point five per cent.

But men still got drunk, and men still reached instinctively for a weapon to kill.

And, incredibly, there were worse things that could happen. The cure was sometimes worse than the disease. "The operation was successful, but the patient died." We're witch doctors, he thought. We don't realize it yet, most of us, but that's what we are. The doctor who only heals is a servant; but the doctor who controls the powers of life and death is a tyrant.

The dark little man across the table had to be made to understand that. Martyn thought he could do it. The man had power—the power of millions of readers, of friends in high places—but he was a genuine, not a professional, lover of democracy.

Now the little man raised his glass, tilted it in a quick, automatic gesture. Martyn saw his throat pulse, like the knotting of a fist, as he swallowed. He set the glass down, and the soft rosy light from the bar made dragons' eyes of his spectacles.

"Well, Dr. Martyn?" he said. His voice was crisp and rapid, but amiable. This man lived with tension; he was acclimated to it, like a swimmer in swift waters.

Martyn gestured with his glass, a slow, controlled movement. "I want you to see something first," he said. "Then we'll talk. I asked you to meet me here for two reasons. One is that it's an out-of-the-way place, and, as you'll understand, I have to be careful. The other has to do with a man who comes here every night. His name is Ernest Fox; he's a machinist, when he works. Over there at the bar. The big man in the checkered jacket. See him?"

The other flicked a glance that way; he did not turn his head. "Yeah. The one with the snootful?"

"Yes. You're right, he's very drunk. I don't think it will take much longer."

"How come they serve him?"

"You'll see in a minute," Martyn said.

Ernest Fox was swaying slightly on the bar stool. His choleric face was flushed, and his nostrils widened visibly with each breath he took. His eyes were narrowed, staring at the man to his left—a wizened little fellow in a big fedora.

Suddenly he straightened and slammed his glass down on the bar. Liquid spread over the surface in a glittering flood. The wizened man looked up at him nervously. Fox drew his fist back.

Martyn's guest had half-turned in his seat. He was watching, relaxed and interested.

The big man's face turned abruptly as if someone had spoken to him. He stared at an invisible something six inches away, and his raised arm slowly dropped. He appeared to be listening. Gradually his face lost its anger and became sullen. He muttered something, looking down at his hands. He listened again. Then he turned to the wizened man and spoke, apparently in apology; the little man waved his hand as if to say, "Forget it," and turned back to his drink.

The big man slumped again on the bar stool, shaking his head and muttering. Then he scooped up his change from the bar, got up and walked out. Someone else took his place almost immediately.

"That happens every night, like clockwork," said Martyn. "That's why they serve him. He never does any harm, and he never will. He's a good customer."

The dark little man was facing him alertly once more. "And?"

"A year and a half ago," Martyn said, "no place in the Loop would let him in the door, and he had a police record as long as your arm. He liked to get drunk, and when he got drunk he liked to start fights. Compulsive. No cure for it, even if there were facilities for such cases. He's *still* incurable. He's just the same as he was—just as manic, just as hostile. But—he doesn't cause any trouble now."

"All right, doctor, I check to you. Why not?"

"He's got an analogue," said Martyn. "In the classical sense, he is even less sane than he was before. He has auditory, visual and tactile hallucinations—a complete, integrated set. That's enough to get you entry to most in-

stitutions, crowded as they are. But, you see, these hallucinations are pre-societal. They were put there, deliberately.
He's an acceptable member of society, *because* he has
them."

The dark man looked interested and irritated at the
same time. He said, "He sees things. What does he see,
exactly, and what does it say to him?"

"Nobody knows that except himself. A policeman, maybe,
or his mother as she looked when he was a child. Someone
whom he fears, and whose authority he acknowledges. The
subconscious has its own mechanism for creating these
false images; all we do is stimulate it—it does the rest.
Usually, we think, it just warns him, and in most cases
that's enough. A word from the right person at the right
moment is enough to prevent ninety-nine out of a hundred
crimes. But in extreme cases, the analogues can actually
oppose the patient physically—as far as he's concerned,
that is. The hallucination is complete, as I told you."

"Sounds like a good notion."

"A very good notion—rightly handled. In another ten
years it will cut down the number of persons institution-
alized for insanity to the point where we can actually hope
to make some progress, both in study and treatment, with
those that are left."

"Sort of a personal guardian angel, tailored to fit."

"That's exactly it," said Martyn. "The analogue always
fits the patient because it *is* the patient—a part of his own
mind, working against his conscious purposes whenever
they cross the prohibition we lay down. Even an excep-
tionally intelligent man can't defeat his analogue, because
the analogue is just as intelligent. Even knowing you've
had the treatment doesn't help, although ordinarily the
patient doesn't know. The analogue, to the patient, is absolutely indistinguishable from a real person—but it doesn't
have any of a real person's weaknesses."

The other grinned. "Could I get one to keep me from
drawing to inside straights?"

Martyn did not smile. "That isn't quite as funny as it
sounds," he said. "There's a very real possibility that you
could, about ten years from now. And that's precisely the
catastrophe that I want you to help prevent."

The tall, black-haired young man got out of the pickup and strolled jauntily into the hotel lobby. He wasn't thinking about what he was going to do; his mind was cheerfully occupied with the decoration of the enormous loft he had just rented on the lower East Side. It might be better, he thought, to put both couches along one wall, and arrange the bar opposite. Or put the Capehart there, with an easy chair on either side.

The small lobby was empty except for the clerk behind his minuscule desk and the elevator operator lounging beside the cage. The young man walked confidently forward.

"Yes, sir?" said the clerk.

"Listen," said the young man, "there's a man leaning out of a window upstairs, shouting for help. He looked sick."

"What? Show me."

The clerk and the elevator operator followed him out to the sidewalk. The young man pointed to two open windows. "It was one of those, the ones in the middle of the top floor."

"Thanks, mister," said the clerk.

The young man said, "Sure," and watched the two men hurry into the elevator. When the doors closed behind them, he strolled in again and watched the indicator rise. Then, for the first time, he looked down at the blue carpet that stretched between elevator and entrance. It was almost new, not fastened down, and just the right size. He bent and picked up the end of it.

"Drop it," said a voice.'

The young man looked up in surprise. It was the man, the same man that had stopped him yesterday in the furniture store. Was he being followed?

He dropped the carpet. "I thought I saw a coin under there," he said.

"I know what you thought," the man said. "Beat it."

The young man walked out to his pickup truck and drove away. He felt chilly inside. Suppose this happened *every* time he wanted to take something—?

The dark man looked shrewdly at Martyn. He said, "All right, doctor. Spill the rest of it. Let's have it all, not just the background. I'm not a science reporter, you know."

"The Institute," Martyn said, "has already arranged for a

staff of lobbyists to start working for the first stage of its program when the world legislature returns to session this fall. Here's what they want for a beginning:

"One, analogue treatment for all persons convicted of crime 'while temporarily insane,' as a substitute for either institutionalization or punishment. They will argue that society's real purpose is to prevent the repetition of the crime, not to punish."

"They'll be right," said the little man.

"Of course. But wait. Second, they want government support for a vast and rapid expansion of analogue services. The goal is to restore useful citizens to society, and to ease pressure on institutions, both corrective and punitive."

"Why not?"

"No reason why not—if it would stop there. But it won't." Martyn took a deep breath and clasped his long fingers together on the table. It was very clear to him, but he realized that it was a difficult thing for a layman to see—or even for a technically competent man in his own field. And yet it was inevitable, it was going to happen, unless he stopped it.

"It's just our bad luck," he said, "that this development came at this particular time in history. It was only thirty years ago, shortly after the Third World War, that the problem of our wasted human resources really became so acute that it couldn't be evaded any longer. Since then we've seen a great deal of progress, and public sentiment is fully behind it. New building codes for big cities. New speed laws. Reduced alcoholic content in wine and liquor. Things like that. The analogue treatment is riding the wave.

"It's estimated by competent men in the field that the wave will reach its maximum about ten years from now. And that's when the Institute will be ready to put through the second stage of its program. Here it is:

"One, analogue treatment against crimes of violence to be compulsory for *all* citizens above the age of seven."

The dark man stared at him. "Blue balls of fire," he said. "Will it work, on that scale?"

"Yes. It will completely eliminate any possibility of a future war, and it will halve our police problem."

The dark man whistled. "Then what?"

"Two," said Martyn, "analogue treatment against peculation, collusion, bribery, and all the other forms of corruption to be compulsory for all candidates for public office. And that will make the democratic system foolproof, for all time."

The dark man laid his pencil down. "Dr. Martyn," he said, "you're confusing me. I'm a libertarian, but there's *got* to be some method of preventing this race from killing itself off. If this treatment will do what you say it will do, I don't care if it does violate civil rights. I want to go on living, and I want my grandchildren—I have two, by the way—to go on living. Unless there's a catch you haven't told me about this thing, I'm for it."

Martyn said earnestly, "This treatment is a crutch. It is not a therapy, it does not cure the patient of anything. As a matter of fact, as I told you before, it makes him less nearly sane, not more. The causes of his irrational or antisocial behavior are still there, they're only repressed—temporarily. They can't ever come out in the same way, that's true; we've built a wall across that particular channel. But they will express themselves in some other way, sooner or later. When a dammed-up flood breaks through in a new place, what do you do?"

"Build another levee."

"Exactly," said Martyn. "And after that? Another, and another, and another—

"It's basically wrong!"

Nicholas Dauth, cold sober, stared broodingly at the boulder that stood on trestles between the house and the orchard. It was a piece of New England granite, marked here and there with chalk lines.

It had stood there for eight months, and he had not touched a chisel to it.

The sun was warm on his back. The air was still; only the occasional hint of a breeze ruffled the treetops. Behind him he could hear the clatter of dishes in the kitchen, and beyond that the clear sounds of his wife's voice.

Once there had been a shape buried in the stone. Every stone had its latent form, and when you carved it, you felt as if you were only helping it to be born.

Dauth could remember the shape he had seen buried in

this one: a woman and child—the woman kneeling, half bent over the child in her lap. The balancing of masses had given it grace and authority, and the free space had lent it movement.

He could remember it; but he couldn't see it any more.

There was a quick, short spasm in his right arm and side, painful while it lasted. It was like the sketch of an action: turning, walking to where there was whiskey—meeting the guard who wouldn't let him drink it, turning away again. All that had squeezed itself now into a spasm, a kind of tic. He didn't drink now, didn't try to drink. He dreamed about it, yes, thought of it, felt the burning ache in his throat and guts. But he didn't try. There simply wasn't any use.

He looked back at the unborn stone, and now, for an instant, he could not even remember what its shape was to have been. The tic came again. Dauth had a feeling of pressure building intolerably inside him, of something restrained that demanded exit.

He stared toward the stone, and saw its form drift away slowly into an inchoate gray sea; then nothing.

He turned stiffly toward the house. "Martha!" he called.

The clatter of dishware answered him.

He stumbled forward, holding his arms away from his body. "Martha!" he shouted. *"I'm blind!"*

"Correct me if I'm wrong," said the dark man. "It seems to me that you'd only run into trouble with the actual mental cases, the people who really have strong complications. And, according to you, those are the only ones who should get the treatment. Now, the average man doesn't have any compulsion to kill, or steal, or what have you. He may be tempted to, once in his life. If somebody stops him, that one time, will it do him any harm?"

"For a minute or two, he will have been insane," said Martyn. "But I agree with you that if that were the end of it, no great harm would be done. At the Institute, the majority believe that that will be the end of it. They're wrong, they're tragically wrong. Because there's one provision that the Institute hasn't included in its program, but that would be the first thought of any lawmaker in the world. *Treatment against any attempt to overthrow the government.*"

The dark man sat silent.

"And from there," said Martyn, "it's only one short step to a tyranny that will last till the end of time."

The other nodded. "You're right," he said. "You are so right. What do you want me to do?"

"Raise funds," said Martyn. "At present the Institute is financed almost entirely by the members themselves. We have barely enough to operate on a minimum scale, and expand very slowly, opening one new center a year. Offer us a charitable contribution—tax-deductible, remember—of half a million, and we'll grab it. The catch is this: the donors, in return for such a large contribution, ask the privilege of appointing three members to the Institute's board of directors. There will be no objection to that, so long as my connection with the donation is kept secret, because three members will not give the donors control. But it will give me majority on this one issue—the second stage of the Institute's program.

"This thing is like an epidemic. Give it a few years, and nothing can stop it. But act now, and we can scotch it while it's still small enough to handle."

"Good enough," said the dark man. "I won't promise to hand you half a million tomorrow, but I know a few people who might reach into their pockets if I told them the score. I'll do what I can. I'll get the money if I have to steal it. You can count on me."

Martyn smiled warmly, and caught the waiter as he went by. "No, this is mine," he said, forestalling the little man's gesture. "I wonder if you realize what a weight you've taken off my shoulders?"

He paid, and they strolled out into the warm summer night. "Incidentally," Martyn said, "there's an answer to a point you brought up in passing—that the weakness of the treatment applies only to the genuinely compulsive cases, where it's most needed. There are means of getting around that, though not of making the treatment into a therapy. It's a crutch, and that's all it will ever be. But for one example, we've recently worked out a technique in which the analogue appears, not as a guardian but as the object of the attack—when there is an attack. In that way, the patient relieves himself instead of being further repressed, but he still doesn't harm anybody but a phantom."

"It's going to be a great thing for humanity," said the little man seriously, "instead of the terrible thing it might have been except for you, Dr. Martyn. Good night!"

"Good night," said Martyn gratefully. He watched the other disappear into the crowd, then walked toward the El. It was a wonderful night, and he was in no hurry.

The waiter whistled under his breath, as unconscious of the conflicting melody the band was playing as he was of the air he breathed. Philosophically, he picked up the two untouched drinks that stood at one side of the table and drained them one after the other.

If a well-dressed, smart-looking guy like that wanted to sit by himself all evening, talking and buying drinks for somebody who wasn't there, was there any harm in it?

No harm at all, the waiter told himself.

⚙ *Fredric Brown*

IMMORTALITY

FROM *"Great Lost Discoveries"*

The third great discovery made and lost in the twentieth century was the secret of immortality. It was the discovery of an obscure Moscow chemist named Ivan Ivanovitch Smetakovsky, in 1978. Smetakovsky left no record of how he made his discovery or of how he knew before trying it that it would work, for the simple reason that it scared him stiff, for two reasons.

He was afraid to give it to the world, and he knew that once he had given it even to his own government the secret would eventually leak through the Curtain and cause chaos. The U.S.S.R. could handle anything, but in the more barbaric and less disciplined countries the inevitable result of an immortality drug would be a population explosion that would most assuredly lead to an attack on the enlightened Communist countries.

And he was afraid to take it himself because he wasn't sure he *wanted* to become immortal. With things as they were even in the U.S.S.R.—not to consider what they must be outside it—was it really worth while to live forever or even indefinitely?

He compromised by neither giving it to anyone else nor taking it himself, for the time being, until he could make up his mind about it.

Meanwhile he carried with him the only dose of the drug he had made up. It was only a minute quantity that fitted into a tiny capsule that was insoluble and could be carried in his mouth. He attached it to the side of one of his dentures, so that it rested safely between denture and cheek and he would be in no danger of swallowing it inadvertently.

But if he should so decide at any time he could reach into his mouth, crush the capsule with a thumbnail, and become immortal.

He so decided one day when, after coming down with lobar pneumonia and being taken to a Moscow hospital, he learned from overhearing a conversation between a doctor and nurse, who erroneously thought he was asleep, that he was expected to die within a few hours.

Fear of death proved greater than fear of immortality, whatever immortality might bring, so, as soon as the doctor and the nurse had left the room, he crushed the capsule and swallowed its contents.

He hoped that, since death might be so imminent, the drug would work in time to save his life. It did work in time, although by the time it had taken effect he had slipped into semicoma and delirium.

Three years later, in 1981, he was still in semicoma and delirium, and the Russian doctors had finally diagnosed his case and ceased to be puzzled by it.

Obviously Smetakovsky had taken some sort of immortality drug—one which they found it impossible to isolate or analyze—and it was keeping him from dying and would no doubt do so indefinitely if not forever.

But unfortunately it had also made immortal the pneumococci in his body, the bacteria (diplococci pneumoniae) that had caused his pneumonia in the first place and would now continue to maintain it forever. So the doctors, being realists and seeing no reason to burden themselves by giving him custodial care in perpetuity, simply buried him.

SHADOW SHOW

I

Bayard Lodge, chief of Life Team No. 3, sat at his desk and stared across it angrily at Kent Forester, the team's psychologist.

"The Play must go on," said Forester. "I can't be responsible for what might happen if we dropped it even for a night or two. It's the one thing that holds us all together. It is the unifying glue that keeps us sane and preserves our sense of humor. And it gives us something to think about."

"I know," said Lodge, "but with Henry dead . . ."

"They'll understand,' Forester promised. "I'll talk to them. I know they'll understand.

"They'll understand all right," Lodge agreed. "All of us recognize the necessity of the Play. But there is something else. One of those characters was Henry's."

Forester nodded. "I've been thinking of that, too."

"Do you know which one?"

Forester shook his head.

"I thought you might," said Lodge. "You've been beating out your brains to get them figured out, to pair up the characters with us."

Forester grinned sheepishly.

"I don't blame you," said Lodge. "I know why you're doing it."

"It would be a help," admitted Forester. "It would give me a key to every person here. Just consider—when a character went illogical . . ."

"They're all illogical," said Lodge. "That's the beauty of them."

"But the illogic runs true to a certain zany pattern," Forester pointed out. "You can use that very zaniness and set up a norm."

"You've done that?"

"Not as a graph," said Forester, "but I have it well in mind. When the illogic deviates it's not too hard to spot it."

"It's been deviating?"

Forester nodded. "Sharply at times. The problem that we have—the way that they are thinking . . ."

"Call it attitude," said Lodge.

For a moment the two of them were silent. Then Forester asked, "Do you mind if I ask why you insist on attitude?"

"Because it is an attitude," Lodge told him. "It's an attitude conditioned by the life we lead. An attitude traceable to too much thinking, too much searching of the soul. It's an emotional thing, almost a religious thing. There's little of the intellectual in it. We're shut up too tightly. Guarded too closely. The importance of our work is stressed too much. We aren't normal humans. We're off balance all the time. How in the world can we be normal humans when we lead no normal life?"

"It's a terrible responsibility," said Forester. "They face it each day of their lives."

"The responsibility is not theirs."

"Only if you agree that the individual counts for less than the race. Perhaps not even then, for there are definite racial implications in this project, implications that can become terribly personal. Imagine making—"

"I know," said Lodge impatiently. "I've heard it from every one of them. Imagine making a human being not in the image of humanity."

"And yet it would be human," Forester said. "That is the point, Bayard. Not that we would be manufacturing life, but that it would be human life in the shape of monsters. You wake up screaming, dreaming of those monsters. A monster itself would not be bad at all, if it were no more than a monster. After centuries of traveling to the stars, we are used to monsters."

Lodge cut him off. "Let's get back to the Play."

"We'll have to go ahead," insisted Forester.

"There'll be one character missing," Lodge warned him. "You know what that might do. It might throw the entire thing off balance, reduce it to confusion. That would be worse than no Play at all. Why can't we wait a few days and start over, new again? With a new Play, a new set of characters."

"We can't do that," said Forester, "because each of us has identified himself or herself with a certain character. That character has become a part, an individual part, of each of us. We're living split lives, Bayard. We're split personalities. We have to be to live. We have to be because not a single one of us could bear to be himself alone."

"You're trying to say that we must continue the Play as an insurance of our sanity."

"Something like that. Not so grim as you make it sound. In ordinary circumstances there'd be no question we could dispense with it. But this is no ordinary circumstance. Every one of us is nursing a guilt complex of horrendous magnitude. The Play is an emotional outlet, a letdown from the tension. It gives us something to talk about it. It keeps us from sitting around at night washing out the stains of guilt. It supplies the ridiculous in our lives—it is our daily comic strip, our chuckle or our belly laugh."

Lodge got up and paced up and down the room.

"I said attitude," he declared, "and it is an attitude—a silly, crazy attitude. There is no reason for the guilt complex. But they coddle it as if it were a thing that kept them human, as if it might be the one last identity they retain with the outside world and the rest of mankind. They come to me and they talk about it—as if I could do something about it. As if I could throw up my hands and say, well, all right, then, let's quit. As if I didn't have a job to do.

"They say we're taking a divine power into our hands, that life came to be by some sort of godly intervention, that it's blasphemous and sacrilegious for mere man to try to duplicate that feat.

"And there's an answer to that one—a logical answer, but they can't see the logic, or won't listen to it. Can Man do anything divine? If life is divine, then Man cannot create it in his laboratories no matter what he does, cannot put it on a mass production basis. If Man can create life out of his chemicals, out of his knowledge, if he can make one living cell by the virtue of his technique and his knowledge, then that will prove divine intervention was unnecessary to the genesis of life. And if we have that proof —if we know that a divine instrumentality is unnecessary for the creation of life, doesn't that very proof and fact rob it of divinity?"

"They are seeking an escape," said Forester, trying to calm him. "Some of them may believe what they say, but there are others who are merely afraid of the responsibility —the moral responsibility. They start thinking how it would be to live with something like that the rest of their lives. You had the same situation a thousand years ago when men discovered and developed atomic fission. They did it and they shuddered. They couldn't sleep at night. They woke up screaming. They knew what they were doing— that they were unloosing terrible powers. And we know what we are doing."

Lodge went back to his desk and sat down.

"Let me think about it, Kent," he said. "You may be right. I don't know. There are so many things that I don't know."

"I'll be back," said Forester.

II

He closed the door quietly when he left.

The Play was a never-ending soap opera, the *Old Red Barn* extended to unheard of reaches of the ridiculous. It had a touch of Oz and a dash of alienness and it went on and on and on.

When you put a group of people on an asteroid, when you throw a space patrol around them, when you lead them to their laboratories and point out the problem to be solved, when you keep them at that problem day after endless day, you must likewise do something to preserve their sanity.

To do this there may be books and music, films, games, dancing of an evening—all the old standby entertainment values the race has used for millennia to forget its troubles.

But there comes a time when these amusements fail to serve their purpose, when they are not enough.

Then you hunt for something new and novel—and basic —for something in which each of the isolated group may participate, something with which they can establish close personal identity and lose themselves, forgetting for a time who they are and what may be their purpose.

That's where the Play came in.

In the older days, many years before, in the cottages of Europe and the pioneer farmsteads of North America, a father would provide an evening's entertainment for his children by means of shadow pictures. He would place a lamp or candle on a table opposite a blank wall, and sitting between the lamp and wall, he would use his hands to form the shadows of rabbit and of elephant, of horse and man and bear and many other things. For an hour or more the shadow show would parade across the wall, first one and then another—rabbit nibbling clover, the elephant waving trunk and ears, the wolf howling on a hilltop. The children would sit quiet and spellbound, for these were wondrous things.

Later, with the advent of movies and of television, of the comic book and the cheap plastic dime-store toy, the shadows were no longer wondrous and were shown no longer, but that is not the point.

Take the principle of the shadow pictures, add a thousand years of know-how, and you have the Play.

Whether the long-forgotten genius who first conceived the Play had ever known of the shadow pictures is something that's not known. But the principle was there, although the approach was different in that one used his mind and thought instead of just his hands.

And instead of rabbits and elephants appearing in one-dimensional black-and-white, in the Play the characters were as varied as the human mind might make them (since the brain is more facile than the hand) and three-dimensional in full color.

The screen was a triumph of electronic engineering with its memory banks, its rows of sonic tubes, its color selectors, ESP antennae and other gadgets, but it was the minds of the audience that did the work, supplying the raw material for the Play upon the screen. It was the audience that conceived the characters, that led them through their actions, that supplied the lines they spoke. It was the combined will of the audience that supplied the backdrops and dreamed up the properties.

At first the Play had been a haphazard thing, with the characters only half developed, playing at cross purposes, without personalities, and little more than cartoons paraded on the stage. At first the backdrops and the properties were the crazy products of many minds flying off at tangents. At times no fewer than three moons would be in the sky simultaneously, all in different phases. At times snow would be falling at one end of the stage and bright sunlight would pour down on palm trees at the other end.

But in time the Play developed. The characters grew to full stature, without missing arms and legs, acquired personalities, rounded out into full-blown living beings. The background became the result of a combined effort to achieve effective setting rather than nine different people trying desperately to fill in the blank spots.

In time direction and purpose had been achieved so that the action flowed smoothly, although there never came a time when any of the nine were sure of what would happen next.

That was the fascination of it. New situations were continually being introduced by one character or another, with the result that the human creators of the other characters were faced with the need of new lines and action to meet the changing situations.

It became in a sense a contest of wills, with each participant seeking advantages for his character, or, on the other hand, forced to backtrack to escape disaster. It became, after a time, a never-ending chess game in which each player pitted himself or herself against the other eight.

And no one knew, of course, to whom any of the characters belonged. Out of this grew up a lively guessing game and many jokes and sallies, and this was to the good, for that was what the Play was for: to lift the minds of the participants out of their daily work and worries.

Each evening after dinner the nine gathered in the theater, and the screen sprang into life and the nine characters performed their parts and spoke their lines: the Defenseless Orphan, the Mustached Villain, the Proper Young Man, the Beautiful Bitch, the Alien Monster and all the others.

Nine of them—nine men and women, and nine characters.

But now there would be only eight, for Henry Griffith had died, slumped against his bench with the notebook at his elbow.

And the Play would have to go on with one missing character—the character that had been controlled and motivated by the man who now was dead.

Lodge wondered which character would be the missing one. Not the Defenseless Orphan, certainly, for that would not have been down Henry's alley. But it might be the Proper Young Man or the Out-At-Elbows Philosopher or the Rustic Slicker.

"Wait a minute there," said Lodge. "Not the Rustic Slicker. The Rustic Slicker's me."

He sat idly speculating on which belonged to whom. It would be exactly like Sue Lawrence to dream up the Beautiful Bitch—a character as little like her prim, practical self as one could well imagine. He remembered that he had taunted her once concerning his suspicion and that she had been very cold to him for several days thereafter.

Forester said the Play must go on, and maybe he was right. They might adjust. God knows, they should be able to adjust to anything after participating in the Play each evening for months on end.

It was a zany thing, all right. Never getting anywhere. Not even episodic, for it never had a chance to become episodic. Let one trend develop and some joker was sure to throw in a stumbling block that upset the trend and sent the action angling off in some new direction.

With that kind of goings-on, he thought, the disappearance of a single character shouldn't throw them off their stride.

He got up from his desk and walked to the great picture window. He stood there looking out at the bleak loneliness of the asteroid. The curved roofs of the research center fell away beneath him, shining in the starlight, to the blackness of the cragged surface. Above the jagged northern horizon lay a flush of light and in a little while it would be dawn, with the weak, watch-sized sun sailing upward to shed its feeble light upon this tiny speck of rock. He watched the flushed horizon, remembering Earth, where the dawn was morning and sunset marked the beginning of the night. Here no such scheme was possible, for the days and nights were so erratic and so short that they could not be used to divide one's time. Here morning came at a certain hour, evening came at another hour, regardless of the sun, and one might sleep out a night with the sun high in the sky.

It would have been different, he thought, if we could have stayed on Earth, for there we would have had normal human contacts. We would not have thought so much or brooded; we could have rubbed away the guilt on the hides of other people.

But normal human contacts would have meant the start of rumors, would have encouraged leaks, and in a thing of this sort there could be no leaks.

For if the people of the Earth knew what they were doing, or, more correctly, what they were trying to do, they would raise a hubbub that might result in calling off the project.

Even here, he thought—even here, there are those who have their doubts and fears.

A human being must walk upon two legs and have two arms and a pair of eyes, a brace of ears, one nose, one mouth, be not unduly hairy. He must walk; he must not hop or crawl or slither.

A perversion of the human form, they said; a scrapping of human dignity; a going-too-far, farther than Man in all his arrogance was ever meant to go.

There was a rap upon the door. Lodge turned and called, "Come in."

It was Dr. Susan Lawrence. She stood in the open doorway, a stolid, dumpy, dowdy woman with an angular face that had a set of stubbornness and of purpose in it. She did not see him for a moment and stood there, turning her head, trying to find him in the dusky room.

"Over here, Sue," he called.

She closed the door and crossed the room, and stood by his side looking out the window.

Finally she said, "There was nothing wrong with him, Bayard. Nothing organically wrong. I wonder . . ."

She stood there, silent, and Lodge could feel the practical bleakness of her thoughts.

"It's bad enough," she said, "when they die and you know what killed them. It's not so bad to lose them if you've had a fighting chance to save them. But this is different. He just toppled over. He was dead before he hit the bench."

"You've examined him?"

She nodded. "I put him in the analyzers. I've got three reels of stuff. Ill check it all—later. But I'll swear there was nothing wrong."

She reached out a hand and put it on his arm, her pudgy fingers tightening.

"He didn't want to live," she said. "He was afraid to live. He thought he was close to finding something and he was afraid to find it."

"We have to find it, Sue."

"For what?" she asked. "So we can fashion humans to live on planets where humans in their present form wouldn't have a chance? So we can take a human mind and spirit and enclose it in a monster's body, hating itself . . ."

"It wouldn't hate itself," Lodge told her. "You're thinking in anthropomorphic terms. A thing is never ugly to itself because it knows itself. Have we any proof that bipedal man is any happier than an insect or a toad?"

"But why?" she persisted. "We do not need those planets. We have more now than we can colonize. Enough Earth-type planets to last for centuries. We'll be lucky if we even colonize them all, let alone develop them, in the next five hundred years."

"We can't take the chance," he said. "We must take control while we have the chance. It was all right when we were safe and snug on Earth, but that is true no longer. We've gone out to the stars. Somewhere in the universe there are other intelligences. There have to be. Eventually we'll meet. We must be in a strong position."

"And to get into that strong position we plant colonies of human monsters. I know, Bayard—it's clever. We can design the bodies, the flesh and nerves and muscles, the organs of communication—all designed to exist upon a planet where a normal human could not live a minute. We are clever, all right, and very good technicians, but we can't breathe life into them. There's more to life than just the colloidal combination of certain elements. There's something else, and we'll never get it."

"We will try," said Lodge.

"You'll drive good technicians out of their sanity," she said. "You'll kill some of them—not with your hands, but with your insistence. You'll keep them cooped up for years and you'll give them a Play so they'll last the longer—but you won't find life, for life is not Man's secret."

"Want to bet?" he asked, laughing at her fury.

She swung around and faced him.

"There are times," she said, "when I regret my oath. A little cyanide . . ."

He caught her by the arm and walked her to the desk.

"Let's have a drink," he said. "You can kill me later."

III

They dressed for dinner.

That was a rule. They always dressed for dinner.

It was, like the Play, one of the many little habits that they cultivated to retain their sanity, not to forget that they were a cultured people as well as ruthless seekers after knowledge—a knowledge that any one of them would have happily forsworn.

They laid aside their scalpels and their other tools, they boxed their microscopes, they ranged the culture bottles neatly in place, they put the pans of saline solutions and their varying contents carefully away. They took their aprons off and went out and shut the door. And for a few hours they forgot, or tried to forget, who they were and what their labors were.

They dressed for dinner and assembled in the so-called drawing room for cocktails and then went in to dinner, pretending that they were no more than normal human beings —and no less.

The table was set with exquisite china and fragile glass, and there were flowers and flaming tapers. They began with an entree and their meal was served in courses by accomplished robots, and they ended with cheese and fruit and brandy and there were cigars for those who wanted them.

Lodge sat at the table's head and looked down the table at them and for a moment saw Sue Lawrence looking back

at him and wondered if she were scowling or if the seeming
scowl was no more than the play of candlelight upon her
face.

They talked as they always talked at dinner—the incon-
sequential social chatter of people without worry and with
little purpose. For this was the moment of forgetting and
escape. This was the hour to wash away the guilt and to
ignore the stain.

But tonight, he noticed, they could not pull themselves
away entirely from the happenings of the day—for there
was talk of Henry Griffith and of his sudden dying and
they spoke of him in soft tones and with strained and sober
faces. Henry had been too intense and too strange a man
for anyone to know him well, but they held him in high
regard, and although the robots had been careful to arrange the seating so his absence left no gap, there was a
real and present sense that one of them was missing.

Chester Sifford said to Lodge, "We'll be sending Henry
back?"

Lodge nodded. "We'll call in one of the patrol and it'll
take him back to Earth. We'll have a short service for him
here."

"But who?"

"Craven, more than likely. He was closer to Henry than
any of the rest. I spoke to him about it. He agreed to say
a word or two."

"Is there anyone on Earth? Henry never talked a lot."

"Some nephews and nieces. Maybe a brother or a sister.
That would be all, I think."

Hugh Maitland said, "I understand we'll continue with
the Play."

"That's right," Lodge told him. "Kent recommended it
and I agreed. Kent knows what's best for us."

Sifford agreed. "That's his job. He's a good man at it."

"I think so, too," said Maitland. "Most psych men stand
outside the group. Posing as your conscience. But Kent
doesn't work that way."

"He's a chaplain," Sifford said. "Just a goddamn chaplain."

Helen Gray sat to the left, and Lodge saw that she was
not talking with anyone but only staring at the bowl of
roses which this night served as a centerpiece.

Tough on her, he thought. For she had been the one who had found Henry dead and, thinking that he was merely sleeping, had taken him by the shoulder and shaken him to wake him.

Down at the other end of the table, sitting next to Forester, Alice Page was talking far too much, much more than she had ever talked before, for she was a strangely reserved woman, with a quiet beauty that had a touch of darkness in it. Now she leaned toward Forester, talking tensely, as if she might be arguing in a low tone so the others would not hear her, with Forester listening, his face masked with patience against a feeling of alarm.

They are upset, thought Lodge—far more than I had suspected. Upset and edgy, ready to explode.

Henry's death had hit them harder than he knew.

Not a lovable man, Henry still had been one of them. One of them, he thought. Why not one of us? But that was the way it always was—unlike Forester, who did his best work by being one of them, he must stand to one side, must keep intact that slight, cold margin of reserve which was all that preserved against an incident of crisis the authority which was essential to his job.

Sifford said, "Henry was close to something."

"So Sue told me."

"He was writing up his notes when he died," said Sifford. "It may be . . ."

"We'll have a look at them," Lodge promised. "All of us together. In a day or two."

Maitland shook his head. "We'll never find it, Bayard. Not the way we're working. Not in the direction we are working. We have to take a new approach."

Sifford bristled. "What kind of approach?"

"I don't know," said Maitland. "If I knew . . ."

"Gentlemen," said Lodge.

"Sorry," Sifford said. "I'm a little jumpy."

Lodge remembered Dr. Susan Lawrence, standing with him, looking out the window at the bleakness of the tumbling hunk of rock on which they lived and saying, "He didn't want to live. He was afraid to live."

What had she been trying to tell him? That Henry Griffith had died of intellectual fear? That he had died because he was afraid to live?

Would it actually be possible for a psychosomatic syndrome to kill a man?

IV

You could feel the tension in the room when they went to the theater, although they did their best to mask the tension. They chatted and pretended to be light-hearted, and Maitland tried a joke which fell flat upon its face and died, squirming beneath the insincerity of the laughter that its telling had called forth.

Kent was wrong, Lodge told himself, feeling a wave of terror washing over him. This business was loaded with deadly psychological dynamite. It would not take much to trigger it and it could set off a chain reaction that could wash up the team.

And if the team were wrecked the work of years was gone—the long years of education, the necessary months to get them working together, the constant, never-ending battle to keep them happy and from one another's throats. Gone would be the team confidence which over many months had replaced individual confidence and doubt, gone would be the smooth cooperation and coordination which worked like meshing gears, gone would be a vast percentage of the actual work they'd done, for no other team, no matter how capable it might be, could take up where another team left off, even with the notes of the first team to guide them on their way.

The curving screen covered one end of the room, sunken into the wall, with the flare of the narrow stage in front of it.

Back of that, thought Lodge, the tubes and generators, the sonics and computers—mechanical magic which turned human thought and will into the moving images that would parade across the screen. Puppets, he thought—puppets of the human mind, but with a strange and startling humanity about them that could not be achieved by carven hunks of wood.

And the difference, of course, was the difference between the mind and hand, for no knife, no matter how sharp, guided by no matter how talented and artistic a hand, could carve a dummy with half the precision or fidelity with which the mind could shape a human creature.

First, Man had created with hands alone, chipping the flint, carving out the bow and dish; then he achieved machines which were extensions of his hands and they turned out artifacts which the hands alone were incapable of making; and now, Man created not with his hands nor with extensions of his hands, but with his mind and extensions of his mind, although he still must use machinery to translate and project the labor of his brain.

Someday, he thought, it will be mind alone, without the aid of machines, without the help of hands.

The screen flickered and there was a tree upon it, then another tree, a bench, a duck pond, grass, a distant statue, and behind it all the dim, tree-broken outlines of city towers.

That was where they had left it the night before, with the cast of characters embarked upon a picnic in a city park—a picnic that was almost certain to remain a picnic for mere moments only before someone should turn it into something else.

Tonight, he hoped, they'd let it stay a picnic, let it run its course, take it easy for a chance, not try any fancy stuff—for tonight, of all nights, there must be no sudden jolts, no terrifying turns. A mind forced to guide its character through the intricacies of a suddenly changed plot or some outlandish situation might crack beneath the effort.

As it was, there'd be one missing character and much would depend upon which one it was.

The scene stood empty, like a delicate painting of a park in springtime with each thing fixed in place.

Why were they waiting? What were they waiting for? They had set the stage. What were they waiting for?

Someone thought of a breeze and you could hear the whisper of it, moving in the trees, ruffling the pond.

Lodge brought his character into his mind and walked him on the stage, imagining his gangling walk, the grass stem stuck in his mouth, the curl of unbarbered hair above his collar.

Someone had to start it off. Someone—

The Rustic Slicker turned and hustled back off stage.

He hustled back again, carrying a great hamper. "Forgot m' basket," he said, with rural sheepishness.

Someone tittered in the darkened room.

Thank God for that titter! It is going all right. *Come on, the rest of you!*

The Out-At-Elbows Philosopher strode on stage. He was a charming fellow, with no good intent at all—a cadger, a bum, a fullfledged fourflusher behind the façade of his flowered waistcoat, the senatorial bearing, the long, white, curling locks.

"My friend," he said. "My friend."

"Y' ain't m' friend," the Rustic Slicker told him, "till y' pay me back m' three hundred bucks."

Come on, the rest of you!

The Beautiful Bitch showed up with the Proper Young Man, who any moment now was about to get dreadfully disillusioned.

The Rustic Slicker had squatted on the grass and opened his hamper. He began to take out stuff—a ham, a turkey, a cheese, a vacuum jug, a bowl of Jello, a tin of kippered herring.

The Beautiful Bitch made exaggerated eyes at him and wiggled her hips. The Rustic Slicker blushed, ducking his head.

Kent yelled from the audience: "Go ahead and ruin him!"

Everyone laughed.

It was going to be all right. It would be all right.

Get the audience and the players kidding back and forth and it was bound to be all right.

"Ah think that's a good idee, honey," said the Beautiful Bitch. "Ah do believe Ah will."

She advanced upon the Slicker.

The Slicker, with his head still ducked, kept on taking things out of the hamper—more by far than could have been held in any ten such hampers.

He took out rings of bologna, stacks of wieners, mounds of marshmallows, a roast goose—and a diamond necklace.

The Beautiful Bitch pounced on the necklace, shrieking with delight.

The Out-At-Elbows Philosopher had jerked a leg off

the turkey and was eating it, waving it between bites to emphasize the flowery oration he had launched upon.

"My friends—" he orated between bites—"my friends, in this vernal season it was right and proper, I said right and proper sir, that a group of friends should forgather to commune with nature in her gayest aspects, finding retreat such as this even in the heart of a heartless city . . ."

He would go on like that for hours unless something intervened to stop him. The situation being as it was, something was almost bound to stop him.

Someone had put a sportive, if miniature, whale into the pond, and the whale, acting much more like a porpoise than a whale, was leaping about in graceful curves and scaring the hell out of the flock of ducks which resided on the pond.

The Alien Monster sneaked in and hid behind a tree. You could see with half an eye that he was bent upon no good.

"Watch out!" yelled someone in the audience, but the actors paid no attention to the warning. There were times when they could be incredibly stupid.

The Defenseless Orphan came on stage on the arm of the Mustached Villain (and there was no good intent in that situation, either) with the Extra-Terrestrial Ally trailing along behind them.

"Where is the Sweet Young Thing?" asked the Mustached Villain. "She's the only one who's missing."

"She'll be along," said the Rustic Slicker. "I saw her at the corner saloon building up a load—"

The Philosopher stopped his oration in midsentence, halted the turkey drumstick in mid-air. His silver mane did its best to bristle, and he whirled upon the Rustic Slicker.

"You are a cad, sir," he said, "to say a thing like that, a most contemptible cad!"

"I don't care," said the Slicker. "No matter what y' say, that's what she was doing."

"You lay off him," shrilled the Beautiful Bitch, fondling the diamond necklace. "He's mah frien' and you can't call him a cad."

"Now, B.B.," protested the Proper Young Man. "you keep out of this."

She spun on him. "You shut yoah mouth," she said. "You mealy hypocrite. Don't you tell me what to do. Too nice to call me by mah rightful name, but using just initials. You prissy-panted high-binder, don't you speak to me."

The Philosopher stepped ponderously forward, stooped down and swung his arm. The half-eaten drumstick took the Slicker squarely across the chops.

The Slicker rose slowly to his feet, one hand grasping the roast goose.

"So y' want to play," he said.

He hurled the goose at the Philosopher. It struck square on the flowered waistcoat. It was greasy and it splashed.

Oh, Lord, thought Lodge. Now the fat's in the fire for sure! Why did the Philosopher act the way he did? Why couldn't they have left it a simple, friendly picnic, just this once? Why did the person whose character the Philosopher was make him swing that drumstick?

And why had he, Bayard Lodge, made the Slicker throw the goose?

He went cold all over at the question, and when the answer came he felt a hand reach into his belly and start twisting at his guts.

For the answer was: He hadn't!

He hadn't made the Slicker throw the goose. He'd felt a flare of anger and a hard, cold hatred, but he had not willed his character to retaliatory action.

He kept watching the screen, seeing what was going on, but with only half his mind, while the other half quarreled with itself and sought an explanation.

It was the machine that was to blame—it was the machine that had made the Slicker throw the goose, for the machine would know, almost as well as a human knew, the reaction that would follow a blow upon the face. The machine had acted automatically, without waiting for the human thought. Sure, perhaps, of what the human thought would be.

It's logical, said the arguing part of his mind—it's logical that the machine would know, and logical once again that being sure of knowing, it would react automatically.

The Philosopher had stepped cautiously backward after he had struck the blow, standing at attention, presenting arms, after a manner of speaking, with the mangy drumstick.

The Beautiful Bitch clapped her hands and cried, "Now you-all got to fight a duel!"

"Precisely, miss," said the Philosopher, still stiffly at attention. "Why else do you think I struck him?"

The goose grease dropped slowly off his ornate vest, but you never would have guessed for so much as an instant that he thought he was anything but faultlessly turned out.

"But it should have been a glove," protested the Proper Young Man.

"I didn't have a glove, sir," said the Philosopher, speaking a truth that was self-evident.

"It's frightfully improper," persisted the Proper Young Man.

The Mustached Villain flipped back his coattails and reaching into his back pockets, brought out two pistols.

"I always carry them," he said with a frightful leer, "for occasions such as this."

We have to break it up, thought Lodge. We have to stop it. We can't let it go on.

He made the Rustic Slicker say, "Now lookit here, now. I don't want to fool around with firearms. Someone might get hurt."

"You have to fight," said the leering Villain, holding both pistols in one hand and twirling his mustaches with the other.

"He has the choice of weapons," observed the Proper Young Man. "As the challenged party . . ."

The Beautiful Bitch stopped clapping her hands.

"You keep out of this," she screamed. "You sissy—you just don't want to see them fight."

The Villain bowed. "The Slicker has the choice," he said.

The Extra-Terrestrial Ally piped up. "This is ridiculous," it said. "All you humans are ridiculous."

The Alien Monster stuck his head out from behind the tree.

"Leave 'em alone," he bellowed in his frightful brogue. "If they want to fight, let 'em go ahead and fight."

Then he curled himself into a wheel by the simple procedure of putting his tail into his mouth, and started to roll. He rolled around the duck pond at a fearful pace, chanting all the while: "Leave 'em fight. Leave 'em fight.

Leave 'em fight." Then he popped behind his tree again.

The Defenseless Orphan complained, "I thought this was a picnic."

And so did all the rest of us, thought Lodge.

Although you could have bet, even before it started, that it wouldn't stay a picnic.

"Your choice, please," said the Villain to the Slicker, far too politely. "Pistols, knives, swords, battle axes—"

Ridiculous, thought Lodge.

Make it ridiculous.

He made the Slicker say, "Pitchforks at three paces."

The Sweet Young Thing tripped lightly on the stage. She was humming a drinking song, and you could see that she'd picked up quite a glow.

But she stopped at what she saw before her: the Philosopher dripping goose grease, the Villain clutching a pistol in each hand, the Beautiful Bitch jangling a diamond necklace, and she asked, "What is going on here?"

The Out-At-Elbows Philosopher relaxed his post and rubbed his hands together with smirking satisfaction.

"Now," he said, oozing good fellowship and cheer, "isn't this a cozy situation? All nine of us are here—"

In the audience, Alice Page leaped to her feet, put her hands up to her face, pressed her palms tight against her temples, closed her eyes quite shut and screamed and screamed and screamed.

V

There had been, not eight characters, but nine.

Henry Griffith's character had walked on with the rest of them.

"You're crazy, Bayard," Forester said. "When a man is dead, he's dead. Whether he still exists or not, I don't profess to know, but if he does exist it is not on the level of his previous existence; it is on another plane, in another state of being, in another dimension, call it what you will, religionist or spiritualist, the answer is the same."

Lodge nodded his agreement. "I was grasping at straws. Trying to dredge up every possibility. I know that Henry's dead. I know the dead stay dead. And yet, you'll have to admit, it is a natural thought. Why did Alice scream? Not because the nine characters were there. But because of why there might be nine of them. The ghost in us dies hard."

"It's not only Alice," Forester told him. "It's all the others, too. If we don't get this business under control, there'll be a flare-up. The emotional index was already stretched pretty thin when this happened—doubt over the purpose of the research, the inevitable wear and tear of nine people living together for months on end, a sort of cabin fever. It all built up. I've watched it building up and I've held my breath."

"Some joker out there subbed for Henry," Lodge said. "How does that sound to you? Someone handled his own character and Henry's, too."

"No one could handle more than one character," said Forester.

"Someone put a whale into that duck pond."

"Sure, but it didn't last long. The whale jumped a time or two and then was gone. Whoever put it there couldn't keep it there."

"We all cooperate on the setting and the props. Why couldn't someone pull quietly out of that cooperation and concentrate all his mind on two characters?"

Forester looked doubtful. "I suppose it could be done. But the second character probably would be out of whack. Did you notice any of them that seemed a little strange?"

"I don't know about strange," said Lodge, "but the Alien Monster hid—"

"Henry's character wasn't the Alien Monster."

"How can you be sure?"

"Henry wasn't the kind of man to cook up an alien monster."

"All right, then. Which one is Henry's character?"

Forester slapped the arm of his chair impatiently. "I've told you, Bayard, that I don't know who any of them are. I've tried to match them up and it can't be done."

"It would help if we knew. Especially . . ."

"Especially Henry's character," said Forester. He left the chair and paced up and down the office.

"Your theory of some joker putting on Henry's character

is all wrong," he said. "How would he know which one?"

Lodge raised his hand and smote the desk. "The Sweet Young Thing!" he shouted.

"What's that?"

"The Sweet Young Thing. She was the last to walk on. Don't you remember? The Mustached Villain asked where she was and the Rustic Slicker said he saw her in a saloon and—"

"Good Lord!" breathed Forester. "And the Out-At-Elbows Philosopher was at great pains to announce that all of them were there. Needling us! Jeering at us!"

"You think the Philosopher is the one, then? He's the joker. The one who produced the Sweet Young Thing— the ninth member of the cast. The ninth one to appear would have to be Henry's character, don't you see. You said yourself it couldn't be done because you wouldn't know which one it was. But you could know—you'd know when eight were on the stage that the missing one was Henry's character."

"Either there was a joker," Forester said, "or the cast itself is somehow sentient—has come half way alive."

Lodge scowled. "I can't buy that one, Kent. They're images of our minds. We call them up, we put them through their paces, we dismiss them. They depend utterly on us. They couldn't have a separate identity. They're creatures of our mind and that is all."

"It wasn't exactly along that line that I was thinking," said Forester. "I was thinking of the machine itself. It takes the impressions from our minds and shapes them. It translates what we think into the images on the screen. It transforms our thoughts into seeming actualities . . ."

"A memory . . ."

"I think the machine may have a memory," Forester declared. "God knows it has enough sensitive equipment packed into it to have almost anything. The machine does more of it than we do, it contributes more than we do. After all, we're the same drab old mortals that we always were. We've just got clever, that is all. We've built extensions of ourselves. The machine is an extension of our imagery."

"I don't know," protested Lodge. "I simply do not know. This going around in circles. This incessant speculation."

But he did know, he told himself. He did know that the machine could act independently, for it had made the Slicker throw the goose. But that was different from handling a character from scratch, different from putting on a character that should not appear. It had simply been a matter of an induced, automatic action—and it didn't mean a thing.

Or did it?

"The machine could walk on Henry's character," Forester persisted. "It could have the Philosopher mock us."

"But why?" asked Lodge and even as he asked it, he knew why the machine might do just that, and the thought of it made icy worms go crawling up his back.

"To show us," Forester said, "that it was sentient, too."

"But it wouldn't do that," Lodge argued. "If it were sentient it would keep quiet about it. That would be its sole defense. We could smash it. We probably would smash it if we thought it had come alive. We could dismantle it; we could put an end to it."

He sat in the silence that fell between them and felt the dread that had settled on this place—a strange dread compounded of an intellectual and moral doubt, of a man who had fallen dead, of one character too many, of the guarded loneliness that hemmed in their lives.

"I can't think," he said. "Let's sleep on it."

"Okay," said Forester.

"A drink?"

Forester shook his head.

He's glad to drop it, too, thought Lodge. He's glad to get away.

Like a hurt animal, he thought. All of us, like hurt animals, crawling off to be alone, sick of one another, poisoned by the same faces eternally sitting across the table or meeting in the halls, of the same mouths saying the same inane phrases over and over again until, when you meet the owner of a particular mouth, you know before he says it what he is going to say.

"Good night, Bayard."

"Night, Kent. Sleep tight."

"See you."

"Sure," said Lodge.

The door shut softly.
Good night. Sleep tight. Don't let the bedbugs bite.

VI

He woke, screaming in the night.

He sat bolt upright in the middle of the bed and searched with numbed mind for the actuality, slowly, clumsily separating the actuality from the dream, becoming aware again of the room he slept in, of the furniture, of his own place and who he was and what he did and why he happened to be there.

It was all right, he told himself. It had been just a dream. The kind of dream that was common here. The kind of dream that everyone was having.

The dream of walking down a street or road, or walking up a staircase, of walking almost anywhere and of meeting something—a spider-like thing, or a worm-like thing, or a squatting monstrosity with horns and drooling mouth or perhaps something such as could be fabricated only in a dream and have it stop and say hello and chat—for it was human, too, just the same as you.

He sat and shivered at the memory of the one he'd met, of how it had put a hairy, taloned claw around his shoulder, of how it had drooled upon him with great affection and had asked him if he had the time to catch a drink because it had a thing or two it wanted to talk with him about. Its odor had been overpowering and its shape obscene, and he'd tried to shrink from it, had tried to run from it, but could neither shrink nor run, for it was a man like him, clothed in different flesh.

He swung his legs off the bed and found his slippers with searching toes and scuffed his feet into them. He found his robe and stood up and put it on and went out to the office.

There he mixed himself a drink.

Sleep tight, he thought. God, how can a man sleep tight? Now it's got me as well as all the others.

The guilt of it—the guilt of what mankind meant to do.

Although, despite the guilt, there was a lot of logic in it.

There were planets upon which no human could have lived for longer than a second, because of atmospheric pressure, because of overpowering gravity, because of lack of atmosphere or poison atmosphere, or because of any one or any combination of a hundred other reasons.

And yet these planets had economic and strategic value, every one of them. Some of them had both great economic and great strategic value. And if Man were to hold the galactic empire which he was carving out against the possible appearance of some as yet unknown alien foe, he must man all economic and strategic points, must make full use of all the resources of his new empire.

For that somewhere in the galaxy there were other intelligences as yet unmet by men there could be little doubt. The sheer mathematics of pure chance said there had to be. Given an infinite space, the possibility of such an intelligence also neared infinity. Friend or foe: you couldn't know. But you couldn't take a chance. So you planned and built against the day of meeting.

And in such planning, to bypass planets of economic and strategic value was sheer insanity.

Human colonies must be planted on those planets—must be planted there and grow against the day of meeting so that their numbers and their resources and their positioning in space might be thrown into the struggle if the struggle came to be.

And if Man, in his natural form, could not exist there— why, then you changed his form. You manufactured bodies that could live there, that could fit into the planets' many weird conditions, that could live on those planets and grow and build and carry out Man's plans.

Man could build those bodies. He had the technique to compound the flesh and bone and nerve, he had the skill to duplicate the mechanisms that produced the hormones, he had ferreted out the secrets of the enzymes and the animo acids and had at his fingertips all the other know-how to construct a body—any body, not just a human body. Biological engineering had become an exact science and biological blueprints could be drawn up to meet any conceivable set of planetary conditions. Man was all set to go on his project for colonization by humans in strange nonhuman forms.

Ready except for one thing: he could make everything but life.

Now the search for life went on, a top-priority, highly

classified research program carried out here and on other asteroids, with the teams of biochemists, metabolists, endocrinologists and others isolated on the tumbling slabs of rock, guarded by military patrols operating out in space, hemmed in by a million regulations and uncounted security checks.

They sought for life, working down in that puzzling gray area where nonlife was separated from life by a shadow zone and a strange unpredictability that was enough to drive one mad, working with the viruses and crystals which at one moment might be dead and the next moment half alive and no man as yet who could tell why this was or how it came about.

That there was a definite key to life, hidden somewhere against Man's searching, was a belief that never wavered in the higher echelons, but on the guarded asteroids there grew up a strange and perhaps unscientific belief that life was not a matter of fact to be pinned down by formula or equation, but rather a matter of spirit, with some shading to the supernatural—that it was not something that Man was ever meant to know, that to seek it was presumptuous and perhaps sacrilegious, that it was a tangled trap into which Man had lured himself by his madcap hunt for knowledge.

And I, thought Bayard Lodge, I am one of those who drive them on in this blind and crazy search for a thing that we were never meant to find, that for our peace of mind and for our security of soul we never should have sought. I reason with them when they whisper out their fears, I kid them out of it when they protest the inhumanity of the course we plan, I keep them working and I kill each of them just a little every day, kill the humanity of them inch by casual inch—and I wake up screaming because a *human* thing I met put its arm around me and asked me to have a drink with it.

He finished off his drink and poured another one and this time did not bother with the mix.

"Come on," he said to the monster of the dream. "Come on, friend. I'll have that drink with you."

He gulped it down and did not notice the harshness of the uncut liquor.

"Come on," he shouted at the monster. "Come on and have that drink with me!"

He stared around the room, waiting for the monster.

"What the hell," he said, "we're all human, aren't we?"

He poured another one and held it in a fist that suddenly was shaky.

"Us humans," he said, still talking to the monster, "have to stick together."

VII

All of them met in the lounge after breakfast, and Lodge, looking from face to face, saw the terror that lay behind the masks they kept in front of them, could sense the unvoiced shrieking that lay inside of them, held imprisoned by the iron control of breeding and of discipline.

Kent Forester carefully lit a cigarette and when he spoke his voice was conversationally casual, and Lodge, watching him as he talked, knew the price he paid to keep his voice casual.

"This is something," Forester said, "that we can't allow to keep on eating on us. We have to talk it out."

"You mean rationalize it?" asked Sifford.

Forester shook his head. "Talk it out, I said. This is once we can't kid ourselves."

"There were nine characters last night," said Craven.

"And a whale," said Forester.

"You mean one of . . ."

"I don't know. If one of us did, let's speak up and say so. There's not a one among us who can't appreciate a joke."

"A grisly joke," said Craven.

"But a joke," said Forester.

"I would like to think it was a joke," Maitland declared. "I'd feel a lot easier if I knew it was a joke."

"That's the point," said Forester. "That's what I'm getting at."

He paused a moment. "Anyone?" he asked.

No one said a word.

They waited.

"No one, Kent," said Lodge.

"Perhaps the joker doesn't want to reveal himself," said Forester. "I think all of us could understand that. Maybe we could hand out slips of paper."

"Hand them out," Sifford grumbled.

Forester took sheets of folded paper from his pocket, carefully tore the strips. He handed out the strips.

"If anyone played a joke," Lodge pleaded, "for God's sake let us know."

The slips came back. Some of them said "no," others said "no joke," one said "I didn't do it."

Forester wadded up the strips.

"Well, that lets that idea out," he said. "I must admit I didn't have much hope."

Craven lumbered to his feet. "There's one thing that all of us have been thinking," he said, "and it might as well be spoken. It's not a pleasant subject."

He paused and looked around him at the others, as if defying them to stop him.

"No one liked Henry too well," he said. "Don't deny it. He was a hard man to like. A hard man any way you look at him. I was closer to him than any of you. I've agreed to say a few words for him at the service this afternoon. I am glad to do it, for he was a good man despite his hardness. He had a tenacity of will, a stubbornness such as you seldom find even in a hard man. And he had moral scruples that none of us could guess. He would talk to me a little— really talk—and that's something that he never did with the rest of you.

"Henry was close to something. He was scared. He died.

"There was nothing wrong with him."

Craven looked at Dr. Lawrence.

"Was there, Susan?" he asked. "Was there anything wrong with him?"

"Not a thing," said Dr. Susan Lawrence. "He should not have died."

Craven turned to Lodge. "He talked with you recently."

"A day or two ago," said Lodge. "He seemed quite normal then."

"What did he talk about?"

"Oh, the usual thing. Minor matters."

"Minor matters?" Mocking.

"All right, then. If you want it that way. He talked

about not wanting to go on. He said our work was unholy. That's the word he used—unholy."

Lodge looked around the room. "That's one the rest of you have never thought to use. Unholy."

"He was more insistent than usual?"

"Well, no," said Lodge. "It was the first time he had ever talked to me about it. The only person engaged in the research here, I believe, who had not talked with me about it at one time or another."

"And you talked him into going back."

"We discussed it."

"You killed the man."

"Perhaps," said Lodge. "Perhaps I'm killing all of you. Perhaps you're killing yourselves and I myself. How am I to know?"

He said to Dr. Lawrence, "Sue, could a man die of a psychosomatic illness brought about by fear?"

"Clinically, no," said Susan Lawrence. "Practically, I'm afraid, the answer might be yes."

"He was trapped," said Craven.

"Mankind's trapped," snapped Lodge. "If you must point your finger, point it at all of us. Point it at the whole community of Man."

"I don't think," Forester interrupted, "that this is pertinent."

"It is," insisted Craven, "and I will tell you why. I'd be the last to admit the existence of a ghost—"

Alice Page came swiftly to her feet. "Stop it!" she cried. "Stop it! Stop it! Stop it!"

"Miss Page, please," said Craven.

"But you're saying . . ."

"I'm saying that if there ever was a situation where a departed spirit had a motive—and I might even say a right—to come back and haunt his place of death, this is it."

"Sit down, Craven," Lodge commanded, sharply.

Craven hesitated angrily, then sat down, grumbling to himself.

Lodge said, "If there's any point in continuing the discussion along these lines, I insist that it be done objectively."

Maitland said, "There's no point to it I can see. As scientists who are most intimately concerned with life we must recognize that death is an utter ending."

"That," objected Sifford, "is open to serious question and you know it."

Forester broke in, his voice cool. "Let's defer the matter for a moment. We can come back to it. There is another thing."

He hurried on. "Another thing we should know. Which of the characters was Henry's character?"

No one said a word.

"I don't mean," said Forester, "to try to find which belonged to whom. But by a process of elimination . . ."

"All right," said Sifford. "Hand out the slips again."

Forester brought out the paper in his pocket, tore more strips.

Craven protested. "Not just slips," he said. "I won't fall for a trick like that."

Forester looked up from the slips.

"Trick?"

"Of course," said Craven harshly. "Don't deny it. You've been trying to find out."

"I don't deny it," Forester told him. "I'd have been derelict in my duty if I hadn't tried."

Lodge said, "I wonder why we keep this secret thing so closely to ourselves. It might be all right under normal circumstances, but these aren't normal circumstances. I think it might be best if we made a clean breast of it. I, for one, am willing. I'll lead off if you only say the word."

He waited for the word.

There was no word.

They all stared back at him and there was nothing in their faces—no anger, no fear, nothing at all that a man could read.

Lodge shrugged the defeat from his shoulders.

He said to Craven, "All right then. What were you saying?"

"I was saying that if we wrote down the names of our characters it would be no better than standing up and shouting them aloud. Forester knows our handwriting. He could spot every slip."

Forester protested. "I hadn't thought of it. I ask you to believe I hadn't. But what Craven says is true."

"All right, then?" asked Lodge.

"Ballots," Craven said. "Fix up ballots with the characters' names upon them."

"Aren't you afraid we might be able to identify your X's?"

Craven looked levelly at Lodge. "Since you mention it, I might be."

Forester said, wearily, "We have a batch of dies down in the labs. Used for stamping specimens. I think there's an X among them."

"That would satisfy you?" Lodge asked Craven.

Craven nodded that it would.

Lodge heaved himself out of the chair.

"I'll get the stamp," he said. "You can fix the ballots while I'm after it."

Children, he thought. Just so many children. Suspicious and selfish and frightened, like cornered animals. Cornered between the converging walls of fear and guilt, trapped in the corner of their own insecurity.

He walked down the stairs to the laboratories, his heels ringing on the metal treads, with the sound of his walking echoing from the hidden corners of the fear and guilt.

If Henry hadn't died right now, he thought, it might have been all right. We might have muddled through.

But he knew that probably was wrong. For if it had not been Henry's death, it would have been something else. They were ready for it—more than ready for it. It would not have taken much at any time in the last few weeks to have lit the fuse.

He found the die and ink pad and tramped back upstairs again.

The ballots lay on the table and someone had found a shoe box and cut a slit out of its lid to make a ballot box.

"We'll all sit over on this side of the room," said Forester, "and we'll go up, one by one, and vote."

And if anyone saw the ridiculous side of speaking of what they were about to do as voting, he pointedly ignored it.

Lodge put the die and ink pad down on the table top and walked across the room to take his seat.

"Who wants to start off?" asked Forester.

No one said a word.

Even afraid of this, thought Lodge.

Then Maitland said he would.

They sat in utter silence as each walked forward to mark a ballot, to fold it and to drop it in the box. Each of them waited for the one to return before another walked to the table.

Finally it was done, and Forester went to the table, took up the box and shook it, turning it this way and that to change the order of the ballots, so that no one might guess by their position to whom they might belong.

"I'll need two monitors," he said.

His eyes looked them over. "Craven," he said. "Sue."

They stood up and went forward.

Forester opened the box. He took out a ballot, unfolded it and read it, passed it on to Dr. Lawrence, and she passed it on to Craven.

"The Defenseless Orphan."

"The Rustic Slicker."

"The Alien Monster."

"The Beautiful Bitch."

"The Sweet Young Thing."

Wrong on that one, Lodge told himself. But who else could it be? She had been the last one on. She had been the ninth.

Forester went on, unfolding the ballots and reading them.

"The Extra-Terrestrial Ally."

"The Proper Young Man."

Only two left now. Only two. The Out-At-Elbows Philosopher and the Mustached Villain.

I'll make a guess, Lodge said to himself. I'll make a bet. I'll bet on which one was Henry.

He was the Mustached Villain.

Forester unfolded the last ballot and read aloud the name.

"The Mustached Villain."

So I lose the bet, thought Lodge.

He heard the rippling hiss of indrawn breath from those around him, the swift, stark terror of what the balloting had meant.

For Henry's character had been the most self-assertive and dominant in last night's Play: the Philosopher.

VIII

The script in Henry's notebook was close and crabbed, with a curtness to it, much like the man himself. His symbols and his equations were a triumph of clarity, but the written words had a curious backward, petulant slant and the phrases that he used were laconic to the point of rudeness—although whom he was being rude to, unless it were himself, was left a matter of conjecture.

Maitland closed the book with a snap and shoved it away from him, out into the center of the table.

"So that was it," he said.

They sat in quietness, their faces pale and drawn, as if in bitter face they might have seen the ghost of Craven's hinting.

"That's the end of it," snapped Sifford. "I won't—"

"You won't what?" asked Lodge.

Sifford did not answer. He just sat there with his hands before him on the table, opening and closing them, making great tight fists of them, then straightening out his fingers, stretching them as if he meant by sheer power of will to bend them back farther than they were meant to go.

"Henry was crazy," said Susan Lawrence curtly. "A man would have to be to dream up that sort of evidence."

"As a medical person," Maitland said, "we could expect that reaction from you."

"I work with life," said Susan Lawrence. "I respect it and it is my job to preserve it as long as it can be kept within the body. I have a great compassion for the things possessing it."

"Meaning we haven't?"

"Meaning you have to live with it and come to know it for its power and greatness, for the fine thing that it is, before you can appreciate or understand its wondrous qualities."

"But, Susan—"

"And I know," she said, rushing on to head him off, "I know that it is more than decay and breakdown, more than the senility of matter. It is something greater than disease. To argue that life is the final step to which matter is reduced, the final degradation of the nobility of soil and ore and water is to argue that a static, unintelligent, purposeless existence is the norm of the universe."

"We're getting all tangled up semantically," suggested Forester. "As living things the terms we use have no comparative values with the terms that might be used for universal purpose, even if we knew those universal terms."

"Which we don't," said Helen Gray. "What you say would be true especially if what Henry had thought he had found was right."

"We'll check Henry's notes," Lodge told them grimly. "We'll follow him step by step. I think he's wrong, but on the chance he isn't, we can't pass up an angle."

Sifford bristled. "You mean even if he were right you would go ahead? That you would use even so humanly degrading a piece of evidence to achieve our purpose?"

"Of course I would," said Lodge. "If life is a disease and a senility, all right, then, it is disease and senility. As Kent and Helen pointed out, the terms are not comparative when used in a universal sense. What is poison for the universe is—well, is life for us. If Henry was right, his discovery is no more than the uncovering of a fact that has existed since time untold."

"You don't know what you're saying," Sifford said.

"But I do," Lodge told him bluntly. "You have grown neurotic. You and some of the others. Maybe I, myself. Maybe all of us. We are ruled by fear—you by the fear of your job, I by the fear that the job will not be done. We've been penned up, we've been beating out our brains against the stone walls of our conscience and a moral value suddenly furbished up and polished until it shines like the shield of Galahad. Back on the Earth you wouldn't give this thing a second thought. You'd gulp a little, maybe, then you'd swallow it, if it were proved true, and you'd go ahead to track down that principle of decay and of disease we happen to call life. The principle itself would be only one more factor for your consideration, one more tool to work with, another bit of knowledge. But here you claw at the wall and scream."

"Bayard!" shouted Forester. "Bayard, you can't—"

"I can," Lodge told him, "and I am. I'm sick of all their whimpering and baying. I'm tired of spoon-fed fanatics who drove themselves to their own fanaticism by their own synthetic fears. It takes men and women with knife-sharp minds to lick this thing we're after. It takes guts and intelligence."

Craven was white-lipped with fury. "We've worked," he shouted. "Even when everything within us, even when all our decency and intelligence and our religious instincts told us not to work, we worked. And don't say you kept us at it, you with your mealy words and your kidding and your back slapping. Don't say you laughed us into it."

Forester pounded the table with a fist. "Let's quit this arguing," he cried. "Let's get down to cases."

Craven settled back in his chair, face still white with anger. Sifford kept on making fists.

"Henry wrote a conclusion," said Forester. "Well, hardly a conclusion. Let's call it a suspicion. Now what do you want to do about it? Ignore it, run from it, test it for its proof?"

"I say, test it," Craven said. "It was Henry's work. Henry's gone and can't speak for his own beliefs. We owe at least that much to him."

"If it can be tested," Maitland qualified. "To me it sounds more like philosophy than science."

"Philosophy runs hand in hand with science," said Alice Page. "We can't simply brush it off because it sounds involved."

"I didn't say involved," Maitland objected. "What I meant was—oh, hell, let's go ahead and check it."

"Check it," Sifford said.

He swung around on Lodge. "And if it checks out, if it comes anywhere near to checking, if we can't utterly disprove it, I'm quitting. I'm serving notice now."

"That's your privilege, Sifford, any time you wish."

"It might be hard to prove anything one way or the other," said Helen Gray. "It might not be any easier to disprove than prove."

Lodge saw Sue Lawrence looking at him and there was grim laughter and something of grudging admiration and a touch of confused cynicism in her face, as if she might be saying to him, *Well, you've done it again. I didn't think you would—not this time, I didn't. But you did. Although you won't always do it. There'll come a time . . .*

"Want to bet?" he whispered at her.

She said, "Cyanide."

And although he laughed back at her, he knew that she was right—righter than she knew. For the time had already come and this was the end of Life Team No. 3.

They would go on, of course, stung by the challenge Henry Griffith had written in his notebook, still doggedly true to their training and their charge, but the heart was out of them, the fear and the prejudice too deeply ingrained within their souls, the confused tangle of their thinking too much a part of them.

If Henry Griffith had sought to sabotage the project, Lodge told himself, he had done it perfectly. In death he had done it far better than he could have alive.

He seemed to hear in the room the dry, acerbic chuckling of the man and he wondered at the imagined chuckle, for Henry had had no humor in him.

Although Henry had been the Out-At-Elbows Philosopher and it was hard to think of Henry as that sort of character—an old humbug who hid behind a polished manner and a golden tongue. For there was nothing of the humbug in Henry, either, and his manner was not polished nor did he have the golden gift of words. He slouched and he rarely talked, and when he did he growled.

A joker, Lodge thought—had he been, after all, a joker?

Could he have used the Philosopher to lampoon the rest of them, a character who derided them and they not knowing it?

He shook his head, arguing with himself.

If the Philosopher had kidded them, it had been gentle kidding, so gentle that none of them had known it was going on, so subtle that it had slid off them without notice.

But that wasn't the terrifying aspect of it—that Henry might have been quietly making fun of them. The terrible thing was that the Philosopher had been second on the stage. He had followed the Rustic Slicker and during the whole time had been much in evidence—munching on the turkey leg and waving it to emphasize the running fire of pompous talk that had never slacked. The Philosopher had been, in fact, the most prominent player in the entire Play.

And that meant that no one could have put him on the stage, for no one, in the first place, could have known so soon which of the nine was Henry's character, and no one, not having handled him before, could have put the Philosopher so realistically through his paces. And none of those who had sent on their characters early in the Play could have handled two characters convincingly for any length of time—especially when the Philosopher had talked all the blessed time.

And that would cancel out at least four of those sitting in the room.

Which could mean:

That there was a ghost.

Or that the machine itself retained a memory.

Or that the eight of them had suffered mass hallucination.

He considered that last alternative and it wilted in the middle. So did the other two. None of the three made sense. Not any of it made sense—none of it at all.

Take a team of trained men and women, trained objectively, trained to look for facts, conditioned to skepticism and impatience of anything outside the pale of fact: What did it take to wreck a team like that? Not simply the cabin fever of a lonely asteroid. Not simply the nagging of awakened conscience against well-established ethics. Not the atavistic, Transylvanian fear of ghosts.

There was some other factor. Another factor that had not been thought of yet—like the new approach that Maitland had talked about at dinner, saying they would have to take a new direction to uncover the secret that they sought. We're going at it wrong, Maitland had said. We'll have to find a new approach.

And Maitland had meant, without saying so, that in their research the old methods of ferreting out the facts were no longer valid, that the scientific mind had operated for so long in the one worn groove that it knew no other, that they must seek some fresh concept to arrive at the fact of life.

Had Henry, Lodge wondered, supplied that fresh approach? And in the supplying of it and in dying, wrecked the team as well?

Or was there another factor, as Maitland had said there must be a new approach—a factor that did not fit in with the conventional thinking or standard psychology?

The Play, he wondered. Was the Play a factor? Had the

Play, designed to keep the team intact and sane, somehow turned into a two-edged sword?

They were rising from the table now, ready to leave, ready to go to their rooms and to dress for dinner. And after dinner, there would be the Play again.

Habit, Lodge thought. Even with the whole thing gone to pot, they still conformed to habit.

They would dress for dinner; they would stage the Play. They would go back tomorrow morning to their work-rooms and they'd work again, but the work would be a futile work, for the dedicated purpose of their calling had been burned out of them by fear, by the conflict of their souls, by death, by ghosts.

Someone touched his elbow and he saw that Forester stood beside him.

"Well, Kent?"

"How do you feel?"

"Okay," said Lodge. Then he said, "You know, of course, it's over."

"We'll try again," said Forester.

Lodge shook his head. "Not me. You, maybe. You're a younger man than I. I'm burned out too."

IX

The Play started in where it had left off the night before, with the Sweet Young Thing coming on the stage and all the others there, with the Out-At-Elbows Philosopher rubbing his hands together smugly and saying, "Now this is a cozy situation. All of us are here."

Sweet Young Thing (*tripping lightly*): Why, Philosopher, I know that I am late, but what a thing to say. Of course we all are here. I was unavoidably detained.

Rustic Slicker (*speaking aside, with a rural leer*): By a Tom Collins and a slot machine.

Alien Monster (*sticking out its head from behind the tree*): Tsk hrstlgn vglater, tsk . . .

And there was something wrong, Lodge told himself.

There was a certain mechanical wrongness, something out of place, a horrifying alienness that sent a shiver through you even when you couldn't spot the alienness.

There was something wrong with the Philosopher, and the wrongness was not that he should not be there, but something else entirely. There was a wrongness about the Sweet Young Thing and the Proper Young Man and the Beautiful Bitch and all the others.

There was a great deal wrong with the Rustic Slicker, and he, Bayard Lodge, knew the Rustic Slicker as he knew no other man—knew the blood and guts and brains of him, knew his thoughts and dreams and his hidden yearnings, his clodhopperish conceit, his smart-aleck snicker, the burning inferiority complex that drove him to social exhibitionism.

He knew him as every member of the audience must know his own character, as something more than an imagined person, as someone more than another person, something more than friend. For the bond was strong—the bond of the created and creator.

And tonight the Rustic Slicker had drawn a little way apart, had cut the apron strings, had stood on his own with the first dawning of independence.

The Philosopher was saying: "It's quite natural that I should have commented on all of us being here. For one of us is dead . . ."

There was no gasp from the audience, no hiss of indrawn breath, no stir, but you could feel the tension snap tight like a whining violin string.

"We have been consciences," said the Mustached Villain. "Projected conscience playing out our parts . . ."

The Rustic Slicker said: "The consciences of mankind."

Lodge half rose out of his chair.

I didn't make him say that! I didn't want him to say that. I thought it, that was all. So help me God, I just thought it, that was all!

And now he knew what was wrong. At last, he knew the strangeness of the characters this night.

They weren't on the screen at all! They were on the stage, the little width of stage which ran before the screen!

They were no longer projected imaginations—they were flesh and blood. They were mental puppets come to sudden life.

He sat there, cold at the thought of it—cold and rigid in

the quickening knowledge that by the power of mind alone —by the power of mind and electronic mysteries, Man had created life.

A new approach, Maitland had said.

Oh, Lord! A new approach!

They had failed at their work and triumphed in their play, and there'd be no longer any need of life teams, grubbing down into that gray area where life and death were interchangeable. To make a human monster you'd sit before a screen and you'd dream him up, bone by bone, hair by hair, brains, innards, special abilities and all. There'd be monsters by the billions to plant on those other planets. And the monsters would be human, for they'd be dreamed by brother humans working from a blueprint.

In just a little while the characters would step down off the stage and would mingle with them. And their creators? What would their creators do? Go screaming, raving mad?

What would he say to the Rustic Slicker?

What *could* he say to the Rustic Slicker?

And, more to the point, what would the Rustic Slicker have to say to him?

He sat, unable to move, unable to say a word or cry out a warning, waiting for the moment when they would step down.

☼ *J. G. Ballard*

CHRONOPOLIS

His trial had been fixed for the next day. Exactly when, of course, neither he nor anyone else knew. Probably it would be during the afternoon, when the principles concerned—judge, jury and prosecutor—managed to converge on the same courtroom at the same time. With luck his defense attorney might also appear at the right moment, though the case was such an open and shut one that Newman hardly expected him to bother—besides, transport to and from the old penal complex was notoriously difficult, involved endless waiting in the grimy depot below the prison walls.

Newman had passed the time usefully. Luckily, his cell faced south and sunlight traversed it for most of the day. He divided its arc into ten equal segments, the effective daylight hours, marking the intervals with a wedge of mortar prised from the window ledge. Each segment he further subdivided into twelve smaller units.

Immediately he had a working timepiece, accurate to within virtually a minute (the final subdivision into fifths he made mentally). The sweep of white notches, curving down one wall, across the floor and metal bedstead, and up the other wall, would have been recognizable to anyone who stood with his back to the window, but no one ever did. Anyway, the guards were too stupid to understand, and the sun dial had given Newman a tremendous advantage over them. Most of the time, when he wasn't recalibrating the dial, he would press against the grill, keeping an eye on the orderly room.

"Brocken!" he would shout out at 7:15, as the shadow line hit the first interval. "Morning inspection! On your feet, man!" The sergeant would come stumbling out of his bunk in a sweat, cursing the other warders as the reveille bell split the air.

Later Newman sang out the other events on the daily roster: roll call, cell fatigues, breakfast, exercise and so on round to the evening roll just before dusk. Brocken regularly won the block merit for the best-run cell deck and he relied on Newman to program the day for him, anticipate the next item on the roster and warn him if anything went on for too long—in some of the blocks fatigues were usually over in three minutes while breakfast or exercise could go on for hours, none of the warders knowing when to stop, the prisoners insisting that they had only just begun.

Brocken never inquired how Newman organized everything so exactly; once or twice a week, when it rained or was overcast, Newman would be strangely silent and the resulting confusion reminded the sergeant forcefully of the merits of cooperation. Newman was kept in cell privileges and all the cigarettes he needed. It was a shame that a date for the trial had finally been named.

Newman, too, was sorry. Most of his research so far had been inconclusive. Primarily his problem was that, given a northward-facing cell for the bulk of his sentence, the task of estimating the time might become impossible. The inclination of the shadows in the exercise yards or across the towers and walls provided too blunt a reading. Calibration would have to be visual; an optical instrument would soon be discovered.

What he needed was an internal timepiece, an unconsciously operating psychic mechanism regulated, say, by his pulse or respiratory rhythms. He had tried to train his time sense, running an elaborate series of tests to estimate its minimum built-in error, and this had been disappointingly large. The chances of conditioning an accurate reflex seemed slim.

However, unless he could tell the exact time at any given moment, he knew he would go mad.

His obsession, which now faced him with a charge of murder, had revealed itself innocently enough.

As a child, like all children, he had noticed the occasional ancient clock tower, bearing the same white circle with its twelve intervals. In the seedier areas of the city the round characteristic dials often hung over cheap jewelry stores, rusting and derelict.

"Just signs," his mother explained. "They don't mean anything, like stars or rings."

Pointless embellishment, he had thought.

Once, in an old furniture shop, they had seen a clock with hands, upside down in a box full of fire irons and miscellaneous rubbish.

"Eleven and twelve," he had pointed out. "What does it mean?"

His mother had hurried him away, reminding herself never to visit that street again. Time Police were still supposed to be around, watching for any outbreak. "Nothing," she told him sharply. "It's all finished." To herself she added experimentally: Five and twelve. Five *to* twelve. Yes.

Time unfolded at its usual sluggish, half confused pace. They lived in a ramshackle house in one of the amorphous suburbs, a zone of endless afternoons. Sometimes he went to school, until he was ten spent most of his time with his mother queueing outside the closed food stores. In the evenings he would play with the neighborhood gang around the abandoned railway station, punting a homemade flat car along the overgrown tracks, or break into one of the unoccupied houses and set up a temporary command post.

He was in no hurry to grow up; the adult world was unsynchronized and ambitionless. After his mother died he spent long days in the attic, going through her trunks and old clothes, playing with the bric-a-brac of hats and beads, trying to recover something of her personality.

In the bottom compartment of her jewelry case he came across a small flat gold-cased object, equipped with a wrist strap. The dial had no hands but the twelve-numbered face intrigued him and he fastened it to his wrist.

His father choked over his soup when he saw it that evening.

"Conrad, my God! Where in heaven did you get that?"

"In Mamma's bead box. Can't I keep it?"

"No. Conrad, give it to me! Sorry, son." Thoughtfully: "Let's see, you're fourteen. Look, Conrad, I'll explain it all in a couple of years."

With the impetus provided by this new taboo there was no need to wait for his father's revelations. Full knowledge came soon. The older boys knew the whole story, but strangely enough it was disappointingly dull.

"Is that all?" he kept saying. "I don't get it. Why worry so much about clocks? We have calendars, don't we?"

Suspecting more, he scoured the streets, carefully inspecting every derelict clock for a clue to the real secret. Most of the faces had been mutilated, hands and numerals torn off, the circle of minute intervals stripped away, leaving a shadow of fading rust. Distributed apparently at random all over the city, above stores, banks and public buildings, their real purpose was hard to discover. Sure enough, they measured the progress of time through twelve arbitrary intervals, but this seemed barely adequate grounds for outlawing them. After all, a whole variety of timers were in general use: in kitchens, factories, hospitals, wherever a fixed period of time was needed. His father had one by his bed at night. Sealed into the standard small black box, and driven by miniature batteries, it emitted a high penetrating whistle shortly before breakfast the next morning, woke him if he overslept. A clock was no more than a calibrated timer, in many ways less useful, as it provided you with a steady stream of irrelevant information. What if it was half-past three, as the old reckoning put it, if you weren't planning to start or finish anything then?

Making his questions sound as naïve as possible, he conducted a long careful poll. Under fifty no one appeared to know anything at all about the historical background, and even the older people were beginning to forget. He also noticed that the less educated they were the more they were willing to talk, indicating that manual and lower-class workers had played no part in the revolution and consequently had no guilt-charged memories to repress. Old Mr. Crichton, the plumber who lived in the basement apartment, reminisced without any prompting, but nothing he said threw any light on the problem.

"Sure, there were thousands of clocks then, millions of them, everybody had one. Watches we called them, strapped to the wrist, you had to screw them up every day."

"But what did you *do* with them, Mr. Crichton?" Conrad pressed.

"Well, you just—looked at them, and you knew what time it was. One o'clock, or two or half past seven—that was when I'd go off to work."

"But you go off to work now when you've had breakfast. And if you're late the timer rings."

Crichton shook his head. "I can't explain it to you, lad. You ask your father."

But Mr. Newman was hardly more helpful. The explanation promised for Conrad's sixteenth birthday never materialized. When his questions persisted Mr. Newman, tired of sidestepping, shut him up with an abrupt: "Just stop thinking about it, do you understand? You'll get yourself and the rest of us into a lot of trouble."

Stacey, the young English teacher, had a wry sense of humor, liked to shock the boys by taking up unorthodox positions on marriage or economics. Conrad wrote an essay describing an imaginary society completely preoccupied with elaborate rituals revolving around a minute-by-minute observance of the passage of time.

Stacey refused to play, however, gave him a noncommittal beta plus, after class quietly asked Conrad what had prompted the fantasy. At first Conrad tried to back away, then finally came out with the question that contained the central riddle.

"Why is it against the law to have a clock?"

Stacey tossed a piece of chalk from one hand to the other.

"Is it against the law?"

Conrad nodded. "There's an old notice in the police station offering a bounty of one hundred pounds for every clock or wrist watch brought in. I saw it yesterday. The sergeant said it was still in force."

Stacey raised his eyebrows mockingly. "You'll make a million. Thinking of going into business?"

Conrad ignored this. "It's against the law to have a gun because you might shoot someone. But how can you hurt anybody with a clock?"

"Isn't it obvious? You can time him, know exactly how long it takes him to do something."

"Well?"

"Then you can make him do it faster."

At seventeen, on a sudden impulse, he built his first clock. Already his preoccupation with time was giving him a marked lead over his classmates. One or two were more intelligent, others more conscientious, but Conrad's ability to organize his leisure and homework periods allowed him to make the most of his talents. When the others were lounging around the railway yard on their way home Conrad had already completed half his prep, allocating his time according to its various demands.

As soon as he finished he would go up to the attic playroom, now his workshop. Here, in the old wardrobes and trunks, he did his first experimental constructions: calibrated candles, crude sun dials, sand glasses, an elaborate clockwork contraption developing about half a horse power that drove its hands progressively faster and faster in an unintentional parody of Conrad's obsession.

His first serious clock was water-powered, a slowly leaking tank holding a wooden float that drove the hands as it sank downward. Simple but accurate, it satisfied Conrad for several months while he carried out his ever-widening search for a real clock mechanism. He soon discovered that although there were innumerable table clocks, gold pocket watches and timepieces of every variety rusting in junk shops and in the back drawers of most homes, none of them contained their mechanisms. These, together with the hands, and sometimes the digits, had always been removed. His own attempts to build an escapement that would regulate the motion of the ordinary clockwork motor met with no success; everything he had heard about clock movements confirmed that they were precision instruments of exact design and construction. To satisfy his secret ambition—a portable timepiece, if possible an actual wrist watch—he would have to find one, somewhere, in working order.

Finally, from an unexpected source, a watch came to him. One afternoon in a cinema an elderly man sitting next to Conrad had a sudden heart attack. Conrad and two members of the audience carried him out to the manager's office. Holding one of his arms, Conrad noticed in the dim aisle light a glint of metal inside the sleeve. Quickly he felt the wrist with his fingers, identified the unmistakable lens-shaped disc of a wrist watch.

As he carried it home its tick seemed as loud as a death knell. He clamped his hand around it, expecting everyone in the street to point accusingly at him, the Time Police to swoop down and seize him.

In the attic he took it out and examined it breathlessly, smothering it in a cushion whenever he heard his father shift about in the bedroom below. Later he realized that its noise was almost inaudible. The watch was of the same pattern as his mother's, though with a yellow and not a red face. The gold case was scratched and peeling, but the movement seemed to be in perfect condition. He pried off the rear plate, watched the frenzied flickering world of miniature cogs and wheels for hours, spellbound. Frightened of breaking the main spring, he kept the watch only half wound, packed away carefully in cotton wool.

In taking the watch from its owner he had not, in fact, been motivated by theft; his first impulse had been to hide the watch before the doctor discovered it, feeling for the man's pulse. But once the watch was in his possession he abandoned any thought of tracing the owner and returning it.

That others were still wearing watches hardly surprised him. The water clock had demonstrated that a calibrated timepiece added another dimension to life, organized its energies, gave the countless activities of everyday existence a yardstick of significance. Conrad spent hours in the attic gazing at the small yellow dial, watching its minute hand revolve slowly, its hour hand press on imperceptibly, a compass charting his passage through the future. Without it he felt rudderless, adrift in a gray purposeless limbo of timeless events. His father began to seem idle and stupid, sitting around vacantly with no idea when anything was going to happen.

Soon he was wearing the watch all day. He stitched together a slim cotton sleeve, fitted with a narrow flap below which he could see the face. He timed everything—the length of classes, football games, meal breaks, the hours of daylight and darkness, sleep and waking. He amused himself endlessly by baffling his friends with demonstrations of this private sixth sense, anticipating the frequency of their heart beats, the hourly newscasts on the radio, boiling a series of identically consistent eggs without the aid of a timer.

Then he gave himself away.

Stacey, shrewder than any of the others, discovered that he was wearing a watch. Conrad had noticed that Stacey's English classes lasted exactly forty-five minutes, let himself slide into the habit of tidying his desk a minute before Stacey's timer piped up. Once or twice he noticed Stacey looking at him curiously, but he could not resist the temptation to impress Stacey by always being the first one to make for the door.

One day he had stacked his books and clipped away his pen when Stacey pointedly asked him to read out a précis he had done. Conrad knew the timer would pip out in less than ten seconds, and decided to sit tight and wait for the usual stampede to save him the trouble.

Stacey stepped down from the dais, waiting patiently. One or two boys turned around and frowned at Conrad, who was counting away the closing seconds.

Then, amazed, he realized that the timer had failed to sound! Panicking, he first thought his watch had broken, just restrained himself in time from looking at it.

"In a hurry, Newman?" Stacey asked dryly. He sauntered down the aisle to Conrad, smiling sardonically. Baffled, and face reddening with embarrassment, Conrad fumbled open his exercise book, read out the précis. A few minutes later, without waiting for the timer, Stacey dismissed the class.

"Newman," he called out. "Here a moment."

He rummaged behind the rostrum as Conrad approached. "What happened then?" he asked. "Forget to wind up your watch this morning?"

Conrad said nothing. Stacey took out the timer, switched off the silencer and listened to the pip that buzzed out.

"Where did you get it from? Your parents? Don't worry, the Time Police were disbanded years ago."

Conrad examined Stacey's face carefully. "It was my mother's," he lied. "I found it among her things." Stacey held out his hand and Conrad nervously unstrapped the watch and handed it to him.

Stacey slipped it half out of its sleeve, glanced briefly at the yellow face. "Your mother, you say? Hmh."

"Are you going to report me?" Conrad asked.

"What, and waste some overworked psychiatrist's time even further?"

"Isn't it breaking the law to wear a watch?"

"Well, you're not exactly the greatest living menace to public security." Stacey started for the door, gesturing Conrad with him. He handed the watch back. "Cancel whatever you're doing on Saturday afternoon. You and I are taking a trip."

"Where?" Conrad asked.

"Back into the past," Stacey said lightly. "To Chronopolis, the Time City."

Stacey had hired a car, a huge battered mastodon of chromium and fins. He waved jauntily to Conrad as he picked him up outside the public library.

"Climb into the turret," he called out. He pointed to the bulging briefcase Conrad slung onto the seat between them. "Have you had a look at those yet?"

Conrad nodded. As they moved off around the deserted square he opened the briefcase and pulled out a thick bundle of road maps. "I've just worked out that the city covers over 500 square miles. I'd never realized it was so big. Where is everybody?"

Stacey laughed. They crossed the main street, cut down into a long tree-lined avenue of semi-detached houses. Half of them were empty, windows wrecked and roofs sagging. Even the inhabited houses had a makeshift appearance, crude water towers on homemade scaffolding lashed to their chimneys, piles of logs dumped in overgrown front gardens.

"Thirty million people once lived in this city," Stacey remarked. "Now the population is little more than two, and still declining. Those of us left hang on in what were once the distal suburbs, so that the city today is effectively an enormous ring, fifty miles in width, encircling a vast dead center forty or fifty miles in diameter."

They wove in and out of various back roads, past a small factory still running although work was supposed to end at noon, finally picked up a long straight boulevard that carried them steadily westwards. Conrad traced their progress across successive maps. They were nearing the edge of the annulus Stacey had described. On the map it was overprinted in green so that the central interior appeared a flat uncharted gray, a massive terra incognita.

They passed the last of the small shopping thoroughfares he remembered, a frontier post of mean terraced houses, dismal streets spanned by massive steel viaducts. Stacey pointed up at one as they drove below it. "Part of the elaborate railway system that once existed, an enormous network of stations and junctions that carried fifteen million people into a dozen terminals every day."

For half an hour they drove on, Conrad hunched against the window, Stacey watching him in the driving mirror. Gradually, the landscape began to change. The houses were taller, with colored roofs, the sidewalks were railed off and fitted with pedestrian lights and turnstiles. They had entered the inner suburbs, completely deserted streets with multi-level supermarkets, towering cinemas and department stores.

Chin in one hand, Conrad stared out silently. Lacking any means of transport he had never ventured into the uninhabited interior of the city, like the other children always headed in the opposite direction for the open country. Here the streets had died twenty or thirty years earlier; plate glass shopfronts had slipped and smashed into the roadway, old neon signs, window frames and overhead wires hung down from every cornice, trailing a ragged webwork of disintegrating metal across the pavements. Stacey drove slowly, avoiding the occasional bus or truck abandoned in the middle of the road, its tires peeling off their rims.

Conrad craned up at the empty windows, into the narrow alleys and sidestreets, but nowhere felt any sensation of fear or anticipation. These streets were merely derelict, as unhaunted as a half-empty dustbin.

One suburban center gave way to another, to long intervening stretches of congested ribbon developments. Mile by mile, the architecture altered its character; buildings were larger, ten or fifteen-story blocks, clad in facing materials of green and blue tiles, glass or copper sheathing.

They were moving forward in time rather than, as Conrad had expected, back into the past of a fossil city.

Stacey worked the car through a nexus of side streets towards a six-lane expressway that rose on tall concrete buttresses above the rooftops. They found a side road that circled up to it, leveled out and then picked up speed sharply, spinning along one of the clear center lanes.

Conrad craned forward. In the distance, two or three miles away, the tall rectilinear outlines of enormous apartment blocks reared up thirty or forty stories high, hundreds of them lined shoulder to shoulder in apparently endless ranks, like giant dominoes.

"We're entering the central dormitories here," Stacey told him. On either side buildings overtopped the motorway, the congestion mounting so that some of them had been built right up against the concrete palisades.

In a few minutes they passed between the first of the apartment batteries, the thousands of identical living units with their slanting balconies shearing up into the sky, the glass in-falls of the aluminum curtain walling speckling in the sunlight. The smaller houses and shops of the outer suburbs had vanished. There was no room on the ground level. In the narrow intervals between the blocks there were small concrete gardens, shopping complexes, ramps banking down into huge underground car parks.

And on all sides there were the clocks. Conrad noticed them immediately, at every street corner, over every archway, three-quarters of the way up the sides of buildings, covering every conceivable angle of approach. Most of them were too high off the ground to be reached by anything less than a fireman's ladder and still retained their hands. All registered the same time: 12:01.

Conrad looked at his wrist watch, noted that it was just 2:45 P.M.

"They were driven by a master clock," Stacey told him. "When that stopped they all ceased at the same moment. One minute after midnight, thirty-seven years ago."

The afternoon had darkened, as the high cliffs cut off the sunlight, the sky a succession of narrow vertical intervals opening and closing around them. Down on the canyon floor it was dismal and oppressive, a wilderness of concrete and frosted glass. The expressway divided and pressed on westward. After a few more miles the apartment blocks gave way to the first office buildings in the central zone. These were even taller, sixty or seventy stories high, linked by spiraling ramps and causeways. The expressway was fifty feet off the ground yet the first floors of the office blocks were level with it, mounted on massive stilts that straddled the glass-enclosed entrance bays of lifts and escalators. The streets were wide but featureless. The sidewalks of parallel roadways merged below the buildings, forming a continuous concrete apron. Here and there were the remains of cigarette kiosks, rusting stairways up to restaurants and arcades built on platforms thirty feet in the air.

Conrad, however, was looking only at the clocks. Never had he visualized so many, in places so dense that they obscured each other. Their faces were multi-colored: red, blue, yellow, green. Most of them carried four or five hands. Although the master hands had stopped at a minute past twelve, the subsidiary hands had halted at varying positions, apparently dictated by their color.

"What were the extra hands for?" he asked Stacey. "And the different colors?"

"Time zones. Depending on your professional category and the consumer-shifts allowed. Hold on, though, we're almost there."

They left the expressway and swung off down a ramp that fed them into the northeast corner of a wide open plaza, eight hundred yards long and half as wide, down the center of which had once been laid a continuous strip of lawn, now rank and overgrown. The plaza was empty, a sudden block of free space bounded by tall glass-faced cliffs that seemed to carry the sky.

Stacey parked, and he and Conrad climbed out and stretched themselves. Together they strolled across the wide pavement toward the strip of waist-high vegetation. Looking down the vistas receding from the plaza Conrad grasped fully for the first time the vast perspectives of the city, the massive geometric jungle of buildings.

Stacey put one foot up on the balustrade running around the lawn bed, pointed to the far end of the plaza, where Conrad saw a low-lying huddle of buildings of unusual architectural style, nineteenth-century perpendicular, stained by the atmosphere and badly holed by a number of explosions. Again, however, his attention was held by the clock face built into a tall concrete tower just behind the older buildings. This was the largest clock dial he had ever seen, at least a hundred feet across, huge black hands halted at a minute past twelve. The dial was white, the first they had seen, but on wide semicircular shoulders built out off the tower below the main face were a dozen smaller faces, no more than twenty feet in diameter, running the full spectrum of colors. Each had five hands, the inferior three halted at random.

"Fifty years ago," Stacey explained, gesturing at the ruins below the tower, "that collection of ancient buildings was one of the world's greatest legislative assemblies." He gazed at it quietly for a few moments, then turned to Conrad. "Enjoy the ride?"

Conrad nodded fervently. "It's impressive, all right. The people who lived here must have been giants. What's really remarkable is that it looks as if they left only yesterday. Why don't we go back?"

"Well, apart from the fact that there aren't enough of us now, even if there were we couldn't control it. In its heyday this city was a fantastically complex social organism. The communications problems are difficult to imagine merely by looking at these blank façades. It's a tragedy of this city that there appeared to be only one way to solve them."

"Did they solve them?"

"Oh, yes, certainly. But they left themselves out of the equation. Think of the problems, though. Transporting fifteen million office workers to and from the center every day, routing in an endless stream of cars, buses, trains, helicopters, linking every office, almost every desk, with a videophone, every apartment with television, radio, power, water, feeding and entertaining this enormous number of people, guarding them with ancillary services, police, fire squads, medical units—it all hinged on one factor."

Stacey threw a fist out at the great tower clock. "Time! Only by synchronizing every activity, every footstep forward or backward, every meal, bus halt and telephone call, could the organism support itself. Like the cells in

your body, which proliferate into mortal cancers if allowed
to grow in freedom, every individual here had to subserve
the overriding needs of the city or fatal bottlenecks threw
it into total chaos. You and I can turn on the tap any hour
of the day or night, because we have our own private
water cisterns, but what would happen here if everybody
washed the breakfast dishes within the same ten minutes?"

They began to walk slowly down the plaza toward the
clock tower. "Fifty years ago, when the population was only
ten million, they could just provide for a potential peak
capacity, but even then a strike in one essential service
paralyzed most of the others; it took workers two or three
hours to reach their offices, as long again to queue for
lunch and get home. As the population climbed the first
serious attempts were made to stagger hours; workers in
certain areas started the day an hour earlier or later than
those in others. Their railway passes and car number plates
were colored accordingly, and if they tried to travel outside the permitted periods they were turned back. Soon
the practice spread; you could only switch on your washing machine at a given hour, post a letter or take a bath
at a specific period."

"Sounds feasible," Conrad commented, his interest mounting. "But how did they enforce all this?"

"By a system of colored passes, colored money, an elaborate set of schedules published every day like the TV or
radio programs. And, of course, by all the thousands of
clocks you can see around you here. The subsidiary hands
marked out the number of minutes remaining in any activity period for people in the clock's color category."

Stacey stopped, pointed to a blue-faced clock mounted
on one of the buildings overlooking the plaza. "Let's say,
for example, that a lower-grade executive leaving his office
at the allotted time, twelve o'clock, wants to have lunch,
change a library book, buy some aspirin, and telephone
his wife. Like all executives, his identity zone is blue. He
takes out his schedule for the week, or looks down the
blue-time columns in the newspaper, and notes that his
lunch period for that day is twelve-fifteen to twelve-thirty.
He has fifteen minutes to kill. Right, he then checks the
library. Time code for today is given as three, that's the third

hand on the clock. He looks at the nearest blue clock, the third hand says thirty-seven minutes past—he has twenty-three minutes, ample time, to reach the library. He starts down the street, but finds at the first intersection that the pedestrian lights are only shining red and green and he can't get across. The area's been temporarily zoned off for lower-grade women office workers—reds, and manuals—greens."

"What would happen if he ignored the lights?" Conrad asked.

"Nothing immediately, but all blue clocks in the zoned area would have returned to zero, and no shops or the library would serve him, unless he happened to have red or green currency and a forged set of library tickets. Anyway, the penalties were too high to make the risk worthwhile, and the whole system was evolved for his convenience, no one else's. So, unable to reach the library, he decides on the chemist. The time code for the chemist is five, the fifth, smallest hand. It reads fifty-four minutes past: he has six minutes to find a chemist and make his purchase. This done, he still has five minutes before lunch, decides to phone his wife. Checking the phone code he sees that no period has been provided for private calls that day—or the next. He'll just have to wait until he sees her that evening."

"What if he did phone?"

"He wouldn't be able to get his money in the coin box, and even then, his wife, assuming she is a secretary, would be in a red time zone and no longer in her office for that day—hence the prohibition on phone calls. It all meshed perfectly. Your time program told you when you could switch on your TV set and when to switch off. All electric appliances were fused, and if you strayed outside the programmed periods you'd have a hefty fine and repair bill to meet. The viewer's economic status obviously determined the choice of program, and vice versa, so there was no question of coercion. Each day's program listed your permitted activities: you could go to the hairdresser's, cinema, bank, cocktail bar, at stated times, and if you went then you were sure of being served quickly and efficiently."

They had almost reached the far end of the plaza. Facing them on its tower was the enormous clock face, dominating its constellation of twelve motionless attendants.

"There were a dozen socio-economic categories: blue for executives, gold for professional classes, yellow for military and government officials—incidentally, it's odd your parents ever got hold of that wrist watch, none of your family ever worked for the government—green for manual workers and so on. But, naturally subtle subdivisions were possible. The lower-grade executive I mentioned left his office at twelve, but a senior executive, with exactly the same time codes, would leave at eleven-forty-five, have an extra fifteen minutes, would find the streets clear before the lunch hour rush of clerical workers."

Stacey pointed up at the tower. "This was the Big Clock, the master from which all others were regulated. Central Time Control, a sort of Ministry of Time, gradually took over the old parliamentary buildings as their legislative functions diminished. The programmers were, effectively, the city's absolute rulers."

As Stacy continued Conrad gazed up at the battery of timepieces, poised helplessly at 12:01. Somehow Time itself seemed to have been suspended, around him the great office buildings hung in a neutral interval between yesterday and tomorrow. If one could only start the master clock the entire city would probably slide into gear and come to life, in an instant be repeopled with its dynamic jostling millions.

They began to walk back toward the car. Conrad looked over his shoulder at the clock face, its gigantic arms upright on the silent hour.

"Why did it stop?" he asked.

Stacey looked at him curiously. "Haven't I made it fairly plain?"

"What do you mean?" Conrad pulled his eyes off the scores of clocks lining the plaza, frowned at Stacey.

"Can you imagine what life was like for all but a few of the thirty million people here?"

Conrad shrugged. Blue and yellow clocks, he noticed, outnumbered all others; obviously the major governmental agencies had operated from the plaza area. "Highly organized but better than the sort of life we lead," he replied finally, more interested in the sights around him. "I'd rather have the telephone for one hour a day than not at all. Scarcities are always rationed, aren't they?"

"But this was a way of life in which everything was scarce. Don't you think there's a point beyond which human dignity is surrendered?"

Conrad snorted. "There seems to be plenty of dignity here. Look at these buildings, they'll stand for a thousand years. Try comparing them with my father. Anyway, think of the beauty of the system, engineered as precisely as a watch."

"That's all it was," Stacey commented dourly. "The old metaphor of the cog in the wheel was never more true than here. The full sum of your existence was printed for you in the newspaper columns, mailed to you once a month from the Ministry of Time."

Conrad was looking off in some other direction and Stacey pressed on in a slightly louder voice. "Eventually, of course, revolt came. It's interesting that in any industrial society there is usually one social revolution each century, and that successive revolutions receive their impetus from progressively higher social levels. In the eighteenth century it was the urban proletariat, in the nineteenth the artisan classes, in this revolt the white-collar office worker, living in his tiny so-called modern flat, supporting through credit pyramids an economic system that denied him all freedom of will or personality, chained him to a thousand clocks . . ." He broke off. "What's the matter?"

Conrad was staring down one of the side streets. He hesitated, then asked in a casual voice: "How were these clocks driven? Electrically?"

"Most of them. A few mechanically. Why?"

"I just wondered . . . how they kept them all going." He dawdled at Stacey's heels, checking the time from his wrist watch and glancing to his left. There were twenty or thirty clocks hanging from the buildings along the side street, indistinguishable from those he had seen all afternoon.

Except for the fact that one of them was working!

It was mounted in the center of a black glass portico over an entrance way fifty yards down the right-hand side, about eighteen inches in diameter, with a faded blue face. Unlike the others its hands registered 3:15, the correct time. Conrad had nearly mentioned this apparent coincidence to Stacey when he had suddenly seen the minute hand move on an interval. Without doubt someone had restarted the clock; even if it had been running off an inexhaustible battery, after thirty-seven years it could never have displayed such accuracy.

He hung behind Stacey, who was saying: "Every revolution has its symbol of oppression . . ."

The clock was almost out of view. Conrad was about to bend down and tie his shoelace when he saw the minute hand jerk downward, tilt slightly from the horizontal.

He followed Stacey toward the car, no longer bothering to listen to him. Ten yards from it he turned and broke away, ran swiftly across the roadway toward the nearest building.

"Newman!" he heard Stacey shout. "Come back!" He reached the pavement, ran between great concrete pillars carrying the building. He paused for a moment behind an elevator shaft, saw Stacey climbing hurriedly into the car. The engine coughed and roared out, and Conrad sprinted on below the building into a rear alley that led back to the side street. Behind him he heard the car accelerating, a door slam as it picked up speed.

When he entered the side street the car came swinging off the plaza thirty yards behind him. Stacey swerved off the roadway, bumped up onto the pavement and gunned the car toward Conrad, throwing on the brakes in savage lurches, blasting the horn in an attempt to frighten him. Conrad sidestepped out of its way, almost falling over the bonnet, hurled himself up a narrow stairway leading to the first floor and raced up the steps to a short landing that ended in tall glass doors. Through them he could see a wide balcony that ringed the building. A fire escape crisscrossed upward to the roof, giving way on the fifth floor to a cafeteria that spanned the street to the office building opposite.

Below he heard Stacey's feet running across the pavement. The glass doors were locked. He pulled a fire extinguisher from its bracket, tossed the heavy cylinder against the center of the plate. The glass slipped and crashed to the tiled floor in a sudden cascade, splashing down the steps. Conrad stepped through onto the balcony, began to climb the stairway. He had reached the third floor when he saw Stacey below, craning upward. Hand over hand, Conrad pulled himself up the next two flights, swung over a bolted metal turnstile into the open court of the cafeteria. Tables and chairs lay about on their sides, mixed up with the splintered remains of desks thrown down from the upper floors.

The doors into the covered restaurant were open, a large pool of water lying across the floor. Conrad splashed through it, went over to a window and peered down past an old plastic plant into the street. Stacey seemed to have given up. Conrad crossed the rear of the restaurant, straddled the counter and climbed through a window onto the open terrace running across the street. Beyond the rail he could see into the plaza, the double line of tire marks curving into the street below.

He had almost crossed to the opposite balcony when a shot roared out into the air. There was a sharp tinkle of falling glass and the sound of the explosion boomed away among the empty canyons.

For a few seconds he panicked. He flinched back from the exposed rail, his eardrums numbed, looking up at the great rectangular masses towering above him on either side, the endless tiers of windows like the faceted eyes of gigantic insects. So Stacey had been armed, almost certainly was a member of the Time Police!

On his hands and knees Conrad scurried along the terrace, slid through the turnstiles and headed for a half-open window on the balcony.

Climbing through, he quickly lost himself in the building.

He finally took up a position in a corner office on the sixth floor, the cafeteria just below him to the right, the stairway up which he had escaped directly opposite.

All afternoon Stacey drove up and down the adjacent streets, sometimes free-wheeling silently with the engine off, at others blazing through at speed. Twice he fired into the air, stopping the car afterward to call out, his words lost among the echoes rolling from one street to the next. Often he drove along the pavements, swerved about below the buildings as if he expected to flush Conrad from behind one of the banks of escalators.

Finally he appeared to drive off for good, and Conrad turned his attention to the clock in the portico. It had moved on to 6:45, almost exactly the time given by his own watch. Conrad reset this to what he assumed was the correct time, then sat back and waited for whoever had wound it to appear. Around him the thirty or forty other clocks he could see remained stationary at 12:01.

For five minutes he left his vigil, scooped some water off the pool in the cafeteria, suppressed his hunger and shortly after midnight fell asleep in a corner behind the desk.

He woke the next morning to bright sunlight flooding into the office. Standing up, he dusted his clothes, turned around to find a small gray-haired man in a patched tweed suit surveying him with sharp eyes. Slung in the crook of his arm was a large black-barreled weapon, its hammers menacingly cocked.

The man put down a steel ruler he had evidently tapped against a cabinet, waited for Conrad to collect himself.

"What are you doing here?" he asked in a testy voice. Conrad noticed his pockets were bulging with angular objects that weighed down the sides of his jacket.

"I . . . er . . ." Conrad searched for something to say. Something about the old man convinced him that this was the clockwinder. Suddenly he decided he had nothing to lose by being frank, and blurted out: "I saw the clock working down there on the left. I want to help wind them all up again."

The old man watched him shrewdly. He had an alert birdlike face, twin folds under his chin like a cockerel's.

"How do you propose to do that?" he asked.

Stuck by this one, Conrad said lamely: "I'd find a key somewhere."

The old man frowned. "One key? That wouldn't do much good." He seemed to be relaxing slowly, shook his pockets with a dull chink.

For a few moments neither of them said anything. Then Conrad had an inspiration, bared his wrist. "I have a watch," he said. "It's seven-forty-five."

"Let me see." The old man stepped forward, briskly took Conrad's wrist, examined the yellow dial. "Movado

Supermatic," he said to himself. "CYC issue." He stepped back, lowering the shotgun, seemed to be summing Conrad up. "Good," he remarked at last. "Let's see. You probably need some breakfast."

They made their way out of the building, began to walk quickly down the street.

"People sometimes come here," the old man said. "Sightseers and police. I watched your escape yesterday, you were lucky not to be killed." They swerved left and right across the empty streets, the old man darting between the stairways and buttresses. As he walked he held his hands stiffly to his sides, preventing his pockets from swinging. Glancing into them, Conrad saw that they were full of keys, large and rusty, of every design and combination.

"I presume that was your father's watch," the old man remarked.

"Grandfather's," Conrad corrected. He remembered Stacey's lecture, and added: "He was killed in the plaza."

The old man frowned sympathetically, for a moment held Conrad's arm.

They stopped below a building, indistinguishable from the others nearby, at one time a bank. The old man looked carefully around him, eyeing the high cliff walls on all sides, then led the way up a stationary escalator

His quarters were on the second floor, beyond a maze of steel grills and strongdoors, a stove and hammock slung in the center of a large workshop. Lying about on thirty or forty desks in what had once been a typing pool, was an enormous collection of clocks, all being simultaneously repaired. Tall cabinets surrounded them, loaded with thousands of spare parts in neatly labeled correspondence trays —escapements, ratchets, cogwheels, barely recognizable through the rust.

The old man led Conrad over to a wall chart, pointed to the total listed against a column of dates. "Look at this. There are now two hundred seventy-eight running continuously. Believe me, I'm glad you've come. It takes me half my time to keep them wound."

He made breakfast for Conrad, told him something about himself. His name was Marshall. Once he had worked in Central Time Control as a programmer, had survived the revolt and the Time Police, ten years later returned to the city. At the beginning of each month he cycled out to one of the perimeter towns to cash his pension and collect supplies. The rest of the time he spent winding the steadily increasing number of functioning clocks and searching for others he could dismantle and repair.

"All these years in the rain hasn't done them any good," he explained, "and there's nothing I can do with the electrical ones."

Conrad wandered off among the desks, gingerly feeling the dismembered timepieces that lay around like the nerve cells of some vast unimaginable robot. He felt exhilarated and yet at the same time curiously calm, like a man who has staked his whole life on the turn of a wheel and is waiting for it to spin.

"How can you make sure that they all tell the same time?" he asked Marshall, wondering why the question seemed so important.

Marshall gestured irritably. "I can't, but what does it matter? There is no such thing as a perfectly accurate clock. Although you never know when, it *is* absolutely accurate twice a day."

Conrad went over to the window, pointed to the great clock visible in an interval between the rooftops. "If only we could start that, and run all the others off it."

"Impossible. The entire mechanism was dynamited. Only the chimer is intact. Anyway, the wiring of the electrically driven clocks perished years ago. It would take an army of engineers to recondition them."

Conrad nodded, looked at the scoreboard again. He noticed that Marshall appeared to have lost his way through the years—the completion dates he listed were seven and a half years out. Idly, Conrad reflected on the significance of this irony, but decided not to mention it to Marshall.

For three months Conrad lived with the old man, following him on foot as he cycled about on his rounds, carrying the ladder and the satchel full of keys with which Marshall wound up the clocks, helping him to dismantle recoverable ones and carry them back to the workshop. All day, and often through half the night, they worked together,

repairing the movements, restarting the clocks and returning them to their original positions.

All the while, however, Conrad's mind was fixed upon
the great clock in its tower dominating the plaza. Once a
day he managed to sneak off and make his way into the
ruined Time buildings. As Marshall had said, neither the
clock nor its twelve satellites would ever run again. The
movement house looked like the engine room of a sunken
ship, a rusting tangle of rotors and drive wheels exploded
into contorted shapes. Every week he would climb the
long stairway up to the topmost platform two hundred
feet above, look out through the bell tower at the flat
roofs of the office blocks stretching away to the horizon.
Once he kicked one of the treble trips playfully, sent a
dull chime out across the plaza.

The sound drove strange echoes into his mind.

Slowly he began to repair the chimer mechanism, rewir-
ing the hammers and the pulley systems, trailing fresh wire
up the great height of the tower, dismantling the winches
in the movement room below and renovating their clutches.

He and Marshall never discussed their self-appointed
tasks. Like animals obeying an instinct they worked tire-
lessly, barely aware of their own motives. When Conrad
told him one day that he intended to leave and continue
the work in another sector of the city, Marshall agreed
immediately, gave Conrad as many tools as he could spare
and bade him good-bye.

Six months later, almost to the day, the sounds of the
great clock chimed out across the rooftops of the city,
marking the hours, the half-hours and the quarter-hours,
steadily tolling the progress of the day. Thirty miles away,
in the towns forming the perimeter of the city, people
stopped in the streets and in the doorways, listening to the
dim haunted echoes reflected through the long aisles of
apartment blocks on the far horizon, involuntarily counting
the slow final sequences that told the hour. Older people
whispered to each other: "Four o'clock, or was it five?
They have started the clock again. It seems strange after
these years."

And all through the day they would pause as the quarter-

and half-hours reached across the miles to them, a voice
from their childhoods reminding them of the ordered world
of the past. They began to reset their timers by the
chimes, at night before they slept they would listen to
the long count of midnight, wake to hear them again in
the thin clear air of the morning.

Some went down to the police station and asked if they
could have their watches and clocks back again.

After sentence, twenty years for the murder of Stacey,
five for fourteen offenses under the Time Laws, to run
concurrently, Newman was led away to the holding cells
in the basement of the court. He had expected the sentence and made no comment when invited by the judge.
After waiting trial for a year the afternoon in the courtroom
was nothing more than a momentary intermission.

He made no attempt to defend himself against the
charge of killing Stacey, partly to shield Marshall, who
would be able to continue their work unmolested, and
partly because he felt indirectly responsible for the policeman's death. Stacey's body, skull fractured by a twenty-
or thirty-story fall, had been discovered in the back seat
of his car in a basement garage not far from the plaza.
Presumably Marshall had discovered him prowling around
and dealt with him single-handed. Newman recalled that
one day Marshall had disappeared altogether and had
been curiously irritable for the rest of the week.

The last time he had seen the old man had been during
the three days before the police arrived. Each morning as
the chimes boomed out across the plaza Newman had seen
his tiny figure striding briskly down the plaza toward him,
waving up energetically at the tower, bareheaded and un-
afraid.

Now Newman was faced with the problem of how to
devise a clock that would chart his way through the coming twenty years. His fears increased when he was taken
the next day to the cell block which housed the long-term
prisoners—passing his cell on the way to meet the superintendent he noticed that his window looked out onto a small
shaft. He pumped his brains desperately as he stood to
attention during the superintendent's homilies, wondering

how he could retain his sanity. Short of counting the seconds, each one of the 86,400 in every day, he saw no possible means of assessing the time.

Locked into his cell, he sat limply on the narrow bed, too tired to unpack his small bundle of possessions. A moment's inspection confirmed the uselessness of the shaft. A powerful light mounted half way up masked the sunlight that slipped through a steel grill fifty feet above.

He stretched himself out on the bed and examined the ceiling. A lamp was recessed into its center, but a second, surprisingly, appeared to have been fitted to the cell. This was on the wall, a few feet above his head. He could see the curving bowl of the protective case, some ten inches in diameter.

He was wondering whether this could be a reading light when he realized that there was no switch.

Swinging round, he sat up and examined it, then leapt to his feet in astonishment.

It was a clock! He pressed his hands against the bowl, reading the circle of numerals, noting the inclination of the hands, 4:53, near enough the present time. Not simply a clock, but one in running order! Was this some sort of macabre joke, or a misguided attempt at rehabilitation?

His pounding on the door brought a warder.

"What's all the noise about? The clock? What's the matter with it?" He unlocked the door and barged in, pushing Newman back.

"Nothing. But why is it here? They're against the law."

"Oh, is that what's worrying you?" The warder shrugged. "Well, you see, the rules are a little different in here. You lads have got a lot of time ahead of you, it'd be cruel not to let you know where you stood. You know how to work it, do you? Good." He slammed the door, bolted it fast, smiled at Newman through the case. "It's a long day here, son, as you'll be finding out, that'll help you get through it."

Gleefully, Newman lay on the bed, his head on a rolled blanket at its foot, staring up at the clock. It appeared to be in perfect order, electrically driven, moving in rigid half-minute jerks. For an hour after the warder left he watched it without a break, then began to tidy up his cell, glancing over his shoulder every few minutes to reassure himself that it was still there, still running efficiently. The irony of the situation, the total inversion of justice, delighted him, even though it would cost him twenty years of his life.

He was still chuckling over the absurdity of it all two weeks later when for the first time he noticed the clock's insanely irritating tick . . .

❋ *Avram Davidson*

OR ALL THE SEAS WITH OYSTERS

When the man came in to the F & O Bike Shop, Oscar greeted him with a hearty "Hi, there!" Then, as he looked closer at the middle-aged visitor with the eyeglasses and business suit, his forehead creased and he began to snap his thick fingers.

"Oh, say, I know you," he muttered. "Mr.—um—name's on the tip of my tongue, doggone it . . ." Oscar was a barrel-chested fellow. He had orange hair.

"Why, sure you do," the man said. There was a Lion's emblem in his lapel. "Remember, you sold me a girl's bicycle with gears, for my daughter? We got to talking about that red French racing bike your partner was working on—"

Oscar slapped his big hand down on the cash register. He raised his head and rolled his eyes up. "Mr. Whatney!" Mr. Whatney beamed. "Oh, *sure*. Gee, how could I forget? And we went across the street afterward and had a couple a beers. Well, how you *been*, Mr. Whatney? I guess the bike—it was an English model, wasn't it? Yeah. It must of given satisfaction or you would of been back, huh?"

Mr. Whatney said the bicycle was fine, just fine. Then he said, "I understand there's been a change, though. You're all by yourself now. Your partner . . ."

Oscar looked down, pushed his lower lip out, nodded. "You heard, huh? Ee-up. I'm all by myself now. Over three months now."

The partnership had come to an end three months ago,

but it had been faltering long before then. Ferd liked books, long-playing records and high-level conversation. Oscar liked beer, bowling and women. Any women. Any time.

The shop was located near the park; it did a big trade in renting bicycles to picnickers. If a woman was barely old enough to be *called* a woman, and not quite old enough to be called an *old* woman, or if she was anywhere in between, and if she was alone, Oscar would ask, "How does that machine feel to you? All right?"

"Why . . . I guess so."

Taking another bicycle, Oscar would say, "Well, I'll just ride along a little bit with you, to make sure. Be right back, Ferd." Ferd always nodded gloomily. He knew that Oscar would not be right back. Later, Oscar would say, "Hope you made out in the shop as good as I did in the park."

"Leaving me all alone here all that time," Ferd grumbled.

And Oscar usually flared up. "Okay, then, next time *you* go and leave *me* stay here. See if I begrudge you a little fun." But he knew, of course, that Ferd—tall, thin, pop-eyed Ferd—would never go. "Do you good," Oscar said, slapping his sternum. "Put hair on your chest."

Ferd muttered that he had all the hair on his chest that he needed. He would glance down covertly at his lower arms; they were thick with long black hair, though his upper arms were slick and white. It was already like that when he was in high school, and some of the others would laugh at him—call him "Ferdie the Birdie." They knew it bothered him, but they did it anyway. How was it possible —he wondered then; he still did now—for people deliberately to hurt someone else who hadn't hurt them? How was it possible?

He worried over other things. All the time.

"The Communists—" He shook his head over the newspaper. Oscar offered an advice about the Communists in two short words. Or it might be capital punishment. "Oh, what a terrible thing if an innocent man was to be executed," Ferd moaned. Oscar said that was the guy's tough luck.

"Hand me that tire iron," Oscar said.

And Ferd worried even about other people's minor concerns. Like the time the couple came in with the tandem and the baby basket on it. Free air was all they took; then the woman decided to change the diaper and one of the safety pins broke.

"Why are there never any safety pins?" the woman fretted, rummaging here and rummaging there. "There are *never* any safety pins."

Ferd made sympathetic noises, went to see if he had any; but, though he was sure there'd been some in the office, he couldn't find them. So they drove off with one side of the diaper tied in a clumsy knot.

At lunch, Ferd said it was too bad about the safety pins. Oscar dug his teeth into a sandwich, tugged, tore, chewed, swallowed. Ferd liked to experiment with sandwich spreads —the one he liked most was cream cheese, olives, anchovy and avocado, mashed up with a little mayonnaise—but Oscar always had the same pink luncheon meat.

"It must be difficult with a baby," Ferd nibbled. "Not just traveling, but raising it."

Oscar said, "Jeez, there's drugstores in every block, and if you can't read, you can at least reckernize them."

"Drugstores? Oh, to buy safety pins, you mean."

"Yeah. Safety pins."

"But . . . you know . . . it's true . . . there's never any safety pins when you look."

Oscar uncapped his beer, rinsed the first mouthful around. "Aha! Always plenny of coat hangers, though. Throw 'em out every month, next month same closet's full of 'm again. Now whatcha wanna do in your spare time, you invent a device which it'll make safety pins outa clothes hangers."

Ferd nodded abstractedly. "But in my spare time I'm working on the French racer . . ." It was a beautiful machine, light, low-slung, swift, red and shining. You felt like a bird when you rode it. But, good as it was, Ferd knew he could make it better. He showed it to everybody who came in the place until his interest slackened.

Nature was his latest hobby, or, rather, reading about Nature. Some kids had wandered by from the park one day with tin cans in which they had put salamanders and toads, and they proudly showed them to Ferd. After that, the work on the red racer slowed down and he spent his spare time on natural history books.

"Mimicry!" he cried to Oscar. "A wonderful thing!"

Oscar looked up interestedly from the bowling scores in the paper. "I seen Edie Adams on TV the other night, doing her imitation of Marilyn Monroe. Boy, oh, boy."

Ferd was irritated, shook his head. "Not that kind of mimicry. I mean how insects and arachnids will mimic the shapes of leaves and twigs and so on, to escape being eaten by birds or other insects and arachnids."

A scowl of disbelief passed over Oscar's heavy face. "You mean they change their *shapes?* What are you giving me?"

"Oh, it's true. Sometimes the mimicry is for aggressive purposes, though—like a South African turtle that looks like a rock and so the fish swim up to it and then it catches them. Or that spider in Sumatra. When it lies on its back, it looks like a bird dropping. Catches butterflies that way."

Oscar laughed, a disgusted and incredulous noise. It died away as he turned back to the bowling scores. One hand groped at his pocket, came away, scratched absently at the orange thicket under the shirt, then went patting his hip pocket.

"Where's that pencil?" he muttered, got up, stomped into the office, pulled open drawers. His loud cry of "Hey!" brought Ferd into the tiny room.

"What's the matter?" Ferd asked.

Oscar pointed to a drawer. "Remember that time you claimed there were no safety pins here? Look—whole gah-damn drawer is full of 'em."

Ferd stared, scratched his head, said feebly that he was certain he'd looked there before . . .

A contralto voice from outside asked, "Anybody here?"

Oscar at once forgot the desk and its contents, called, "Be right with you," and was gone. Ferd followed him slowly.

There was a young woman in the shop, a rather massively built young woman, with muscular calves and a deep chest. She was pointing out the seat of her bicycle to Oscar, who was saying "Uh-huh" and looking more at her than at anything else. "It's just a little too far forward ["Uh-huh"], as you can see. A wrench is all I need ["Uh-huh"]. It was silly of me to forget my tools."

Oscar repeated, "Uh-huh" automatically, then snapped

to. "Fix it in a jiffy," he said, and—despite her insistence that she could do it herself—he did fix it. Though not quite in a jiffy. He refused money. He prolonged the conversation as long as he could.

"Well, thank *you*," the young woman said. "And now I've got to go."

"That machine feel all right to you now?"

"Perfectly. Thanks—"

"Tell you what, I'll just ride along with you a little bit, just—"

Pear-shaped notes of laughter lifted the young woman's bosom. "Oh, you couldn't keep up with me! My machine is a *racer!*"

The moment he saw Oscar's eyes flit to the corner, Ferd knew what he had in mind. He stepped forward. His cry of "No" was drowned out by his partner's loud, "Well, I guess this racer here can keep up with yours!"

The young woman giggled richly, said, well, they would see about that, and was off. Oscar, ignoring Ferd's outstretched hand, jumped on the French bike and was gone. Ferd stood in the doorway, watching the two figures, hunched over their handlebars, vanish down the road into the park. He went slowly back inside.

It was almost evening before Oscar returned, sweaty but smiling. Smiling broadly. "Hey, what a babe!" he cried. He wagged his head, he whistled, he made gestures, noises like escaping steam. "Boy, oh, boy, what an afternoon!"

"Give me the bike," Ferd demanded.

Oscar said, yeah, sure; turned it over to him and went to wash. Ferd looked at the machine. The red enamel was covered with dust; there was mud spattered and dirt and bits of dried grass. It seemed soiled—degraded. He had felt like a swift bird when he rode it . . .

Oscar came out wet and beaming. He gave a cry of dismay, ran over.

"Stand away," said Ferd, gesturing with the knife. He slashed the tires, the seat and seat cover, again and again.

"You crazy?" Oscar yelled. "You outa your mind? Ferd, no, don't, Ferd—"

Ferd cut the spokes, bent them, twisted them. He took the heaviest hammer and pounded the frame into shapelessness, and then he kept on pounding till his breath was gasping.

"You're not only crazy," Oscar said bitterly, "you're rotten jealous. You can go to hell." He stomped away.

Ferd, feeling sick and stiff, locked up, went slowly home. He had no taste for reading, turned out the light and fell into bed, where he lay awake for hours, listening to the rustling noises of the night and thinking hot, twisted thoughts.

They didn't speak to each other for days after that, except for the necessities of the work. The wreckage of the French racer lay behind the shop. For about two weeks, neither wanted to go out back where he'd have to see it.

One morning Ferd arrived to be greeted by his partner, who began to shake his head in astonishment even before he started speaking. "How did you *do* it, how did you *do* it, Ferd? Jeez, what a beautiful job—I gotta hand it to you —no more hard feelings, huh, Ferd?"

Ferd took his hand. "Sure, sure. But what are you talking about?"

Oscar led him out back. There was the red racer, all in one piece, not a mark or scratch on it, its enamel bright as ever. Ferd gaped. He squatted down and examined it. It *was* his machine. Every change, every improvement he had made, was there.

He straightened up slowly. "Regeneration . . ."

"Huh? What say?" Oscar asked. Then, "Hey, kiddo, you're all white. Whad you do, stay up all night and didn't get no sleep? Come on in and siddown. But I still don't see how you done it."

Inside, Ferd sat down. He wet his lips. He said, "Oscar —listen—"

"Yeah?"

"Oscar. You know what regeneration is? No? Listen. Some kinds of lizards, you grab them by the tail, the tail breaks off and they grow a new one. If a lobster loses a claw, it regenerates another one. Some kinds of worms— and hydras and starfish—you cut them into pieces, each piece will grow back the missing parts. Salamanders can regenerate lost hands, and frogs can grow legs back."

"No kidding, Ferd. But, uh, I mean: Nature. Very interesting. But to get back to the bike now—how'd you manage to fix it so good?"

"I never touched it. It regenerated. Like a newt. Or a lobster."

Oscar considered this. He lowered his head, looked up at Ferd from under his eyebrows. "Well, now, Ferd . . . Look . . . How come all broke bikes don't do that?"

"This isn't an ordinary bike. I mean it isn't a real bike." Catching Oscar's look, he shouted, "Well, it's *true!*"

The shout changed Oscar's attitude from bafflement to incredulity. He got up. "So for the sake of argument, let's say all that stuff about the bugs and the eels or whatever the hell you were talking about is true. But they're alive. A bike ain't." He looked down triumphantly.

Ferd shook his leg from side to side, looked at it. "A crystal isn't, either, but a broken crystal can regenerate itself if the conditions are right. Oscar, go see if the safety pins are still in the desk. Please, Oscar?"

He listened as Oscar, muttering, pulled the desk drawers out, rummaged in them, slammed them shut, tramped back.

"Naa," he said. "All gone. Like that lady said that time, and you said, there never are any safety pins when you want 'em. They disap—Ferd? What're—"

Ferd jerked open the closet door, jumped back as a shoal of clothes hangers clattered out.

"And like *you* say," Ferd said with a twist of his mouth, "on the other hand, there are always plenty of clothes hangers. There weren't any here before."

Oscar shrugged. "I don't see what you're getting at. But anybody could of got in here and took the pins and left the hangers. *I* could of—but I didn't. Or *you* could of. Maybe—" He narrowed his eyes. "Maybe you walked in your sleep and done it. You better see a doctor. Jeez, you look rotten."

Ferd went back and sat down, put his head in his hands. "I feel rotten. I'm scared, Oscar. Scared of what?" He breathed noisily. "I'll tell you. Like I explained before, about how things that live in the wild places, they mimic other things there. Twigs, leaves . . . toads that look like rocks. Well, suppose there are . . . things . . . that live in people places. Cities. Houses. These things could imitate—well, other kinds of things you find in people places—"

"*People* places, for crise sake!"

"Maybe they're a different kind of life form. Maybe they get their nourishment out of the elements in the air. You know what safety pins *are*—these other kinds of them? Oscar, the safety pins are the pupa forms and then they, like, *hatch*. Into the larval forms. Which look just like coat hangers. They feel like them, even, but they're not. Oscar, they're not, not really, not really, not . . ."

He began to cry into his hands. Oscar looked at him. He shook his head.

After a minute, Ferd controlled himself somewhat. He snuffled. "All these bicycles the cops find, and they hold them waiting for owners to show up, and then we buy them at the sale because no owners show up because there aren't any, and the same with the ones the kids are always trying to sell us, and they say they just found them, and they really did because they were never made in a factory. They grew. They grow. You smash them and throw them away, they regenerate."

Oscar turned to someone who wasn't there and waggled his head. "Hoo, boy," he said. Then, to Ferd: "You mean one day there's a safety pin and the next day instead there's a coat hanger?"

Ferd said, "One day there's a cocoon; the next day there's a moth. One day there's an egg; the next day there's a chicken. But with . . . these it doesn't happen in the open daytime where you can see it. But at night, Oscar—at night you can *hear* it happening. All the little noises in the night-time, Oscar—"

Oscar said, "Then how come we ain't up to our belly-button in bikes? If I had a bike for every coat hanger—"

But Ferd had considered that, too. If every codfish egg, he explained, or every oyster spawn grew to maturity, a man could walk across the oceans on the backs of all the codfish or oysters there'd be. So many died, so many were eaten by predatory creatures, that Nature had to produce a maximum in order to allow a minimum to arrive at maturity. And Oscar's question was: then who, uh, eats the, uh, coat hangers?

Ferd's eyes focused through wall, buildings, park, more

buildings, to the horizon. "You got to get the picture. I'm not talking about real pins or hangers. I got a name for the others—'false friends,' I call them. In high school French we had to watch out for French words that looked like English words, but really were different. *'Faux amis,'* they call them. False friends. Pseudo-pins. Pseudo-hangers . . . Who eats them? I don't know for sure. Pseudo-vacuum cleaners, maybe?"

His partner, with a loud groan, slapped his hands against his thighs. He said, "Ferd, Ferd, for crise sake. You know what's the trouble with you? You talk about oysters, but you forgot what they're good for. You forgot there's two kinds of people in the world. Close up them books, them bug books and French books. Get out, mingle, meet people. Soak up some brew. You know what? The next time Norma —that's this broad's name with the racing bike—the next time she comes here, *you* take the red racer and *you* go out in the woods with her. I won't mind. And I don't think she will, either. Not *too* much."

But Ferd said no. "I never want to touch the red racer again. I'm afraid of it."

At this, Oscar pulled him to his feet, dragged him protestingly out to the back and forced him to get on the French machine. "Only way to conquer your fear of it!"

Ferd started off, white-faced, wobbling. And in a moment was on the ground, rolling and thrashing, screaming. Oscar pulled him away from the machine.

"It threw me!" Ferd yelled. "It tried to kill me! Look—blood!"

His partner said it was a bump that threw him—it was his own fear. The blood? A broken spoke. Grazed his cheek. And he insisted Ferd get on the bicycle again, to conquer his fear.

But Ferd had grown hysterical. He shouted that no man was safe—that mankind had to be warned. It took Oscar a long time to pacify him and to get him to go home and into bed.

He didn't tell all this to Mr. Whatney, of course. He merely said that his partner had gotten fed up with the bicycle business.

"It don't pay to worry and try to change the world," he

pointed out. "I always say take things the way they **are.** If you can't lick 'em, join 'em."

Mr. Whatney said that was his philosophy, exactly. He asked how things were, since.

"Well . . . not *too* bad. I'm engaged, you know. Name's Norma. Crazy about bicycles. Everything considered, things aren't bad at all. More work, yes, but I can do things all my own way, so . . ."

Mr. Whatney nodded. He glanced around the shop. "I see they're still making drop-frame bikes," he said, "though with so many women wearing slacks, I wonder they bother."

Oscar said, "Well, I dunno. I kinda like it that way. Ever stop to think that bicycles are like people? I mean, of all the machines in the world, only bikes come male and female."

Mr. Whatney gave a little giggle, said that was *right,* he had never thought of it like that before. Then Oscar asked if Mr. Whatney had anything in particular in mind—not that he wasn't always welcome.

"Well I wanted to look over what you've got. My boy's birthday is coming up—"

Oscar nodded sagely. "Now here's a job," he said, "which you can't get it in any other place but here. Specialty of the house. Combines the best features of the French racer and the American standard, but it's made right here, and it comes in three models—Junior, Intermediate and Regular. Beautiful, ain't it?"

Mr. Whatney observed that, say, that might be just the ticket. "By the way," he asked, "what's become of the French racer, the red one, used to be here?"

Oscar's face twitched. Then it grew bland and innocent and he leaned over and nudged his customer. "Oh, *that* one. Old Frenchy? Why, I put *him* out to stud!"

And they laughed and they laughed, and after they told a few more stories they concluded the sale, and they had a few beers and they laughed some more. And then they said what a shame it was about poor Ferd, poor old Ferd, who had been found in his own closet with an unraveled coat hanger coiled tightly around his neck.

❀ *Arthur C. Clarke*

PATENT PENDING

There are no subjects that have not been discussed, at some time or other, in the saloon bar of the White Hart— and whether or not there are ladies present makes no difference whatsoever. After all, they came in at their own risk. Three of them, now I come to think of it, have eventually gone out again with husbands. So perhaps the risk isn't on their side at all. . . .

I mention this because I would not like you to think that all our conversations are highly erudite and scientific, and our activities purely cerebral. Though chess is rampant, darts and shove-ha'penny also flourish. The *Times Literary Supplement*, the *Saturday Review*, the *New Statesman and* the *Atlantic Monthly* may be brought in by some of the customers, but the same people are quite likely to leave with the latest issue of *Staggering Stories of Pseudoscience*.

A great deal of business also goes on in the obscurer corners of the pub. Copies of antique books and magazines frequently change hands at astronomical prices, and on almost any Wednesday at least three well-known dealers may be seen smoking large cigars as they lean over the bar, swapping stories with Drew. From time to time a vast guffaw announces the denouement of some anecdote and provokes a flood of anxious inquiries from patrons who are afraid they may have missed something. But, alas, delicacy forbids that I should repeat any of these interesting tales here. Unlike most things in this island, they are not for export. . . .

Luckily, no such restrictions apply to the tales of Mr.

Harry Purvis, B.Sc. (at least), Ph.D. (probably) F.R.S. (personally I don't think so, though it *has* been rumored). None of them would bring a blush to the cheeks of the most delicately nurtured maiden aunts, should any still survive in these days.

I must apologize. This is too sweeping a statement. There was one story which might, in some circles, be regarded as a little daring. Yet I do not hesitate to repeat it, for I know that you, dear reader, will be sufficiently broadminded to take no offense.

It started in this fashion. A celebrated Fleet Street reviewer had been pinned into a corner by a persuasive publisher, who was about to bring out a book of which he had high hopes. It was one of the riper productions the "and-then-the-house-gave-another-lurch-as-the-termites-finished-the-east-wing" school of fiction. Eire had already banned it, but that is an honor which few books escape nowadays, and certainly could not be considered a distinction. However, if a leading British newspaper could be induced to make a stern call for its suppression, it would become a best seller overnight. . . .

Such was the logic of its publisher, and he was using all his wiles to induce cooperation. I heard him remark, apparently to allay any scruples his reviewer friend might have, "Of course not! If they can understand it, they *can't* be corrupted any further!" And then Harry Purvis, who has an uncanny knack of following half a dozen conversations simultaneously, so that he can insert himself in the right one at the right time, said in his peculiarly penetrating and non-interruptable voice: "Censorship does raise some very difficult problems, doesn't it? I've always argued that there's an inverse correlation between a country's degree of civilization and the restraints it puts on its press."

A New England voice from the back of the room cut in: "On *that* argument, Paris is a more civilized place than Boston."

"Precisely," answered Purvis. For once, he waited for a reply.

"OK." said the New England voice mildly. "I'm not arguing. I just wanted to check."

"To continue," said Purvis, wasting no more time in doing so, "I'r̩ reminded of a matter which has not yet concerned the censor, but which will certainly do so before long. It began in France, and so far has remained there. When it *does* come out into the open, it may have a greater impact on our civilization than the atom bomb.

"Like the atom bomb, it arose out of equally academic research. *Never*, gentlemen, underestimate science. I doubt if there is a single field of study so theoretical, so remote from what is laughingly called everyday life, that it may not one day produce something that will shake the world.

"You will appreciate that the story I am telling you is, for once in a while, second-hand. I got it from a colleague at the Sorbonne last year while I was over there at a scientific conference. So the names are all fictitious: I was told them at the time, but I can't remember them now.

"Professor—ah—Julian was an experimental physiologist at one of the smaller, but less impecunious, French universities. Some of you may remember that rather unlikely tale we heard here the other week from that fellow Hinckelberg, about his colleague who'd learned how to control the behavior of animals through feeding the correct currents into their nervous systems. Well, if there *was* any truth in that story—and frankly I doubt it—the whole project was probably inspired by Julian's papers in *Comptes Rendus*.

"Professor Julian, however, never published his most remarkable results. When you stumble on something which is really terrific, you don't rush into print. You wait until you have overwhelming evidence—unless you're afraid that someone else is hot on the track. Then you may issue an ambiguous report that will establish your priority at a later date, without giving too much away at the moment—like the famous cryptogram that Huygens put out when he detected the rings of Saturn.

"You may well wonder what Julian's discovery was, so I won't keep you in suspense. It was simply the natural extension of what man has been doing for the last hundred years. First the camera gave us the power to capture scenes. Then Edison invented the phonograph, and sound was mastered. Today, in the talking film, we have a kind of mechanical memory which would be inconceivable to our forefathers. But surely the matter cannot rest there. Eventually science must be able to catch and store thoughts and sensations themselves, and feed them back into the mind so that, whenever it wishes, it can repeat any experience in life, down to its minutest detail."

"That's an old idea!" snorted someone. "See the 'feelies' in *Brave New World*."

"All good ideas have been thought of by somebody before they are realized," said Purvis severely. "The point is that what Huxley and others had talked about, Julian actually did. My goodness, there's a pun there! Aldous—Julian—oh, let it pass!

"It was done electronically, of course. You all know how the encephalograph can record the minute electrical impulses in the living brain—the so-called 'brain waves,' as the popular press calls them. Julian's device was a much subtler elaboration of this well-known instrument. And, having recorded cerebral impulses, he could play them back again. It sounds simple, doesn't it? So was the phonograph, but it took the genius of Edison to think of it.

"And now, enter the villain. Well, perhaps that's too strong a word, for Professor Julian's assistant Georges—Georges Dupin—is really quite a sympathetic character. It was just that, being a Frenchman of a more practical turn of mind than the Professor, he saw at once that there were some milliards of francs involved in this laboratory toy.

"The first thing was to get it out of the laboratory. The French have an undoubted flair for elegant engineering, and after some weeks of work—with the full cooperation of the Professor—Georges had managed to pack the "playback" side of the apparatus into a cabinet no larger than a television set, and containing not very many more parts.

"Then Georges was ready to make his first experiment. It would involve considerable expense, but as someone so rightly remarked you cannot make omelettes without breaking eggs. And the analogy is, if I may say so, an exceedingly apt one.

"For Georges went to see the most famous *gourmet* in France, and made an interesting proposition. It was one that the great man could not refuse, because it was so unique a tribute to his eminence. Georges explained patiently that he had invented a device for registering (he said nothing about storing) sensations. In the cause of science, and for the honor of the French *cuisine,* could he be privileged to analyze the emotions, the subtle nuances of gustatory discrimination, that took place in Monsieur le Baron's mind when he employed his unsurpassed talents? Monsieur could name the restaurant, the *chef* and the menu—everything would be arranged for his convenience. Of course, if he was too busy, no doubt that well-known epicure, Le Compte de—

"The Baron, who was in some respects a surprisingly coarse man, uttered a word not to be found in most French dictionaries. '*That* cretin!' he exploded. 'He would be happy on English cooking! No, *I* shall do it.' And forthwith he sat down to compose the menu, while Georges anxiously estimated the cost of the items and wondered if his bank balance would stand the strain. . . .

"It would be interesting to know what the chef and the waiters thought about the whole business. There was the Baron, seated at his favorite table and doing full justice to his favorite dishes, not in the least inconvenienced by the tangle of wires that trailed from his head to that diabolical-looking machine in the corner. The restaurant was empty of all other occupants, for the last thing Georges wanted was premature publicity. This had added very considerably to the already distressing cost of the experiment. He could only hope that the results would be worth it.

"They were. The only way of *proving* that, of course, would be to play back Georges' recording.' We have to take his word for it, since the utter inadequacy of words in such matters is all too well known. The Baron *was* a genuine connoisseur, not one of those who merely pretend to powers of discrimination they do not possess. You know Thurber's 'Only a naïve domestic Burgundy, but I think you'll admire its presumption.' The Baron would have known at the first sniff whether it was domestic or not—and if it had been presumptuous he'd have smacked it down.

"I gather that Georges had his money's worth out of that recording, even though he had not intended it merely for personal use. It opened up new worlds to him, and clarified the ideas that had been forming in his ingenious brain. There was no doubt about it: all the exquisite sensations that had passed through the Baron's mind during the consumption of that Lucullan repast had been captured, so that anyone else, however untrained he might be in such matters, could savor them to the full. For, you see, the recording dealt purely with emotions: intelligence did not come into the picture at all. The Baron needed a lifetime of knowledge and training before he could *experience* these sensations. But once they were down on tape, anyone, even if in real life he had no sense of taste at all, could take over from there.

"Think of the glowing vistas that opened up before Georges' eyes! There were other meals, other gourmets. There were the collected impressions of all the vintages of Europe—what would connoisseurs not pay for them? When the last bottle of a rare wine had been broached, its incorporeal essence could be preserved, as the voice of Melba can travel down the centuries. For, after all, it was not the wine itself that mattered, but the sensations it evoked . . .

"So mused Georges. But this, he knew, was only a beginning. The French claim to logic I have often disputed, but in Georges' case it cannot be denied. He thought the matter over for a few days: then he went to see his *petite dame*.

" 'Yvonne, *ma cheri*,' he said. 'I have a somewhat unusual request to make of you . . .' "

Harry Purvis knew when to break off in a story. He turned to the bar and called, "Another Scotch, Drew." No one said a word while it was provided.

"To continue," said Purvis at length, "the experiment, unusual though it was, even in France, was successfully carried out. As both discretion and custom demanded, all was arranged in the lonely hours of the night. You will have gathered already that Georges was a persuasive person, though I doubt if Mam'selle needed much persuading.

"Stifling her curiosity with a sincere but hasty kiss, Georges saw Yvonne out of the lab and rushed back to his apparatus. Breathlessly, he ran through the playback. It worked—not that he had ever had any real doubts. Moreover—do please remember I have only my informant's word for this—it was indistinguishable from the real thing. At that moment something approaching religious awe overcame Georges. This was, without a doubt, the greatest invention in history. He would be immortal as well as wealthy, for he had achieved something of which all men had dreamed, and had robbed old age of one of its terrors. . . .

"He also realized that he could now dispense with Yvonne, if he so wished. This raised implications that would require further thought. *Much* further thought.

"You will, of course, appreciate that I am giving you a highly condensed account of events. While all this was going on, Georges was still working as a loyal employee of the Professor, who suspected nothing. As yet, indeed, Georges had done little more than any research worker might have in similar circumstances. His performances had been somewhat beyond the call of duty, but could all be explained away if need be.

"The next step would involve some very delicate negotiations and the expenditure of further hard-won francs. Georges now had all the material he needed to prove, beyond a shadow of doubt, that he was handling a very valuable commercial property. There were shrewd businessmen in Paris who would jump at the opportunity. Yet a certain delicacy, for which we must give him full credit, restrained Georges from using his second—er—recording as a sample of the wares his machine could purvey. There was no way of disguising the personalities involved, and Georges was a modest man. 'Besides,' he argued, again with great good sense, 'when the gramophone company wishes to make a *disque*, it does not enregister the performance of some amateur musician. *That* is a matter for professionals. And so, *ma foi*, is *this*.' Whereupon, after a further call at his bank, he set forth again for Paris.

"He did not go anywhere near the Place Pigalle, because that was full of Americans and prices were accordingly exorbitant. Instead, a few discreet inquiries and some understanding cab drivers took him to an almost oppressively respectable suburb, where he presently found himself in a pleasant waiting room, by no means as exotic as might have been supposed.

"And there, somewhat embarrassed, Georges explained his mission to a formidable lady whose age one could have no more guessed than her profession. Used though she was to unorthodox requests, *this* was something she had never encountered in all her considerable experience. But the customer was always right, as long as he had the cash, and so in due course everything was arranged. One of the young ladies and her boy friend, an *apache* of somewhat overwheming masculinity, traveled back with Georges to the provinces. At first they were, naturally, somewhat suspicious, but as Georges had already found, no expert can ever resist flattery. Soon they were all on excellent terms. Hercule and Susette promised Georges that they would give him every cause for satisfaction.

"No doubt some of you would be glad to have further details, but you can scarcely expect me to supply them. All I can say is that Georges—or rather his instrument— was kept very busy, and that by the morning little of the recording material was left unused. For it seems that Hercule was indeed appropriately named. . . .

"When this piquant episode was finished, Georges had very little money left, but he did possess two recordings that were quite beyond price. Once more he set off to Paris, where, with practically no trouble, he came to terms with some businessmen who were so astonished that they gave him a very generous contract before coming to their senses. I am pleased to report this, because so often the scientist emerges second best in his dealings with the world of finance. I'm equally pleased to record that Georges had made provision for Professor Julian in the contract. You may say cynically that it was, after all, the Professor's invention, and that sooner or later Georges would have had to square him. But I like to think that there was more to it than that.

"The full details of the scheme for exploiting the device are, of course, unknown to me. I gather that Georges had been expansively eloquent—not that much eloquence was needed to convince anyone who had once experienced one or both of his playbacks. The market would be enormous, unlimited. The export trade alone could put France on her feet again and would wipe out her dollar deficit overnight —once certain snags had been overcome. Everything would have to be managed through somewhat clandestine channels, for think of the hub-bub from the hypocritical Anglo-Saxons when they discovered just what was being imported into their countries. The Mother's Union, The Daughters of the American Revolution, The Housewives League, and *all* the religious organizations would rise as one. The lawyers were looking into the matter very carefully, and as far as could be seen the regulations that still excluded *Tropic of Capricorn* from the mails of the English-speaking countries could not be applied to this case—for the simple reason that no one had thought of it. But there would be such a shout for new laws that Parliament and Congress would have to do something, so it was best to keep under cover as long as possible.

"In fact, as one of the directors pointed out, if the recordings were banned, so much the better. They could make more money on a smaller output, because the price would promptly soar and all the vigilance of the Customs Officials couldn't block every leak. It would be Prohibition all over again.

"You will scarcely be surprised to hear that by this time Georges had somewhat lost interest in the gastronomical angle. It was an interesting but definitely minor possibility of the invention. Indeed, this had been tacitly admitted by the directors as they drew up the articles of association, for they had included the pleasures of the *cuisine* among 'subsidiary rights.'

"Georges returned home with his head in the clouds, and a substantial check in his pocket. A charming fancy had struck his imagination. He thought of all the trouble to which the gramophone companies had gone so that the world might have the complete recordings of the Forty-Eight Preludes and Fugues or the Nine Symphonies. Well, *his* new company would put out a complete and definite set of recordings, performed by experts versed in the most esoteric knowledge of East and West. How many *opus* numbers would be required? That, of course, had been a subject of profound debate for some thousands of years. The Hindu textbooks, Georges had heard, got well into three figures. It would be a most interesting research, combining profit with pleasure in an unexampled manner. . . . He had already begun some preliminary studies, using treatises which even in Paris were none too easy to obtain.

"If you think that while all this was going on, Georges had neglected his usual interests, you are all too right. He was working literally night and day, for he had not yet revealed his plans to the Professor and almost everything had to be done when the lab was closed. And one of the interests he had had to neglect was Yvonne.

"Her curiosity had already been aroused, as any girl's would have been. But now she was more than intrigued—she was distracted. For Georges had become so remote and cold. He was no longer in love with her.

"It was a result that might have been anticipated. Publicans have to guard against the danger of sampling their own wares too often—I'm sure *you* don't, Drew—and Georges had fallen into this seductive trap. He had been through that recording too many times, with somewhat debilitating results. Moreover, poor Yvonne was not to be compared with the experienced and talented Susette. It was the old story of the professional versus the amateur.

"All that Yvonne knew was that Georges was in love with someone else. That was true enough. She suspected that he had been unfaithful to her. And *that* raises profound philosophical questions we can hardly go into here.

"This being France, in case you had forgotten, the outcome was inevitable. Poor Georges! He was working late one night at the lab, as usual, when Yvonne finished him off with one of those ridiculous ornamental pistols which are *de rigueur* for such occasions. Let us drink to his memory."

"That's the trouble with all your stories," said John Beynon. "You tell us about wonderful inventions, and then at the end it turns out that the discoverer was killed, so no one can do anything about it. For I suppose, as usual, the apparatus was destroyed?"

"But no," replied Purvis. "Apart from Georges, this is one of the stories that has a happy ending. There was no trouble at all about Yvonne, of course. Georges' grieving sponsors arrived on the scene with great speed and prevented any adverse publicity. Being men of sentiment as well as men of business, they realized that they would have to secure Yvonne's freedom. They promptly did this by playing the recording to *le Maire* and *le Préfet*, thus convincing them that the poor girl had experienced irresistible provocation. A few shares in the new company clinched the deal, with expressions of the utmost cordiality on both sides. Yvonne even got her gun back."

"Then when—" began someone else.

"Ah, these things take time. There's the question of mass production, you know. It's quite possible that distribution has already commenced through private—*very* private—channels. Some of those dubious little shops and notice boards around Leicester Square may soon start giving hints."

"Of course," said the New England voice disrespectfully, "you wouldn't know the *name* of the company."

You can't help admiring Purvis at times like this. He scarcely hesitated.

"*Le Société Anonyme d'Aphrodite*," he replied. "And I've just remembered something that will cheer *you* up. They hope to get round your sticky mails regulations and establish themselves before the inevitable congressional inquiry starts. They're opening up a branch in Nevada: apparently you can still get away with anything there." He raised his glass.

"To Georges Dupin," he said solemnly. "Martyr to science. Remember him when the fireworks start. And one other thing—"

"Yes?" we all asked.

"Better start saving now. And sell your TV sets before the bottom drops out of the market."

✿ *Julian Kawalec*

I KILL MYSELF

Translated from the Polish by HARRY STEVENS

Today I shall destroy the Zeta bomb. I shall do it this evening, when I begin my tour of duty in the army laboratory. Today I have achieved the capacity for sacrifice; I realized that when I looked at the slender, mournful boughs of the trees; I can't say why it was just at the moment when I noticed the trees.

I am walking along an avenue in the park. I feel a keen rawness in the air. People go past me. They pay no attention to me. They don't know that I, a homely-looking man in a gray raincoat, with big ears and a mole on the cheek, am capable of great self-sacrifice; that this evening I shall turn the key in the door of an iron safe, open it, and take out something which looks like a large goose egg. That's the Zeta bomb. The distance between the contact pin and the critical point of the bomb is three millimeters. That is the distance to which Professor Lombard set the contact pin when he solicitously laid the Zeta in its plush case. The Zeta rests like a child in swaddling clothes; today I shall destroy the steel child, for today I have achieved the capacity to make this great sacrifice of myself.

I must do it, I must free humanity from the terrible nightmare and that powerful mite. Why should a tiny steel pin have power of life and death over people? . . . So long as it doesn't touch the critical point, the sun will go on shining; when it does touch, night will fall, all men will die, and the birds will drop like meteors. By the force of its explosion the Zeta bomb exceeds the most powerful hydrogen bomb a billion times. If it were to explode, the result would not be death, for death is an equal partner with life—one can argue with it, one can quarrel and be reconciled with it. In comparison with the consequences of an explosion of Zeta, death is something anodyne. The term "death" doesn't apply to the effects of that. One must create a new word for it.

I'm walking along the park avenues, waiting for the evening. When evening comes, I shall destroy Professor Lombard's "iron child." I shall unscrew the contact pin; I shall throw the bomb into a marsh, and the pin into a river some five kilometers distant from the marsh. The Zeta and the pin will never meet again. And if they don't meet, the world will continue to exist. I shall burn the documents giving the sketches and specifications of the bomb, and tread the ashes into the ground. Professor Lombard will not live long enough to give birth to a second "iron child."

I shall destroy the Zeta bomb. I shall do it for the sake of the trees, the animals, the birds, the people, the insects. I shall do it for my own sake, and for the sake of that young man with black hair who is sitting on a bench hidden among the trees, waiting for a girl; for you, gnarled elm, and for your inhabitant the woodpecker, and for you, black worm corkscrewing through the earth.

In the midst of all these people and trees I feel an enormous and oppressive loneliness. I cannot tell anyone what I'm planning to do. I'm afraid they might stop me from destroying the bomb. But after all, great sacrifice demands great loneliness. If I talk about it, I'm sharing it with others, reducing its greatness. But the feeling of loneliness doesn't weaken my determination.

The sky withdraws from the far end of the avenue, a sign that evening will soon be coming on. I leave the park. Today I shall walk to the laboratory. I take a road which shows up white among the small houses and crisscrossed fallow land. On my left someone is singing; on my right a gentle breeze is noisily tousling withered branches. After a moment the singing and the sound of the wind both stop. All is still.

Beyond a small pine wood I come to the first control barrier. They shine a beam of light toward me. They've recognized me. The guards know the senior laboratory assistant very well; he's a quiet sort and docile, with large ears and a mole on the cheek. I pass the first control barrier; the road is as smooth as a table top; the army laboratory has good roads leading to it. In a clump of leafy trees I come to the second control barrier. They pick me out with three beams of light; as they do so a single bird wakes up in a tree and begins to twitter. They scrutinize me closely, though all of them know me, though they know I'm the senior laboratory assistant and initiated into all the secrets. Beyond the second control barrier the road passes underground. Now I'm walking along a lighted tunnel. The side walls of the tunnel have innumerable little windows, through which guards poke their heads. One must walk steadily and calmly along the tunnel; the best thing is to whistle.

In a small hall, brilliantly lit, I show my identity papers, then I enter a narrow corridor. A tall guard opens an iron door for me. Now I'm in the anteroom of the laboratory. I am alone. I set to work. I bend over the secret drawer which contains the keys; it is known only to Professor Lombard, the commander-in-chief, and myself.

I pick up the key. In the third room of the laboratory I disconnect the alarm signal fixed to the iron safe. I open a drawer and take the Zeta bomb out of its plush case. Zeta is cold and slippery. I could destroy it here, in the laboratory; I could thaw it out; but that would take time, and the three junior laboratory assistants will be arriving in a few minutes. I conceal the bomb and the sketches in the broad pocket of my light raincoat, which I hang over my arm. I telephone to Professor Lombard, using a one-figure number known only to me and the commander-in-chief. I tell him I've forgotten to bring important reagents from the store and I must go for them myself at once.

In a minute or two I am on my way. I am not detained at the control points. The commander of the guard has been informed that it is a question of getting important reagents swiftly.

I have passed the last control barrier. Now there are no more lights. I turn off the main road. I'm going across flat, soft ground, in the direction of an alder grove. Surely this must be a sown field. It is night. Cold. I put on my raincoat. I have it, I have the bomb; with every step I take I feel it knocking against my ribs. Now and again I put my hand into the raincoat pocket to make sure it's there. It is, it is. I touch it with my hand. It is cold, slippery. Professor Lombard polished it, smoothed it. He gave it the gleam of a monstrous distorting mirror. Under my forefinger I feel the tiny head of the contact pin. All I have to do is to slip back the safety catch, press that little head, and then only invisible, inchoate fragments will be left of everything. However, the words "visible" and "invisible" wouldn't have any meaning whatever then. But that will never happen. Quite soon now I shall throw the Zeta bomb into the marsh. I shall throw it with all my strength, so that it flies into the very middle, where the mud is thinnest, where it will sink most easily and swiftly. I shall throw the contact pin into the river. Who will ever find a pin only a little thicker than a needle?

And then? Then I must go into hiding. I must find a good hiding place, for they are sure to search for me. I dare say the whole of the police force, the special military departments and forces, and the secret service will all be called in to search for me. I can already see, already hear, the orders being issued, the instructions intercrossing; how they'll be shouting, how they'll be whispering, all to find out where I am. But the great sacrifice to which I have dedicated myself cares nothing for such things. The great sacrifice must even require such things. And yet the great sacrifice doesn't require that after I've destroyed the bomb I should voluntarily and even frivolously put myself in the hands of those who have produced it. No, I cannot give them that pleasure. I cannot do anything which would give those wicked people the least satisfaction. And so, after I've destroyed Professor Lombard's "iron child," I must conceal myself thoroughly. The people, for whom I am making this great sacrifice, will not defend me. It will be a long time before they even learn of my exploit, before they have any realization of its benefits. They will stop to consider the matter; they will discuss, doubt, suspect; they will pluck up courage and succumb to cowardice; and maybe they will be ready to come to my defense only when it's too late. So I must seek out a good hiding place. But if they come upon my tracks, if I hear their steps, the clatter of belts hung about with weapons, the rustle of uniforms, and the snorting of highly sensitive, perfectly trained dogs, shall I leave my hiding place with my hands up? Does my self-sacrifice call for putting up a valiant resistance or for valiant renunciation of resistance? For resistance, for valiant resistance. But my sacrifice connotes prudent resistance, which in certain circumstances demands that I should hide from the enemy, should deceive the enemy. So I shall not go out to meet the police with my hands up. Rather, the moment they see me I shall spring at the throat of the nearest policeman. If I had a revolver I could kill several before I died. If I had a machine gun I could mow down several dozen from my hiding place.

The ground over which I'm now walking is longer even and soft; it is hard and crowded with little tussocks. So it must be quite close to the alder grove. I think I see a dark patch in front. Yes, that surely is the alder grove. The marsh lies just beyond it. I am coming across more and more of those little tussocks. My steps are inevitably becoming broken, and short. At times my feet slip farther down than I expect. Then my body is subjected to an involuntary jolt. Then Zeta strikes more violently against my ribs. It reminds me more insistently of its presence. I swiftly thrust my hand into my raincoat pocket. It's there, it's there. It's not so cold now as it was, it's rather warmer. Its shape also isn't so ugly. But it's a monster threatening something which cannot be called death or silence, or by any word from a modern dictionary. It's a tiny sleeping monster.

The dark patch grows blacker. Now the alder grove is very close. All around is still.

Now I can hear the gentle murmur of the trees. I am in the alder grove. I'm walking along a narrow path. The trees surround me with a friendly air; they're whispering something to me. The Zeta bomb must be destroyed so that the alders can live. Beyond the alder grove the ground turns soft again. But it's not the softness of a sown field, it's the springy softness of India rubber. I am conscious of the marsh; I can hear it. It too has its voice. The voice of the marsh is like the heavy breathing of a dying man. I can still go on for the time being; my feet are not sinking in yet; I know I shall go on safely as far as the first clump of tall spear grass. So now only minutes are left. The ground is getting softer and softer. Now I am at the spot, by a clump of spear grass. I hurriedly thrust my hand into my raincoat pocket. The bomb is warm. I hold its warm, smooth metal a long time in my palm. Then I cautiously take Zeta out of my pocket. Now it is lying on my palm. And so, in a moment *that* will be happening. In a moment the world will be freed from multitudinous death. But the world knows nothing about it. The world is quiet, indifferent, and sluggish. Is it possible that such a great deed can be accomplished in such great silence? I put the thumb and forefinger of my right hand on the safety catch. But just as I do so I hear a loud rustling. I seize the safety catch between my fingers and release it. I'm being pursued. No, it's only the wind running over the reeds . . . But if it were indeed a pursuit, if dogs picking up my trail began to bark at the edge of the marsh, if the first policemen were to put in an appearance . . . after all, I could threaten them with the bomb. I could shout to them: "Halt. I've got the Zeta bomb in my hand. With the safety catch released. The contact pin is one millimeter away from the critical point. If you advance a single step I shall press the pin. And don't try shooting at me, for if I fall the bomb will be given a violent jolt and it will explode. You'll perish!" But I wouldn't be the only one to perish. And not only would they perish. Millions of innocent people would perish. Such reasoning is not worthy of a man who has decided to sacrifice himself. And yet, the police will not move one step if I threaten them with the bomb. They're cowards. So nothing will happen to the world. My courage, which should accompany my sacrifice, will not suffer either, for I shall threaten the police, not because they're afraid, but because they're in the service of those who produce the bomb, those I hate. So that threat and that hatred should be included in the program of sacrifice. I cling to this thought: I consider it fine and pure, for I can hold the makers of the Zeta bomb, and their assistants, under threat; I can do as I like with them. That's a wise sacrifice. I can command them to march to a hollow between hills and leave them there, and starve them. I can send Professor Lombard there, and even the chief of staff, himself. I'm grateful to that rustle in the reeds. It has brought about a judicious change in my thinking.

I shan't destroy the Zeta bomb today. Pity I didn't bring the plush box also when I brought it away, I'd have had something in which to keep it. I shall keep Zeta and devote it to the service of the good. I'm astonished that I could ever have forgotten the great significance of the bomb in this kind of service.

Blind self-sacrifice made me regard it only as the source of a great evil. Prudence, which I now associate with the desire for sacrifice, makes it possible for me to consider Zeta from various aspects. With Zeta's aid I can see the world free from Zeta. By using it as a threat, I can order the laboratories in which it was to have serial production to be destroyed. I can render Professor Lombard harmless, and all the experts on the bomb, and its guards. I can do this if I screw the contact pin to a distance of one millimeter from the critical point. The threat of its explosion will compel them to submit and be absolutely obedient to me. With Zeta in my possession I can destroy every wicked man. With Zeta I can do much, I can do almost everything. Why do I say "almost"? I'm in a position not only to achieve general reforms, but to break into the life of every man on this earth and arbitrarily change it. If I wish, the wealthiest of merchants will hand over his store to me. If I wish, Mrs. Emilia will forsake the husband she loves, will bow to me and go wandering about the world. If I wish, the daughter of the chief of staff will present herself naked to me. If I give the order, the Nestor of science will shave off his beard and climb a tree in the city park in broad daylight. I imagine the scene and laugh: the Nestor of science climbing to the top of the tree with the agility of a monkey. I already see people coming from all over the world and bowing to me and handing me all sorts of articles and titles. One gives me a sumptuous villa at the seaside; another proposes that I should accept a doctorate of all the sciences; a third humbly explains that kingship is the finest form of government and that I am highly suited to be king, for I have a fine bearing and profound intelligence. Someone tells me I have very handsome ears.

I try to cast out these thoughts. For I am to serve the good. I must set about the destruction of evil. That's why I'm keeping Zeta. In order to destroy evil I must divide the people into wicked and good.

I can do that: I shall be the supreme judge. But why the future tense? I am the supreme judge. There is no one higher than I. I touch Zeta. I stroke it. How beautiful it has become, how smooth and pleasant it is, how brilliantly it shines. I press Zeta to my heart, I kiss it. What am I saying, what am I doing? But why ask? I'm doing and performing that which ought to be done; all this is included within my enlarged, human program of sacrifice. I cannot hesitate—I should be ridiculous if I hesitated. I am Caesar, Napoleon, Alexander the Great; I am the supreme judge, I am God, I surpass God. I shout: "I am God." The trees already know; they bow down to the ground. The human beings don't know it yet. I hurry back to the city by the shortest route. To judgment. I shall judge. All human beings are wicked; they must all be destroyed. I alone am good. I ALONE AM GOOD, FOR I POSSESS ZETA.

✿ *Alfred Bester*

THE MEN WHO MURDERED MOHAMMED

There was a man who mutilated history. He toppled empires and uprooted dynasties. Because of him, Mount Vernon should not be a national shrine, and Columbus, Ohio, should be called Cabot, Ohio. Because of him the name Marie Curie should be cursed in France, and no one should swear by the beard of the Prophet. Actually, these realities did not happen, because he was a mad professor; or, to put it another way, he only succeeded in making them unreal for himself.

Now, the patient reader is too familiar with the conventional mad professor, undersized and overbrowed, creating monsters in his laboratory which invariably turn on their maker and menace his lovely daughter. This story isn't about that sort of make-believe man. It's about Henry Hassel, a genuine mad professor in a class with such better-known men as Ludwig Boltzmann (*see* Ideal Gas Law), Jacques Charles and André Marie Ampère (1775-1836).

Everyone ought to know that the electrical ampere was so named in honor of Ampère. Ludwig Boltzmann was a distinguished Austrian physicist, as famous for his research on black-body radiation as on Ideal Gases. You can look him up in Volume Three of the *Encyclopaedia Britannica*, BALT to BRAI. Jacques Alexandre César Charles was the first mathematician to become interested in flight, and he invented the hydrogen balloon. These were real men.

They were also real mad professors. Ampère, for example, was on his way to an important meeting of scientists in Paris. In his taxi he got a brilliant idea (of an electrical nature, I assume) and whipped out a pencil and jotted the equation on the wall of the hansom cab. Roughly, it was: $dH = ipdl/r^2$ in which p is the perpendicular distance from P to the line of the element dl; or $dH = i \sin \phi \, dl/r^2$. This is sometimes known as Laplace's Law, although he wasn't at the meeting.

Anyway, the cab arrived at the Académie. Ampère jumped out, paid the driver and rushed into the meeting to tell everybody about his idea. Then he realized he didn't have the note on him, remembered where he'd left it, and had to chase through the streets of Paris after the taxi to recover his runaway equation. Sometimes I imagine that's how Fermat lost his famous "Last Theorem," although Fermat wasn't at the meeting either, having died some two hundred years earlier.

Or take Boltzmann. Giving a course in Advanced Ideal Gases, he peppered his lectures with involved calculus, which he worked out quickly and casually in his head. He had that kind of head. His students had so much trouble trying to puzzle out the math by ear that they couldn't keep up with the lectures, and they begged Boltzmann to work out his equations on the blackboard.

Boltzmann apologized and promised to be more helpful in the future. At the next lecture he began, "Gentlemen, combining Boyle's Law with the Law of Charles, we arrive at the equation $pv = p_0 v_0 (1 + at)$. Now, obviously, if $_aS^b = f(x)dx(a)$, then $pv = RT$ and $S f (x,y,z) \, dV = O$. It's as simple as two plus two equals four." At this point Boltzmann remembered his promise. He turned to the blackboard, conscientiously chalked $2 + 2 = 4$, and then breezed on, casually doing the complicated calculus in his head.

Jacques Charles, the brilliant mathematician who discovered Charles' Law (sometimes known as Gay-Lussac's Law), which Boltzmann mentioned in his lecture, had a lunatic passion to become a famous paleographer—that is, a discoverer of ancient manuscripts. I think that being forced to share credit with Gay-Lussac may have unhinged him.

He paid a transparent swindler named Vrain-Lucas 200,000 francs for holograph letters purportedly written by Julius Caesar, Alexander the Great, and Pontius Pilate.

Charles, a man who could see through any gas, ideal or not, actually believed in these forgeries despite the fact that the maladroit Vrain-Lucas had written them in modern French on modern notepaper bearing modern watermarks. Charles even tried to donate them to the Louvre.

Now, these men weren't idiots. They were geniuses who paid a high price for their genius because the rest of their thinking was other-world. A genius is someone who travels to truth by an unexpected path. Unfortunately, unexpected paths lead to disaster in everyday life. This is what happened to Henry Hassel, professor of Applied Compulsion at Unknown University in the year 1980.

Nobody knows where Unknown University is or what they teach there. It has a faculty of some two hundred eccentrics, and a student body of two thousand misfits—the kind that remain anonymous until they win Nobel prizes or become the First Man on Mars. You can always spot a graduate of U.U. when you ask people where they went to school. If you get an evasive reply like: "State," or "Oh, a fresh-water school you never heard of," you can bet they went to Unknown. Someday I hope to tell you more about this university, which is a center of learning only in the Pickwickian sense.

Anyway, Henry Hassel started home from his office in the Psychotic Psenter early one afternoon, strolling through the Physical Culture arcade. It is not true that he did this to leer at the nude coeds practicing Arcane Eurythmics; rather, Hassel liked to admire the trophies displayed in the arcade in memory of great Unknown teams which had won the sport of championships that Unknown teams win—in sports like Strabismus, Occlusion and Botulism. (Hassel had been Frambesia singles champion three years running.) He arrived home uplifted, and burst gaily into the house to discover his wife in the arms of a man.

There she was, a lovely woman of thirty-five, with smoky red hair and almond eyes, being heartily embraced by a person whose pockets were stuffed with pamphlets, microchemical apparatus and a patella-reflex hammer—a typical campus character of U.U., in fact. The embrace was so concentrated that neither of the offending parties noticed Henry Hassel glaring at them from the hallway.

Now, remember Ampère and Charles and Boltzmann. Hassel weighed one hundred and ninety pounds. He was muscular and uninhibited. It would have been child's play for him to have dismembered his wife and her lover, and thus simply and directly achieve the goal he desired—the end of his wife's life. But Henry Hassel was in the genius class; his mind just didn't operate that way.

Hassel breathed hard, turned and lumbered into his private laboratory like a freight engine. He opened a drawer labeled DUODENUM and removed a .45-caliber revolver. He opened other drawers, more interestingly labeled, and assembled apparatus. In exactly seven and one half minutes (such was his rage), he put together a time machine (such was his genius).

Professor Hassel assembled the time machine around him, set a dial for 1902, picked up the revolver and pressed a button. The machine made a noise like defective plumbing and Hassel disappeared. He reappeared in Philadelphia on June 3, 1902, went directly to No. 1218 Walnut Street, a red-brick house with marble steps, and rang the bell. A man who might have passed for the third Smith Brother opened the door and looked at Henry Hassel.

"Mr. Jessup?" Hassel asked in a suffocated voice.

"Yes?"

"You are Mr. Jessup?"

"I am."

"You will have a son, Edgar? Edgar Allan Jessup—so named because of your regrettable admiration for Poe?"

The third Smith Brother was startled. "Not that I know of," he said. "I'm not married yet."

"You will be," Hassel said angrily. "I have the misfortune to be married to your son's daughter, Greta. Excuse me." He raised the revolver and shot his wife's grandfather-to-be.

"She will have ceased to exist," Hassel muttered, blowing smoke out of the revolver. "I'll be a bachelor. I may even be married to somebody else . . . Good God! Who?"

Hassel waited impatiently for the automatic recall of the time machine to snatch him back to his own laboratory. He rushed into his living room. There was his red-headed wife, still in the arms of a man.

Hassel was thunderstruck.

"So that's it," he growled. "A family tradition of faithlessness. Well, we'll see about that. We have ways and means." He permitted himself a hollow laugh, returned to his laboratory, and sent himself back to the year 1901, where he shot and killed Emma Hotchkiss, his wife's maternal grandmother-to-be. He returned to his own home in his own time. There was his redheaded wife, still in the arms of another man.

"But I *know* the old bitch was her grandmother," Hassel muttered. "You couldn't miss the resemblance. What the hell's gone wrong?"

Hassel was confused and dismayed, but not without resources. He went to his study, had difficulty picking up the phone, but finally managed to dial the Malpractice Laboratory. His finger kept oozing out of the dial holes.

"Sam?" he said. "This is Henry."

"Who?"

"Henry."

"You'll have to speak up."

"Henry Hassel!"

"Oh, good afternoon, Henry."

"Tell me all about time."

"Time? Hmmm . . ." The Simplex-and-Multiplex Computer cleared its throat while it waited for the data circuits to link up. "Ahem. Time. (1) Absolute. (2) Relative. (3) Recurrent. (1) Absolute: period, contingent, duration, diurnity, perpetuity—"

"Sorry, Sam. Wrong request. Go back. I want time, reference to succession of, travel in."

Sam shifted gears and began again. Hassel listened intently. He nodded. He grunted. "Uh huh. Uh huh. Right. I see. Thought so. A continuum, eh? Acts performed in past must alter future. Then I'm on the right track. But act must be significant, eh? Mass-action effect. Trivia cannot divert existing phenomena streams. Hmmm. But how trivial is a grandmother?"

"What are you trying to do, Henry?"

"Kill my wife," Hassel snapped. He hung up. He returned to his laboratory. He considered, still in a jealous rage.

"Got to do something significant," he muttered. "Wipe Greta out. Wipe it all out. All right, by God! I'll show 'em."

Hassel went back to the year 1775, visited a Virginia farm and shot a young colonel in the brisket. The colonel's name was George Washington, and Hassel made sure he was dead. He returned to his own time and his own home. There was his redheaded wife, still in the arms of another.

"Damn!" said Hassel. He was running out of ammunition. He opened a fresh box of cartridges, went back in time and massacred Christopher Columbus, Napoleon, Mohammed and half a dozen other celebrities. "That ought to do it, by God!" said Hassel.

He returned to his own time, and found his wife as before.

His knees turned to water; his feet seemed to melt into the floor. He went back to his laboratory, walking through nightmare quicksands.

"What the hell is significant?" Hassel asked himself painfully. "How much does it take to change futurity? By God, I'll really change it this time. I'll go for broke."

He traveled to Paris at the turn of the twentieth century and visited a Madame Curie in an attic workshop near the Sorbonne. "Madame," he said in his execrable French, "I am a stranger to you of the utmost, but a scientist entire. Knowing of your experiments with radium— Oh? You haven't got to radium yet? No matter. I am here to teach you all of nuclear fission."

He taught her. He had the satisfaction of seeing Paris go up in a mushroom of smoke before the automatic recall brought him home. "That'll teach women to be faithless," he growled . . . "Guhhh!" The last was wrenched from his lips when he saw his redheaded wife still— But no need to belabor the obvious.

Hassel swam through fogs to his study and sat down to think. While he's thinking I'd better warn you that this is not a conventional time story. If you imagine for a moment that Henry is going to discover that the man fondling his wife is himself, you're mistaken. The viper is not Henry Hassel, his son, a relation, or even Ludwig Boltzmann (1844-1906). Hassel does not make a circle in time, ending where the story begins—to the satisfaction of nobody and the fury of everybody—for the simple reason that time isn't circular, or linear, or tandem, discoid, syzygous, longinquitous, or pandicularted. Time is a private matter, as Hassel discovered.

"Maybe I slipped up somehow," Hassel muttered. "I'd better find out." He fought with the telephone, which seemed to weigh a hundred tons, and at last managed to get through to the library.

"Hello, Library? This is Henry."

"Who?"

"Henry Hassel."

"Speak up, please."

"HENRY HASSEL!"

"Oh. Good afternoon, Henry."

"What have you got on George Washington?"

Library clucked while her scanners sorted through her catalogues. "George Washington, first president of the United States, was born in—"

"First president? Wasn't he murdered in 1775?"

"Really, Henry. That's an absurd question. Everybody knows that George Wash—"

"Doesn't anybody know he was shot?"

"By whom?"

"Me."

"When?"

"In 1775."

"How did you manage to do that?"

"I've got a revolver."

"No, I mean, how did you do it two hundred years ago?"

"I've got a time machine."

"Well, there's no record here," Library said. "He's still doing fine in my files. You must have missed."

"I did not miss. What about Christopher Columbus? Any record of his death in 1489?"

"But he discovered the New World in 1492."

"He did not. He was murdered in 1489."

"How?"

"With a forty-five slug in the gizzard."

"You again, Henry?"

"Yes."

"There's no record here," Library insisted. "You must be one lousy shot."

"I will not lose my temper," Hassel said in a trembling voice.

"Why not, Henry?"

"Because it's lost already," he shouted. "All right! What about Marie Curie? Did she or did she not discover the fission bomb which destroyed Paris at the turn of the century?"

"She did not. Enrico Fermi—"

"She did."

"She didn't."

"I personally taught her. Me. Henry Hassel."

"Everybody says you're a wonderful theoretician, but a lousy teacher, Henry. You—"

"Go to hell, you old biddy. This has got to be explained."

"Why?"

"I forget. There was something on my mind, but it doesn't matter now. What would you suggest?"

"You really have a time machine?"

"Of course I've got a time machine."

"Then go back and check."

Hassel returned to the year 1775, visited Mount Vernon, and interrupted the spring planting. "Excuse me, Colonel," he began.

The big man looked at him curiously. "You talk funny, stranger," he said. "Where are you from?"

"Oh, a fresh-water school you never heard of."

"You look funny too. Kind of misty, so to speak."

"Tell me, Colonel, what do you hear from Christopher Columbus?"

"Not much," Colonel Washington answered. "Been dead two, three hundred years."

"When did he die?"

"Year fifteen hundred some-odd, near as I remember."

"He did not. He died in 1489."

"Got your dates wrong, friend. He discovered America in 1492."

"Cabot discovered America. Sebastian Cabot."

"Nope. Cabot came a mite later."

"I have infallible proof!" Hassel began, but broke off as a stocky and rather stout man, with a face ludicrously reddened by rage, approached. He was wearing baggy gray slacks and a tweed jacket two sizes too small for him. He was carrying a .45 revolver. It was only after he had stared for a moment that Henry Hassel realized that he was looking at himself and not relishing the sight.

"My God!" Hassel murmured. "It's me, coming back to murder Washington that first time. If I'd made this second trip an hour later, I'd have found Washington dead. Hey!" he called. "Not yet. Hold off a minute. I've got to straighten something out first."

Hassel paid no attention to himself; indeed, he did not appear to be aware of himself. He marched straight up to Colonel Washington and shot him in the gizzard. Colonel Washington collapsed, emphatically dead. The first murderer inspected the body, and then, ignoring Hassel's attempt to stop him and engage him in dispute, turned and marched off, muttering venomously to himself.

"He didn't hear me," Hassel wondered. "He didn't even feel me. And why don't I remember myself trying to stop me the first time I shot the colonel? What the hell is going on?"

Considerably disturbed, Henry Hassel visited Chicago and dropped into the Chicago University squash courts in the early 1940's. There, in a slippery mess of graphite bricks and graphite dust that coated him, he located an Italian scientist named Fermi.

"Repeating Marie Curie's work, I see, *dottore?*" Hassel said.

Fermi glanced about as though he had heard a faint sound.

"Repeating Marie Curie's work, *dottore?*" Hassel roared.

Fermi looked at him strangely. "Where you from, *amico?*"

"State."

"State Department?"

"Just State. It's true, isn't it, *dottore*, that Marie Curie discovered nuclear fission back in nineteen ought ought?"

"No! No! No!" Fermi cried. "We are the first, and we are not there yet. Police! Police! Spy!"

"This time I'll go on record," Hassel growled. He pulled out his trusty .45, emptied it into Dr. Fermi's chest, and awaited arrest and immolation in newspaper files. To his amazement, Dr. Fermi did not collapse. Dr. Fermi merely explored his chest tenderly and, to the men who answered his cry, said, "It is nothing. I felt in my within a sudden sensation of burn which may be a neuralgia of the cardiac nerve, but is most likely gas."

Hassel was too agitated to wait for the automatic recall of the time machine. Instead he returned at once to Unknown University under his own power. This should have given him a clue, but he was too possessed to notice. It was at this time that I (1913-1975) first saw him—a dim figure tramping through parked cars, closed doors and brick walls, with the light of lunatic determination on his face.

He oozed into the library, prepared for an exhaustive discussion, but could not make himself felt or heard by the catalogues. He went to the Malpractice Laboratory, where Sam, the Simplex-and-Multiplex Computer, has installations sensitive up to 10,700 angstroms. Sam could not see Henry, but managed to hear him through a sort of wave-interference phenomenon.

"Sam," Hassel said, "I've made one hell of a discovery."

"You're always making discoveries, Henry," Sam complained. "Your data allocation is filled. Do I have to start another tape for you?"

"But I need advice. Who's the leading authority on time, reference to succession of, travel in?"

"That would be Israel Lennox, spatial mechanics, professor of, Yale."

"How do I get in touch with him?"

"You don't, Henry. He's dead. Died in '75."

"What authority have you got on time, travel in, living?"

"Wiley Murphy."

"Murphy? From your own Trauma Department? That's a break. Where is he now?"

"As a matter of fact, Henry, he went over to your house to ask you something."

Hassel went home without walking, searched through his laboratory and study without finding anyone, and at last floated into the living room, where his redheaded wife was still in the arms of another man. (All this, you understand, had taken place within the space of a few moments after the construction of the time machine; such is the nature of time and time travel.) Hassel cleared his throat once or twice and tried to tap his wife on the shoulder. His fingers went through her.

"Excuse me, darling," he said. "Has Wiley Murphy been in to see me?"

Then he looked closer and saw that the man embracing his wife was Murphy himself.

"Murphy!" Hassel exclaimed. "The very man I'm looking for. I've had the most extraordinary experience." Hassel at once launched into a lucid description of his extraordinary experience, which went something like this: "Murphy, $u - v = (u^{1/2} - v^{1/4})$ $(u^a + u^x v^y + v^b)$ but when George Washington $F(x)y^2 dx$ and Enrico Fermi $F(u^{1/2})$ dxdt one half of Marie Curie, then what about Christopher Columbus times the square root of minus one?"

Murphy ignored Hassel, as did Mrs. Hassel. I jotted down Hassel's equations on the hood of a passing taxi.

"Do listen to me, Murphy," Hassel said. "Greta dear, would you mind leaving us for a moment? I— For heaven's sake, will you two stop that nonsense? This is serious."

Hassel tried to separate the couple. He could no more touch them than make them hear him. His face turned red again and he became quite choleric as he beat at Mrs. Hassel and Murphy. It was like beating an Ideal Gas. I thought it best to interfere.

"Hassel!"

"Who's that?"

"Come outside a moment. I want to talk to you."

He shot through the wall. "Where are you?"

"Over here."

"You're sort of dim."

"So are you."

"Who are you?"

"My name's Lennox. Israel Lennox."

"Israel Lennox, spatial mechanics, professor of, Yale?"

"The same."

"But you died in '75."

"I disappeared in '75."

"What d'you mean?"

"I invented a time machine."

"By God! So did I," Hassel said. "This afternoon. The

idea came to me in a flash—I don't know why—and I've had the most extraordinary experience. Lennox, time is not a continuum."

"No?"

"It's a series of discrete particles—like pearls on a string."

"Yes?"

"Each pearl is a 'Now.' Each 'Now' has its own past and future. But none of them relate to any others. You see? If $a = a_1 + a_2ji + \phi ax(b_1)$—"

"Never mind the mathematics, Henry."

"It's a form of quantum transfer of energy. Time is emitted in discrete corpuscles or quanta. We can visit each individual quantum and make changes within it, but no change in any one corpuscle affects any other corpuscle. Right?"

"Wrong," I said sorrowfully.

"What d'you mean, 'Wrong'?" he said, angrily gesturing through the cleavage of a passing coed. "You take the trochoid equations and—"

"Wrong," I repeated firmly. "Will you listen to me, Henry?"

"Oh, go ahead," he said.

"Have you noticed that you've become rather insubstantial? Dim? Spectral? Space and time no longer affect you?"

"Yes."

"Henry, I had the misfortune to construct a time machine back in '75."

"So you said. Listen, what about power input? I figure I'm using about 7.3 kilowatts per—"

"Never mind the power input, Henry. On my first trip into the past, I visited the Pleistocene. I was eager to photograph the mastodon, the giant ground sloth, and the saber-toothed tiger. While I was backing up to get a mastodon fully in the field of view at f/6.3 at 1/100th of a second, or on the LVS scale—"

"Never mind the LVS scale," he said.

"While I was backing up, I inadvertently trampled and killed a small Pleistocene insect."

"Aha!" said Hassel.

"I was terrified by the incident. I had visions of returning to my world to find it completely changed as a result of this single death. Imagine my surprise when I returned to my world to find that nothing had changed."

"Oho!" said Hassel.

"I became curious. I went back to the Pleistocene and killed the mastodon. Nothing was changed in 1975. I returned to the Pleistocene and slaughtered the wild life—still with no effect. I ranged through time, killing and destroying, in an attempt to alter the present."

"Then you did it just like me," Hassel exclaimed. "Odd we didn't run into each other."

"Not odd at all."

"I got Columbus."

"I got Marco Polo."

"I got Napoleon."

"I thought Einstein was more important."

"Mohammed didn't change things much—I expected more from *him*."

"I know. I got him too."

"What do you mean, you got him too?" Hassel demanded.

"I killed him September 16, 599. Old Style."

"Why, I got Mohammed, January 5, 598."

"I believe you."

"But how could you have killed him after I killed him?"

"We both killed him."

"That's impossible."

"My boy," I said, "time is entirely subjective. It's a private matter—a personal experience. There is no such thing as objective time, just as there is no such thing as objective love, or an objective soul."

"Do you mean to say that time travel is impossible? But we've done it."

"To be sure, and many others, for all I know. But we each travel into our own past, and no other person's. There is no universal continuum, Henry. There are only billions of individuals, each with his own continuum; and one continuum cannot affect the other. We're like millions of strands of spaghetti in the same pot. No time traveler can ever meet another time traveler in the past or future. Each of us must travel up and down his own strand alone."

"But we're meeting each other now."

"We're no longer time travelers, Henry. We've become the spaghetti sauce."

"Spaghetti sauce?"

"Yes. You and I can visit any strand we like, because we've destroyed ourselves."

"I don't understand."

"When a man changes the past he only affects his own past—no one else's. The past is like memory. When you erase a man's memory, you wipe him out, but you don't wipe out anybody else. You and I have erased our past. The individual worlds of the others go on, but we have ceased to exist." I paused significantly.

"What d'you mean, 'ceased to exist'?"

"With each act of destruction we dissolved a little. Now we're all gone. We've committed chronicide. We're ghosts. I hope Mrs. Hassel will be very happy with Mr. Murphy. . . . Now let's go over to the Académie. Ampére is telling a great story about Ludwig Boltzmann."

✿ *Walter M. Miller, Jr.*

A CANTICLE FOR LEIBOWITZ

Brother Francis Gerard of Utah would never have discovered the sacred document, had it not been for the pilgrim with girded loins who appeared during that young monk's Lenten fast in the desert. Never before had Brother Francis actually seen a pilgrim with girded loins, but that this one was the bona fide article he was convinced at a glance. The pilgrim was a spindly old fellow with a staff, a basket hat, and a brushy beard, stained yellow about the chin. He walked with a limp and carried a small waterskin over one shoulder. His loins truly were girded with a ragged piece of dirty burlap, his only clothing except for hat and sandals. He whistled tunelessly on his way.

The pilgrim came shuffling down the broken trail out of the north, and he seemed to be heading toward the Brothers of Leibowitz Abbey six miles to the south. The pilgrim and the monk noticed each other across an expanse of ancient rubble. The pilgrim stopped whistling and stared. The monk, because of certain implications of the rule of solitude for fast days, quickly averted his gaze and continued about his business of hauling large rocks with which to complete the wolf-proofing of his temporary shelter. Somewhat weakened by a ten-day diet of cactus fruit, Brother Francis found the work made him exceedingly dizzy; the landscape had been shimmering before his eyes and dancing with black specks, and he was at first uncertain that the bearded apparition was not a mirage induced by hunger, but after a moment it called to him cheerfully, *"Ola allay!"*

It was a pleasant musical voice.

The rule of silence forbade the young monk to answer, except by smiling shyly at the ground.

"Is this here the road to the abbey?" the wanderer asked.

The novice nodded at the ground and reached down for a chalklike fragment of stone. The pilgrim picked his way toward him through the rubble. "What you doing with all the rocks?" he wanted to know.

The monk knelt and hastily wrote the words "Solitude & Silence" on a large flat rock, so that the pilgrim—if he could read, which was statistically unlikely—would know that he was making himself an occasion of sin for the penitent and would perhaps have the grace to leave in peace.

"Oh, well," said the pilgrim. He stood there for a moment, looking around, then rapped a certain large rock with his staff. "*That* looks like a handy crag for you," he offered helpfully, then added: "Well, good luck. And may you find a Voice, as y' seek."

Now Brother Francis had no immediate intuition that the stranger meant "Voice" with a capital V, but merely assumed that the old fellow had mistaken him for a deaf mute. He glanced up once again as the pilgrim shuffled away whistling, sent a swift silent benediction after him for safe wayfaring, and went back to his rock work, building a coffin-sized enclosure in which he might sleep at night without offering himself as wolf bait.

A sky-herd of cumulus clouds, on their way to bestow moist blessings on the mountains after having cruelly tempted the desert, offered welcome respite from the searing sunlight, and he worked rapidly to finish before they were gone again. He punctuated his labors with whispered prayers for the certainty of a true Vocation, for this was the purpose of his inward quest while fasting in the desert.

At last he hoisted the rock which the pilgrim had suggested.

The color of exertion drained quickly from his face. He backed away a step and dropped the stone as if he had uncovered a serpent.

A rusted metal box lay half-crushed in the rubble . . . only a rusted metal box.

He moved toward it curiously, then paused. There were things, and then there were Things. He crossed himself hastily, and muttered brief Latin at the heavens. Thus fortified, he readdressed himself to the box.

"*Apage Satanas!*"

He threatened it with the heavy crucifix of his rosary.

"Depart, O Foul Seductor!"

He sneaked a tiny aspergillum from his robes and quickly spattered the box with holy water before it could realize what he was about.

"If thou be creature of the Devil, begone!"

The box showed no signs of withering, exploding, melting away. It exuded no blasphemous ichor. It only lay quietly in its place and allowed the desert wind to evaporate the sanctifying droplets.

"So be it," said the brother, and knelt to extract it from its lodging. He sat down on the rubble and spent nearly an hour battering it open with a stone. The thought crossed his mind that such an archaeological relic—for such it obviously was—might be the Heaven-sent sign of his vocation but he suppressed the notion as quickly as it occurred to him. His abbot had warned him sternly against expecting any direct personal Revelation of a spectacular nature. Indeed, he had gone forth from the abbey to fast and do penance for forty days that he might be rewarded with the inspiration of a calling to Holy Orders, but to expect a vision or a voice crying "Francis, where art thou?" would be a vain presumption. Too many novices had returned from their desert vigils with tales of omens and signs and visions in the heavens, and the good abbot had adopted a firm policy regarding these. Only the Vatican was qualified to decide the authenticity of such things. "An attack of sunstroke is no indication that you are fit to profess the solemn vows of the order," he had growled. And certainly it was true that only rarely did a call from Heaven come through any device other than the *inward* ear, as a gradual congealing of inner certainty.

Nevertheless, Brother Francis found himself handling the old metal box with as much reverence as was possible while battering at it.

It opened suddenly, spilling some of its contents. He

stared for a long time before daring to touch, and a cool thrill gathered along his spine. Here was antiquity indeed! And as a student of archaeology, he could scarcely believe his wavering vision. Brother Jeris would be frantic with envy, he thought, but quickly repented this unkindness and murmured his thanks to the sky for such a treasure.

He touched the articles gingerly—they were real enough —and began sorting through them. His studies had equipped him to recognize a screwdriver—an instrument once used for twisting threaded bits of metal into wood—and a pair of cutters with blades no longer than his thumbnail, but strong enough to cut soft bits of metal or bone. There was an odd tool with a rotted wooden handle and a heavy copper tip to which a few flakes of molten lead had adhered, but he could make nothing of it. There was a toroidal roll of gummy black stuff, too far deteriorated by the centuries for him to identify. There were strange bits of metal, broken glass, and an assortment of tiny tubular things with wire whiskers of the type prized by the hill pagans as charms and amulets, but thought by some archaeologists to be remnants of the legendary *machina analytica*, supposedly dating back to the Deluge of Flame. All these and more he examined carefully and spread on the wide flat stone. The documents he saved until last. The documents, as always, were the real prize, for so few papers had survived the angry bonfires of the Age of Simplification, when even the sacred writings had curled and blackened and withered into smoke while ignorant crowds howled vengeance.

Two large folded papers and three hand-scribbled notes constituted his find. All were cracked and brittle with age, and he handled them tenderly, shielding them from the wind with his robe. They were scarcely legible and scrawled in the hasty characters of pre-Deluge English—a tongue now used, together with Latin, only by monastics and in the Holy Ritual. He spelled it out slowly, recognizing words but uncertain of meanings. One note said: *Pound pastrami, can kraut, six bagels, for Emma.* Another ordered: *Don't forget to pick up form 1040 for Uncle Revenue.* The third note was only a column of figures with a circled total from which another amount was subtracted and finally a percentage taken, followed by the word *damn!* From this he could deduce nothing, except to check the arithmetic, which proved correct.

Of the two larger papers, one was tightly rolled and began to fall to pieces when he tried to open it; he could make out the words RACING FORM, but nothing more. He laid it back in the box for later restorative work.

The second large paper was a single folded sheet, whose creases were so brittle that he could only inspect a little of it by parting the folds and peering between them as best he could.

A diagram . . . a web of white lines on dark paper!

Again the cool thrill gathered along his spine. It was a *blueprint*—that exceedingly rare class of ancient document most prized by students of antiquity, and usually most challenging to interpreters and searchers for meaning.

And, as if the find were not enough of a blessing, among the words written in a block at the lower corner of the document was the name of the founder of his order—of the Blessed Leibowitz *himself!*

His trembling hands threatened to tear the paper in their happy agitation. The parting words of the pilgrim tumbled back to him: "May you find a Voice, as y' seek." Voice indeed, with V capitalized and formed by the wings of a descending dove and illuminated in three colors against a background of gold leaf. V as in *Vere dignum* and *Vidi aquam,* at the head of a page of the Missal. V, he saw quite clearly, as in Vocation.

He stole another glance to make certain it was so, then breathed, *"Beate Leibowitz, ora pro me. . . . Sancte Leibowitz, exaudi me,"* the second invocation being a rather daring one, since the founder of his order had not yet been declared a saint.

Forgetful of his abbot's warning, he climbed quickly to his feet and stared across the shimmering terrain to the south in the direction taken by the old wanderer of the burlap loincloth. But the pilgrim had long since vanished. Surely an angel of God, if not the Blessed Leibowitz himself, for had he not revealed this miraculous treasure by pointing out the rock to be moved and murmuring that prophetic farewell?

Brother Francis stood basking in his awe until the sun lay red on the hills and evening threatened to engulf him in its shadows. At last he stirred, and reminded himself of the wolves. His gift included no guarantee of charismata for subduing the wild beast, and he hastened to finish his enclosure before darkness fell on the desert. When the stars came out, he rekindled his fire and gathered his daily repast of the small purple cactus fruit, his only nourishment except the handful of parched corn brought to him by the priest each Sabbath. Sometimes he found himself staring hungrily at the lizards which scurried over the rocks, and was troubled by gluttonous nightmares.

But tonight his hunger was less troublesome than an impatient urge to run back to the abbey and announce his wondrous encounter to his brethren. This, of course, was unthinkable. Vocation or no, he must remain here until the end of Lent, and continue as if nothing extraordinary had occurred.

A cathedral will be built upon this site, he thought dreamily as he sat by the fire. He could see it rising from the rubble of the ancient village, magnificent spires visible for miles across the desert . . .

But cathedrals were for teeming masses of people. The desert was home for only scattered tribes of huntsmen and the monks of the abbey. He settled in his dreams for a shrine, attracting rivers of pilgrims with girded loins . . . He drowsed. When he awoke, the fire was reduced to glowing embers. Something seemed amiss. Was he quite alone? He blinked about at the darkness.

From beyond the bed of reddish coal, the dark wolf blinked back. The monk yelped and dived for cover.

The yelp, he decided as he lay trembling within his den of stones, had not been a serious breach of the rule of silence. He lay hugging the metal box and praying for the days of Lent to pass swiftly, while the sound of padded feet scratched about the enclosure.

Each night the wolves prowled about his camp, and the darkness was full of their howling. The days were glaring nightmares of hunger, heat, and scorching sun. He spent them at prayer and wood-gathering, trying to suppress his impatience for the coming of Holy Saturday's high noon, the end of Lent and of his vigil.

But when at last it came, Brother Francis found himself too famished for jubilation. Wearily he packed his pouch, pulled up his cowl against the sun, and tucked his precious box beneath one arm. Thirty pounds lighter and several degrees weaker than he had been on Ash Wednesday, he staggered the six-mile stretch to the abbey where he fell exhausted before its gates. The brothers who carried him in and bathed him and shaved him and anointed his desiccated tissues reported that he babbled incessantly in his delirium about an apparition in a burlap loincloth, addressing it at times as an angel and again as a saint, frequently invoking the name of Leibowitz and thanking him for a revelation of sacred relics and a racing form.

Such reports filtered through the monastic congregation and soon reached the ears of the abbot, whose eyes immediately narrowed to slits and whose jaw went rigid with the rock of policy.

"Bring him," growled that worthy priest in a tone that sent a recorder scurrying.

The abbot paced and gathered his ire. It was not that he objected to miracles, as such, if duly investigated, certified, and sealed; for miracles—even though always incompatible with administrative efficiency, and the abbot was administrator as well as priest—were the bedrock stuff on which his faith was founded. But last year there had been Brother Noyen with his miraculous hangman's noose, and the year before that, Brother Smirnov who had been mysteriously cured of the gout upon handling a probable relic of the Blessed Leibowitz, and the year before that . . . *Faugh!* The incidents had been too frequent and outrageous to tolerate. Ever since Leibowitz' beatification, the young fools had been sniffing around after shreds of the miraculous like a pack of good-natured hounds scratching eagerly at the back gate of Heaven for scraps.

It was quite understandable, but also quite unbearable. Every monastic order is eager for the canonization of its founder, and delighted to produce any bit of evidence to serve the cause of advocacy. But the abbot's flock was getting out of hand, and their zeal for miracles was making the Albertian Order of Leibowitz a laughing stock at

New Vatican. He had determined to make any new bearers of miracles suffer the consequences, either as a punishment for impetuous and impertinent credulity, or as payment in penance for a gift of grace in case of later verification.

By the time the young novice knocked at his door, the abbot had projected himself into the desired state of carnivorous expectancy beneath a bland exterior.

"Come in, my son," he breathed softly.

"You sent for . . ." The novice paused, smiling happily as he noticed the familiar metal box on the abbot's table. ". . . for me, Father Juan?" he finished.

"Yes . . ." The abbot hesitated. His voice smiled with a withering acid, adding: "Or perhaps you would prefer that I come *to you*, hereafter, since you've become such a famous personage."

"O, no, Father!" Brother Francis reddened and gulped.

"You are seventeen, and plainly an idiot."

"That is undoubtedly true, Father."

"What improbable excuse can you propose for your outrageous vanity in believing yourself fit for Holy Orders?"

"I can offer none, my ruler and teacher. My sinful pride is unpardonable."

"To imagine that it is so great as to be unpardonable is even a vaster vanity," the priest roared.

"Yes, Father. I am indeed a worm."

The abbot smiled icily and resumed his watchful calm. "And you are now ready to deny your feverish ravings about an angel appearing to reveal to you this . . ." He gestured contemptuously at the box. ". . . this assortment of junk?"

Brother Francis gulped and closed his eyes. "I—I fear I cannot deny it, my master."

"What?"

"I cannot deny what I have seen, Father."

"Do you know what is going to happen to you now?"

"Yes, Father."

"Then prepare to take it!"

With a patient sigh, the novice gathered up his robes about his waist and bent over the table. The good abbot produced his stout hickory ruler from the drawer and whacked him soundly ten times across the bare buttocks. After each whack, the novice dutifully responded with a

"*Deo Gratias!*" for this lesson in the virtue of humility.

"Do you *now* retract it?" the abbot demanded as he rolled down his sleeve.

"Father, I cannot."

The priest turned his back and was silent for a moment. "Very well," he said tersely. "Go. But do not expect to profess your solemn vows this season with the others."

Brother Francis returned to his cell in tears. His fellow novices would join the ranks of the professed monks of the order, while he must wait another year—and spend another Lenten season among the wolves in the desert, seeking a vocation which he felt had already been granted to him quite emphatically. As the weeks passed, however, he found some satisfaction in noticing that Father Juan had not been entirely serious in referring to his find as "an assortment of junk." The archaeological relics aroused considerable interest among the brothers, and much time was spent at cleaning the tools, classifying them, restoring the documents to a pliable condition, and attempting to ascertain their meaning. It was even whispered among the novices that Brother Francis had discovered true relics of the Blessed Leibowitz—especially in the form of the blueprint bearing the legend OP COBBLESTONE, REQ LEIBOWITZ & HARDIN, which was stained with several brown splotches which might have been his blood—or equally likely, as the abbot pointed out, might be stains from a decayed apple core. But the print was dated in the Year of Grace 1956, which was—as nearly as could be determined—during that venerable man's lifetime, a lifetime now obscured by legend and myth, so that it was hard to determine any but a few facts about the man.

It was said that God, in order to test mankind, had commanded wise men of that age, among them the Blessed Leibowitz, to perfect diabolic weapons and give them into the hands of latter-day Pharaohs. And with such weapons Man had, within the span of a few weeks, destroyed most of his civilization and wiped out a large part of the population. After the Deluge of Flame came the plagues, the madness, and the bloody inception of the Age of Simplification when the furious remnants of humanity had torn politicians, technicians, and men of learning limb from limb, and burned all records that might contain information that could once more lead into paths of destruction. Nothing had been so fiercely hated as the written word, the learned man. It was during this time that the word *simpleton* came to mean *honest, upright, virtuous citizen,* a concept once denoted by the term *common man.*

To escape the righteous wrath of the surviving simple-tons, many scientists and learned men fled to the only sanctuary which would try to offer them protection. Holy Mother Church received them, vested them in monks' robes, tried to conceal them from the mobs. Sometimes the sanctuary was effective; more often it was not. Monasteries were invaded, records and sacred books were burned, refugees seized and hanged. Leibowitz had fled to the Cistercians, professed their vows, become a priest, and after twleve years had won permission from the Holy See to found a new monastic order to be called "the Albertians," after St. Albert the Great, teacher of Aquinas and patron saint of scientists. The new order was to be dedicated to the preservation of knowledge, secular and sacred, and the duty of the brothers was to memorize such books and papers as could be smuggled to them from all parts of the world. Leibowitz was at last identified by simpletons as a former scientist, and was martyred by hanging; but the order continued, and when it became safe again to possess written documents, many books were transcribed from memory. Precedence, however, had been given to sacred writings, to history, the humanities, and social sciences—since the memories of the memorizers were limited, and few of the brothers were trained to understand the physical sciences. From the vast store of human knowledge, only a pitiful collection of hand-written books remained.

Now, after six centuries of darkness, the monks still preserved it, studied it, recopied it, and waited. It mattered not in the least to them that the knowledge they saved was useless—and some of it even incomprehensible. The knowledge was there, and it was their duty to save it, and it would still be with them if the darkness in the world lasted ten thousand years.

Brother Francis Gerard of Utah returned to the desert the following year and fasted again in solitude. Once more he returned, weak and emaciated, to be confronted by the abbot, who demanded to know if he claimed further conferences with members of the Heavenly Host, or was prepared to renounce his story of the previous year.

"I cannot help what I have seen, my teacher," the lad repeated.

Once more did the abbot chastise him in Christ, and once more did he postpone his profession. The document, however, had been forwarded to a seminary for study, after a copy had been made. Brother Francis remained a novice, and continued to dream wistfully of the shrine which might someday be built upon the site of his find.

"Stubborn boy!" fumed the abbot. "Why didn't somebody else see his silly pilgrim, if the slovenly fellow was heading for the abbey as he said? One more escapade for the Devil's Advocate to cry hoax about. Burlap loincloth indeed!"

The burlap had been troubling the abbot, for a tradition related that Leibowitz had been hanged with a burlap bag for a hood.

Brother Francis spent seven years in the novitiate, seven Lenten vigils in the desert, and became highly proficient in the imitation of wolf calls. For the amusement of his brethren, he would summon the pack to the vicinity of the abbey by howling from the walls after dark. By day, he served in the kitchen, scrubbed the stone floors, and continued his studies of the ancients.

Then one day a messenger from the seminary came riding to the abbey on an ass, bearing tidings of great joy. "It is known," said the messenger, "that the documents found near here are authentic as to date of origin, and that the blueprint was somehow connected with your founder's work. It's being sent to New Vatican for further study."

"Possibly a true relic of Leibowitz, then?" the abbot asked calmly.

But the messenger could not commit himself to that extent, and only raised a shrug of one eyebrow. "It is said that Leibowitz was a widower at the time of his ordination. If the name of his deceased wife could be discovered . . ."

The abbot recalled the note in the box concerning certain articles of food for a woman, and he too shrugged an eyebrow.

Soon afterwards, he summoned Brother Francis into his presence. "My boy," said the priest, actually beaming, "I believe the time has come for you to profess your solemn vows. And may I commend you for your patience and persistence. We shall speak no more of your, ah . . . encounter with the, ah, desert wanderer. You are a good simpleton. You may kneel for my blessing, if you wish."

Brother Francis sighed and fell forward in a dead faint. The abbot blessed him and revived him, and he was permitted to profess the solemn vows of the Albertian Brothers of Leibowitz, swearing himself to perpetual poverty, chastity, obedience, and observance of the rule.

Soon afterwards, he was assigned to the copying room, apprentice under an aged monk named Horner, where he would undoubtedly spend the rest of his days illuminating the pages of algebra texts with patterns of olive leaves and cheerful cherubim.

"You have five hours a week," croaked his aged overseer, "which you may devote to an approved project of your own choosing, if you wish. If not, the time will be assigned to copying the *Summa Theologica* and such fragmentary copies of the Britannica as exist."

The young monk thought it over, then, asked: "May I have the time for elaborating a beautiful copy of the Leibowitz blueprint?"

Brother Horner frowned doubtfully. "I don't know, son —our good abbot is rather sensitive on this subject, I'm afraid . . ."

Brother Francis begged him earnestly.

"Well, perhaps," the old man said reluctantly. "It seems like a rather brief project, so—I'll permit it."

The young monk selected the finest lambskin available and spent many weeks curing it and stretching it and stoning it to a perfect surface, bleached to a snowy whiteness. He spent more weeks at studying copies of his precious document in every detail, so that he knew each tiny line and marking in the complicated web of geometric markings and mystifying symbols. He pored over it until he could see the whole amazing complexity with his eyes closed. Additional weeks were spent searching painstakingly through the monastery's library for any information at all that might lead to some glimmer of understanding of the design.

Brother Jeris, a young monk who worked with him in

the copy room and who frequently teased him about miraculous encounters in the desert, came to squint at it over his shoulder and asked: "What, pray, is the meaning of *Transistorized Control System for Unit Six-B?*"

"Clearly, it is the name of the thing which this diagram represents," said Francis, a trifle crossly since Jeris had already read the title of the document aloud.

"Surely," said Jeris. "But what is the thing the diagram represents?"

"The transistorized control system for unit six-B, obviously."

Jeris laughed mockingly.

Brother Francis reddened. "I should imagine," said he, "that it represents an abstract concept, rather than a concrete *thing*. It's clearly not a recognizable picture of an object, unless the form is so stylized as to require special training to see it. In my opinion, *Transistorized Control System* is some high abstraction of transcendental value."

"Pertaining to what field of learning?" asked Jeris, still smiling smugly.

"Why . . ." Brother Francis paused. "Since our Beatus Leibowitz was an electronicist prior to his profession and ordination, I suppose the concept applies to the lost art called *electronics.*"

"So it is written. But what was the subject matter of that art, Brother?"

"That too is written. The subject matter of electronics was the Electron, which one fragmentary source defines as a Negative Twist of Nothingness."

"I am impressed by your astuteness," said Jeris. "Now perhaps you can tell me how to negate nothingness?"

Brother Francis reddened slightly and squirmed for a reply.

"A negation of nothingness should yield somethingness, I suppose," Jeris continued. "So the Electron must have been a twist of *something*. Unless the negation applies to the 'twist,' and then we would be 'Untwisting Nothing,' eh?" He chuckled. "How clever they must have been, these ancients. I suppose if you keep at it, Francis, you will learn how to untwist a nothing, and then we shall have the Electron in our midst. Where would we put it? On the high altar, perhaps?"

"I couldn't say," Francis answered stiffly. "But I have a certain faith that the Electron must have existed at one time, even though I can't say how it was constructed or what it might have been used for."

The iconoclast laughed mockingly and returned to his work. The incident saddened Francis, but did not turn him from his devotion to his project.

As soon as he had exhausted the library's meager supply of information concerning the lost art of the Albertians' founder, he began preparing preliminary sketches of the designs he meant to use on the lambskin. The diagram itself, since its meaning was obscure, would be redrawn precisely as it was in the blueprint, and penned in coal-black lines. The lettering and numbering, however, he would translate into a more decorative and colorful script than the plain block letters used by the ancients. And the text contained in a square block marked SPECIFICATIONS would be distributed pleasingly around the borders of the document, upon scrolls and shields supported by doves and cherubim. He would make the black lines of the diagram less stark and austere by imagining the geometric tracery to be a trellis, and decorate it with green vines and golden fruit, birds and perhaps a wily serpent. At the very top would be a representation of the Triune God, and at the bottom the coat of arms of the Albertian Order. Thus was the Transistorized Control System of the Blessed Leibowitz to be glorified and rendered appealing to the eye as well as to the intellect.

When he had finished the preliminary sketch, he showed it shyly to Brother Horner for suggestions or approval. "I can see," said the old man a bit remorsefully, "that your project is not to be as brief as I had hoped. But . . . continue with it anyhow. The design is beautiful, beautiful indeed."

"Thank you, Brother."

The old man leaned close to wink confidentially. "I've heard the case for Blessed Leibowitz' canonization has been speeded up, so possibly our dear abbot is less troubled by you-know-what than he previously was."

The news of the speed-up was, of course, happily received by all monastics of the order. Leibowitz' beatification had long since been effected, but the final step in

declaring him to be a saint might require many more years,
even though the case was under way; and indeed there
was the possibility that the Devil's Advocate might uncover
evidence to prevent the canonization from occurring at all.

Many months after he had first conceived the project,
Brother Francis began actual work on the lambskin. The
intricacies of scrollwork, the excruciatingly delicate work of
inlaying the gold leaf, the hair-fine detail, made it a labor
of years; and when his eyes began to trouble him, there
were long weeks when he dared not touch it at all for
fear of spoiling it with one little mistake. But slowly, painfully, the ancient diagram was becoming a blaze of beauty.
The brothers of the abbey gathered to watch and murmur
over it, and some even said that the inspiration of it was
proof enough of his alleged encounter with the pilgrim
who might have been Blessed Leibowitz.

"I can't see why you don't spend your time on a *useful*
project," was Brother Jeris' comment, however. The skeptical monk had been using his own free-project time to make
and decorate sheepskin shades for the oil lamps in the chapel.

Brother Horner, the old master copyist, had fallen ill.
Within weeks, it became apparent that the well-loved monk
was on his deathbed. In the midst of the monastery's grief,
the abbot quietly appointed Brother Jeris as master of the
copy room.

A Mass of Burial was chanted early in Advent, and the
remains of the holy old man were committed to the earth
of their origin. On the following day, Brother Jeris informed Brother Francis that he considered it about time
for him to put away the things of a child and start doing
a man's work. Obediently, the monk wrapped his precious
project in parchment, protected it with heavy board, shelved
it, and began producing sheepskin lampshades. He made
no murmur of protest, and contented himself with realizing
that someday the soul of Brother Jeris would depart by the
same road as that of Brother Horner, to begin the life for
which this copy room was but the staging ground; and afterwards, please God, he might be allowed to complete his
beloved document.

Providence, however, took an earlier hand in the matter.
During the following summer, a monsignor with several
clerks and a donkey train came riding into the abbey and

announced that he had come from New Vatican, as Leibowitz advocate in the canonization proceedings, to investigate such evidence as the abbey could produce that might
have bearing on the case, including an alleged apparition of
the beatified which had come to one Francis Gerard of Utah.

The gentleman was warmly greeted, quartered in the
suite reserved for visiting prelates, lavishly served by six
young monks responsive to his every whim, of which he
had very few. The finest wines were opened, the huntsman
snared the plumpest quail and chaparral cocks, and the
advocate was entertained each evening by fiddlers and a
troupe of clowns, although the visitor persisted in insisting
that life go on as usual at the abbey.

On the third day of his visit, the abbot sent for Brother
Francis. "Monsignor di Simone wishes to see you," he said.
"If you let your imagination run away with you, boy, we'll
use your gut to string a fiddle, feed your carcass to the
wolves, and bury the bones in unhallowed ground. Now get
along and see the good gentleman."

Brother Francis needed no such warning. Since he had
awakened from his feverish babblings after his first Lenten
fast in the desert, he had never mentioned the encounter
with the pilgrim except when asked about it, nor had he
allowed himself to speculate any further concerning the
pilgrim's identity. That the pilgrim might be a matter for
high ecclesiastical concern frightened him a little, and his
knock was timid at the monsignor's door.

His fright proved unfounded. The monsignor was a
suave and diplomatic elder who seemed keenly interested
in the small monk's career.

"Now about your encounter with our blessed founder,"
he said after some minutes of preliminary amenities.

"Oh, but I never said he was our Blessed Leibo—"

"Of course you didn't, my son. Now I have here an
account of it, as gathered from other sources, and I would
like you to read it, and either confirm it or correct it." He
paused to draw a scroll from his case and handed it to
Francis. "The sources for this version, of course, had it on
hearsay only," he added, "and only *you* can describe it
first hand, so I want you to edit it *most* scrupulously."

"Of course. What happened was really very simple,
Father."

But it was apparent from the fatness of the scroll that the hearsay account was not so simple. Brother Francis read with mounting apprehension which soon grew to the proportions of pure horror.

"You look white, my son. Is something wrong?" asked the distinguished priest.

"This . . . this . . . it wasn't like this *at all!*" gasped Francis. "He didn't say more than a few words to me. I only saw him once. He just asked me the way to the abbey and tapped the rock where I found the relics."

"No heavenly choir?"

"Oh, no!"

"And it's not true about the nimbus and the carpet of roses that grew up along the road where he walked?"

"As God is my judge, nothing like that happened at all!"

"Ah, well," sighed the advocate. "Travelers' stories are always exaggerated."

He seemed saddened, and Francis hastened to apologize, but the advocate dismissed it as of no great importance to the case. "There are other miracles, carefully documented," he explained, "and anyway—there is one bit of good news about the documents you discovered. We've unearthed the name of the wife who died before our founder came to the order."

"Yes?"

"Yes. It was Emily."

Despite his disappointment with Brother Francis' account of the pilgrim, Monsignor di Simone spent five days at the site of the find. He was accompanied by an eager crew of novices from the abbey, all armed with picks and shovels. After extensive digging, the advocate returned with a small assortment of additional artifacts, and one bloated tin can that contained a desiccated mess which might once have been sauerkraut.

Before his departure, he visited the copy room and asked to see Brother Francis' copy of the famous blueprint. The monk protested that it was really nothing, and produced it with such eagerness his hands trembled.

"Zounds!" said the monsignor, or an oath to such effect. "Finish it, man, finish it!"

The monk looked smilingly at Brother Jeris. Brother Jeris swiftly turned away; the back of his neck gathered color.

The following morning, Francis resumed his labors over the illuminated blueprint, with gold leaf, quills, brushes, and dyes.

And then came another donkey train from New Vatican, with a full complement of clerks and armed guards for defense against highwaymen, this time headed by a monsignor with small horns and pointed fangs (or so several novices would later have testified), who announced that he was the *Advocatus Diaboli,* opposing Leibowitz' canonization, and he was here to investigate—and perhaps fix responsibility, he hinted—for a number of incredible and hysterical rumors filtering out of the abbey and reaching even high officials at New Vatican. He made it clear that he would tolerate no romantic nonsense.

The abbot greeted him politely and offered him an iron cot in a cell with a south exposure, after apologizing for the fact that the guest suite had been recently exposed to smallpox. The monsignor was attended by his own staff, and ate mush and herbs with the monks in refectory.

"I understand you are susceptible to fainting spells," he told Brother Francis when the dread time came. "How many members of your family have suffered from epilepsy or madness?"

"None, Excellency."

"I'm not an 'Excellency,'" snapped the priest. "Now we're going to get the truth out of you." His tone implied that he considered it to be a simple straightforward surgical operation which should have been performed years ago.

"Are you aware that documents can be aged artificially?" he demanded.

Francis was not so aware.

"Did you know that Leibowitz' wife was named Emily, and that Emma is *not* a diminutive for Emily?"

Francis had not known it, but recalled from childhood that his own parents had been rather careless about what they called each other. "And if Blessed Leibowitz chose to call her Emma, then I'm sure . . ."

The monsignor exploded, and tore into Francis with semantic tooth and nail, and left the bewildered monk wondering whether he had ever really seen a pilgrim at all.

Before the advocate's departure, he too asked to see the

illuminated copy of the print, and this time the monk's hands trembled with fear as he produced it, for he might again be forced to quit the project. The monsignor only stood gazing at it however, swallowed slightly, and forced himself to nod. "Your imagery is vivid," he admitted, "but then, of course, we all knew that, didn't we?"

The monsignor's horns immediately grew shorter by an inch, and he departed the same evening for New Vatican.

The years flowed smoothly by, seaming the faces of the once young and adding gray to the temples. The perpetual labors of the monastery continued, supplying a slow trickle of copied and recopied manuscript to the outside world. Brother Jeris developed ambitions of building a printing press, but when the abbot demanded his reasons, he could only reply, "So we can mass-produce."

"Oh? And in a world that's smug in its illiteracy, what do you intend to do with the stuff? Sell it as kindling paper to the peasants?"

Brother Jeris shrugged unhappily, and the copy room continued with pot and quill.

Then one spring, shortly before Lent, a messenger arrived with glad tidings for the order. The case for Leibowitz was complete. The College of Cardinals would soon convene, and the founder of the Albertian Order would be enrolled in the Calendar of Saints. During the time of rejoicing that followed the announcement, the abbot—now withered and in his dotage—sumoned Brother Francis into his presence, and wheezed:

"His Holiness comands your presence during the canonization of Isaac Edward Leibowitz. Prepare to leave.

"Now don't faint on me again," he added querulously.

The trip to New Vatican would take at least three months, perhaps longer, the time depending on how far Brother Francis could get before the inevitable robber band relieved him of his ass, since he would be going unarmed and alone. He carried with him only a begging bowl and the illuminated copy of the Leibowitz print, praying that ignorant robbers would have no use for the latter. As a precaution, however, he wore a black patch over his right eye, for the peasants, being a superstitious lot, could often be put to flight by even a hint of the evil eye. Thus armed and equipped, he set out to obey the summons of his high priest.

Two months and some odd days later he met his robber on a mountain trail that was heavily wooded and far from any settlement. His robber was a short man, but heavy as a bull, with a glazed knob of a pate and a jaw like a block of granite. He stood in the trail with his legs spread wide and his massive arms folded across his chest, watching the approach of the little figure on the ass. The robber seemed alone, and armed only with a knife which he did not bother to remove from his belt thong. His appearance was a disappointment, since Francis had been secretly hoping for another encounter with the pilgrim of long ago.

"Get off," said the robber.

The ass stopped in the path. Brother Francis tossed back his cowl to reveal the eye-patch, and raised a trembling finger to touch it. He began to lift the patch slowly as if to reveal something hideous that might be hidden beneath it. The robber threw back his head and laughed a laugh that might have sprung from the throat of Satan himself. Francis muttered an exorcism, but the robber seemed untouched.

"You black-sacked jeebers wore that one out years ago," he said. "Get off."

Francis smiled, shrugged, and dismounted without protest.

"A good day to you, sir," he said pleasantly. "You may take the ass. Walking will improve my health, I think." He smiled again and started away.

"Hold it," said the robber. "Strip to the buff. And let's see what's in that package."

Brother Francis touched his begging bowl and made a helpless gesture, but this brought only another scornful laugh from the robber.

"I've seen that alms-pot trick before too," he said. "The last man with a begging bowl had half a heklo of gold in his boot. Now strip."

Brother Francis displayed his sandals, but began to strip. The robber searched his clothing, found nothing, and tossed it back to him.

"Now let's see inside the package."

"It is only a document, sir," the monk protested. "Of value to no one but its owner."

"Open it."

Silently Brother Francis obeyed. The gold leaf and the colorful design flashed brilliantly in the sunlight that filtered through the foliage. The robber's craggy jaw dropped an inch. He whistled softly.

"What a pretty! Now wouldn't me woman like it to hang on the shanty wall!"

He continued to stare while the monk went slowly sick inside. *If Thou hast sent him to test me, O Lord,* he pleaded inwardly, *then help me to die like a man, for he'll get it over the dead body of Thy servant, if take it he must.*

"Wrap it up for me," the robber commanded, clamping his jaw in sudden decision.

The monk whimpered softly. "Please, sir, you would not take the work of a man's lifetime. I spent fifteen years illuminating this manuscript, and . . ."

"Well! Did it yourself, did you?" The robber threw back his head and howled again.

Francis reddened. "I fail to see the humor, sir . . ."

The robber pointed at it between guffaws. "You! Fifteen years to make a paper bauble. So that's what you do. Tell me why. Give me one good reason. For fifteen years. Ha!"

Francis stared at him in stunned silence and could think of no reply that would appease his contempt.

Gingerly, the monk handed it over. The robber took it in both hands and made as if to rip it down the center.

"*Jesus, Mary, Joseph!*" the monk screamed, and went to his knees in the trail. "For the love of God, sir!"

Softening slightly, the robber tossed it on the ground with a snicker. "Wrestle you for it."

"Anything, sir, anything!"

They squared off. The monk crossed himself and recalled that wrestling had once been a divinely sanctioned sport—and with grim faith, he marched into battle.

Three seconds later, he lay groaning on the flat of his back under a short mountain of muscle. A sharp rock seemed to be severing his spine.

"Heh heh," said the robber, and arose to claim his document.

Hands folded as if in prayer, Brother Francis scurried

after him on his knees, begging at the top of his lungs.

The robber turned to snicker. "I believe you'd kiss a boot to get it back."

Francis caught up with him and fervently kissed his boot.

This proved too much for even such a firm fellow as the robber. He flung the manuscript down again with a curse and climbed aboard the monk's donkey. The monk snatched up the precious document and trotted along beside the robber, thanking him profusely and blessing him repeatedly while the robber rode away on the ass. Francis sent a glowing cross of benediction after the departing figure and praised God for the existence of such selfless robbers.

And yet when the man had vanished among the trees, he felt an aftermath of sadness. Fifteen years to make a paper bauble . . . The taunting voice still rang in his ears. Why? Tell one good reason for fifteen years.

He was unaccustomed to the blunt ways of the outside world, to its harsh habits and curt attitudes. He found his heart deeply troubled by the mocking words, and his head hung low in the cowl as he plodded along. At one time he considered tossing the document in the brush and leaving it for the rains—but Father Juan had approved his taking it as a gift, and he could not come with empty hands. Chastened, he traveled on.

The hour had come. The ceremony surged about him as a magnificent spectacle of sound and stately movement and vivid color in the majestic basilica. And when the perfectly infallible Spirit had finally been invoked, a monsignor—it was di Simone, Francis noted, the advocate for the saint—arose and called upon Peter to speak, through the person of Leo XXII, commanding the assemblage to hearken.

Whereupon, the Pope quietly proclaimed that Isaac Edward Leibowitz was a saint, and it was finished. The ancient and obscure technician was of the heavenly hagiarchy, and Brother Francis breathed a dutiful prayer to his new patron as the choir burst into the *Te Deum*.

The Pontiff strode quickly into the audience room where the little monk was waiting, taking Brother Francis by surprise and rendering him briefly speechless. He knelt

quickly to kiss the Fisherman's ring and receive the blessing. As he arose, he found himself clutching the beautiful
document behind him as if ashamed of it. The Pope's eyes
caught the motion, and he smiled.

"You have brought us a gift, our son?" he asked.

The monk gulped, nodded stupidly, and brought it out.
Christ's Vicar stared at it for a long time without apparent
expression. Brother Francis' heart went sinking deeper as
the seconds drifted by.

"It is a nothing," he blurted, "a miserable gift. I am
ashamed to have wasted so much time at . . ." He choked
off.

The Pope seemed not to hear him. "Do you understand
the meaning of Saint Isaac's symbology?" he asked, peering
curiously at the abstract design of the circuit.

Dumbly the monk shook his head.

"Whatever it means . . ." the Pope began, but broke off.
He smiled and spoke of other things. Francis had been so
honored not because of any official judgment concerning
his pilgrim. He had been honored for his role in bringing to light such important documents and relics of the
saint, for such they had been judged, regardless of the
manner in which they had been found.

Francis stammered his thanks. The Pontiff gazed again
at the colorful blaze of his illuminated diagram. "Whatever it means," he breathed once more, "this bit of learning, though dead, will live again." He smiled up at the
monk and winked. "And we shall guard it till that day."

For the first time, the little monk noticed that the Pope
had a hole in his robe. His clothing, in fact, was thread-
bare. The carpet in the audience room was worn through
in spots, and plaster was falling from the ceiling.

But there were books on the shelves along the walls.
Books of painted beauty, speaking of incomprehensible
things, copied by men whose business was not to understand but to save. And the books were waiting.

"Good-by, beloved son."

And the small keeper of the flame of knowledge trudged
back toward his abbey on foot. His heart was singing as
he approached the robber's outpost. And if the robber happened to be taking the day off, the monk meant to sit
down and wait for his return. This time he had an answer.

BIOGRAPHICAL NOTES

J. G. BALLARD, who was born in Shanghai, China, is one of the best known of the "new" group of science-fiction writers that has grown up about the British magazine *New Worlds Science Fiction*, in which "Chronopolis" first appeared (1961). Mr. Ballard is the author of two novels, *The Wind from Nowhere* and *The Drowned World*, and of two collections of stories, *The Voices of Time* and *Billenium*.

ALFRED BESTER, born in New York in 1913, attended the University of Pennsylvania and Columbia Law School. He spent a year as a public relations man for the Metropolitan Opera, then turned to writing and directing radio and television shows, and to authoring a monthly column in *Holiday* magazine. He has been writing science fantasy since 1939, and is the author of two collections of stories, and of three novels (one of which, *The Demolished Man*, won a "Hugo" Award for the Best Science Fiction Novel of the year, in 1953.) "The Men Who Murdered Mohammed" was first published in the *Magazine of Fantasy and Science Fiction* in 1958.

RAY BRADBURY, born in Waukegan, Illinois, in 1920, is possibly the most generally famous of today's science-fiction writers: his stories and novels, written in haunting, almost poetic prose, earned him a complimentary citation from the American Academy of Arts and Letters in 1954. Among his collections of stories are *The Martian Chronicles* and *The Illustrated Man;* his two novels are *Dandelion Wine* and *Something Wicked This Way Comes*. "There Will Come Soft Rains" was originally published in *Collier's* in 1950.

FREDRIC BROWN, born in Cincinnati, Ohio, in 1906, has

authored over twenty-five books in the mystery and science-fiction fields. He is undoubtedly today's most prolific purveyor of short-short science fantasy: his two collections, *Honeymoon in Hell* and *Nightmares and Geezenstacks*, alone contain sixty-eight stories averaging well under five pages in length. The story reproduced here, "Immortality," is the third in a series of vignettes in which Mr. Brown relates the history of the great discoveries "made, and tragically lost, during the twentieth century"; it was published previously in *Nightmares and Geezenstacks* (1961).

JOHN C. M. BRUST, graduated from Harvard College in 1958, where he was Ibis (Vice-President) of the humor magazine, the *Lampoon*. "The Red White and Blue Rum Collins" first appeared in that publication, as did Mr. Brust's well-known lyric poem "Armadillo." Mr. Brust, who has since got involved in the New York business world, now lives in Old Lyme, Connecticut.

ARTHUR C. CLARKE is one of Britain's outstanding exponents of science-fiction. He is also a scientist and lecturer of note: among his most remarkable achievements is a detailed plan for a system of communications satellites similar to the Syncom project, formulated several years before the first Sputnik was launched in 1957. "Patent Pending" is from his collection *Tales from the White Hart* (1957), of which Mr. Clarke writes: "It seems to me there is a long unfelt want for what might be called the 'tall' science-fiction story. By this I mean stories that are *intentionally* unbelievable, not as is too often the case, unintentionally so."

ROALD DAHL, born in South Wales in 1916, is a six-foot-six Englishman who has been, among other things, an explorer, an RAF fighter pilot, and a representative of the Shell Oil Company in Dar-es-Salaam, Tanganyika. More important, he is the author of two collections of short stories, *Someone Like You* (1953) and *Kiss Kiss* (1960), which have earned him a reputation as one of today's top fantasy writers. "The Great Automatic Grammatisator" appeared in the latter volume.

AVRAM DAVIDSON is the magnificently bearded former editor-in-chief of the *Magazine of Fantasy and Science Fiction*. "Or All the Seas with Oysters," the title of Mr. Davidson's first collection, won the World Science Fiction Writers' "Hugo" Award as the best short story of 1957. It first appeared in *Galaxy* magazine.

MARTIN GARDNER, born in Tulsa, Oklahoma, in 1914, is a regular columnist for the *Scientific American*. He was the editor of the famous *The Annotated Snark* and *The Annotated Alice*, and has authored, in addition, several books on science and mathematics for the layman. Studying the antics and writings of "mad" scientists has always been a special hobby of his: his book *In the Name of Science* (1952) portrays some of the more delightful escapades of history's scientific crackpots. Mr. Gardner's story "No-Sided Professor" betrays his interest in cranks, but it is so scientifically well based that it has been designated "required reading" in several college mathematics courses.

JOSÉ MARIA GIRONELLA, born in Gerona, Spain, in 1917, is the author of a well-known trilogy of novels about the Spanish Civil War, the first of which—*The Cypresses Believe in God*—won the Thomas More Association Medal for 1955. "The Death of the Sea" is a selection from Mr. Gironella's *Los Fantasmas de Mi Cerebro* (1958)—published in the United States as part of the book *Phantoms and Fugitives*—which represented a complete reversal from the factual realism of his earlier work. The inspiration was a period of severe mental illness: "Upon penetrating into a world of pain and of thoughts that came like lightning bolts," Gironella writes, "I understood that, just as the stars which our eyes can see are not the *only* stars, so what our hands can touch are not the *only* truths."

JULIAN KAWALEC, who was born near Sandomierz, Poland, pursues the dual careers of journalist and short-story writer. A graduate of the University of Krakow, Mr. Kawalec is a member of what has been called the "modern school of Polish satire." He has published two collections of short stories, *Paths Within the Streets* and *Scars*.

DAMON KNIGHT (who formerly called himself damon knight, but has apparently given up attempting to get editors to honor his requests for low-case billing) was born in 1922. He is the author of two science-fiction collections, *Far Out* and *In Deep*, and is also one of the top critics in the science-fiction field: an anthology of his critical essays and reviews, *In Search of Wonder*, has been published in book form. "The Analogues" was originally published in *Astounding Science-Fiction Magazine* (1952), and later appeared as the first chapter of Mr. Knight's novel, *Hell's Pavement*.

C. M. KORNBLUTH was born in New York City in 1923; before he had reached twenty-one he was one of America's most prolific authors. Under "eighteen or nineteen" pseudonyms, Mr. Kornbluth published literally scores of stories in the early war years. Writes Frederik Pohl, who collaborated with Mr. Kornbluth on two science-fiction novels—*The Space Merchants* and *Search the Sky*— "There were magazines which, for the *total* length of theirs careers, published more words originally set on paper by Kornbluth than by all other contributors combined." After serving in World War II, Mr. Kornbluth settled down to writing the more polished, bitterly satirical, almost humorous stories of which "The Rocket of 1955" (from the magazine *Worlds Beyond*, 1951) is an example. He died in 1958, at the age of thirty-five, one of the most respected science-fantasy writers in the United States.

WALTER M. MILLER, JR., was born in 1923 and originally studied to be an electrical engineer, but after serving as a flyer in World War II (he flew more than fifty missions over Italy and the Balkans), he decided to turn to writing as a career. His first published story appeared in the *American Mercury* in 1950. Mr. Miller is one of the few writers to win two "Hugo" awards from the World Science-Fiction Writers' Convention: his novelette *The*

Darfsteller was a prize-winner in 1955, and in 1960 *A Canticle for Leibowitz,* an expanded version of the story in this volume, was chosen as the year's best science-fiction novel. (The story, as it appears here, was published in the *Magazine of Fantasy and Science Fiction* in 1956.)

IDRIS SEABRIGHT, born in Hutchinson, Kansas, in 1911, was educated in the public schools of her birthplace, and at the University of California, from which she received a master's degree. She has written numerous short fantasy stories, most of which display a uniquely grisly sense of humor. "An Egg a Month from All Over" originally appeared in the *Magazine of Fantasy and Science Fiction,* in 1952.

ROBERT SHECKLEY, born in New York City in 1928, is a graduate of New York University. While at college, he met his wife-to-be in a writing course given by Irwin Shaw. Among his collections of science-fantasy stories are *Untouched by Human Hands, The Shards of Space,* and *Citizen in Space.* "Something for Nothing" originally appeared in *Galaxy* magazine, in 1954.

CLIFFORD SIMAK, born in Wisconsin in 1904, attended the University of Wisconsin, and has gone on from there to pursue a successful career in journalism. Throughout much of his life he has turned out science-fiction stories at a steady, if not rapid, rate. Mr. Simak was the winner of a "Hugo" Award at the 1959 World Science Fiction Convention for his novelette, *The Big Front Yard.* "Shadow Show" appeared in his collection *Strangers in the Universe* (1956).

THEODORE STURGEON, born in New York City in 1918, has had a long and checkered career: merchant mariner, short-order cook, door-to-door salesman, bulldozer operator, and assorted other jobs. Since his early twenties he has also written science-fiction—among his accolades is the International Fantasy Award, presented to him for his novel *More Than Human.* Under a pseudonym, Mr. Sturgeon wrote *I, Libertine* (1956) to satisfy the extraordinary demand created by New York disk jockey Jean

Shepherd's advertisements for a then nonexistent novel of that title. "And Now the News" first appeared in the *Magazine of Fantasy and Science Fiction.*

WILLIAM STYRON, born in Newport News, Virginia, in 1925, is a graduate of Duke University. He is the author of two acclaimed novels, *Lie Down in Darkness* and *Set This House on Fire,* and of a novella, *The Long March,* which has been called by critics "a small classic." "Pie in the Sky," an early Styron venture into a field of writing very different from his accustomed one, is published here for the first time.

JOHN WYNDHAM (John Benyon Harris) is a native Britisher born in 1903. After attending the Bedales School, he settled down briefly to a life of gentleman-farming, then moved on to law, advertising, and commercial art, in that order. In 1933 he at last turned to writing; after the war his first successful novel, *The Day of the Triffids,* was published. Since then he has written several books, including the novel *The Midwich Cuckoos,* upon which the motion picture *The Village of the Damned* was based. "Random Quest" is reprinted from Mr. Wyndham's collection, *The Infinite Moment* (1961).